A WARRIOR'S PATH

SAGA
OF THE
KNOWN LANDS

BOOK FIVE

By

JACOB PEPPERS

Visit the author's website: http://www.jacobpeppersauthor.com.

This is to my wife, Andrea. My partner. My helper and friend.

As we travel through life together,

You watch the path so that I might close my eyes and dream of dragons,

And I am grateful to you for that, as I am for so much else.

I love ya, babe. It's been a heck of a ride so far but hold on tight—

We're just getting started.

Sign up for the author's mailing list and for a limited time receive a FREE copy of *The Silent Blade*, prequel to the bestselling fantasy series *The Seven Virtues*.

Go to JacobPeppersAuthor.com to get your free book now!

CHAPTER ONE

MATT was alone.

He stood in a castle full of dozens of servants and guardsmen, all eager to do his bidding. He stared out his castle window at a city of tens of thousands of men and women who called him king...

Yet he had never felt more alone.

It was as if he stood not within the walls of his castle but instead within the confines of a cell, one in which the bars were growing closer and closer. Soon, it seemed to him, they would crush him. And considering how he had been feeling lately, considering how his dreams had been plagued by madness and horrors, he was not so sure that would be a bad thing.

He turned at the sound of a door opening to see Healer Malden. The old healer bowed as he stepped inside, carrying a small bag. "Forgive me, Majesty, for taking so long," he said. "I'm afraid all my apprentices are sleeping."

"I'm glad someone can," Matt said. "And please, if anyone needs forgiving its me—I should have waited until morning, shouldn't have woken you. Only..." He shrugged, not really knowing how to finish. The truth was he had woken in the middle of the night in a terrible sweat. He had done so before, of course, many times since Emma, the Feyling, had possessed him. But lately, these awakenings—and his dreams—had been different. Worse.

He had not woken just to a feeling of general unease, but in a state of panic, gasping for breath, shaking with terror. As with the other times, he could not remember the particulars of the dream, could remember no more than vague pictures, what might have been faces and forms of all kinds. Dozens, hundreds of monstrous figures of all shapes and sizes, sneering at him and baring their teeth.

That terror, those images, had cast him out of his bed, banishing any thought of renewing his sleep, driving him here, to the healer's chambers.

"Think nothing of it, Majesty," Healer Malden said, offering him a tired smile. "I find that the older I get the more sleep I need, and the less I manage. It is as if my ancient bones, knowing they approach their end, begrudge me each moment of sleep, wishing not to waste any time. Had you not come, I would have awoken soon anyway." He shrugged. "Still, if cracking knees and hairy ears are the price of making it to old age, then they are ones I pay gladly. After all, many of my contemporaries followed the army during the Fey War and were not so lucky. Had they still the faculty of speech, I imagine they would have far worthier complaints than lack of sleep."

"Still," Matt said. "I am sorry."

The healer waved the apology away, moving forward and offering the bag he carried to Matt. Matt took it, catching a strong smell of several herbs even before he opened it to reveal ground up leaves. "What is it?" he asked.

"A mixture of several herbs, all of which should serve to help you, Majesty. There is valerian root, of course, along with lavender and chamomile."

"Something...minty, too," Matt said.

The healer bobbed his head like a duelist acknowledging a point. "You have a good nose, Majesty," he said. "There is also some spearmint and peppermint, both of which should serve to give more shape to your dreams, to make them more vivid, while the thyme—"

"*More* vivid?" Matt asked, feeling a brief swell of panic. "Forgive me, Malden, but that's the *last* thing I want."

"Perhaps, Majesty," the old healer said apologetically, "but now, as is so often the case, what we want and what we need are rarely the same. You see, there is nothing man fears like the unknown. And while you cannot remember your dreams, while they do not have shape and substance, they remain something to be feared, feared in the same way a man might fear a dark, unfamiliar room. But give the same man a lantern, pull back the curtains and let the sunlight in..."

"And the room isn't scary anymore," Matt finished. "It's just a room."

"And the dream just a dream," the old man said, smiling. "I'll instruct the Mistress of Servants, Madam Olaphasia, on the proper way to make the tea, so that she might show her charges. It needs to be taken once at night, before you sleep, and again in the morning."

"And...this'll help?" Matt asked, frowning doubtfully, for tea seemed a small thing when held against those monstrosities which had driven him from sleep.

"It will, Majesty," the healer said, giving him a small smile. "Problems with sleep can often seem bigger than they are...we make them bigger, you see, Highness, for in the night, in the dark, everything seems worse than it really is."

"So...it isn't a big deal?"

"I make no claims of that, Majesty," Malden said. "I mean only that you need not fret—the tea will work. What fears you have are natural, but they are also unnecessary. Children, after all, do not often see ghosts in the daytime, do they? They see them in the dark, in those moments when sleep has begun to creep in but has yet to fully claim them or, alternatively, in those moments when they have begun to shake off their slumber but have not yet fully ridden themselves of the vestiges of their dreams. Such is the same with what plagues you. The tea will help, Highness. You will sleep, and you will dream, and within those dreams you will find that there is naught to fear."

Matt nodded, feeling a little better now. It was the man's confidence, the way he was so sure. Matt didn't just feel better. He felt...even a little embarrassed. A child who saw a tunic hanging on a chair and made of it, in the darkness, a monster come to eat him up. He sighed. "Thank you, Malden," he said. "I...I feel foolish."

"There is never anything foolish, sire, about the man who seeks help. But there is plenty of foolishness in the man who does not."

Matt nodded. "Thank you," he said. "I'll leave you now. I apologize again for interrupting your night." He opened the door then paused. "May you sleep well."

"May we both, Majesty," the old man said, bowing his head.

Matt gave the man a weary smile and left.

He passed several servants and guardsmen in the castle hallways—more of both than he normally would have. Since the murder of the serving girl, servants had been set to working in pairs, and the guard patrols within the castle had been doubled, both at Commander Malex's suggestion.

None of those he passed seemed to think anything odd of Matt being out at so late an hour, only bowing as he passed. But then, why should they? After all, Matt had spent many of the last nights wandering the hallways when the nightmares drove him from his bed. He'd told himself, at such times, that he had risen because he needed to tend to the needs of his body or because he already felt well-rested from sleep but neither of those things were true, and he knew it.

The truth was, on those early mornings or late nights, he had not risen from his bed—he had fled from it. Fled from the unclear images he could ill-define from his nightmares, images that seemed to fade and vanish even as he tried to examine them, leaving only a vague color in their place, a lambent emerald that flashed in his mind from time to time, an impression of it, this all-consuming green, driving into him, through him. That and one other thing.

A steady, rhythmic beating, as if the beating of some great heart. A beating that had seemed to come from inside him, that had seemed to shake his body, his soul.

But it was nothing. He knew that now. As Malden had said, such night terrors might be caused by any number of things, chief among them stress. And if anyone had reason to be stressed, who better than the king who had sent his father and uncle on a suicide mission to the Black Wood, who had been visited, only days ago, by an assassin coming to his room and, before that, been possessed by a Fey creature?

Oh yes, there were plenty of things over which he might worry, plenty of things that might turn his dreams into nightmares. So he told himself to relax, that the tea would work as the healer said it would. He was still telling himself as much when he reached his quarters and the two guards stationed outside bowed.

"*Majesty,*" they said in unison.

"Vorrun," Matt said, offering one of the men a smile, for they had become well acquainted over the last week. "How are the children?"

"As much hellions now as ever, Majesty," the man said, grinning. "Thanks for asking."

"Of course." Matt turned to the other guard. "And Blake? The new wife? Everything is well, I hope?"

The man nodded. "Of course, Your Grace. My Addy, she's mad at me just now, but I'll sort it out."

"I hope so," Matt said. "My mother, she used to tell me that I would be alright in marriage, just so long as I understood that my wife was always right. Even when she's wrong."

The two laughed. "I'm just now startin' to learn that myself, Majesty."

Vorrun, the older of the two, sighed, shaking his head. "I been tryin' to tell 'em but some folks got to leap headfirst into the fire 'fore they decide it's hot."

Matt laughed. "Well, you two have a goodnight."

"You too, sire," Vorrun said. "Sleep well."

Here's to hoping, Matt thought as he walked through the door, closing it behind him, but the truth was he felt better. Speaking with Malden had done much to allay his concerns and what little had remained had largely been brushed away by his brief conversation with the two guardsmen. Malden was right. Sometimes, the dark could play tricks on people, that was all. In the night, in the stillness, it seemed anything was possible, that the shadows could move, that they had teeth.

But it was just a child's fancy, nothing more, one which he was far too old to entertain. He fixed the tea according to the healer's instructions, then drank. It tasted better than he had expected and soon he was finished, lying back down in his bed.

His eyelids were heavy, and so he closed them. Malden had told him that the fear he felt upon waking was only a fear of the unknown, the same fear a man might feel upon hearing a branch fall when wandering through a dark wood. An innocuous sound but without being able to see it, to know it for what it was, he might imagine it was anything. The footfalls of some monster come to claim him, perhaps.

But it was only a branch, only a sound.

It was only the darkness.

So he told himself, as he lay there, his breathing slowing, feeling as if he were slowly sinking into the bed by degrees as the tea took hold.

And then, in minutes, he slept.

And in his sleep...

He dreamed.

He felt as if he floated, as if he was being carried along by some invisible tether, dragged through the star-lit darkness of the sky. On and on he went.

Beneath him, so far beneath him as to appear like little more than toys, were cities and villages, homes and people. All those people of the Known Lands, it seemed to him.

And then whatever force pulled at him tugged him farther, beyond the Known Lands, where the great expanse of the Black Wood seemed to stretch on forever, into the horizon and beyond it. Great sentinels of trees, their shadowed limbs reaching out as if clawing at the world, meaning to tear and rend it. And somewhere, from up ahead, there was a sound.

A beating.

A beating like that of some great monstrous heart in a cavernous chest, one of a size with the wood itself.

Thump.

A beating so powerful it seemed to shake his very being, inside and out as he was dragged farther into the wood.

Thump.

Each beat was louder than the last as he drew nearer to the source of that thundering, earth-shaking beating.

Thump.

As he sailed farther through the sky, he began to think that it was the beating that pulled him after all. That great heart. He could not see it, but he felt from the sound that he must see it soon. It had to lie somewhere near, up ahead beyond the trees or in the mist that seemed to cover the ground beneath their canopies, blocking it from view.

He was carried onward.

Thump.

Thump.

Thump.

Faster now, a staccato rhythm, so powerful he felt as if he would be torn apart, that he would surely burst into thousands of pieces, each piece carried away like fallen leaves in a high wind.

Just when he thought he could take no more, just when he was sure that the invisible force that pulled at him would indeed rip him apart, that it *meant* to rip him apart...

Silence.

A silence that, following that thundering beat, felt deafening. He was being pulled forward no longer but left to hover high in the sky. It was beautiful up there. High enough that the problems of man and beast were as nothing. High enough that the stars shined like great lanterns in the firmament, and the air was crisp and clean. High enough that, for a moment, he was able to forget about everything.

He forgot his fears, his worries, and his shames. Forgot, too, his obligations, his desires, his dreams. There was nothing but him and the darkness and the stars. Even the Black Wood, at this distance, lost much of its menace.

As he hovered there for what might have been minutes or weeks or years, he forgot even himself. At least in so much as he might have considered himself *separate,* apart from everything. He was not separate—he was part. He *was* everything, and, at the same time, he was nothing. There was something very freeing, very comforting about that.

He even found himself smiling, and the stars seemed to twinkle brighter, smiling with him.

That was when he moved.

Abruptly, he was hovering no longer—he was falling. Plummeting through the air, yet there was no sound, and he did not feel the wind rushing by his face. Felt nothing at all. He screamed, but he could not hear it. There was only the silence and him.

Not a part of everything after all but only him, or at least if he were a part then he was a part cast off, discarded as if of no worth.

He fell...and he fell...and he fell.

And then, suddenly, he fell no longer.

He froze in the air a hundred feet above the midnight canopy of the Black Wood. And then whatever force had propelled him pulled him forward, slowly now, and while the tops of the trees, coupled with the mist, blocked most of the forest floor from view, he caught snatches of it here and there. And in those brief spots, he saw movement.

Creatures of all sorts and sizes, some as large as houses he'd seen, stalked through the forest beneath him. None seemed to mark his passage above their heads, yet despite that, despite the fact that he hovered a hundred feet above them, far out of their reach, Matt felt a wave of revulsion and fear pass through him.

But as the seconds turned into minutes, that fear, so powerful at first, began to fade. The creatures had not noticed him, and it seemed that they would not. And even if they *did* they would be able to do nothing to him up here, so far away. Or so he hoped.

And as his fear began to fade, a thought crept into his mind—more, a question, really. As he watched more and more of the creatures skulking through the wood, moving beneath the trees, he wondered what it was they moved *toward.*

His first thought, his first fear, was that they moved toward the Known Lands, that the Fey had gathered their forces and prepared to renew a war that had been over for a decade and more. But as he continued to watch, he realized that this fear, at least, was unfounded, for the creatures were not moving toward the border of the Known Lands. In fact, they were going in the opposite direction, deeper into the Wood, in the direction from which that powerful, thunderous beating had come.

Matt wondered what could possibly cause so many of the Fey—if not all of them then what he thought, what he *hoped* was a majority—to move toward the same place, the same direction. He mused over what it might be, what it *could be,* until finally his flight brought him over a rise in the forest.

Beyond the rise was a large, open clearing. And within that glade were thousands, tens of thousands of Fey, their numbers so great that Matt felt his fear rise. There were so many that should they choose to march on the Known Lands, to renew the war, he could not imagine how his people might survive it.

The creatures had separated themselves into two groups, opening an empty avenue of space between them.

Matt gazed at that opening, wondering what had drawn all their attention, what they had created such a space for. At first, he thought it must be some sort of royalty—if the Fey even had royalty. The truth was, he knew nothing of them, nothing except for what he'd heard in the stories, but since they'd had a king, the Fey King Yeladrian, then he supposed they must have royalty.

But as his gaze alighted on a small group moving through the mass of creatures, and on one figure in particular, a rush of terror surged through him. He no longer needed to wonder what had drawn the Fey deeper into the wood, did not need to wonder why they had opened an avenue amongst their midst, for he knew.

It was not royalty that had caused that parting, that drew them. Nor was it some ritual of their people.

It was Cutter.

It was his father.

Matt had heard the names others used for his father, of course. The Fey called him the Destroyer, but he was known by other names, too. Before his exile, even his own people had feared him, feared his anger and his ferocity, his love for violence. They had called him the Crimson Prince, a moniker that Matt suspected had never been truer than it was now.

His father was covered in blood and dirt from head to toe, practically dripping the stuff. His face was tense, strained, and for the first time Matt could remember, he looked...old.

He had the look of a man who had traveled a very long, hard road and even through that strain, even through his narrow set eyes and trudging walk, Matt thought he saw some hint of what might have been relief. Relief that he had reached the road's end, maybe? Relief that it would all be over soon?

That thought sent a shiver of fear through Matt. He told himself that his father was the most feared warrior walking the face of the world, that he had sent countless hundreds, Fey and mortal alike, to their deaths. The histories—some by Petran Quinn but certainly not all—spoke often of his father, of him leading his people across the great seas to finally arrive here, to the Known Lands. They recounted his father's actions during the Fey War. Those accounts varied in small, sometimes very large ways, but one thing on which they were all in agreement was this—the Crimson Prince was a master of war, a man who wielded his axe the same way a master bard might wield his lute.

And the effect he'd had, they all also agreed, was far more shocking, far more pronounced than any bard or poet could ever hope to attain.

He was, quite simply, the greatest warrior the world had ever known.

But what matter did such a thing make? For even the world's greatest warrior might fall before the thousands surrounding him. With so many, even Matt—a fledgling warrior at best—knew that skill and training meant nothing. His father had slain hundreds, but now he faced countless thousands, their numbers stretching on as far as Matt could see in every direction.

He did not know the number, and he did not need to know it. There were enough, that was all.

More than enough.

But as he watched his father move forward without hesitating, watched the creatures parting on either side of him, he could not help but be impressed even as he was terrified. His father was surrounded by all manner of creatures, creatures whose sometimes haunting, sometimes monstrous, but always alien visages regarded him with a hate and a hunger that was clear even despite their unfamiliar features. Yet he moved forward as if he belonged there, as if all of those creatures who wanted nothing more than to kill him—some of which were even now being physically restrained by their brethren—caused him no concern at all.

He seemed confident, capable, and despite the fact that many of those creatures surrounding him were far larger than Cutter himself, he seemed to loom over them, to loom in the same way that a fully grown male might loom over children. And for as many that tried to go after him and forced their brethren to restrain them, there were just as many that recoiled as he passed, hissing and spitting and sputtering in a mixture of hatred and fear.

For his part, Cutter barely seemed to notice, immune to their hatred and fear alike. He marched on stoically, a grim expression on his face, his axe—the weapon the Fey knew as the Breaker of Pacts—held loosely in one hand, and Matt thought it spoke to his father's weariness and exhaustion that the axe dragged along the ground as he walked, as if he lacked the strength to even raise it.

But as exhausted as he looked, covered in blood and dirt as if he had been through some terrible trial—a trial Matt had sent him on, and he winced at a sharp pang of shame—he looked positively spritely compared to his brother, Feledias.

Matt's uncle currently lay draped over Cutter's left shoulder, hanging there the way a hunter might lug a deer carcass after a day's work. The man's limp form bounced with each step Matt's father took, and his eyes were closed, both of which might have been enough to have convinced Matt that he was asleep—or something worse—save for the grimace of pain on his face, one that seemed to grow worse with each thudding impact of Cutter's feet on the forest path.

He was alive, but judging by his obvious pain and the weak, emaciated look of him, it was unclear how long that might remain the case. But then the same could have been said for Cutter himself. After all, the Fey held no love for the Crimson Prince, the man who was solely responsible for killing their king. True, he had done so to protect Feledias, but Matt doubted they would care about such a tale, even if they waited long enough to hear it before attacking.

The only real surprise to Matt was that the creatures had not attacked them already. They seemed to be waiting for something, and as Cutter continued down the empty avenue toward a lone figure waiting up ahead, Matt realized the reason for their hesitation. Cutter was to be judged, then, and it was clear from the deference the Fey paid to the ten-foot-tall creature that waited for him, that here was the one who would do the judging. The creature's body was a deep, vertiginous green. Its face was as dark as night itself and its eyes, which were several times larger than a man's, shone a vibrant green.

Cutter moved to stand before the creature and even before it spoke Matt felt a stab of terror, for he recognized the creature from his and his father's foray into the Black Woods when they'd fled Brighton. And how could he not? After all, it was a visage that had haunted his dreams on more than one night, one that he was not likely to forget as long as he lived.

The creature spoke then, in a voice that seemed somehow like the rushing of wind through treetops, like the shifting of some great stone edifice, but it was not the sound of the creature's words which struck true fear into Matt's heart. Instead, it was their content—death.

There was a brief conversation, if conversation it could be called, and then, suddenly, the air was filled with the thundering roars and shouts and cries of all manner of creatures.

The very ground seemed to shake at the tumultuous cacophony of their voices, and Matt's father knelt, laying Feledias, his brother, onto the ground with surprising gentleness before rising again. It took a visible effort for him to heft the axe in both hands, but heft it he did, staring around him at the creatures with an expression that seemed more at peace than Matt had ever seen the man.

That left him wondering not just how the man might feel peaceful at that moment of all things, but also of what might have given him that peace. He was still wondering it when the roars and cries reached a great, reverberating crescendo and, like ants swarming over a kicked anthill, the creatures all rushed forward as one, toward his father who watched them come, his expression unreadable.

Matt screamed, meaning to add his shout of defiance and terror for his father to the cries of those slavering beasts, but he found that he was silent, without a voice. And a moment later, he was without eyes, for darkness suddenly rushed into him, filling him up, and there was nothing else in all the world.

As the echoes of those terrible, horrifying wails and screams sounded in his mind, Matt jerked awake. Here, he had a voice, and he used it, screaming into the darkness.

"*Majesty!*" came a muffled cry, but Matt barely heard it, was barely aware that he had shot straight up to sit, gasping and covered in sweat, in his bed at the castle. He did not see the room around him, not truly. Instead, he saw that glade, those creatures, all charging toward his father and uncle, his father and uncle who were only there to be charged at because *he* had sent them.

"Open the damned door!" another shout came, but still it barely registered in Matt's mind, as did the reply.

"I c-can't," a young voice said, panic clear in it, *"th-the key, it's stuck!"*

"Then damn the key!"

Matt was still trying to pull himself out of that glade and back to the present, still trying to hear anything save the horrible, alien screeches and wails that filled his mind, when there came another, distinct sound.

The sound of splintering wood.

He glanced over, dumbly, to see an axe head appear through the door to his quarters as if by magic. The door was thick and strong, built to last, to defend the Known Lands' sovereign ruler, to keep him safe while he was inside his quarters. But here, as with all things, it was easier to destroy than to create, and even as he watched, the axe head was ripped free and, accompanied by a bellowed cry, tore into the wood again.

Another two blows did the trick, and in what felt like moments Guardsman Vorrun and Guardsman Blake charged into his room. Vorrun held an axe in two hands. His jerkin was covered in slivers of wood, and he had several fresh, shallow scratches on his face and hands from the splintering door.

Blake had his sword out and was looking around the room pale-faced and terrified.

"Guardsman Vorrun," Matt said in a hoarse, shocked voice. "Wha—"

"Where is he, Majesty?" the guardsman asked, speaking over him, his eyes scanning the room.

"Sorry...where is who?"

The guardsman frowned around the room then turned to regard Matt. "The assassin, Majesty. Where is he?"

Matt blinked, and a moment later his face heated as he realized what had happened. "Vorrun there...there is no assassin."

"No assassin?" Guardsman Blake asked. "Then why—"

"Forgive me, Majesty," Vorrun interrupted, shooting his fellow guardsman a quick glance before looking back to Matt. "We heard you scream and thought you had been attacked."

Matt winced, feeling embarrassed and ashamed and stupid all at once. "Forgive me, Vorrun. It...it was a bad dream, that's all." Only, the truth was he wasn't sure of that, but then he didn't think it would do any good to tell the man as much.

The guardsman shook his head instantly. "There's nothing to forgive, Majesty. Dreams...they're funny things. I s'pose I've had some doozies myself."

Matt thought back to the dream. Even now he could hear the screams of those creatures. Even now he could see his father's eyes as he watched his death come. He could almost smell the blood and dirt that had covered him, could almost feel his uncle's pained groans as if they were his own. "Yes..." he croaked. "I...I suppose it was a doozy indeed, Vorrun."

"But...it was just a dream," Guardsman Blake said, and Matt felt his face heat.

Vorrun frowned at the younger guardsman. "Forgive him, Majesty. He does not mean to give offense, I assure you. It is ignorance which guides his tongue—as is so often the case with the young, I find—not malice."

Matt found a small smile coming to his face as he glanced at the younger of the two guardsmen, a man who was, it had to be said, at least five years his senior. Vorrun followed his gaze and seemed to read his thoughts, for the man let out sputtering cough.

"That is, Majesty...some mature quicker than others, it is true. And we guardsmen cannot imagine what sort of pressures and difficulties your lofty—and well earned—position puts on you."

Matt found his smile widening. "It is okay, Vorrun," he said, then he glanced Blake. "You're right to be surprised at such a strong reaction to a dream, as I am surprised myself. I am embarrassed, and I can only say that I am sorry."

Guardsman's Blake's eyes went wide at that. "Th-there's no apology necessary, Highness."

"Are you sure you're alright, Majesty?" Vorrun pressed.

"Positive," Matt lied, for the truth was he did not think he was alright, not at all. In fact, he thought it had been some time since he was alright. He promised himself that, as soon as he was done here, he would go and see Malden. Perhaps it was something in the tincture and mixture of herbs the man had given him that had caused such vivid dreams—whatever the cause, he intended to find out. "Anyway," he said, more to himself than the guardsman, "it was just a dream." He tried to give the man a smile, but it felt fragile on his face, and in another moment he let it drop.

"Forgive me, Majesty," Vorrun said slowly. "I don't mean to argue, but..." He hesitated, then gave a shake of his head. "Never mind—it's not important."

"No, please, Vorrun," Matt said. "If you have some thoughts I would gladly hear them."

The old guard gave him a bit of a surprised look at that.

"What?" Matt asked. "Is everything okay?"

"Sure," the man said, then cleared his throat. "Of course, Your Majesty. Only..." He gave a soft, uncomfortable laugh. "I s'pose I'm not accustomed to someone of your position wonderin' much on the opinion of someone in mine."

"I admit I don't know much about being a king, Vorrun," Matt said, "but it seems to me that I would be a poor ruler indeed, if I didn't listen to others."

The guard nodded slowly. "I see."

"What is it?" Matt asked, sensing that the man had more to say.

Vorrun winced. "If you're alright, Majesty, we really ought to go and get some men to fix the door. We can find quarters for you to finish your sleep and—"

"I think it's safe to say I'm done sleeping for the night, Vorrun," Matt interrupted. "Now, please. Tell me what's troubling you." As he spoke the words, they seemed to echo in his mind with his desire to know the man's thought.

Vorrun tensed, as if struck, a dazed look coming over his face. "Of course, Majesty. See, you say it'd be a poor ruler that'd not take his people's concerns into account," the guardsman said, the words seeming to spill out of him, "but your uncle, during the years since your father's exile, didn't seem to care. As for your father, well, he was always too concerned with where he was going to sheathe his axe next to be bothered worrying over—" The man cut off, his eyes going wide, his face paling, as he no doubt realized exactly what he'd said. "Forgive me, Majesty," he stammered, dropping to his knees, his head bowed. "I didn't mean...that is, I don't know why I said that, where it came from. I...I'll leave, of course, and—"

"Don't be ridiculous, Vorrun," Matt said. "Please, rise." He moved forward, helping the guard to his feet, and the man winced as if expecting a blow.

The guardsman blinked, looking confused, lost. "F-forgive me, Majesty, I—"

"There's nothing to forgive," Matt said, feeling confused himself. "I asked for your opinion and you gave it—that's all. And I'm grateful that you did. I understand your feelings, truly I do. But I can only tell you that my father, he is not the man he once was. He has grown. Has changed. He is a better man now."

"Of course, Majesty," the guard said quickly. A bit too quickly as far as Matt was concerned, and although the man schooled his features well, Matt was somehow possessed of the feeling—no, the *certainty*—that the man was not saying what he really thought. He was as sure of it as if the words were scrawled across the man's forehead.

Men such as the Crimson Prince do not change.

The words rang in Matt's mind, and although they were spoken in his own voice, the voice he always heard in his head, he did not think that they were *his* words, did not think that they were his thoughts. It was a strange feeling, a scary one, particularly following the nightmare he'd woken from, and he gave his head a shake in an effort to clear it. "And the rest? What you were saying about dreams?"

"It's nothing, Majesty," Vorrun said, giving an apologetic wince. "Just, well, you put me in mind of somethin' my gram used to tell me when I was a boy, that's all."

"Oh?" Matt said. "What's that?"

"Forgive me, Majesty, but it's just silly words, that's all. You have to understand, my gram, she was an odd woman. Odd even when she was young, the folks of my village said, and odder still when she got older. I didn't think nothin' of it at the time as I was just a boy, and at that age I reckon just about everythin' in the world seems magical, even if she seemed the most." He shook his head. "Had some funny ideas, my gram, but nothin' to distract you with."

"I have just woken from a terrible nightmare and had my door beaten down, Vorrun," Matt said with a small smile. "Distract me."

The man returned the smile, as Matt had hoped he would, and gave a nod, clearly feeling more at ease. "Ain't nothin' really, Majesty," Vorrun said. "It's just that she—my gram—she used to say that there's dreams and then there's *dreams.* Accordin' to her, dreams always mean somethin'. Sometimes, most times, really, dreams reflect our worries and our fears, the concerns we bury in other thoughts throughout the day, the worries we spend so much of our wakin' hours doin' our best to distract ourselves from."

"And the other times?" Matt asked, suddenly feeling unexplainably nervous and on edge.

Some of his feelings must have communicated themselves either in his voice or his expression, for Vorrun shook his head. "As I said, Majesty, she was strange—even those as loved her, like I did, would say as much. I wouldn't put—"

"What of the other times?" Matt asked again, aware that his voice sounded strained, even to his own ears, the voice of a man who was close to losing it...or had he lost it already?

Vorrun nodded slowly. "Well, my gram, she said that sometimes dreams weren't dreams at all—sometimes they were windows. Windows that a body might see through, sure, but more than that. Sometimes—and this rarely, understand—sometimes they were windows a body might open. Windows a body might climb through. And sometimes it weren't the person who climbed out of the window—instead, accordin' to my gran, sometimes it was the dream that crawled in it."

"The dream crawled in," Matt repeated slowly, thinking it over. It sounded like being haunted to him, and certainly that felt right, for he *felt* haunted. "Your gram," he said. "Did she ever know anybody that such a thing happened to? Where the dream crawled in the window, I mean?"

Vorrun frowned. "Everythin' alright, Majesty? Maybe I could talk to the cook, get you somethin' to eat. I know it always helps me to have a full belly and—"

"Please, Vorrun," Matt said. "Answer the question."

The guard winced. "Once, she said she did," he said slowly. "Fella had some real issues—I was a kid and even I remember that much. Couldn't ever sleep for fear of the dream, whatever it was—

he wouldn't ever tell anybody 'ceptin' my gram. Anyway, he was troubled, that's for sure. He went on not sleepin' and went on gettin' worse. Seein' things that weren't there, that sort of thing. He had fits, too. Fits where he'd just start a screamin' and carryin' on so terrible you'd think he was bein' tortured, and I don't doubt he was. Only, whenever anyone went to check on him he was always alone, thrashin' and a shoutin' as if in the worst kind of pain and with no source, so far as anyone could see. Least so far as my gram. She thought she knew—said the dream'd crawled through the window, then into him." The guard shrugged. "Anyway. That's what she said. But then gram said a lot of things, Majesty," the man offered in a tone that made it clear he was trying to put Matt at ease. "As I said, she was a strange woman."

Matt nodded. "Thank you, Vorrun—for telling me. And thanks also, for...you know," he paused, glancing at the broken in door.

The guard blinked, obviously surprised to be thanked. "Of course, Majesty."

"Perhaps I could use something to eat after all," he said after a moment. "I wonder, Vorrun, would you mind—"

"Not at all, Majesty," the guard said, and Matt wondered whether or not he imagined the note of eagerness he heard in the man's tone. "I'll go talk to the cook personally."

"Thank you," Matt said, and the guards bowed before starting for what remained of the door.

"Vorrun?"

The guard turned back. "Majesty?"

"The man—the one your gram said the dream crawled into. What happened to him?"

He went mad and died.

The words seemed to come to Matt's mind out of nowhere, and he frowned. Vorrun hesitated for a moment then gave a thoughtful expression, tapping his chin. "As I recall, Majesty," the guard said, "he got better. Started sleepin' and all of it went away."

A lie. Matt knew it as much as he knew anything and never mind the fact that he didn't know *how* he knew it. The other words, those that had resonated in his mind but had never been spoken out loud, felt far truer. "I see," Matt said. "Thank you, Vorrun."

"Of course, Majesty," the man said, then he glanced at the doorway. "And if you need anything—like another door steps out of line and needs seein' to—"

Matt gave the man a smile he didn't feel. "I'll be sure to let you know."

The guardsman gave a small frown, as if he saw some of the turmoil inside Matt. "Majesty, if—"

"Good day, Vorrun," Matt interrupted, suddenly desperate to be alone. "And thanks again for your help, both of you."

The guard winced, nodding. "Thank you, Majesty. Good day."

A moment later they were gone, both men disappearing through the doorway without a look back which was just as well, for had they glanced behind them they would have seen their king collapse into the chair by his reading table and bury his face in his hands.

Matt, though, could spare no more thoughts for the guardsmen. His heart was racing in his chest, and the memory of the dream—or nightmare, for if any dream had ever qualified as such, then that had certainly been it—of his father raising his axe grimly as thousands, tens of thousands of Fey creatures rushed toward him was still fresh in his mind.

And as bad as the dream was, as unnerving as it had been, made worse by his door being broken in, that was not the only worry plaguing Matt. What of the strange thoughts he'd had when speaking to Vorrun? What of the way he'd felt as though he knew the man's mind, knew whether he was lying or not, as if by magic? And then what of what the guardsman had said regarding his grandmother, and the man into whom the dream had crawled?

Relax, he told himself. *Be easy,* he told his heart, currently hammering in his chest. *The man Vorrun spoke of, he was crazy, that's all. You're not crazy. You're not crazy and dreams don't crawl into people, don't slither into them like snakes. You're fine— everything is fine.*

But whatever strangeness had made him feel as if he could tell whether Vorrun was being truthful or not, he did not need it now to recognize those thoughts for what they were—lies. Everything was not fine. Things were not okay. *He* was not okay. And as bad as things were, he was possessed of the sinking but undeniable feeling that they were getting worse. That *he* was getting worse.

True. It was true, and he knew it and never mind that it didn't make sense.

He should have been getting better. After all, he'd killed Emma, destroyed her utterly. His mind should be his own, his thoughts his own. Whatever part of him she'd taken, he should have back. Or so he had thought. Now, though, he wasn't so sure. If someone stole a man's coin purse, he could track that person down, could take it back. That was how he had thought of it, how he'd rationalized what Emma had done to him.

Perhaps that was wrong.

Perhaps Emma had been less like a thief and more like a lion, or a shark. If a man is attacked by a lion, if a lion sinks its teeth into him, even if that man somehow manages to best the beast, to destroy it, that does not mean that the part of him which the lion consumed would be returned to him. It was gone, that part, beyond even the faintest hope of retrieval.

Matt sat there, his face buried in his hands, his heart racing, and he thought of dreams, of monsters crawling through open windows.

He was still thinking of it, still replaying the nightmare of his father and uncle in his mind when suddenly there was a hand on his shoulder. Matt had been so absorbed in his own thoughts, so focused on simply surviving the raging storm of emotions within him, of fear and doubt, that he had not even been aware that anyone had entered the room. In his surprise, he let out a cry that was a mixture of anger and fear, spinning and lashing out without conscious thought.

Too late he realized that it was Priest, but the blow was already landing, hitting the man in the arm he'd raised in his own defense. Priest stumbled backward from the force of the blow, striking the wall.

"Priest I'm sorry!" Matt said, hurrying forward. "You surprised me—are you alright?"

Priest winced, giving his arm a shake. "I'm fine, Majesty—it's my fault. I should have announced myself. If you don't mind my saying so, you have your father's strength."

Matt felt an odd mixture of pride and shame at that. "I'm really sorry," he said again. "Come, we can get you to the healer and—"

"That is quite alright, Majesty," Priest said. "I will be okay, though in future I will make sure to announce my arrival," he continued, giving Matt a small smile. "It is only that I saw you sitting there, and you seemed...troubled."

"I'm fine," Matt said quickly—perhaps, he thought, a bit too quickly.

"I see," Priest said, glancing around the room with one eyebrow raised, taking in the sheets and coverlet—in disarray and covered in sweat—then the broken, splintered wreckage of the door. "It has been an eventful morning, I see."

Matt frowned. He knew that the man wanted to ask him again what was wrong just as he knew that he would not. Priest was gentle—if anything could be said about the man, it was that. Capable of great violence when necessary, it was true, but if the man had once possessed a violent nature then he'd managed to tame it, had learned to control it instead of it controlling him.

In that moment, Matt considered telling his friend everything. He was a *priest*, after all, one who had managed to leave behind his violent nature and become the kindest person Matt had ever known. One who, at least until very recent events, had seemed always to be filled with a peace and a confidence that nothing could touch.

In the end, though, Matt decided against it. After all, the Priest before him was very different than the one he'd met in the Black Wood with his father what felt like a lifetime ago. That Priest had been confident in a humble way, wise in a quiet, abiding fashion. His simple presence had been enough, on many occasions, to temper Matt's fear and worry, to assure him that, in the end, no matter how dark the night got, the sun would come again.

Now, though, Priest no longer felt like that. The man before him seemed as doubtful and distrusting, as worried as everyone else—perhaps even more so. And whatever the man had faith in now, Matt was confident of this much at least—he no longer wanted to share it.

"I'm fine," he said again.

Priest nodded. "I see. And the door?"

"Yes," Matt said, glancing at it. "I suppose I'll need a new one."

"That is not what I meant, Majesty," Priest said. "But then I think you know that."

Matt did, and he realized that while he didn't want to tell Priest everything—certainly he had no intention of telling the man about the feeling he'd had of being able to read Vorrun's mind—he would have to tell him something. "I had a bad dream," he said, wincing. "A nightmare, I suppose you'd call it."

"Is that what *you* would call it?" Priest asked.

A haunting, a premonition, a presentiment of doom. The words came into Matt's mind one after another, but he forced them away. "Yes," he said, aware that the word came out in a dry croak. "A nightmare."

"I see," Priest said. "And the door?"

"I must have cried out in my sleep," Matt said, not having to fake his embarrassment. "The guards heard and came to make sure that everything was okay."

"And was it, Majesty?"

Matt frowned. "I haven't been assassinated, if that's what you mean. I think that's the sort of thing I'd remember."

Priest gave him a small, gentle smile, one that immediately made Matt feel bad for snapping. "Listen, Matt, I do not mean to offend you—I only wish to make sure that you are okay. The last days and weeks...they have been hard. For all of us. Yet as much as we have all gone through, it seems to me that it is you who has suffered most. I am sorry for that, that is all, and I would help you, would share the burden, if I could. If you would let me."

"I'm sorry, Priest," Matt said, feeling very small and very cruel. For whatever inner battle the man was fighting—and he *was* fighting one, of that there was no doubt—still he always set it aside to worry over Matt, to do what he could to protect him. And as thanks, Matt snapped at him. "Really I am," he went on. "It was a nightmare, truly. I dreamed of my father and uncle, in the Black Wood. I dreamed that they had come upon an enormous glade in the forest and, filling that glade was every manner of Fey creature and monster. I dreamed that these monsters all attacked them."

Priest nodded slowly. "I see. And you believe that this dream is somehow real?"

Matt scoffed, opening his mouth to say no, to tell the man that such a thing was ridiculous. Only, it didn't *feel* ridiculous. Not at all. His father, standing there stoically, a grim expression on his face as he raised his axe, had not felt like a dream. Neither had Feledias in his pain, or the creatures who had charged at them. "It felt real," he admitted.

Priest nodded. "Yes, and all the worst nightmares do, as do the best dreams."

"So...so you're saying that's all it was then," Matt said. "Just a dream. That there isn't anything to worry about."

Priest gave him a sad smile. "I am afraid, Majesty, that there is plenty to worry about." The man's smile quickly faded, replaced by an almost haunted look of despair and grief, one that vanished in another moment, covered by an expressionless mask, one which Matt was confident the man had donned for his benefit.

"What happened to you, Priest?" he asked.

Another man might have pretended that he had no idea what Matt was talking about, might have dissembled and played word games in the hope that Matt would let it go. But whatever else had changed in him, Priest was still not the type of man to avoid something because it was uncomfortable. He gave a small shrug. "I lost my faith, Majesty," he said.

"You lost your faith," Matt repeated.

"That's right."

"That's it?"

"That's everything."

Matt didn't say anything, at least not at first. Instead, he found himself thinking of the dream again, of the way the two men had looked surrounded by so many of the Fey. He thought of the look on his father's face as he watched them come on.

His father had faced certain death, and he had stared at that death's approach with relief. It was as if he had stumbled off a cliff, or perhaps walked off it and, in finding himself plummeting to an unavoidable doom, had smiled. And there was only one reason Matt could think of for that smile, one reason for that relief.

It was not a good one.

It was just a dream, he told himself, but while the logical, rational part of him knew that it had to be that, could *only* be that, there was another part. A part that knew it was the truth and never mind the logic. And even if, somehow, it *were* only a dream, what difference did that make? After all, his father and uncle *had* gone to the Black Wood, that much was certain, had traveled directly into the enemy's place of power and had done so at his command.

"Majesty?"

He heard Priest's voice, but it seemed to come from a long way off, not fully penetrating the dark shrouded turmoil of his thoughts. He had sent his father and his uncle to the Black Wood, to their deaths. That had been days ago now. Over a week in fact. How long could any man, even his father, hope to survive against the many dangers and threats of the Black Wood? They would have been there for several days now.

"Matt?"

"I think my father's dead."

The words were out of his mouth before he was even aware he meant to speak and immediately Matt wished he could take them back. But it was too late—they were out there, those words, and some superstitious part of him recoiled in terror, for it seemed to him that his saying it would somehow make it come true. Ridiculous, maybe, illogical, but it was how he felt nonetheless.

He turned to Priest, tears suddenly coming into his eyes. "I think my father's dead," he said again, "and I killed him."

He tried to fight the sadness, the overwhelming despair that came over him then, the memory of his father in the Black Wood so fresh, but he never stood a chance. In a moment, he was hunched over, his face buried in his hands, the tears coming freely, his body shaking with great, terrible, wracking sobs.

This went on for several seconds, until finally the worst of it had passed, and he looked up to see Priest standing in the same spot he had been, staring at him with undisguised helplessness and sadness. Even through his sadness he thought of how different the man was than he'd once been. He remembered the way Priest had comforted the guardsman at the small village of Ferrimore after the Fey's attack, sharing in his grief.

He'd done so without hesitation, seeming to know instinctually the right thing to say, to do. At the time, Matt had been amazed by it, for he never seemed to know the right thing to say in such situations. Now, though, Priest only stood there looking helpless and lost and even a little afraid as tears flowed freely down Matt's face. "Priest...please, tell me that it will be okay. That *they'll* be okay."

The man winced, seeming to pale as if suffering under some great pain, and Matt thought that was right. The man was suffering, that was not in doubt, and never mind that the agony he underwent was not a physical one. "I cannot, Majesty," the man said, and a spasm of grief flashed across the man's face. Only for a moment and then it was gone again, buried, but that moment was enough to see the proof of what he went through. "I would not tell you a lie," he said, "not if I could help it."

Matt nodded, sniffling. He should have known as much—the man had told him, after all, that his faith was gone. "You could have just lied to me," Matt said.

"No," Priest said in a choked whisper. "No, Majesty, I could not. There are some things a man can only say if he believes them."

Matt stared at him for several seconds. He had known things were bad with Priest, but he realized in that moment that he had not known just how bad. Priest was not going through a crisis, was not having a momentary lapse of faith, one from which he might recover.

Priest was breaking. Perhaps he was broken already. The two said nothing for a time, only remaining in silence. Then, finally, Matt gave a slow, shaky nod. "I miss the old you," he said.

"So do I, Majesty."

Matt nodded again, slowly, his breath shaky and uncertain in his chest. "I wish..." he began, but he did not finish. There were simply too many possible ends to that sentence, too many things for which he wished, too many ways in which his heart might break.

"I know," Priest told him.

Then the tears were coming again, tracing lines of grief and pain and regret down Matt's face. He felt that he had lost so much in his life, that sometimes that's all life was. Losing. A man got things, earned things or was given things, only so that he might lose them.

He did not know how long he sat there, his body wracked by sobs, the memory of his father standing there, hefting his axe, playing again and again in his mind. All he knew was that his tears, his sadness, felt as if it flowed up from some great well dug deep into the earth, so deep that there was no end to it. And so he sobbed, and he ached, and he grieved.

In time, he was surprised to feel a hand on his shoulder and raised his head to see Priest kneeling beside him, a tortured look on his own face. "Listen to me, Matt," the man said. "Will you listen?"

"I will," Matt said, aware of how young his voice sounded, how much like a child's voice, one woken in the night to a bad dream and hoping for comfort.

"I cannot say what will happen," Priest said. "I cannot tell you that everything will be okay. Nor can I pretend at faith I do not have, faith in the rightness of things, faith in the gods themselves. For I have no faith left for them. I have no faith left for the idea that good will triumph, no faith left in myself. But I will tell you this, Matt—I have faith in your father. I have faith that he will not be defeated, that he will not be stopped. I believe it for I have seen it, time and time again. Your father is an agent of change. That I know as much as I know anything."

"An agent of change?" Matt asked, confusion making its way past his grief.

Priest nodded slowly. "I had a mentor once, when I first came to the Priesthood, when I first left my old life behind me. He taught me that while the world was full of thousands, maybe millions of people and creatures, not all of them, nor even most of them, were capable of producing real change. If so, then the world would ever be in turmoil, a roaring storm of confusion, and the people upon walking its surface would feel as if they stood in sand that constantly shifted beneath their feet, unable to ever catch their balance. This man, he told me that, instead, the gods had seen fit to choose certain individuals out of that chaos. Or, perhaps it was that those individuals chose themselves—I was never sure on that point. Either way, these men and women possessed the capability to produce great change, whether for good or ill, to reshape the face of the world. Men and women whose footprints across the world could be seen for generations to come. Your father is one such man, one such agent, one of the greatest. Perhaps even *the* greatest. And the fates of ones such as he can never be guessed at or underestimated. Or so my mentor told me."

Matt nodded slowly, finding at least some comfort in the man's words. "This mentor...you believed him?"

"He was my friend, my connection to the good, the one who helped to pull me from the swamp of despair and self-loathing I found myself in. He was also the wisest person I have ever known. Yes, I believed him. Back then, I believed him about everything."

"And now?"

Priest considered that for a moment. "Now I have come to question some of those things which he taught me, but one I have never questioned is this—there are men and women walking the face of the world who are capable of incredible feats, feats which produce equally incredible results. Your father is one such man. I knew that the moment I first met him. He is not just a man but a force, and it is no easy thing to stop a force."

"Not easy..." Matt said. "But not impossible."

Priest gave him a small, fragile smile, one that was clearly meant to offer comfort. "If any man can survive the Black Wood and its denizens, it is your father."

That was not as comforting as Matt would have liked, but then he knew that it was as much as Priest was capable of. And the fact was, he did feel better. Early morning sunlight shined through the window, reaching warm, golden fingers across the room, banishing the shadows that, at night, lurked in the corners.

Here, with the warmth of the sun on his face, with Priest beside him, those cold, lonesome woods of his dream felt very, very far away, and the image of his father standing as thousands of creatures rushed toward him lost some of its power. Not all—far from all—but enough that the terror that had gripped him upon waking loosened its grip. Not much, maybe, but enough that he could move. Enough that he could breathe.

"It is okay that you don't have faith, Priest," he told the man, standing. "I will have enough for the both of us. My father, after all, may find himself in a war, but who better to come out of it than the world's greatest warrior?"

CHAPTER TWO

Cutter had lived the life of a violent man, a life of one battle after another. War unending. A life of sharp steel and bloodshed. And so he knew war, knew violence better than he knew anything at all. It was for this reason that he became aware as those creatures around him which, up to that point, had restrained themselves, began to slip free of those restraints.

There was not a specific sign that he could point to—it was only a feeling. A feeling he recognized as the one that signaled coming violence, coming bloodshed. He knew it well, knew it the way a man who spent each morning and each night standing barefoot on the shore, letting the waters rush over his feet and calves, might know the comings and goings of the tide. He knew it the way a master sculptor might know the perfect moment when the right amount of stone had been carved away, might recognize in that instant when one more stroke might have ruined the work beyond repair.

The sculptor recognized that moment, and how not? For that moment was his, had been his time and time again. Cutter did not know how to sculpt, could not create fine paintings or write ballads. But war he knew. *Death* he knew. The truth was, he knew little else.

And so even as the creatures were yet unaware of what was coming, he knew it, saw it the way a seer might pick the future out of the murky bog of what-ifs and might-have-beens. And, seeing it, he flexed his fingers, trying to work some feeling back into the cold, stiff digits. He rolled his shoulders in a vain effort to loosen them, and cricked his neck first one way, then the other.

"Are you ready, Fel?" he asked quietly.

"Ready?" his brother asked in a slurred voice Cutter did not like. "Sure, 'course I'm ready, never been readier. Waiting on you. Anyway...ready for what? Where are we going?"

Cutter let his gaze travel across the creatures surrounding them in the glade, many of them beginning to shift as if they were waking from a dream, coming awake to the idea of violence. "I don't know, brother. But I promise you this much—wherever it is, we will go there together."

Feledias answered not with words but with a distracted hum. Then he was gone again. He had lost himself several times on the way here, delirious from fever and pain, and it seemed he had done so once more. Cutter thought that, in the end, that might even be for the best. After all, if they were going to die—and it seemed very likely that they were—then at least Feledias's mind would be elsewhere. It would all be over before he was even aware of it.

Or so Cutter hoped.

He felt another burgeoning of that tide of violence, warning of it, and he knew that it would not be long now. He knelt, carefully laying Feledias on the ground. His brother did not answer. His eyes were closed, and he shifted and moved, speaking in a low voice, uttering nonsense words, the language of fever and sickness.

Cutter rose again, then, gripping the haft of his axe in two hands, he hefted it and waited for what would come.

He did not have to wait long.

Kill him! Kill them both!

It was Shadelaresh's voice, one that was like the rushing of wind through the trees, the cracking of dried leaves and the rumbling of distant thunder all at once. The creatures did not hesitate, did not stop to question, for they were as eager as a tamed dog finally let off its leash to hunt, and they came on in a wave.

Cutter knew that he could not defeat so many, knew that it was hopeless. And in fact, he realized as those creatures rushed toward him, that he did not *want* to defeat them, not really. He wished to protect Fel, yes, but he knew that he could not and, failing that, failing a happy ending, then at least he might have *an* ending. An ending to a life of hate and rage and pain.

And so, Cutter watched his death come, and he was glad.

Another man, feeling the same, might have dropped his axe, might have bowed his head, knelt, and waited for that end, greeted it. But Cutter was a fighter. Whatever else he was or had been, a prince, a murderer, a monster, he had always been that. He could no more kneel and peacefully accept his fate than a cow might stand upon two legs and dance a jig.

He was not a man who might meekly accept his fate. He was not a kneeler.

He was what he was.

He was a warrior.

And so he warred.

The creatures came upon him in a cresting wave, and he lunged forward, crashing into that wave with his axe. A beast he had never seen before howled in pain as its taloned hand was torn away by the Breaker of Pacts, the black metal cleaving through it like paper. The creature's cries of pain abruptly cut off as Cutter's backswing removed its head from its shoulders, flinging the bloody object into its fellows.

Another creature was on him then, this one nine feet tall at least, gray-skinned and appearing like nothing so much as a terribly emaciated giant, its long, spindly arms—twice as long as Cutter's—lashing out at him with a clawed hand. Cutter used the flat of his axe head to bat the arms away then moved forward, into the creature's guard even as he released the haft of his weapon with one hand.

The creature might have been tall—incredibly so, towering over Cutter and many of its fellows—but it was skinny, frail, so when Cutter's fist struck its thin stomach it didn't just send the creature backward. Instead, his knuckles tore through the creature's flesh, and it screamed an unearthly wail as his fist erupted from its back in a shower of black ichor and pale gray flesh.

Cutter growled in disgust, ripping his hand free. Or, at least, he tried to. His fist was stuck fast, and he was forced to plant a foot in the creature's midsection and kick the corpse away to pull his hand free. No sooner had he done so than something landed on his shoulder. He reacted by instinct, pivoting into a spin, his axe cutting a lethal line through the air as he did. Another Feyling, this one a squat, piggy creature with close-set eyes and what looked like far too many teeth to fit into its mouth. It let out a sound somewhere between a croak and a gasp as the blade cut deep across its midsection, and it staggered away, short, chubby fingers trying in vain to keep its insides from spilling out.

Cutter still felt the pressure on his shoulder, though, as if someone were grabbing him, and he craned his head to look, stiffening as he saw what had caused it. Not the piggy Feyling, nor one of the other numerous creatures pressing in all around him. Instead, it was a creature that was no more than six inches tall.

A faerie.

But the creature perched on Cutter's shoulder bore little to no resemblance to the mystical, whimsical creatures in the stories, creatures that were far more a product of the author's imagination and childish fancies than anything resembling a living being. This creature did not arouse feelings of delight and whimsy, but instead, disgust and revulsion and disquiet.

It had wings—the stories had this much right, at least. But those wings were not gossamer, transparent things of fragile beauty, and instead were the gray black wings of a wasp. Its ugly features were twisted with insane hate, and in its spindly, hairy fingers it clutched what appeared to be a thorn that was at least two inches long. It currently held its weapon raised high above its head and before Cutter could react, the creature let out a squeal of excitement and drove the thorn into Cutter's shoulder.

He grunted in pain as it went in and a moment later his hand was there, snatching the creature off his shoulder. The creature hissed like a snake, biting into his hand with its misshapen, yellowed teeth. It hurt. A lot. But it had never been in Cutter's nature to avoid those things which hurt him but to destroy them, so instead of reacting as many men would have and jerking their hand away, Cutter squeezed.

He crushed the creature's body between his fingers and palm before tossing it away in disgust as he felt a sickening sort of heat begin to spread through his shoulder where the thorn had stabbed into him.

There was no time to think on it, though, for he caught sight of one creature the size of a dog but with only three legs, one at its front and two at its back, moving in an odd running, jumping fashion toward his brother, Feledias, who lay unconscious, oblivious to the battle waging all around him.

The fight had carried him nearly a dozen feet away from Feledias, and Cutter snarled as he waded forward, batting creatures aside with his axe while his free hand punched and shoved. He reached his brother's side just as the creature was lunging toward him, its elongated snout turned sideways, its mouth opened to reveal rows of jagged teeth. Cutter charged forward, swinging his axe in a wide, arcing uppercut that caught the creature in its mouth.

The head of the Breaker of Pacts struck the creature with tremendous force, and Cutter heard something, likely the creature's jaw, *crack* before it went sailing into the air, coming back to land somewhere beyond his sight in the milling throng of its fellows.

He'd saved Feledias, at least for the moment, but the distraction cost him. Cutter roared as claws traced fiery lines of pain down his back. He spun and lashed out with his free hand to knock his attacker away. Or, at least, he tried. The sickening heat that had come with the faerie's thorn had spread from his shoulder into his arm, all the way to the tips of his fingers, and his arm refused to obey his commands. Instead it just hung there numbly, limply, as the creature—that resembled nothing so much as praying mantis, though one that was the size of a large dog— lashed out again with its front feet.

Cutter recoiled but not quite in time, and he hissed as the creature's clawed feet traced three shallow but painful lines across his chest. He staggered back but barely made it a step before he fetched up against something behind him.

The praying-mantis-like Feyling sprung forward again, its front feet clawing at him, but Cutter brought his axe up, severing the creature's legs. He started forward, meaning to finish the creature, but before he could, something slammed into his back, and he stumbled, falling to one knee. He tried to rise but hadn't managed it when something pounced onto him from behind, claws digging into his shoulders while others slashed at his lower back.

Cutter growled and hissed and spat, letting go of his axe for a moment as he struggled to pull the creature free. Finally he managed it, pulling the creature over his shoulder and slamming it down in front of him on the muddy ground.

He felt more than heard something *crack* as the creature struck, but that didn't stop it from opening its mouth and lunging at him, trying to take a bite out of his face. Cutter recoiled, and the creature's fanged maw snapped closed only inches away from him. His left arm was still numb, his right currently occupied holding the creature down, and even if he had been free to grab his axe, the weapon was currently underneath the creature and therefore out of reach. That left only one option—not a great one but then when fighting for his life a man was rarely presented with the perfect choice.

Cutter waited for the creature to snap at him again then he twisted, leaning forward and biting deep into its neck. Unlike many of those creatures surrounding him, Cutter's teeth were not made for fighting, were not sharpened to easily tear into flesh, but what he lacked in natural gifts he made up for in motivation. He squeezed his teeth together, ignoring the sharp, acrid taste of the creature's flesh and blood in his mouth and shook his head like a dog. One savage shake, then another, and the creature was still.

Cutter hocked and spat out his grisly prize of flesh and blood then used his still-working right arm to throw the creature aside, uncovering his axe where it lay on the muddy ground. He snatched the axe up, starting to his feet, but they were all around him now, all manner of creature pushing in from every side, and he was forced to focus completely on swinging his weapon this way and that to fend them off.

Despite his efforts, the creatures were pressing in closer every second. He knew he needed to get his feet underneath him, knew that the time that he could stand against the waves of creatures would be dramatically reduced if he remained on one knee. All he needed was a moment's respite, a second, no more, to climb his way to his feet. Yet that second, that moment, never came.

His arm was aching from swinging his axe, and his body was covered in dozens of shallow cuts and scratches. None of the creatures had managed a deep wound on him, not yet, but he knew that it was only a matter of time before they would, or before his axe became stuck in one of their bodies, and then it would be over.

As his doom pressed in all around him, Cutter found himself thinking of his son, Matt. Matt who had sent him here to search for peace, an end to the war that Cutter had created when he'd slain the Fey King Yeladrian. *I'm sorry,* he told his son. *For all of it.*

And then, as his enemies pressed in all around him, Prince Bernard, son of King Dalten, the Crimson Prince, did not think or doubt or feel ashamed anymore.

He did what he had always done.

He fought.

CHAPTER THREE

Chall stood in the street and stared glumly at the giant stone building looming in front of him. It seemed to regard him with, if not outright hatred, then certainly a palpable disdain. The windows of the great stone edifice were like eyes weighing him and judging him unworthy. Standing there, Chall felt a very childlike urge to turn and run, to flee from the sight of that strange, alien place, the existence of which was as inimical to his own as a sudden onset of scruples and standards might have been to a prostitute's career.

"Honestly, Chall, you're being ridiculous."

He pulled his gaze slowly away from the building, half convinced that, when he was no longer looking, its door would open like the maw of some enormous beast, and it would lunge forward, consuming him.

"A deer might tell his fellow as much," Chall said, "might tell him he has nothing to worry about, but that won't stop the hunter's arrow from finding its mark. Nor will a hare's casual disregard of his danger stay the lion's teeth. Instruments of destruction are often subtle, Mae. You should know that better than anyone. You know, considering your past."

"True," Maeve said, an unmistakable note of impatience and annoyance in her voice, "but this is not a lion or an arrow. Fire and salt, Chall, it's a *library.*"

"Believe me," he said, frowning, "I know *exactly* what it is, and I know well its dangers."

"What *dangers?*" Maeve demanded in an exasperated voice. "You act as if it's full of soldiers or bloodthirsty madmen but it houses *books,* that's all."

"Books that are full of words," Chall said slowly, "knowledge."

"Fine," Maeve said with a huff. "Let's get this out of the way, so that you can get over it. *Why,* exactly, should anyone be scared of books?"

"It's not the books, Maeve, it's the knowledge. Have you ever heard the saying that ignorance is bliss?"

"Of course I have, but what—"

"Well, take it from someone who has bed his share of...shall we say, previously engaged women—"

"Married," Maeve interrupted, rolling her eyes.

Chall cleared his throat. "Anyway, take it from me—ignorance *is* bliss. Why, had I but known how often an angry husband was going to show up in the wee hours of the morning—when any reasonable person ought to have already found a bed for the night—waving a pitchfork, then I would have spent much of my life in terror and found the experiences of those nights which came before far less enjoyable."

Maeve stared at him for several seconds then, and although her expression would have been unreadable to most, Chall had known her for a very long time, and while he might not have been able to pinpoint why he thought so, he was suddenly overcome with the thought that he was very close to getting stabbed with one of the many knives she always carried about her person. "*Some* people," she said in a dangerous tone, "*most* people, in fact, might find it unwise for a man to speak to his lady about previous conquests. Particularly when that lady has been trained in the art of killing by some of the most lethal people ever to walk the face of the world."

Chall started to open his mouth to speak—he had no idea what he was going to say, only knew that the gist of it was going to be "please don't stab me"—but Maeve held up a warning finger and he snapped his mouth closed again.

"Besides which," she said, "some—and by some I mean anyone with a brain—might say that knowing these harlots were married should serve to dissuade any fool looking to bed them, therefore avoiding angry pitch-fork-wielding husbands altogether. And in that way a man's life would be saved not by his ignorance but by his *knowledge.*"

"Sure, he'd be *alive,*" Chall mumbled, before he could stop himself, "but being alive isn't the same as living."

Fool, he scolded himself the moment the words were out of his mouth. "Maeve, I—"

"Perhaps it is best for both of us—you in particular—if we cut this conversation short. Suffice to say that we *are* going inside. Petran Quinn is here—or at least according to the castle staff he's spent much time here since leaving the castle. And if we are to find out everything we can about these Crimson Wolves—something of a necessity, I'd think, considering they're killing innocent serving women in the castle—who better to ask than a historian?"

Chall could see the fire in her eyes still, could see that he'd upset her, and he thought he understood. He was not given to self-reflection—a state he'd cultivated over years of work and effort—but in that moment he found himself looking at the situation with far more objectivity than he generally liked. No one enjoyed hearing about the previous couplings and excursions of their lovers. It was not easy for anyone, and he imagined it must be all the harder when that person was a notorious lech, once known as the Charmer, a man about whom there were dozens, if not hundreds of stories, often told by drunken bards, regaling his sexual exploits. Never mind the fact that many of those stories weren't true and that some of them—the exact number was a secret he guarded carefully, even from himself—were lies he himself had told, that would not stop the hurt. After all, there were plenty of truths to match the lies, some even worse and they, too, were secrets he guarded carefully, if for very different reasons.

He was not good with words, never had been. At least those words not used as tools to get women into bed—he'd always had a bit of a knack for that. But then, during the height of his fame he had been far younger and far skinnier, and he did not care for the idea of testing his charm once more. Instead, he chose to employ a different strategy, one he usually avoided at all costs.

The truth.

"I love you, Maeve. I love you, and I do not deserve you."

Her eyes went wide at his words. "I know that," she said, but a small smile came to her face, and he thought that it would be alright. "I love you too," she went on. "You damned fool."

There were some jokes he might have made then, but instead he chose another strategy that, most often in his life, he had also foregone—silence.

"Anyway," she said after a moment, the menace gone from her voice as she glanced back at the library, "I know that this may not be your favorite place, but it doesn't bite, and we need any information we can get if we're to figure out what these Crimson Wolves are up to and how to stop them."

"It'd be more fun to spend the afternoon in bed," Chall muttered.

"Yes, it would," she said, smiling, "but we can't spend all day of every day in bed, Chall."

"We could give it a good effort, anyway," he said, then sighed. "Very well, Maeve. If you wish to venture in to mortal danger, then I will not allow you to venture alone. I, your protector, will escort you into the very depths of depravity, of sophistic scholars and haranguing historians, to ensure that you return once more from the land of the dead to the world of the living."

She raised an eyebrow. "I am so very grateful."

"As you should be," he said. "Now, ladies first." He sketched a mock bow and waved in the direction of the library across the street.

"So said the bold knight to the blushing damsel," she said, rolling her eyes again, but she started forward. Chall fell into step gratefully behind her. And that was just about as good as he could have hoped for. After all, he loved Maeve—loved her more than he'd ever thought he could love anyone or anything besides himself—but if that door *was* a mouth, and if it *was* going to chew on someone, he'd just as soon it chew on her first.

***

Five minutes later, they were inside, and while the door had not taken a bite out of him as he had jokingly—or at least mostly jokingly—quipped, the feeling that overcame Chall as they stood inside the entranceway was not relief but a sort of creeping panic.

He had rarely been in a library before—he'd made a point of avoiding them at all costs, much the same way he'd avoided early-arriving husbands—and he was astounded by the sheer number of books lining the shelves. Aisle after aisle of shelf, book after book, scroll after scroll. How many trees had been cut down and stripped to fill those shelves? How many *forests?* Too many, as far as he was concerned. So many that he thought that, had he been alone, he might have feared getting lost, so many shelves that a man might have spent his life wandering them and starved to death before finding his way out. So many books that a man could dedicate his entire life to the reading of them and still die long before even a fraction of the task was finished.

Chall knew that there were people that did just that—scholars, they called themselves. Historians, like Petran Quinn, the man they had come to see. Madmen. After all, the authors of all the books lining the shelves had loved lecturing others, showing off their grandiose wit and knowledge. Had loved it so much that they had decided even death would not keep them from it and had gone and written those lectures down so that they might continue to make people feel inferior and foolish for decades, even centuries beyond their own demise.

And, as maddening as *that* was, more maddening still was the idea that people *voluntarily* subjected themselves to those pretentious ramblings. Better for a man to skip, singing, to his own execution, at least so far as Chall was concerned. At least that bastard would get to lie down soon enough.

Staring at all those shelves lined with books, at the officious, prim and proper men and women walking around with stiff backs, their noses raised high in the air. Chall was reminded of his time in the academy back in Daltenia. He had thought that time was torture—still did, in truth—and had spent several years moping about how his life was over, and he was cursed to do nothing but sit through one lecture after another, endure the gaze of one disapproving tutor after another.

Of course, then the Skaalden had come, and the lives of thousands of Daltenia's citizens had been over in truth. He remembered, standing on the boats as they departed, fleeing into the unknown, feeling not only terror and grief—though those had been there in abundance—but also relief. Relief that he would never have to return to that academy again.

And now he was back—or at least considerably more back than he'd ever thought to be. *It's the damned academy all over again,* he thought.

"Stones and starlight, but they really did a number on you didn't they?"

Chall had been so caught up in his own thoughts that he had practically forgotten he wasn't alone. He glanced over and saw Maeve looking at him with a mixture of annoyance and compassion in her gaze—pretty much the usual way she looked at him. He was about to ask her what she was talking about when he realized he'd unintentionally spoken his thoughts aloud. "You know," he said, deciding it was past time to change the subject, "we probably don't even need to find Petran. Probably we could just ask one of these bowties with legs, and they'd tell us everything we could possibly want to know on the Crimson Wolves."

Maeve raised an eyebrow. "Bowties with legs?"

"Sure," he said, frowning at the librarians moving here and there among the shelves, not missing the glances they cast at him and Maeve—arrogant, snobbish glances. "You know," he said. "Useless, all show and no substance, full of its own importance."

"Wow. You really don't like bowties."

"You ever tried wearing one?" he said, glancing at her. "Because I have." He sighed. "Fire and salt, I have."

She rolled her eyes at that. "Be dramatic all you want—we both know that this has nothing to do with bowties and that you're just trying to avoid Petran. Which is ridiculous, by the way—he's a good man."

"The gods save me from anymore *good* men," Chall muttered. "It was up to me, I'd prefer an honest one. Failing that, how about one that minds his own damn business—a lost art, that is."

"But then, he *is* minding his own business, isn't he?" Maeve said. "After all, we're the ones coming to see him, not the other way around. And your dislike of Petran has nothing to do with him being honest or otherwise—which we both know he is. It's just because he sees through all of your bullshit."

"Don't even joke like that," Chall said. "My bullshit is all I am."

"And here I was thinking you liked honest men."

"I like women too," Chall countered. "Doesn't mean I want to be one." She frowned at that, and he cleared his throat. "That is...woman. I like woman. You. I like you."

She sighed. "Not great, but it'll do, I suppose. After all, we're pressed for time. Now, if you're done bitching—"

"Not even close."

"Then let's go find Petran."

He started to speak—well, to bitch, if he was being honest—but Maeve walked away before he could get a word out, and Chall was forced to swallow it and hurry after her. The last thing he wanted to do, after all, was to be left alone in such a place. Might as well invite one of the somber-dressed men and women shelving books to regale him with some unimportant war or leader of some forgotten kingdom that nobody had thought or cared about for a thousand years.

He chose to follow Maeve.

She walked forward as if not afraid in the slightest—no doubt aided by her experience training among assassins—and went straight for the desk behind which sat a woman with a back so rigid it looked like it was made of iron. Or, perhaps, as if she'd just sat on—

"Be nice," Maeve said beside him in a whisper. "I can see you thinking mean thoughts."

"Wouldn't dream of it," Chall answered. Maeve stepped up to the woman at the desk without hesitation, reminding Chall of nothing so much as those insane men that worked in traveling troupes, the ones who made a career out of sticking their faces and other important bits close to the mouths of creatures who, if they took it in mind, could easily chomp them off.

"Hello, ma'am," Maeve began without preamble, "I was wondering—"

"Shhh," the gray-haired woman said, poking her neck out and further accentuating the way her hair had been severely pulled back into a bun. "It is improper to speak loudly in the library."

She pointed at a nearby sign that indicated as much in bold letters, somehow imbuing the simple gesture with reverence as if it were the word of the gods themselves.

"Well, if the sign says it, then—" Chall cut off his mumbling, letting out a squeak of pain as Maeve kicked him in the shin. Not hard but then, when it came to the shin, he'd learned long ago that it didn't have to be.

"My apologies, madam," Maeve said, and although she seemed to speak in the same way, there was some subtle change to her tone, one that Chall couldn't identify but one that somehow made it sound more proper. "My companion, here, suffers from foolish notions, flights of fancy and, of course, ignorance, all of which I thought might be cured by a visit here."

The stern-faced woman behind the desk studied Maeve for a moment, then slowly her deep frown began to fade, melting away like frost in the sun. "This is the perfect place, of course, to treat such an illness," the woman said, smiling at Maeve and then turning a look on Chall that was a mixture of mild disgust and pity. "Now, tell me, Healer," she said, glancing back at Maeve, the smile reappearing instantly, "how would you begin to treat such a...clearly terrible condition?"

Maeve glanced at Chall, looking him up and down. "Well, a more thorough examination might be called for..." She gave him a small, hidden smile, her eyes twinkling. "But going on what I know—and what he doesn't—" she paused at a soft laugh from the woman behind the desk, her own eyes going wide in surprise, likely trying to figure out what the sound was as Chall suspected she wasn't the type that laughed often—"I suppose histories might be the best place to start."

"Histories?" the woman asked, sounding a bit surprised now. "And that is your professional diagnosis?"

Chall thought that the metaphor had just about run its course—and then run it a few more times for good measure. He was about to say as much, but he didn't get the chance.

"Such is my *humble* diagnosis," Maeve said, shooting Chall a warning glance before turning back to the woman. "After all, what better place to begin than the beginning?"

The woman's head bobbed slowly up and down in what appeared to be an involuntary nod, and she stared at Maeve not with distrust or suspicion now, the way she had when they'd first entered, but instead with something like admiration. "Very wise," she said. "I, myself, am an ardent fan of history, as well as current events."

"Not *too* much, surely," Chall said sourly, "after all, you don't seem to recognize us, and I, at least, am quite fa—"

"Do not call yourself fat," Maeve scolded. "I have told you that there is no purpose to it—eat better, that's all."

Chall frowned. He hadn't been about to say fat but famous and judging by her warning stare Maeve knew it. He shifted uncomfortably, feeling hurt. He glanced down at his ample belly, still there, or at least most of it, and never mind Prince Bernard's best efforts to the contrary in the last months. How a man could take five steps in his own house and lose his coin purse but could walk dozens of miles and not lose his gut was beyond him. He knew that he *was* fat, but that didn't keep it from hurting when someone—particularly Maeve—said as much.

"I wonder," Maeve went on, "I had heard tale that Petran Quinn himself, the Crown's historian, spends time here. Is that true?"

The woman's smile twitched at that. "It...is true that the great Truth Teller has seen fit, from time to time, to grace our humble establishment with his presence since his clever escape from his wrongful imprisonment."

The adjectives on you, Chall thought. "Clever?" he said. "A man doesn't have to be all that clever to walk out of an open ce—" Another shin kick, another squeak.

"You must feel truly blessed," Maeve said. "I wonder, do you have any idea when the next time he might come by would be?" The frown the woman had carried when they'd first entered was slowly beginning to re-emerge and Maeve spoke on quickly. "I just think, who better to educate my poor friend here, than the great Truth Teller, Petran Quinn, himself?"

That was laying it on pretty thick so far as Chall was concerned, but a quick glance at the woman behind the counter showed that, if anything, Maeve could have gone further still. The librarian was nodding appreciatively, smiling so widely now that Chall expected she'd be sore in the morning, working unused muscles and all. "Indeed, such a desperate student may well call for such an incredible teacher," the woman said slowly. "Still...I would not dare seek to presume upon the great historian's time or to speak for him. He is not a teacher, as such, for you see the truly gifted, such as Sir Petran, do not have time for teaching, for his life is spent on great, weighty matters."

Chall rolled his eyes again, unable to suppress the groan that came—not that he tried all that hard.

The woman spun on him with such abruptness—and such anger in her gaze—that he was half-convinced she meant to dive out of her chair, tight bun and all. "One such as you cannot hope to fathom Sir Petran's greatness, nor could you imagine the sacrifices he must endure—*has* endured—in pursuit of the truth. He did not even escape his prison cell for himself but in order to lend his aid to Prince Bernard, as well as Challadius the Cad, and Maeve the Murderous."

There was a sound that was somewhere between a growl and a hiss from Maeve, and this time it was Chall that found himself grinning. "Maeve the Murderous, is it?" he asked.

"That's right," the woman said.

"I hadn't heard that one before," Chall said, not glancing at Maeve—mostly because he didn't dare to. There was a fine line, when it came to assassins, between a funny joke and murder. He wasn't exactly sure where that line was, but he didn't mean to find out just now. "Marvelous, I thought they called her."

The woman behind the desk rolled her eyes. "Yes, that is what the unknowing masses call her, just as many call Challadius the Cad the Charmer instead. But I know better."

Chall nodded slowly. "I see. So you would say that you know a lot about them?" he asked. "Challadius and Maeve, I mean?"

The woman snorted. "Everything."

Another low growl from Maeve, and the woman turned to her. "Is everything quite alright, ma'am?"

"Fine," Maeve hissed through clenched teeth.

"You'll have to forgive her," Chall said, unable to keep the smile from his own face, "my friend here is, I'm afraid, quite infatuated with Challadius the Charmer."

"Cad," the woman corrected instantly, so quickly that it seemed almost involuntary.

"Right," Chall said. "Anyway, she has mooned over him for—" He cut off, grunting in pain, wondering how it was that she managed to hit the *exact* same place on his shin every time.

"I admit," the woman said, glancing at Maeve, "that there was a time when I, too, was infatuated with him, for there is no denying that he was once quite comely to look upon."

"Is that so?" Chall said, his smile widening.

"So it is," the woman said. "I cannot count the nights I dreamt of him, what it might be like to—" She cut off, blushing, and glanced at Maeve. "Well, surely you must know what I mea—"

"Petran Quinn," Maeve said, sounding decidedly frostier than she had before. "Do you know the next time that he will visit the library?"

The woman behind the desk blinked, clearing her throat. "O-of course. That...that is, Sir Petran is here now."

"Then might we speak to him?" Maeve pressed.

"That is really up to Sir Petran. Now, who may I tell him is calling?"

Chall shrugged. "Just tell him a couple of old fr—"

"Tell him Maeve the *Murderous* is here," Maeve said in a tone as sharp as one of her knives. "Along with Challadius the Cad."

The woman let out a soft giggle then glanced at Maeve, cutting off when she took in the woman's deadly-serious expression. "An odd jest, to be sure, but—"

"It is no joke," Maeve said. "Go and tell him."

The librarian gave a nervous laugh. "This is ridiculous. I would recognize Maeve the Murderous and Challadius the Cad if they were standing right in front of..." She trailed off as her gaze traveled to Chall. She squinted, staring at him so closely it was all he could do to keep from fidgeting. She blinked, swallowing hard, and he could almost see her thoughts writ plain on her face as she turned to regard Maeve. Her face paled, and she cleared her throat. "I...that is, oh my...Lady Maeve, please know that I meant no offense by...by what I said. I'm sure that you are of course just as wonderful and marvelous as all the stories claim and—"

"Oh, I would not be so sure," Maeve said. "I am feeling *particularly* murderous at the moment. Now, what of Petran?"

The woman cleared her throat again then she gave a shaky nod. "O-of course. This way, please, I will show you to a conference room and have Sir Petran meet you there as soon as possible."

They followed the woman as she started away, walking in a sort of sideways shuffle as she tried to keep her eyes in front of her and on them at the same time. No doubt she subscribed to the commonly held belief that assassins enjoyed stabbing people in the back. Which, as far as Chall was concerned, was ridiculous—in his experience, they were just as happy when stabbing them in the front.

Eventually they reached a closed door, and the woman—considerably less stern-faced and considerably more terrified-faced than when they'd first met her—removed a keyring from the pocket of her dress. She fumbled desperately to find the right key, all the while shooting frightened glances behind her as if Maeve might, at any moment, decide to attack her. Ridiculous, of course. At least...probably. Chall had known Maeve a long time, and while he might not say that she'd made a hobby of stabbing people, she'd certainly shown an aptitude for it.

Finally, to his and the woman's relief, she found the correct key, and the door swung open to reveal a small office in which sat a table with six chairs surrounding it. "I'll speak to Sir Petran immediately and let him know you're here," the librarian stammered, then she was retreating down the hallway between two shelves, leaving them there in the office, not practically running now but running in truth.

"Hard to look disapproving running like that," Chall observed, then he turned back to Maeve to find her scowling after the departing woman. "You really have a way with people—did I ever tell you that?"

"I always believed in being kind," Maeve observed, still frowning down the hallway. "After all, you can't have too many friends..." She glanced at him then, her expression still hard. "You can always kill them later."

It was Chall's turn to laugh nervously. "She was a funny lady, wasn't she?"

"Hilarious," Maeve said, her expression not changing.

"Right, right," Chall said, glancing at her hands to make sure they didn't happen to be clutching a knife.

He caught sight of a young couple out of the corner of his eye. They were halfway down an aisle, surrounded by books on all sides—not that they were in any danger of reading any of them. They were kissing and groping as if they'd just found out what kissing and groping were. Chall would have applauded them had his hands not been shaking quite so badly. Still, he thought that their being there presented him with an opportunity to go on being unstabbed, so he nodded in their direction. "Sweet, isn't it?" he said. "Young love." Though, truth be told, if it got much sweeter they could charge for admittance.

"What's sweet about it?" Maeve said, eyeing the two of them.

"You know," Chall said, "just...they've got their whole lives ahead of them. And, well, I guess, their innocence, that's what makes it sweet."

"Innocence," Maeve repeated, turning to him.

"Uh...yes?"

Maeve sighed. "She is not young at all but a woman in her thirties—a professional, judging by the way she just lifted his coin purse off him."

"What?" Chall asked, glancing again at the young girl. "You can't be serious, she can't be more than twenty-one, or I'll eat my hat. I'll have to get a hat first, of course, but—"

"Then we'd best go shopping," Maeve said. "Take a look at her neck—right where her throat gives way to her chest."

Chall had been doing that already—the woman had a considerable amount of bosom exposed, and he'd been taking mental guesses at how long it would take before what little was covered by her low-cut dress spilled out in their arduous kissing. Still, he thought it best not to tell Maeve as much. "Sure, if you insist," he said instead.

She looked at him as if he were a fool, likely knowing full well what he'd been eyeing. "Notice the top of her dress—do you see how her skin looks darker there?"

Chall blinked, looking again, and was surprised to find that Maeve was right. "So what? Been out in the sun a bit, that's all."

"With her face and shoulders covered?" Maeve asked, shaking her head. "No, she's used a powder—Madonna Lily, most likely—to make herself appear younger, to hide the wrinkles and imperfections of age. Not to mention her hair."

"What about her hair?" Chall asked, frowning.

"Dyed, obviously," Maeve said. "It is not that dark naturally, I can assure you. There's a method where one cuts leeches apart, stores them in a lead container and—"

"I don't need to know," Chall said. "Anyway, even if she does dye her hair, so what?"

"Women as young as she is pretending to be rarely concern themselves with dying their hair and, if they do, they rarely, if ever, go darker," Maeve said. "An older woman, though, might dye her hair darker to easier hide the gray hairs in her head."

Chall blinked, thinking that women really were complex creatures. Once, he'd wished he could tell what they were thinking by the looking—he was older now, though, and wiser, and so he was only grateful that he could not. "So she's a thief, then?"

"Today," Maeve said, shrugging. "Tomorrow she'll be something else."

"Like what?"

"Whatever she needs to be to survive."

"Well," Chall said, feeling somehow cheated. "At least the fellow seems to love her well enough."

"As much as he'd love any woman who showed that much of her tits," Maeve said sourly. "Anyway, he is no better—were she truly in love with him, he would leave her soon enough, would use her cruelly and abandon her to her own fate without a second thought, breaking her heart and making her wish she could break him."

"How do you know that?" Chall asked, glancing back at him, taking in the man's fine clothes. "Is it because he's wealthy? Or, no, don't tell me, it's because he has a mole on his left cheek, or perhaps his boots—"

"It's because he's a man," Maeve said, as if it were obvious.

Chall was tempted to argue that. After all, *he* was a man, and he didn't like the idea of sitting idly by while his gender was attacked. The problem, of course, was that he'd broken his fair share of hearts over the years, and they both knew it, so instead he only sighed.

"Now come on," Maeve said, starting into the room. "If we're going to be made to wait, I'd just as soon do it sitting down."

Chall glanced one more time at the couple—watching the woman stroke the man's hand, slowly easing a ring off it as she did—then sighed again.

He was in a library, coming to speak to a man whose chosen profession was seeking—and recording—the truth, when Chall spent much of his life doing his best to avoid it. At least one of the workers here thought he was a fool—and was likely right—and, worst of all, his assassin girlfriend was clearly angry with him.

He figured that, at that moment, he was having just about as bad of a day as any man could.

CHAPTER FOUR

Death was all around him. It came for him in gnashing teeth and slicing claws.

Cutter, the villagers of Brighton had named him.

He had not liked the name then, but as he stood over Feledias who'd fallen into fevered unconsciousness, swinging his axe this way and that, he thought that it was as accurate a name as any.

He was Cutter.

A man who had slain a wild boar and much more with his axe.

He was the Crimson Prince, a man who was coated in the blood of his enemies even in that moment, a man who had been so many times.

So he fought. He cut. And one after another, his enemies fell before him.

Only, this time, he knew it would make no difference. There were simply too many. The thing had been decided long before he'd ever raised his axe, long before they had charged him. Soon, their great numbers would tell.

In truth, they were telling already.

For not all the blood that coated him was that of his enemies. Much of it—just how much he couldn't guess—was his own. He'd suffered dozens of scratches and cuts, most shallow, some less so, in the minute since the battle had begun. Already he was beginning to weaken, the loss of blood robbing what little strength the travails of the past days had left him.

Soon, he would become too tired to swing his axe, and then it would be finished. He'd managed to make it to his feet from where he'd fallen once—he knew that it would not happen again. The next time he was knocked down, he would lack the strength to rise. He would die, in that moment, or perhaps the one after. And as for Feledias...his unconscious brother would be left alone, defenseless, forced to rely on the mercy of creatures who had none.

The thought of his brother, of what the creatures would do to him, fanned the spark of Cutter's resolve, his fury, and he roared as he lashed out with the axe, cleaving the creature nearest him in two before he took the head off another with his backswing.

And on it went.

The axe blade rose and fell and blood spilled. Some of his enemy's. Some of his own.

It might have gone on for seconds or hours, or years. It was as if he were stuck in some afterlife in which he would wage perpetual, unending battle. And the worst of that thought was that he would deserve no less. If a man's actions and character in life determined where he found himself after it then surely this was Cutter's place. A world of monsters and death—the Crimson Prince deserved nothing else.

But suddenly a voice came, one that drowned out all the hissing, snarling, growling, screeching of those creatures surrounding him, that seemed to shove them aside the way a grown man might push his way through a group of small children.

Enough.

The word did not seem to be raised, only spoken normally, yet it thundered in the air, reverberating with power and force. The creatures suddenly froze then retreated enough that they left a five-foot circle surrounding Cutter and his brother, a circle that was piled with the corpses of those creatures he'd slain.

Cutter stood in the center of that devastation, as he had so often when the battle was finished or, if not finished, at least when it had reached one of its pauses. The brief moment when a man had slain that enemy which lay before him and another had not yet stepped forward to take its place. Sometimes, he thought that was all life was and peace, the very idea of it, was in fact no more than that fleeting respite a man might find as his next foe moved toward him.

But as the creatures separated into an avenue shirking away, hunched, their faces down the way men might shuffle out of the way and kneel respectfully before an approaching ruler, it was not some hideous visage, some giant monster of their kind, which stalked toward him.

At first, in the seemingly perpetual twilight of what the creature who had escorted him here had called the Glade, Cutter took the figure to be a man. Certainly it was of the right size and shape, albeit it a particularly slender one, one whose walk somehow communicated a quiet authority and strength, reminding Cutter of some of the grandest mountain peaks he'd seen. Mountains did not sputter and spit and make a show as a storm did, but when the storm left, the mountains would remain as they had, unchanged or nearly so. Staring at the figure felt much the same as staring at one of those great edifices.

Cutter would have stood taller than him—had he not been hunched over gasping for breath, his axe dangling loosely from his hand—yet the figure seemed to loom not just over him but over everyone present.

As the stranger drew closer Cutter saw that it was not a man at all but instead an amalgamation of leaves and sticks and twigs and rocks that had been arranged in the shape of one. The pieces which made it up were constantly shifting and moving but retained their overall shape, held together by some incomprehensible magic.

A silence that felt almost sacred had descended on the Glade, the only sound the slight rustling of the creature's steps as it walked toward where Cutter stood. The creature paused at the edge of the devastation Cutter had wrought, its face turning one way, then the other. Although the creature itself was clearly a creation of sticks and branches and various detritus off the forest floor, the spots where a man's eyes might have been were not empty but were instead filled with eyes that were slightly larger than a man's. They were pure gray, the color of an overcast sky, and they shifted as he stared at the corpses like clouds shifting in a tumultuous sky.

The creature was alien, strange, yet Cutter thought he understood its thoughts in that moment, or at least its feelings, for it seemed to radiate a terrible sadness, one far greater than any he had ever felt or thought himself capable of feeling. As the creature regarded the dead, Cutter felt that sadness creeping into him as well.

It is enough, Destroyer, the figure said, its voice like the rustling of leaves in the wind, like the swaying of branches in the breeze. *Let it be enough.*

Cutter found himself frowning. Despite the fact that the creature's form was made of shifting twigs and leaves and rocks, there was something familiar about it. Something familiar, in particular, about its voice. A voice that sounded solemn and ancient and wise and, most surprisingly, kind.

"Do I know you?" Cutter rasped, his voice hoarse and raw from shouting during the bloodshed.

It is rare, indeed, Destroyer, for any living creature to truly know another, rare even for them to know themselves. Yet I do not think that is your true question. Yes, we have met before, not so very long ago.

Cutter blinked as realization dawned. "It's you—from before. The Gray Man."

The figure inclined its head then turned to regard Feledias where he lay unconscious on the ground. *It grieves me to see that your brother fares no better than when last we met.*

"It's been a hard road," Cutter said.

All roads are, Destroyer, the creature responded, *though it cannot be denied that the one you have chosen is perilous indeed. It seems that you have not lost your resolve in your pursuit of peace?*

"I have not."

The creature nodded its head, a gesture that it somehow imbued with a deep sadness, then it turned its gray-eyed, shifting gaze on the dead again before looking back to him. *And I need not ask you how your quest fares, for I can see it well enough.*

What is the meaning of this? a new voice demanded, and this one, too, Cutter recognized. In many ways it sounded similar to the Gray Man's, the voice almost of nature itself. But if the Gray Man's voice was the embodiment of the peace and gentleness of nature, the voice of growing things, of life and creation, then this new voice was that of a raging storm, of trees snapping and the earth being torn asunder beneath the grip of some great maelstrom.

Cutter turned, along with the Gray Man, to see Shadelaresh, the one he had known as the Green Man, walking between the thousands of Fey gathered in the clearing.

Shadelaresh's ten-foot-tall frame shook with rage as he strode closer. It was his face, though, that struck Cutter the most. A face as black as night, shaped the way many men thought a demon's face might be shaped, and within that darkness his eyes shone a furious emerald green.

Shadelaresh marched to stand before them, towering over Cutter and the Gray Man, but if the Gray Man was at all intimidated by Shadelaresh's far greater size he did not show it, only gazed at the newcomer calmly.

Teacher, Shadelaresh hissed in a voice like the sound of limbs snapping in the frost. *I thought you might be the cause of this disruption.*

And I thought you might be behind the attempted murder of this man, but I had hoped otherwise, Youngling.

Youngling.

It was a strange word to call Shadelaresh, a being who, to Cutter's thoughts, seemed eternal, and it was stranger still to imagine the Green Man as a student, even to one as imposing as the Gray Man. Yet the Gray Man had not said the word with disdain or in a patronizing way. Instead, it had sounded almost like a term of endearment, of closeness.

Despite that, Shadelaresh did not seem pleased by the moniker. *I am young no longer, Teacher, in case you have not noticed. I left my youth behind centuries gone now. I am no longer a child to be lectured, to be taught.*

It is the wisest among us, the Gray Man says, *who understands that there is always more to learn.*

One of your favorite platitudes, as I recall, the Green Man said. *And if you wish, we will discuss it further, but not now. Now,* he went on, turning to regard Cutter with eyes that danced with emerald fire, *we have more pressing business. The Destroyer has come among us, has in his arrogance dared to encroach upon our lands, to trespass into the Glade itself.*

"We didn't trespass," Cutter said. He turned behind him to regard the creature perched upon the dead Ferrik's back, the big soldier's form currently knelt as the other Fey. "We were brought here."

Captured, you mean, the Green Man hissed.

"No," Cutter said. "We came of our own free will on a mission given to us by our king."

You would dare speak to the Fey of kings, Shadelaresh growled, *you who stole ours from us? You came seeking to harm the Fey, and so you will die. Both of you will.*

"I did not come seeking violence but peace," Cutter said.

Peace, Shadelaresh hissed. *What does one such as you know of peace, Destroyer? You who, even now, holds the Breaker of Pacts in your hands, its blade slick with the blood of my people?*

You cannot fault any creature, Fey or otherwise, for defending itself, Youngling, the Gray Man said. *It was not the Destroyer who began the bloodshed but you when you ordered him killed.*

And what of it? Shadelaresh demanded. *He must be made to answer for his crimes. He who is responsible for uncountable Fey deaths, who has dared trespass into the Black Wood on several occasions, whose people pushed us back here in the first place, robbing us of our lands, lands which we held for millennia beyond counting.* The Glade was suddenly filled with thousands of angry growls as the gathered Fey reacted to the Green Man's words.

Tell me, Teacher, Shadelaresh went on, imbuing the word with disdain, *would you counsel mercy against one such as this? One who has killed so many of our kind, who has, with his people, stolen our lands, our homes, our very lives?*

It matters not what I might counsel, Shadelaresh. It is the Law that must be obeyed, not me. He has come seeking audience with the king and it is the law of our people that any who come with grievance to the Glade must be given an opportunity to earn their right to speak.

He is not of the people! Shadelaresh growled. *And even if he were his appeal could only fall on deaf ears, for we have no king. We have no king because he took him from us. Took him from us with the very Fey-crafted weapon Yeladrian himself gave to him, an honor unheard of by any of his kind.*

It seems that you are not so finished with my lessons after all, Youngling, the Gray Man said. *For it is in the Law. Whether a king sits upon the throne or not, the one who comes to make appeal must be allowed the opportunity to prove the worth of that appeal.*

You speak to me of the Law when a murderer of our kind stands before us, bloody axe clutched in his hands?

Yes, the Gray Man said, his voice as calm and relaxed as Shadelaresh's was furious. *The Law is inviolate, standing above any and all of us. Even above kings. Otherwise, it is not law at all, and if there is no Law, Shadelaresh, then there is only chaos. Yeladrian knew that much, would tell you as much, if he could.*

But he can't, can he? Shadelaresh snapped. *Yeladrian—my friend—is in the Land Beyond and so out of reach. He is dead. Your son is dead, and before you stands the man responsible for it. Are you truly going to allow him to continue drawing breath when each moment he lives is a mockery to the memory of your beloved son, my dearest friend and the greatest king our people have seen in generations? I cannot believe that you would do that, that you would tarnish your son's memory so frivolously.*

The wind suddenly picked up, and the giant ancient trees surrounding the Glade began to sway in the sudden gusts like saplings in a hurricane. Cutter grunted, holding up his hand against the driving wind, and he was not the only one affected. Several of the smaller Fey such as the faeries were cast about as if they'd been thumped by some giant—not that Cutter minded, he could only hope that all of the little bastards broke their necks in the tumble.

Even the larger Fey were having difficulty keeping their feet, digging and grasping at the ground or at each other for support, sounds and cries that had, a moment ago, been ones of fury and eagerness as they prepared to kill him, suddenly changed to mewling whines of terror.

Do not dare question my love for my son, Shadelaresh, the Gray Man said in a voice that rumbled like the thunder of an approaching storm. *It is a love the depths of which you could not begin to understand, a love that could throw up mountains and cast them down again, that could blot out the sun, that could shake the very foundations of the world. Do you understand?*

Shadelaresh's green eyes danced, and the wanderer stared at his alien face, seeing it contort and twist as he seemed to shrink beneath the gaze of the Gray Man and never mind that he stood ten feet tall to the Gray Man's own five and a half feet. He expected Shadelaresh to lash out in fury, thought that here he might see a battle between two of the most powerful of the Fey, if not *the* most powerful.

But when Shadelaresh finally spoke, Cutter realized by the shaking of his voice that it was not anger that gripped him—or, at least, not mostly that—but fear. *Forgive me, Teacher,* the Green Man said, his voice sounding apologetic and frightened, yet Cutter did not think he imagined the undercurrent of resentment hidden beneath. *I spoke only out of anger, an anger born of my love for my people, for your son. He was like a brother to me, as you know, and his loss is one that has left a hole within me. And not* just *me. Your people suffer too, Teacher. Surely you must see this.*

The wind slowly began to settle, the groaning creak of the trees subsiding into silence. In that abrupt stillness, devoid of the driving wind that had nearly taken Cutter from his feet multiple times, the Black Wood seemed to stop, waiting on what the Gray Man might say, what he might do. *I know well your love for my son, Youngling,* the Gray Man said in a voice that was soft and kind and sad. *Just as I know how he loved you, how I loved you both. It is for this reason that I took you in, that I taught you all that I know, gave you of my heart and soul and spirit. It is why it grieves me so to see the path that you have chosen, the path of hatred and malice, of revenge. For such paths lead only to pain, and I would not see you suffer so, would see you settle yourself upon a different path, one the end of which might end in something besides suffering.*

A different path, Shadelaresh said, his voice shaking with some powerful emotion. *If another exists, Teacher, I do not see it, and would not take it even if I did. I did not set myself on this path— others did.* He paused, turning his furious green eyes on Cutter. *But now that my feet have found it, I will walk it to its end.*

To your end, the Gray Man said sadly.

I think not, the Green Man answered, *but nevertheless, my heart will not be changed. There is only one cure for what ails me, what ails our people, and it is the death of the man who brought our grief upon us.*

Death is never a cure, Youngling, the Gray Man said sadly. *Even the most uneducated of healers could tell you as much. It is what it is—the final answer. But the death of these two mortals, the death of their people, will not fill the hole inside you. It cannot. You cannot create by destroying. You must know this.*

The Green Man stared at his counterpart for several seconds, and Cutter was possessed of the feeling that he was considering the creature's words, that he might, in the end, be swayed. Finally, though, he let out an angry hiss, like the sound of a blade being dragged from its sheath. *Even if it offers no cure, still I would see them all dead. If not to save myself then to save our people. They are the intruders here. They came to our lands, and we offered them friendship. Your son offered it only to find himself on the other end of the very axe that you, his father, imbued with power. I will make sure that these two and all of theirs die for what they've done. We will push them back into the waters from whence they came the way one might sweep away dirt that has gathered at his door.*

It is the rage that speaks for you, Youngling, the Gray Man said, *not your spirit, not your own soul.*

I am rage, Yeladrian hissed. *And forgive me, Teacher, but I do not know how you are not the same. It was your son who was slain in cold blood, so it is you who is owed the price of this one's head,* he finished, turning to regard Cutter with hatred that couldn't have been more obvious despite the creature's alien features. *I do not understand how you can speak of the Law when this, this monster stands here, his bloody axe in hand, corpses of our people around him. If there need be any testament to who he is, to* what *he is, there can be none clearer than that.*

And it is for that very reason—the fact that it is my *son who was slain—that you should understand the importance of my words, Shadelaresh,* the Gray Man said. *It is the Law that holds us together, the Law that binds our people, connects us. Without it, we are nothing, or if we are anything then we are what the mortals believe us to be—monsters. Savages. Beasts.*

There were low rumblings of anger at that from the Fey filling the Glade, but the Gray Man didn't even bother to turn, his eyes locked on Shadelaresh's face. *My son knew this. He gave his life to the Law, and he gave his life for it. You may not see it, Shadelaresh, may be blinded to the truth of it by your own rage, but it is not I who tarnishes Yeladrian's memory—it is you. For he would never have countenanced cold-blooded murder without cause.*

Cutter might have argued with that considering the fact that it had been Yeladrian who had attempted to get him to kill his brother, Feledias, as a blood price to seal the peace between their two kingdoms. But considering that the Gray Man was the only creature in the Glade beside Feledias who didn't want to see him dead he chose to remain silent.

Shadelaresh stared at the Gray Man for several seconds, a pregnant silence falling on the clearing. *You would have me choose the Law over my brother?* he asked, not aggressively but disbelievingly. *You would choose it over your own son?*

Yes, the Gray Man answered, his voice sad and solemn but also confident.

The Green Man stared at his teacher with a betrayed expression on his alien features. *Very well, Teacher,* Shadelaresh said in a voice like limbs snapping in the frost, like dry leaves cracking underfoot. *It will be your way, then. And what would you have us do?*

Follow the Law, the Gray Man said simply. *There is no king to give audience to the petition of these two men and so we must convene the Council of Elders to hear it.*

The Council of Elders, Shadelaresh repeated. *I was just a youngling the last time such a meeting was called. Are you sure that this justifies their calling? These men have come seeking peace between our peoples, Shadelaresh,* the Gray Man said. *Peace that would mean no more bloodshed, no more of our Younglings dead to no purpose. Yes. I believe it justifies their calling. Don't you?*

But how do you even know that they will come? Shadelaresh said. *Many live very deep in the Wood and have not visited the Glade in decades or longer. It may be that they will not share your opinions about the significance of these two men's visit.*

Two men, the two princes of the Known Lands, one known for his ferocity in battle who is said to have slain hundreds of our kind, the other for his tactical genius? Oh yes, Shadelaresh. I believe that they will come. In their fury and their hatred, they will come, for there are few things which drive creatures forward more than such emotions, a truth I think you know well. As the Eldest, I will send out the call. The Council of Elders will meet and hear the petition of these two men. Until that time, they are not to be harmed. He paused, turning to regard the thousands of Fey gathered in the Glade, and despite his diminutive size and the fact that he spoke softly, the Fey bowed their heads and recoiled as if afraid.

All, that was, save for Shadelaresh who stood his ground and, in another moment, went a step further than that. *No.*

The Gray Man turned back to regard his pupil. *No?* he asked, and now Cutter thought he detected a hint of uncertainty in his voice to match that he'd heard in Shadelaresh's earlier. *As Eldest, Shadelaresh, it is my duty to—*

Oh, I do not mean who is allowed to call on the Council, Shadelaresh said, and Cutter did not like the satisfaction he heard in the creature's voice. *You are Eldest and so indeed that is your duty, your honor. No, instead, I mean that the two princes of the Known Lands are not, I'm afraid, going to be allowed to render their petition quite so...easily.*

Shadelaresh, there is really no need to—the Gray Man began, but he never got a chance to finish.

Oh, but I'm afraid there is. The Code of Warriors and the Code of Innocents are very different, as you well know. While an innocent, un-blooded might petition the king—or the Council—simply on the merit of whatever message he carries, those who have shed blood have a different route. For they are not innocent, are not of peace but of war, and so they may not walk the path of peace to air their grievance.

You call him a man of war, yet he comes in search of peace, and peace is the message which he carries.

True, but I am sorry to say that the Law gives no special dispensation to those who come bearing tidings of peace, Shadelaresh said in a voice that made it clear he wasn't sorry in the slightest. *So, it seems, Teacher, that it is I who has a lesson for you. Unless, of course, you wish to go against the Law after all? Unless you mean to disregard it for these two mortal princes when you would not disregard it for me...or your son.*

The Gray Man shifted. That was all. The slightest movement, or so it seemed to Cutter, but the next thing he knew Shadelaresh's ten-foot frame was lying on his back, writhing as if in agony, gasping and hissing. The world suddenly seemed very strange, as if there were some great pressure all around Cutter. It felt as if the sky had dropped low and was preparing to crush him beneath it the way a man might crush a bug beneath his booth. And judging by the whimpers and cries of pain and terror from around him, Cutter was not the only one who felt it.

Twice now you have questioned my love for my son, Shadelaresh, the Gray Man said. *Twice you have thought to use Yeladrian and his death as a weapon against me. There will not be a third. Do you understand?*

I...understand, Shadelaresh said in a gasping, pained voice.

Good, the Gray Man said, and then, suddenly the great pressure Cutter felt eased. The ground no longer seemed to tremble, and the sky seemed to retreat high above head once more. *You are like a son to me, Shadelaresh,* the Gray Man went on, his voice sounding sad and regretful. *I love you, nearly as much as my own kin, but you forget your place. You are not the king of the Fey—the Fey have no king, not anymore. You do not speak for them.*

Shadelaresh climbed to his feet, glancing at Cutter, and in that quick glance Cutter could see that the creature blamed him, personally, for his embarrassment and his shame. Well, he supposed that was alright. They hadn't exactly been on the road to lifelong friendship anyway, and the bastard could only kill him once, if it came to it.

You would turn our people into murderers, the Gray Man said. *But the Fey are not cruel or hateful, Shadelaresh. We are not the monsters that many of the mortals believe us to be.*

Truly? Shadelaresh said. *I am not king—that is true. I could never be, for I am not your true son—you have made that clear. So let me ask the people directly. Who among you,* he said, raising his voice in a sound like cracking thunder in the distance, *would allow these two men, men responsible for the lives of hundreds, thousands, of our kind to speak in open council, to the most revered among us, without trial?*

Silence fell over the glade then, a silence as powerful, in its way, as that which had come when the Gray Man had grown angry.

And within that silence, Shadelaresh smiled. *It seems, Teacher, that I speak for the Fey more than you think. So is it settled, then? Will you abide by the will of your people? Or will you speak for them?*

The Gray Man stood in silence for several seconds, then he glanced at Cutter, an obvious sadness and apology in his gray, stormy eyes, before he turned back to regard Shadelaresh. *Very well, Youngling. I will not stand against the people, though it pains me to see us, to see you, choose the path of blood.*

I did not choose it.

You choose it even now. But if it is to be the Trial, then at least they might have time to rest.

A single sun rise and sunset, Shadelaresh answered, his pleasure clear in his voice. *Such is the law regarding how long a warrior might wait, once coming forward with his grievance, before his trial begins.*

A single day and night? One is unconscious and the other can barely even stand. Even a week would not be enough. A day will be as nothing.

And yet it is what they have, Shadelaresh said. He turned to Cutter then, his demon's face smiling, his green eyes sparkling with cruel joy. *Enjoy your last day, Destroyer. Enjoy it, for it, like all days, comes to an end. But before it does, know this—you killed my brother, and I will kill yours. But before I do, I will visit upon his flesh punishment for the many sins of you and your people. His suffering will be so great that your women will clutch their babies to their chests at the very mention of his name, and your strong fighting men will wilt in fear of sharing his fate. I will make of his torturing a testament, proof against any who might dare to stand against the Fey as you and your people have done. You murdered my brother, Destroyer. I will tear yours apart piece by piece, mind and body and soul until there is nothing left but so much quivering meat.*

Cutter considered planting the axe he still held clutched in his hands in the creature's forehead in that moment, felt some old, familiar part of him—a part that he had thought, or had at least hoped, long dead—rise up like a beast raising its head at the sniff of prey. The Gray Man, when he'd asked Cutter and Feledias to kill Shadelaresh, had told him that the creature had become too strong to be slain by mundane weapons, even an enchanted axe like the one Cutter carried, yet he was still tempted to put that to the test.

What stopped him, in the end, was not fear that it would not work. Cutter had never feared anyone or anything, save himself and that always. Nor was it concern for the creatures surrounding him.

In the end, what stopped him was Matt's voice in his mind. Matt asking him to right the wrongs he'd made. He had not asked him to travel here to kill Shadelaresh—he had asked him to come here and find peace for his people. So for once in his life, perhaps the only time, Cutter, known as the Crimson Prince, let his words do the talking instead of his axe. "You don't like me," he said quietly, staring at the green demon, its eyes shining before him. "I get it. I don't much care for you, either."

Shadelaresh snarled silently at that, then motioned and two Fey stepped forward. One moved toward Cutter, the other toward Feledias. "Touch him and you die." The words were out of Cutter's mouth before he even realized he was going to speak, coming out in a vicious snarl, and he became aware, in the silence, the stillness that followed, that he was gripping the haft of his axe so hard his fingers ached.

Odd words coming from a man who sues for peace, Shadelaresh said. *And how else do you think we will move him, Destroyer? He is unconscious, after all, and we would hate for him not to be ready for the beginning of the Trial on the morrow.*

"Then I will carry him."

Carry him? Shadelaresh said. *You can barely stand.*

"There have been others who have assumed they knew what I was capable of," Cutter observed, staring into that ebony face, the green eyes dancing. "They are all dead now."

There was a pregnant silence then as they stood regarding each other. Part of Cutter thought that the Green Man would rush forward and attack him. Part of him hoped he would. In the end, though, Shadelaresh only inclined his head. *As you wish, Destroyer,* the Green Man said in a humoring voice. *You will have your way— at least for tonight. Tomorrow, though, the Fey will have theirs.*

Cutter watched the creature for another moment then, finally, knelt down and, using his free arm, lifted Feledias. He was weak and tired, yet still he was surprised by how light his brother felt. The fever and their time in the Black Wood had not been kind to Feledias. He had always been leaner built than Cutter. A willow to Cutter's oak, their father had said. Before his exile, Cutter had always envied his brother the natural grace that came with his lean form, had always appreciated the way Feledias, even with less natural skill, seemed to float during a fight whereas Cutter plodded along like some flat-footed grunt.

But Feledias did not look graceful now. The trials and tribulations since they'd entered the Black Wood had stripped pieces of him away the way a sculptor might cut away the excess stone. Only what had been cut away was not excess but the sculpture itself. Feledias looked hollowed out, his cheeks thin, his face gaunt, and his normally muscular, thin frame now just seemed thin.

Cutter frowned, hoisting him onto his shoulder and rising.

Shadelaresh stared at him, and Cutter thought he saw anger and, perhaps, something else there, in his alien visage. Then the Green Man motioned to the two Fey standing on either side of Cutter. The creatures moved toward him, as if considering grabbing him by the arm. He watched them take one step, then another.

They did not take a third. Instead, they looked at him, looked at each other, and started down the avenue of Fey.

Cutter, left with no other option, followed after them.

CHAPTER FIVE

They sat in what was, for Chall, at least, an uncomfortable silence as they waited on Petran Quinn—the *great Truth Teller,* according to the maddening and quite clearly *mad* woman at the library's front desk—to arrive.

Maeve was clearly still sore with him, and while Chall wasn't entirely sure what he'd done he was certain he deserved it. Likely it had something to do with bringing up his previous escapades with other women. That had been careless. When he was younger—and considerably thinner—he could get away with such comments. After all, people had a tendency to accept things from the handsome and the beautiful that they would never accept from those they considered ugly. A hard truth, maybe, an unfair truth, but then that didn't change anything. And despite how hard it was for him to believe, Chall *had* been considered quite handsome once. But then that was a long time ago. What was simple foolish carelessness of speech had, then, been just an appealing sort of eccentricity. Now, though, he was fat and old, and it just made him a fool.

He'd spent the last several minutes trying to think of something to say, some way of apologizing but then he had always been far better at talking himself into trouble than out of it. He was still thinking when the door opened to reveal the woman from before.

She looked considerably less stern this time around than when he'd first seen her, and Chall noted absently—because with women, he missed very little—that her hair, which moments ago had been tied back in a bun so tight it had looked like some sort of special torture, was now hanging free. Salt and pepper hair but surprisingly luxurious for all that. It made her look very different—pretty, in fact, if in a scornful teacher sort of way.

The woman moved into the room, motioning. "Please, Truth Teller, this way, your guests are inside." The woman hurriedly stepped to the side of the door, bowing her head as if in deference to some approaching king. A moment later, Petran Quinn, the no longer exiled Historian to the Crown, stepped into the room.

Clearly the woman held the historian in high regard, but where great kings might have been known for their majesty and presence, Petran Quinn was a small, bookish man and with his glasses perched high on his nose, his hair in disarray, and his fingers and tunic stained with ink he was a far cry from the noble, inspiring kings the bards sung about. But then, Chall supposed that in such a place as this, among men and women who voluntarily wasted their lives away with their noses buried in books, the man might indeed be a bit of a celebrity.

"Please, Elizabeth," the historian said, blushing, "I asked you to call me Petran."

"And I asked *you* to call me Beth," the woman countered, blushing as well.

Petran swallowed, staring at the woman. "Beth," he said.

She smiled shyly. "Petran."

The two stood there staring at each other for several seconds. Maeve shot a look at Chall—the first one for fifteen minutes that didn't look like a prelude to murder—and Chall cleared his throat. Petran and the librarian started at the sound.

"I-if there's nothing else, sir," the librarian stammered, "I'll leave you to it."

"We're good, Beth, thank you," Petran said in a dry, breathy voice.

"Very well," the woman said, inclining her head with a small, nervous smile. "Petran."

The librarian half-walked, half-fled toward the door, disappearing through it in another moment.

Chall watched her go and, when the door was closed behind her, he and Maeve turned to regard the historian who stood fidgeting uncomfortably beneath their gazes.

"Um...hello, Lady Maeve. Sir Challadius. I hope...that is, I hope all is well."

"Better by the minute," Chall said, grinning. "Beth, huh?"

Petran jumped as if he'd just been goosed. "Sorry, what?"

Chall shrugged, enjoying himself now. "Just didn't think she'd have a first name like Beth, that's all."

"What did you think it would be?" Maeve asked, raising an eyebrow.

Chall shrugged again. "I don't know. Miss, maybe?"

Maeve rolled her eyes. "Thank you for seeing us on such short notice, Petran. You've been missed at the castle."

The historian nodded, clearly eager to change the subject as he moved to the table and sat. "Yes, well, I am afraid that castle life proved a bit too...eventful for my tastes." He tried a smile but it wiggled free of his face a moment later.

Chall couldn't blame him for his choice. After all, it hadn't been too long ago that Petran had nearly been killed by the assassin Maeve had ultimately defeated. It was no great surprise the man had chosen to reject the castle's dubious welcome and flee to a library where the loudest sound Chall had heard since entering was people clearing their throat, no doubt after breathing in the dust covering the tomes and books they read. Not the sanctuary Chall would have chosen—his would have had significantly more ale, for one—but then he supposed if everyone picked the same one the sanctuary would get pretty damn crowded. And loud...likely dangerous. Wouldn't really be a sanctuary at all, come to it.

Fun, though. That much Chall knew from experience for he had spent an inordinate amount of time—most of it drunken, some little not—in such places. The ale, the laughing and carousing, the dancing—or drunken stumbling, depending on the way a person decided to look at it—were all quite enjoyable. And then there were the women, of course...

Chall found a smile coming to his face at the memories—not that there were all that many, an inevitable result of the gratuitous amounts of ale he'd imbibed.

He blinked and glanced over to see Maeve staring at him, a frown on her face. Not the imminent-stabbing-frown he'd grown woefully accustomed to, but the considering-stabbing frown he'd also become very familiar with. He didn't believe that Maeve could read minds—at least not completely—a thought that was supported by the fact that he was still alive. But he did think that she, like all women, was dangerously—and completely unfairly—skilled at seeing into a man's thoughts. And given that his last thoughts had been of heaving busts and frothing beers, he thought it best to focus on the task at hand.

He cleared his throat, turning to Petran. "Thanks for coming to see us, Petran," he said. "I hope we didn't interrupt you doing anything too important."

It was meant as a joke, but Maeve was still frowning at him, and so the words lacked Chall's usual sarcastic tone—perfected over years of practice—and were instead breathy and slightly hoarse.

And so, the joke's delivery botched completely, it was no surprise that the man took Chall's question as nothing but genuine. "Thank you, Challadius," he said, "for the thoughtful consideration. But no, it was quite alright." He gave a soft laugh. "That is the thing about dusty old books and tomes, I suppose—they'll keep."

The man sounded surprised by Chall's apology—as well he should as it had not been meant to be an apology at all—but Maeve was not so easily fooled. She was still frowning at him from where she sat beside him, not knowing exactly why she ought to be angry but knowing, by that magic that was the domain of women and women alone, that she should be.

Finally, she turned away from him to regard Petran, and Chall did his best to hide the sigh of relief as she did. "Listen, Petran," she said, "I'm sorry to say this isn't a social visit. A lot has transpired since you left the castle, and we came seeking information."

Petran smiled, suddenly put fully at ease. "Well then," he said, holding his hands up to either side, palms up, "you have come to the right place, Lady Maeve and Sir Challadius. After all, what better place to find the knowledge you seek than—"

"How about you save the propaganda for those poor, dewy-eyed, doomed souls who wander into this place and never find their way ou—" Chall's words turned into a squeak of pain as Maeve gave his foot a stomp, and he winced. "Or say more, please," he told Petran. "It's really whatever you'd like."

Petran glanced between the two of them uncertainly. "Yes, well, as I was saying there is no better place to find the answers to your questions than in an institution and among people who have made it their sole purpose to—"

Chall was saved from anymore prattling by a soft knock on the door. They all turned to see a young man step inside, holding a silver tray aloft. Chall hadn't had breakfast—the thought of going to the library had messed with what was normally an insatiable appetite—and he found his mouth watering at the thought of something to snack on.

That quickly stopped, though, as the man bent—practically kneeled, in truth—before Petran, as if the man were some great king. "Forgive me, Truth Teller, but I thought that, perhaps, you might be thirsty or hungry. I brought tea and a sweet cake—my mother makes them."

Petran blushed, glancing at Maeve and Chall before turning back to the young man. "Thank you, Frederick," he said, taking the single cup and single sweet cake that sat on the tray. The young man continued to watch him expectantly, and the historian blushed further before he took a bite of the proffered cake. He smiled, nodding. "It is really quite good," he said, his voice muffled by the food still in his mouth.

The young man beamed widely at that. "Thank you, sir, she will be gratified to hear it."

There passed several awkward seconds then, and Chall grunted. "Don't worry about us then," he said. "Thankfully we, unlike every other person walking the face of the world, rely neither on food nor water to stay alive. I won't speak for Lady Maeve here, but I, at least, seem to subsist purely off disappointment and great quantities of shame."

The man gave Chall an awkward smile, clearly half-convinced that he was a madman. Chall couldn't blame him. The truth was, he was half-convinced himself. The man turned back to the historian, bowing his head again. "If there is nothing else, Sir Petran, I will leave you to your..." He glanced at Chall and Maeve then back to the historian. "To your business. But should you require anything—anything at all—you need only ring this bell," he said, retrieving a small silver bell from his pocket and setting it upon the table in front of Petran, "and I or another will see to your needs as quickly as possible."

Chall blinked, staring at the bell and at Petran who, at this point, was blushing an alarming shade of crimson. "Thank you, Frederick," the historian said quickly, "but I am quite sure that won't be necessary."

The man gave another nod then turned and hurried away, closing the door softly behind him but not before, Chall saw, he shot an almost worshipful glance at the historian.

Silence settled on the room for several seconds then, each of them staring at the bell sitting on the table. "So," Chall said finally, "I suppose there's no need to worry about how you've been faring away from the castle, Petran. A king in his kingdom, is that it?"

The Historian to the Crown winced. "It is not so glamourous as it appears, I'm sure. I, at least, would liken my position here less that of a king in his kingdom and more like that of a refugee who has found safe haven."

Chall raised an eyebrow. "I saw some refugees during the war. Folks left homeless after the Fey attacked their village or town. Never did see one holding a sweet cake and a warm mug of tea, though."

Petran blushed deeper. "Yes, well, it is true that they are quite kind here."

"Kind to you, anyway," Chall observed, glancing meaningfully at his own hands—quite devoid of dessert or beverage.

Petran nodded, clearing his throat. "It is, perhaps, accurate to say that I enjoy some degree of...renown among the staff and visitors here."

"Which isn't at *all* surprising," Maeve interjected before Chall could speak, giving him a scowl before turning back to the historian. "Not considering your contribution to the recording of our people's history and your unwillingness to ignore the truth even when that unwillingness landed you in a dungeon cell."

"A dungeon cell," Chall offered, smiling, "from which, the story goes, you escaped single-handedly without aid or assistance from anyone else. Not that I don't enjoy a good story, but I did find that one a bit odd. You know, considering that I seem to recall being there, along with the prince, not to mention Maeve and Priest and even our illustrious king."

Petran shifted, obviously uncomfortable. "Yes, well, you know how it is with such things. Stories so often have a way of growing and changing from person to person until the truth is hardly recognizable."

"Or not at all," Chall agreed. "Still, I am surprised that they would continue to believe something that wasn't true, particularly after you no doubt disabused them of its veracity. You know, you, the great *Truth Teller*."

Petran cleared his throat. "Yes, well, I suppose, you know, with everything that's been going on and my trying to get my records up to date—they're woefully behind, you couldn't imagine— well...it's possible that I forgot to mention the exact nature of my liberation from the cell in which I was imprisoned. After all, there has been much to do to get the records caught up. Why, Beth and I—" he paused, clearing his throat. "That is, Elizabeth and I—the Chief Librarian with whom you spoke—have spent countless late nights working on the problem."

"I don't doubt you have," Chall said, a grin coming to his face. "I do not doubt that you and—Beth, wasn't it?—have wiled away many hours together. Why, I wouldn't be surprised if you've both been left sweating and exhausted from the effort."

"Yes, that is quite so, quite so," Petran said, nodding along and clearly not understanding Chall's jibe. Maeve, though, understood it well enough, judging by the scowl he saw her giving him out of the corner of his eye.

"And tell me, Petran, dear Elizabeth, she wouldn't happen to have anything to do with why you haven't quite yet found the time to describe, in detail, the truth of how you came to be free of your prison cell, would she?"

"I'm...I'm quite sure I don't understand what you mean," Petran said, but judging by the squeak in his voice and the way he fidgeted Chall thought he understood well enough. Perhaps it was that old age was making him soft. Maybe it was the fact that Petran was a familiar face in a world where familiar faces were growing increasingly rare. It might have been due to the fact that Maeve was sitting beside him, watching him, and Chall was quite aware of just how many knives she kept tucked about her person.

Whatever the reason, as he watched the man, clearly nervous and just as clearly in love, Chall found himself growing fond of Petran, thinking he had not given the man enough credit after all. As it turned out, he was more than just a lexicon with legs. Beneath that dry, bookish exterior was a real man with a real heart who was as nervous as a young boy at the mention of the woman for whom he had clearly fallen.

He found himself glancing at Maeve, giving her a smile. Countless people had spent countless hours searching for some way to be or at least to *appear* younger. Women wore face paint, men took this potion or that one, but Chall decided that there was really only one way to stave off the years, and that was love. Love made a man young. Took him back to the time when he was an eager young boy, just discovering what women were—or at least rediscovering it in ways that were at once terrifying and incredible. "Forgive me, Petran," he said, meaning it. "I—*we*—haven't come to tease you."

"Are you quite sure of that, Sir Challadius?" the historian asked.

"I am," Chall said, glancing at Maeve and being terribly thankful—and, as always when he thought of it, mystified—that she had chosen him. "The truth is," he said, looking back at the historian, "I wish you all the luck with your librarian, and I am sorry for poking fun at you."

"I-I assure you, Sir Challadius," Petran stammered, "there has been nothing untoward between Be—*Elizabeth* and I. We are only two professionals whose interests and obligations have happened to intertwine." He let out a soft sigh, one Chall was quite sure he wasn't even aware he'd done. "Anyway, I am sure that she would have no interest in a man such as myself. I am at least ten years her senior, besides which, a woman like Elizabeth could have any man she wanted. What possible interest could she have in a man like me?"

"The woman chooses to spend her days surrounded by a forest's worth of books, Petran."

"Actually, much of the pages and lengths of scroll you see are not crafted from trees but are made of plant fibe—"

Chall yawned loudly, and the historian cut off. "My point, Petran," he said, "is that you are just the type of person the woman is looking for, and it'd be clear to a blind man that she likes you. Don't ask me why—" he paused, glancing at Maeve—"there's no understanding why a woman might choose to place her affection in a man who is, inevitably, completely undeserving of it. But then a man who's spent his life in rain doesn't stop to question, when the sun finally comes, why it chose that day of all days to break free of the clouds or to ask why it deigns to shine on him. If he's anything but the world's biggest fool, he just accepts the gift for what it is and enjoys the feel of the sun on his skin as well as he can for as long as he can."

The historian nodded slowly. "I think, perhaps, Challadius, that you missed your calling. You might have made a fine poet. Your words put me in mind of an ancient by the name of Eriocles. He claimed—"

"All I'm saying, Petran," Chall interrupted before he was forced to learn some obscure fact that he couldn't care less about, "is that she likes you, and you like her. That's a fact as unmissable as a fist in the face, though it can be considerably more enjoyable."

"You...you really think she likes me?" Petran said.

"Of course she likes you, you damned fool," Chall said. "The real question is, what are you going to do about it?"

Petran's eyes went wide in terror. "I...I'm not sure, that is, I wouldn't...couldn't..."

"You'd better, Petran," Chall said. "You don't have to today. Or tomorrow. But don't wait too long. After all..." He paused, glancing at Maeve, seeing her smiling at him. "There's plenty of time...until there isn't."

The historian nodded solemnly. "Th-thank you, Challadius. For your advice. I...I will think seriously on it."

It was Chall's turn to blink. Advice. That's what he'd just given, wasn't it? Him, Challadius the Charmer—or the Cad, and the fact was the second was probably closer to the truth. Giving advice. That was a damned horrifying thing. "Anyway, Petran," he said, "the reason we came was to speak to you about a criminal organization, one that hasn't been around in quite some time, as I understand it."

Petran raised an eyebrow. "It *is* to be a history lesson, then? I must confess, Challadius, I had not taken you as the type of man to be interested in the past."

"I'm damned interested in it when that past tries to stick a knife in me," Chall said.

Petran shook his head slowly. "If it's all the same to you, I think I would rather not know. I have trouble enough sleeping as it is. But as for this group you've mentioned, do they have a name?"

Chall glanced at Maeve, making sure that they wanted to confide in the historian. After all, the man was a good enough sort, but telling him the information might not just put others in danger—it might be dangerous for him as well. "Petran, what we wanted to ask you about...the thing is, the stuff we'd have to tell you...it's the kind of stuff that can be dangerous to know. So I guess I'm asking...are you sure you *want* to? Know, I mean."

Petran considered that for a moment finally nodded. "I spent several years in a dungeon for seeking the truth, Challadius, and while I appreciate your concern, my opinion in regard to the importance of that—the importance of men seeking the truth and standing with it, even when it's inconvenient, perhaps *particularly* when it's inconvenient—has, if anything, only grown stronger."

Despite the man's words, Chall studied him for a moment, trying to decide if this had been a good idea or not. After all, it was easy to be brave in the day, with the sun shining, with people walking the streets, laughing and living, the darkness of the night before nothing but a vague memory and that of the night to come seemingly only a distant possibility.

It was quite another thing to be brave when night came, when the shadows stretched out across the world like the great hands of some ancient god, when the shadows had teeth.

The historian met his gaze, scared sure—proof that he wasn't a complete idiot—but determined for all that, his jaw set. The man wanted the truth, had dedicated his life to the seeking of it.

He wanted the truth...so Chall gave it to him. All of it. He and Maeve together. Over the next hour they described everything that had transpired in the castle since the historian left, everything that had transpired in the city as well. They told him of Cutter and Feledias's journey to the Black Wood, of Matt's possession by the Feyling, Emma, and of the servant girl being murdered in the castle. As Petran's expression grew grimmer and grimmer, his face paler and paler, they recounted their meetings with the crime lord,

Nadia, and Catham, as well as all that they knew and had been told by Ned about the Crimson Wolves.

Chall left out nothing save for Ned and Emille's roles in everything that had transpired, for he thought it would be a poor way for him to repay them for all their help by giving up their identities. When he was finished, Chall noticed two things. One was that a heavy silence had descended on the room, one in which Petran sat as if frozen, his face as white as a sheet of parchment. The second was that, as he'd recounted everything together, taking it all in at once, Chall had been overcome by one feeling—certainty. A certainty, specifically, that they were screwed.

"Is...is there anything else?" Petran asked in a trembling voice that made it clear he hoped there wasn't.

"Isn't that enough?" Maeve asked softly.

"I...I had no idea things were so bad," Petran said, taking a sip of his tea, the cup in his hands trembling against the saucer as he raised it, beating a nervous beat as he brought it to his mouth. "I...I'd love to help, truly, but...I'm not sure what I can do."

"You can tell us everything you know about these Crimson Wolves," Maeve said. "We have more than enough to deal with already without worrying about people breaking into the king's quarters, killing serving women. And from what Chall says this Catham the Cautious is a part of it, too."

Chall found himself thinking of the tavern Catham had led them to before betraying them, a tavern full of people that he'd ordered to kill them. And the entire tavern of people had been preparing to do exactly that before Ned showed up and saved their lives, displaying the fact that he was far more than just a carriage driver but was also an empath, an extremely rare user of the Art.

Oh, and his wife was an assassin. And the most interesting thing was that, according to his conversations with Ned and Maeve's conversations with Emille, neither of them knew the truth of the other's hidden identity. He'd heard of married couples keeping secrets, but if there was anything he knew for sure it was that he didn't want to be in the house when those truths started coming to light. Didn't want to be in the city if he could help it.

Petran slowly nodded. "The Crimson Wolves...I have heard of them, of course. A small entry, as I recall, in one of Falidar's works. Or, at least, it *would* have been a small entry." He frowned. "Falidar does so enjoy the sound of his own voice, and oh how he loves to lecture others." He glanced at Chall. "You cannot imagine the frustration when dealing with a man such as that, one who is convinced that he knows everything."

"I'll do my best," Chall said, trying to keep a straight face and, judging by the fact that Maeve nudged him in his arm, shooting him a knowing grin, not doing all that good a job.

"It's in his Treatises on the Criminal Underground and its Role in the Formation of New Daltenia's Economic and Social Structure."

"Say that ten times fast," Maeve said dryly.

"Yes, well, as I believe I mentioned Falidar is nothing if not in love with the sound of his own voice." He rolled his eyes. "I've known him since we were both pupils, and while he is an...*adequate* scholar, it takes him what feels like a lifetime to ever reach the point of anything."

"One sympathizes," Chall said.

Petran blinked. "Oh, right, I'm sorry. You were asking about the Crimson Wolves."

"I think so," Chall said. "It's been so long I can't remember."

Petran colored at that. "My apologies, of course. Anyway, if it's the Crimson Wolves you wish to know about then we'll need to consult Falidar's work, long-winded though it is." He glanced at the bell on the table, leaned forward and had reached halfway to it when he froze, looking at Chall who grinned widely.

"Go on, Majesty," Chall said. "Ring away."

Petran jerked his hand back as if it had been scalded, clearing his throat. "That um...that is quite alright. I remember where it is, I think. No need to trouble anyone else."

"Oh, go ahead, trouble them," Chall said. "I'm sure they'd be honored to find the book for you."

Petran was shaking his head already, though, standing up. "No, no, that's quite unnecessary. If you will give me but a moment, I will return with the book."

He scurried for the door then, disappearing out of it and closing it hastily behind him. Chall chuckled, shaking his head. The man really was a funny one.

"You shouldn't tease him so."

He turned to Maeve and was glad to see that she was smiling at him. "Ah, it's good for him," he said. "Otherwise the poor guy will take himself entirely too seriously."

"A condition that you, at least, have managed to avoid completely."

"It's gratifying to finally see someone appreciating all the work I put in."

Maeve rolled her eyes, but the smile was still in place, so he thought probably that was alright.

"That was nice," she said. "Some of the things you said to him. About the woman, Elizabeth, I mean."

Chall could see that she was pleased with him, was giving him the look that she sometimes did, the one that couldn't fail to get his attention no matter what he might be doing. He opened his mouth to answer and then, deciding that he could only say the wrong thing and screw it up, chose silence instead.

She smiled wider, as if she knew exactly what he was thinking. "All those things you said, is that how you feel?"

"About you?" Chall said. "Of course. You're the best thing that ever happened to me, Maeve," he said honestly. "A damn sight better than I deserve."

She smiled wide then, and he decided that he'd said the right thing, a rare enough occurrence that he thought it shouldn't go unnoticed. "I wish we were back at the castle," she said, running a hand along his arm in a way that sent a tingle running through it, one that reached all the way between his shoulders.

"I tried," he told her, failing to keep the grumble out of his voice, "but you were insistent on a trip to the library."

"I know," she said, and he became aware of her hand on his thigh. "If only there were some way I could make it up to you."

"Oh?" he asked, grinning as she leaned in, her breath soft and warm on his neck. "You have any ideas?"

"A few," she said softly, the words no more than a whisper, and a shiver of anticipation ran through him. "For one, I could—"

The door chose that moment to creak open. Petran was already speaking even as he came inside. "Just where I thought it would be," the historian said, smiling.

"I'll kill you," Chall said abruptly.

"I'm sorry?" Petran said, coming up short.

"Don't mind him," Maeve said, "that is no more than Challadius's attempt at humor."

"Damn if it was," Chall said quietly.

"He's not very good at it, in case you can't tell," Maeve said as if he hadn't spoken. Petran remained silent for a moment, and Maeve nodded at the bundle he carried. "The book?"

The historian blinked, glancing at Chall with a nervous smile before nodding. "Right, right," he said, moving toward the table and setting it down.

Based on the patina of dust covering the giant tome the historian set on the table Chall thought there were others who shared Petran's dislike for his fellow scholar's style.

"I feared that someone might have borrowed the Treatise but apparently no one has," Petran said, and it wasn't fear that Chall saw on the man's expression but pleasure. He glanced at Maeve and she raised an eyebrow at him in return, a small smile on her own face. Men—even spectacled men with ink-stained fingers, it seemed—did love their rivalries.

"Now then, let's see..." Petran said, opening the book and letting out a small cough that upset the dust covering it. "He would have been aided greatly by a glossary, I think, but we will do what we can." He flipped through the pages, seemingly at random. "I seem to recall it being somewhere around here..."

Chall watched the man turn page after page, finding the section he was looking for. A moment later, Petran gave a smile. "Ah, here it is."

Chall stared at him, unable to keep from being impressed. True, Chall could create illusions—a fact that had gotten him into and out of trouble more times than he could count—but the scholar's magic was a kind all his own. After all, the man had, according to him, only read the book once, yet he was able to find, among its sprawling, intimidating pages the passage he'd wanted in no more than a minute. Chall wondered, for a moment, what it would be like to have a memory like that but then, considering some of the things he'd done over the course of his life, many of which he wasn't particularly proud of, he decided he was glad he didn't know.

"You found it?" Maeve asked, leaning forward eagerly, and Chall couldn't blame her. After all, right now they had a lot of questions. It would be good to have some answers for a change. It wouldn't guarantee their safety, but then he figured it'd be a lot easier for a fella to avoid falling into a pit if he knew where the damn thing was.

"Yes, I have it here," Petran said. "I ask that you forgive me for the words—as I said Falidar is nothing if not verbose. Now then...he writes, '*Here it might behoove us to make mention of another criminal organization that exists within New Daltenia's borders. Or, at least, is* said *to exist for there are many—this scholar among them—who discount word of it as no more than rumor. And why not? For the Crimson Wolves—or so they are called—are said to be a group of individuals who perpetrate crimes not against the commonfolk but instead against criminals themselves, robbing thieves and, if the rumors are to be believed, murdering murderers. And, if the stories are indeed true—an eventuality that this scholar finds exceedingly unlikely—then the word that might best be used to describe the group, along with vigilantes, would be brutal. It is said that they are ruthless in the application of what they deem "justice" for the crimes of those who garner their attention, and are not shy about expressing that fact in lurid, gory application.*'"

As Petran paused to take a breath Chall stifled a yawn—the historian had not been lying about his colleague loving to hear himself talk. Falidar's opinion seemed to be that why would a man use a few words when many would do?

"'*Proponents of the existence of the "Wolves" as they are known for short,*' Petran continued, "*point to half a dozen or so murders in the city, all of which involved individuals either known to or expected to take part in criminal enterprises. In this scholar's humble, informed opinion, though, those crimes are far more likely to have been perpetrated by members of rival criminal enterprises seeking to strengthen their position and weaken that of their competition. As for the brutality of the murders themselves, that is no more than an attempt of those responsible to pass the blame onto the specter of what has become, for the criminal element in New Daltenia, at least, the bogeyman.*

"'*Yet now that we have established the dubious nature of the Crimson Wolves and the unlikelihood of their existence and the impossible task of trying to prove the veracity of any of the stories associated with it, we will, for the sake of being exhaustive in our description, share what little is supposedly "known"—in truth no more than guessed and hypothesized—about the organization that is, in all likelihood, non-existent.'"*

"He really knows how to hammer a point home, doesn't he?" Maeve said.

"Sure," Chall agreed, "makes me want to do some murdering myself just listening to him."

Petran winced apologetically. "I can stop, if you would like. Perhaps—"

"No, no, that's alright, Petran," Chall said. "Go on. Who knows? Maybe we'll grow numb to it after a while. Wouldn't that be nice?"

"Very well," the historian said, nodding as he glanced back to the text. "Let's see, where were we...'*They are said to be a group of vigilantes who, sick of the criminals who have taken advantage of the crown's distraction with the Fey War, have taken it upon themselves to right what they consider the wrongs of such individuals. Little is known about them, save that signet members are each said to wear a ring with a stylized wolf's head on it. Though, perhaps unsurprisingly, no such signet has been found or might be produced as evidence of the group's existence.'*"

Chall wondered what the arrogant bastard would have had to say if he'd been the one to stumble onto a dead serving girl clutching a wolf signet. Likely a lot. The man seemed to have a lot to say about everything and had mastered the art of saying a lot without really saying anything at all.

Petran glanced up at the two of them. "He goes on like that for some time," he said, "mostly talking about how they definitely don't exist."

"Is that all, then?" Chall asked, glancing at Maeve and seeing the frown on her face, one to match that on his own. After all, they'd come for answers, and while they'd heard plenty, none of it had been useful.

"Nearly so, I'm afraid," Petran said, "though, I do seem to remember some part referencing the fact that there were said to be three founding members of...ah, right, there it i—"

"Wait a minute," Chall said, a shock running through him. "Did you say *three* founders?"

Petran blinked at the intensity in his voice. "That's correct, yes. Ah yes, here it is. Shall I read it?"

"Please," Chall said, aware that his voice sounded strained.

"'If there is any rumor among those countless tales purporting to describe the deeds and goings-on of the Crimson Wolves that seems to be the most often recounted—though, perhaps unsurprisingly, unsubstantiated—it is likely the supposition that the group is led by three individuals. And these fabricators of such rumors have gone so far in their offensive lies to claim that one of these individuals is none other than Lady Valencia, matron of one of the oldest families of our people with family roots, it is said, that might be traced back to the very beginning of our kingdom. The rumors are no more than ridiculous slander, of course, and claims which I only put forth here in the interest of vindicating a noble citizen of our kingdom. After all, anyone who knows the fair Lady Valencia knows well her commitment to uprightness and goodness, and she is as far from the works of any criminal enterprise as the sun is from the moon with which it constantly wars for dominion over our world.'"

"Damn," Chall heard Maeve say, her voice cutting through his suddenly tumultuous thoughts. "It sounds like your friend here has a certain fondness for Lady Valencia. She sounds like quite the paragon of virtue."

"And wealth," Petran added with a frown. "Lady Valencia is from a very well-to-do family and married into riches, riches which became hers and hers alone when her husband died twenty-five years ago, the two of them never having had children. A very wealthy woman, said to be the wealthiest in all the kingdom, in fact, and one that enjoyed using that wealth to sponsor certain people. Such as artists, musicians, singers..."

"And historians?" Chall asked.

Petran gave him a small smile. "Yes, historians as well. In fact, one of Lady Valencia's servants approached me, once upon a time, but considering my role as Historian to the Crown I was, of course, obligated to decline, and so she extended the offer to another of my peers in my stead."

"And that other peer," Maeve said, "wouldn't happen to be Falidar, the bastard who writes books when sentences will do?"

Petran smiled again. "Falidar does enjoy his luxuries, that is a fact, and Lady Valencia, it is said, is generous to a fault when it comes to those whom she sponsors. Finding oneself in her employ is, for pretty much every artist or scholar, a dream so exciting they hardly dare even contemplate it."

"So this bastard gets a life of luxury, and you get thrown in prison," Chall said, shaking his head. "You ask me, Petran, you made the wrong choice."

"What choice?" the historian asked, his face open, honest. "I do what I do, Sir Challadius, not for money or fame. The truth is its own reward, after all."

"The truth is that I think you're out of your mind," Chall said, grinning. "But I respect your choice, Petran. Maybe you're crazy, but at least you're dedicated to your craziness."

"Thank you...I think?" Petran asked uncertainly.

"Chall doesn't easily pass out compliments," Maeve said. "I'm afraid that's about as good as you're likely to get."

"Then I suppose I'll take it, largely because it seems I have no choice," Petran said.

Maeve laughed at that, nudging Chall, but the truth was he barely noticed. Instead he was thinking of what the historian, Falidar, had written. Maybe the man was a pompous fool—certainly Chall had heard enough to decide as much—but even fools stumbled on the truth from time to time. And, according to the fool in question, there hadn't been two founding members of the Crimson Wolves, as Ned the carriage driver had told him. There had been three.

Ned had told him and Priest that there had only been himself and a clerk named Robert Palden. He had never mentioned a Lady Valencia—Chall was quite certain of that. After all, he'd lived a life largely focused on nothing but women—it was exceedingly unlikely that he, of all people, would forget mention of one, particularly the richest one in all the kingdom.

Which meant that the man had lied. Or, at the least, he had omitted the truth, which Chall had been told again and again by uncountable women was the same thing. And while he'd taken the other end of that argument countless times, he certainly *felt* like a man who had been lied to, who had been betrayed. He felt angry and confused and more than a little frightened. He had never even considered that the carriage driver might have lied to him. After all, the man always seemed so genuine, so simple. A sort of what-you-see-is-what-you-get type of guy. Now, though, Chall wasn't so sure. Not at all. After all, if the man had lied about there being a third member of the Crimson Wolves, what else had he lied about?

"Shit," he breathed. "What if Priest was right all along?"

The words were more for himself than anyone else, but Maeve and the historian cut off the conversation they'd been in—about what, Chall couldn't have guessed—and both looked to him.

"What do you mean, Chall?" Maeve asked. "Right about what?"

"We shouldn't have trusted him, Maeve," Chall said, shaking his head, thinking of just how deeply they'd fallen into believing in the carriage driver. True, the man had saved them from Feledias when they'd first arrived in the city—or at least, he'd appeared to. But then that was another thing, wasn't it? Was it coincidence that he'd happened to be on hand just when they'd needed him? Or was it something else?

He felt so terribly lost, as if he'd been walking a path he'd thought he'd long since memorized, only to find that when he took a corner in the trail, it brought him to a place he had never been, and a glance behind him showed that he had been transported to a world he did not know.

"We need to leave," he told Maeve. "Now. We need to find Priest."

"Are you going to tell me what's upsetting you so much, Chall?" Maeve asked, and it was clear by her expression and the sound of her voice that she was worried. Which was just as well— if Chall was right, if the bastard really was a traitor, then they all should be worried. Particularly considering that they had trusted the man completely, that, because of that trust, he was able to come and go freely in the castle, for his face was known to the guardsmen.

Another thought struck Chall then, a terrible one indeed. What of the woman they'd met, the one who had pretended at being a serving girl but who had killed the real one? They had wondered how she'd gotten in, had wondered, also, how it was possible that Rolph had been killed underneath the nose of the guards. Well, perhaps they had their answer. Ned, after all, would have been allowed to come and go as he pleased, and his presence wouldn't have been remarked upon at all.

"*Shit,*" Chall hissed.

"Chall, you're scaring me," Maeve said. Part of him thought that said a lot, for Maeve was not the type that was easily scared. Most of him, though, was too damn terrified to think anything about it.

"Don't you see, Maeve?" he said, turning on her. "We practically gave the bastard the keys to the kingdom! We have to go—now!"

She started to ask a question, but he didn't think there was time—they'd wasted far too much already. He grabbed her by the hand, pulling her up as he rose himself. "Thanks, Petran—we'll see you later."

He was moving then, rushing toward the door and throwing it open.

"Chall, what *is it?*" Maeve demanded, pulling them to a stop, displaying her surprising strength.

Chall was forced to turn. "Ned, don't you get it, Maeve? It's Ned!"

"*Shhh,*" a sound came, and they both turned to see a heavy-set, middle-aged woman with a rump to rival that of some cows Chall had seen frowning at them, a finger to her lips, her eyebrows drawn down severely.

"*Oh, fuck off!*" Chall yelled back, and the woman's eyes went wide, as if she couldn't imagine living in a world where everyone didn't jump to do exactly as she said.

"How da—"

"One more word," Chall hissed, "and I'll set you on fire." He raised his hand then and, in answer, his gift produced a fire raging above his palm, one that was exactly like real fire except for the small fact that it wasn't. The woman didn't know that, though, and her eyes went wider still, her eyebrows climbing into her hairline, as she let out a squawk of panic that reminded Chall of a moose he'd once heard letting loose a mating call in the north. Then she turned and moved with a speed he wouldn't have credited her, fleeing down an alley of books.

"Good to see you haven't lost your touch with the ladies," Maeve quipped, but it was clear by her face and the sound of her voice that it wasn't genuine. "Chall, please—what do you mean it's Ned?"

They needed to move, to *go,* but Chall knew that Maeve was far cleverer than he was and not just clever—she was also far more skilled in fighting than him. If she didn't want to be moved, he wouldn't be able to move her. "Back when Ned rescued me and Priest," he said quickly, "he told us that there were only two of them that started the Crimson Wolves. Himself and a guy named Robert Palden."

"Yeah, you told me," Maeve said. "So what?"

"So," Chall said, "according to that arrogant prick of a historian there were *three* of them."

She frowned. "So you think...what, Ned lied to you and that somehow that lie means that he's behind the Crimson Wolves?"

"Why lie otherwise?" Chall said. "Take it from a practiced liar, Maeve. Despite common belief, we *always* have a reason."

"But...surely you must see that's ridiculous, Chall," Maeve said. "I mean, you said it yourself, Ned rescued you and Priest. Not to mention rescuing us all when Feledias nearly had us. Why would he do all of that just to turn around and betray us? It doesn't make any sense."

"Doesn't it?" Chall countered. "Think about it—the first time he saved us, what did that do? It made us trust him—for clearly he couldn't have been working with Feledias, right? Not and rescue us from his clutches the way he did. But then, what if it wasn't Feledias he was working for—what if it was someone else?"

"Like who?" Maeve said, sounding exasperated.

"The Crimson Wolves?" Chall asked. "The Fey? Who knows? All I know for sure is that he lied, and if he lied there's a reason for it. And look at how many times we've been attacked here in the castle! Fire and salt, Maeve, he's a *carriage driver.* Who better to know our comings and goings than him? Think about it—it would explain how that damned assassin got into the castle, how that bastard Rolph ended up torn to pieces and never mind the fact that he was in the dungeon."

Maeve frowned, thinking over his words. Finally, she shook her head. "No, it can't be. We *know* Ned, Chall. If all that you're saying is true he isn't just a liar—he's a killer, too. And I don't get that from him. I think I'd know it."

"Would you, Maeve?" Chall countered. "Would you really?" He shrugged. "I don't know. I'm not so sure. See, everyone thinks illusions are hard, and they can be, but the truth is, they aren't all that bad. Not as long as you show people what they expect—or what they *want*—to see. Lying is much the same. And damn if he didn't tell us exactly what we wanted to hear—that he was there to help, that there were people in the city who weren't out to see our heads on pikes."

"But...but it's *Ned,* Chall," Maeve said, shaking her head. "I like him—*you* like him."

"Don't you get it, Maeve?" Chall said. "He's a bloody *empath.* The bastard can make us *feel* however he damned well wants."

That brought her up short. "But...are they really that powerful? Empaths, I mean?"

Chall shrugged. "How should I know? He's the only one I've ever met. But I'll tell you this, Maeve—using his power he made an entire room of people who wanted nothing more than to kill us forget themselves. That was him using it as a hammer. If he were being more subtle? Not a hammer at all but a knife?" Chall shook his head in frustration. "I just don't know."

Another thought came to him then—one that was terrifying in its simplicity. What if Ned wasn't an empath at all? What if the whole situation with Catham and the people at the inn had been no more than play-acting, a show put on for his and Priest's benefit? But no...what would be the point of such a show? To ingratiate him with them? That didn't make sense—after all, he was *already* ingratiated with them. Besides, he had felt it when the man used his power, and Chall knew enough of the Art to recognize when it was being used around him.

No, whatever else he had lied about, Ned *was* an empath. That much was not in doubt. He frowned. Better if it had been. It wasn't enough that they were facing a traitor who was an ex—or maybe not so ex—member of a secret criminal organization, one who had managed to insinuate himself into their lives in countless ways, worse that traitor was an empath, possessing the ability to use the Art in very, very dangerous ways. The academy back at Daltenia, before the Skaalden came, had always searched out empaths, and when they'd found one—Ned—they had kept him sequestered away from everyone else. They had done so not just so that they might work with him, might study him, but also so that they would minimize the amount of damage he could do, if he chose.

After all, when a man could make people feel things they didn't actually feel, make them *believe* things they didn't actually believe, well...such a thing could ruin lives. Could topple kingdoms.

Kingdoms like ours.

"We have to go," he said again, his mouth suddenly terribly dry.

Maeve's expression was caught somewhere between disbelief and terror, but this time when he pulled on her arm she did not resist him.

"But...what about Emille?" Maeve asked as they turned down an alleyway, Chall leading them on the shortest route to get back to the castle.

"What about her?" he huffed—promising himself for the thousandth time that he really would start eating better and knowing even as he thought it that it was a lie. They reached the end of the alley and moved out into Baker's Street.

It was early afternoon. By now, most people would be halfway through their workday. At least those who had work to go to. Many of those who didn't would be several hours into a day of drinking. Still, he was surprised by just how few people were in the street.

Namely...none.

"Guess everybody stopped liking bread at the same time?"

"What bread?" Maeve asked quietly, frowning out at the street.

Chall was preparing to ask what she meant by that, but then he saw it. As he'd noted, there were no people roaming the streets in search of bread or pastries and that was just as well for there was no one to sell them any even if there had been.

Normally at this time of the day the street would be full of the smell of baked bread and meat pies, the air filled with the sound of bakers shouting out their wares and prices. A person might not have thought that men and women who baked bread for a living might be so competitive, but Chall had visited Baker's Street plenty of times—he had a weakness for sweet cakes—and he knew from experience that they could get downright vicious. More than once he'd found himself on the wrong side of such a scuffle and ended up getting some free bruises along with his bread.

But there were no shouts now, no rising loaves, the heat steaming off them. The smell was still in the air, though, as if everything, bakers and bread and all, had been here only a little while ago.

"They're all...vanished," Maeve said quietly.

"Yes, but vanished *where?*" Chall said, frowning.

"I'm more concerned with *why* they went," Maeve said quietly, her eyes studying the buildings around them.

Chall glanced at her. "Baker's strike?"

"Unlikely," she said quietly, her lips barely moving. "Turn around, Chall, now. Get back to the alley. I'll try to hold them off, buy you space."

"Hold who off?" he asked, giving a soft, confused laugh. "The invisible bakers?"

"No," she said softly. "Not bakers. Assassins."

"Assassins?" Chall asked.

"The Guild," Maeve said, staring around at the empty street. "They're here. You need to go—now."

"But we handled the Guild," Chall said, finding himself staring down at the empty buildings, imagining assassins popping out of every door, leaping out of windows and off of rooftops like the tumblers that sometimes accompanied traveling entertainment troupes.

Maeve spared a moment to shoot him a glance. "One doesn't *handle* a guild of assassins, Chall. Now, go for the alley—I'll cover you as best I can."

"No."

"Chall, I'm not making this up," she hissed. "Trust me, they're here, and we don't have time to—"

"I don't think you're making it up," he said. "I do trust you, Maeve, and you can trust that if assassins are coming, I'm not going to be the coward that runs and leaves you alone." He gave her a sickly grin—the best he was capable of just then. "Instead I'll be the coward that stands in the street with you trembling."

She flashed him a smile that vanished in another instant. "Fine," she said, "then we go together. Come on." She grabbed his arm, turning to the nearest alleyway and starting toward it.

They'd barely made it half a dozen steps before a voice rang out.

"Lady Maeve. Sir Challadius."

Chall tensed, hunching his shoulders the way a man might if he expected an arrow in the back—which, of course, was a very distinct possibility—and glanced at Maeve. "Should we run?"

She sighed softly. "They'd catch us."

Chall turned to glance back at the street in the direction they'd been heading. A man stood there, though where he'd come from Chall could only guess—perhaps he really had leapt off the roof of one of the buildings. Whatever the case, he stood calmly now, a small smile on his face. It wasn't the mad grin Chall might have expected, either, but a pleasant, calming gesture, as seemingly innocuous and unthreatening as the man himself. He was short, no more than five and a half feet tall, with a slight frame and short hair pushed back on his scalp. He wore woolen russet robes of the kind a servant might wear.

To Chall he looked like nothing so much as a clerk or, perhaps, the employee of some unremarkable noble family. Not that the man's appearance put Chall at ease. After all, he'd seen how many knives Maeve could hide about her person—in a robe like that, for all he knew the man had an army tucked under one sleeve. "You sure?" he asked quietly out of the corner of his mouth as he returned the man's smile. "He doesn't look all that fast. I'll admit that I'm not in as good shape as I used to be, but I think maybe I could outrun him."

"I doubt it," she said, her eyes locked on the man in the street, "and even if you could it would make no difference. He wouldn't be the one chasing us."

Chall frowned, looking at the man and then at the rest of the street—empty as far as he could see. He was about to ask Maeve what she was talking about when the stranger spoke. "I must say, it is truly an honor to meet you both." He sketched a low bow that would have been at home in the grandest of castle courts. "Sir Challadius, I have heard much of your exploits—it is indeed a pleasure. And Lady Maeve," he went on, turning to regard Maeve and bowing so low that his head nearly scraped the cobbles of the street. "It is the greatest honor of my life to be speaking with you. I hope I cause no offense when I say that the stories have fallen far short of doing your beauty justice."

"This great honor," Chall said, "would it extend to letting us be on our way? We're in a bit of a hurry, truth be told. Perhaps, if you leave us your name, we might set up a time we can all sit together and chat—how'd that be?"

The man smiled humoringly as if Chall had told a joke. "Of course, Sir Challadius," he said, bowing again, "I would not think to impose upon your time. Some mutual...friends, of ours, have asked that I come and extend to you an invitation for dinner."

"That's the thing about invitations," Chall said. "A person can always decline."

He expected the man to snap then, to threaten, but he did not. Instead, he only continued to smile. "I assure you," he said to Maeve as if Chall hadn't spoken, "we will take no more of your time than is absolutely necessary, Lady Maeve. Our friends truly desire the honor of your company."

Chall thought it was funny to hear someone who represented the Assassin's Guild speak so much of honor, but then people were funny creatures—there was no denying that.

"It seems you have us at a disadvantage," Maeve said. "You know both of us, yet I'm afraid I have not gotten your name."

The man winced. "Apologies, ma'am, but I am no one of importance, no more than a messenger sent to extend this...invitation."

Chall didn't much care for the way the man hesitated before saying "invitation," making it clear that it wasn't really an invitation at all. The man might have been still smiling, showing no weapon, but Chall could read Maeve's tense posture, and she knew much more about this sort of thing than he did. Somehow he expected that, should they decline the offer, the pleasantries might grow considerably less pleasant.

"A messenger and that only," Maeve said. "Yet even messengers have names, do they not?"

The man smiled, bowing his head like a duelist acknowledging a point. "Very well, Lady, but you do me honor I do not deserve. My mother, may she rest in peace, bestowed upon me the name of Balderath."

Maeve tensed at the name as if she'd been struck by lightning. "Balderath," she said, her voice breathy. "As in Balderath Reldon?"

The man inclined his head again. "It is flattering indeed, Lady Maeve, to discover that you have heard of me. Very kind of you."

But a quick glance at Maeve and Chall saw that "kind"wasn't the main thing she was feeling. Maeve was the toughest woman he knew—one of the toughest people he knew, in truth. She did not frighten easy. Still, he *had* seen her frightened on numerous occasions, an inevitable result of time spent with the Crimson Prince in a war against the Fey. An outsider, looking at her, might not have noticed the hard set of her jaw or the slight tightening around her eyes, but Chall knew Maeve. Knew her as well as he knew himself, and so he knew that she wasn't just afraid...she was terrified.

"Those who sent you," Maeve said in a voice that was a dry croak, "they only want to see me?"

"Yes, lady," Balderath said, smiling pleasantly. "It was only your esteemed personage that I was sent to escort to them. Sir Challadius may, perhaps, address whatever urgent matter the two of you were about, and you will, I'm sure, catch him up quickly enough."

"*Are* you sure, though?" Chall asked, glancing between the smiling man and Maeve.

"Chall," Maeve said, turning to him, "you need to go. Now."

Chall snorted. "I'll be damned if I do. I'll sit on the bastard before I let him take you anywhere."

"You'd regret it," Maeve said. "He might look innocent enough, but that is Balderath the Brutal," she went on quietly.

Chall frowned. "Don't suppose he's named that as a joke?" he asked in a voice too low for the man to hear. "Like calling a fat man 'Tiny,' that sort of thing?"

"Not a joke," Maeve said quietly, her eyes still trained on the man standing in the street, looking, to Chall, at least, like the clerkiest clerk that ever clerked. "I've heard stories about him," she said. "Everyone in the Guild has. He isn't known as being the subtlest assassin, nor the most accomplished, but if anyone is looking for brutality, to send a message, it's Balderath the Brutal they ask for."

"I see," Chall said, working his tongue around his mouth in a vain effort to gather some saliva in a throat that had suddenly gone terribly, painfully dry. "But that's all the more reason that I won't leave you, Mae," he finished, doing his best to sound courageous, like one of those damned fools the bards loved to sing about, bastards who couldn't seem to wait to strap on their armor and ride off to give their lives for one cause or another. Blushing maidens or kittens in trees, whatever came up. Chall had never been that kind of bastard—he'd been a completely different kind. He always figured the kittens got themselves in the mess, they could get themselves out—or not, it made little difference to him. And as for the maidens, well, he'd never seen reason to brave the dragon to save the maiden imprisoned in some damned high tower—ridiculous as, in his experience, dungeons were nearly always underground—when there were plenty of other maidens that would blush just as prettily as a man pleased, at least for a price.

This, though, was different. This was Maeve. "Where you go I go," he told her. The kind of thing the damned fools in shining armor would say, sure, but damn those fools and damn the bards. He loved her, that was all.

She smiled wide at that, her eyes sparkling, and he thought again how she was the most beautiful thing he'd ever seen. She might not have been as young as she once had been, was no longer the Maeve the Marvelous famous all across the land for her beauty. She was better. Her beauty was still there, so obvious it would take a blind man not to notice, but now with her outside shining not quite as bright as it once had, it made it all the more obvious to see what was inside. And that was a beauty far greater than youth could provide.

"I love you," she said. "Whatever happens."

"I can't imagine why," he said honestly, "but I love you too."

"Lady Maeve, we really must be going, or I fear we'll be late and miss our appointment."

Chall started at the voice, and nearly screamed as he turned to see that the assassin was no longer standing twenty-five feet or so down the street but was instead nearly within reaching distance. *Within* reaching distance if one was wielding a knife, Chall thought unpleasantly.

That scared Chall, the way the man had come upon him so quietly and that made him angry. "You're not taking her anywhere," he snarled, raising his hands to his sides, palm up. Fire erupted from his palms, first one, then the other, dancing in the assassin's eyes.

The man did not recoil, though, as Chall would have thought—as he certainly would have hoped. Instead, he stared at the blazes raging over each of Chall's hands, a firestorm waiting to be unleashed. "Impressive," Balderath said, his smile well in place. "Truly. I had heard tales of your talents, of course, Sir Challadius, but to hear of it and see it in person are two very different things."

"You'll be seeing it a whole lot closer, if you aren't careful," Chall warned, the flames responding to his words, shooting higher.

The man smiled wider. "Quite impressive," he said again. "Why, I can even feel the heat from it."

"You'll feel it a whole lot more if—" But before Chall could finish the threat the man reached out, not quickly, not tentatively, only casually, the way a man might reach for a glass of water, and stuck his hands into the flames.

"It even feels a little warm," the assassin remarked, meeting Chall's eyes. "Remarkable. I wonder, is the warmth from the use of the Art, or is it only my brain which tells me I'm warm, a product of the illusion?"

Chall winced. He'd been hoping the man hadn't realized he was an illusionist and that, even if he had, he might still be intimidated. It had happened before, after all, many times. It was one thing to know in a logical, clinical sort of way that the flames weren't real. It was quite another to risk being burned. It would take a crazy man to do it—and yet he had.

The man was still smiling, but there was a look in his eyes, hidden just beneath the surface, a *madness,* that made Chall think he would risk a lot more than reaching into the flames, would *do* a lot more.

"I need to go, Chall," Maeve said.

"Not without me."

"Yes," she said. "Balderath is right—our errand is important. I...I won't say I'm sure about the...the thing you mentioned, but it bears looking into. Find Priest and tell him—the two of you have to figure out the truth of it."

The man, Balderath, bowed low, offering his arm. "Lady," he said.

"You can shove that lady shit," Chall growled, stepping in front of Maeve. He became aware, the moment he moved, of several forms suddenly seeming to materialize out of thin air at the mouths of the nearby alleyways. As the figures came into view, he saw that there were five in all and three of them held crossbows. He saw, but he didn't care. He'd just gotten Maeve back—just gotten her at all, in fact. He wasn't about to lose her.

He was watching the figures out of the corner of his eye, watching the assassin in front of him, waiting for him to make a move. But the man only raised his hands to either side as if to say he meant no harm. Chall *saw* the hands, saw that they were empty. Which was why he was so surprised when he felt something strike him in the back of the head, hard.

He stumbled forward and would have bumped into the assassin, sending them both sprawling, but the man stepped to the side as casually as he'd reached into the fire. Instead, it was Chall alone who fell, turning as he did to land hard on his back. He lay there, the darkness of unconsciousness seeping into his mind, and tried to figure out how the man had hit him without hitting him. He was still trying to figure it out when Maeve stepped forward and he saw her holding a knife in one hand. He stared at it, at the hard iron handle in particular, and realized in that moment what had struck him. How the man had managed to hit him without hitting him—he hadn't.

Maeve had.

"I'm sorry, Chall," she said, her voice muffled and sounding as if it came from a great distance. "I love you."

"*Feldaplou,*" Chall said in response.

Then he passed out.

CHAPTER SIX

They walked for like felt like an eternity.

His brother had lost weight since they'd come to the Black Wood—they both had—yet the burden of carrying him was increasingly unbearable. Cutter bore it just the same. His back ached, his shoulders burned as if they were on fire, and the muscles in his thighs and calves were numb with fatigue.

He might have set him down, allowed one of the two Feylings to carry Feledias, as Shadelaresh had first suggested, but he did not. The main reason for that was that he simply did not trust the Feylings. Or, rather, he trusted them to want to harm him and his brother as much as possible and it was only a true fool that placed his pet mouse in front of a hungry cat and expected it not to eat.

But, while the main reason for his unwillingness to allow one of the creatures to carry his brother was a distrust for them, it was far from the only one. Even if Priest or Chall or Maeve had been there, still he would not have allowed them to help. Not because he didn't trust them—he trusted the three of them more than he trusted himself. Instead, he would not have allowed it because his brother was his burden to carry.

After all, it was Cutter and he alone who had set about the chain of events which had, eventually, brought them here. Had it not been for his betrayal, had it not been for him slaying Yeladrian, the Fey King, then the Fey War would have likely never started at all, and he and Feledias would not have found themselves venturing into the Black Wood, confronting creatures who would have loved nothing more than to torture and kill them.

No, his brother, the task of making peace with the Fey, whatever would come on the morrow, it was his burden to carry, all of it, and so he would...for as long as he was able.

To where do you lead him? It was the Gray Man's voice. The creature had been walking beside Cutter silently as the two Feylings escorted him. At the sound of his voice, the two stopped, turning.

One of them, a creature who was as tall as Cutter but twice as wide, turned, displaying a face that resembled nothing so much as a lizard. It spoke in a language Cutter did not know, but one that he had heard before—the language of the Fey. It was a melodic language in some ways, one that almost sounded like a song, but there was an ancient sound to it too, one that made him think of quiet places in some hidden glen, places where no man had ever walked since the forming of the world itself.

You mean to take him to Shadelaresh's own place? the Gray Man asked, clearly incredulous, and Cutter understood that, for he didn't love the idea of being placed in the care of a creature whose only care regarding Cutter and his brother was how quickly he could see them dead.

Cutter's escort responded, and while he might not have understood its words he understood its angry tone easily enough, just as he understood the gesture it made back at the clearing.

I do not care what Shadelaresh said, the Gray Man said. *He is not an Elder, however much he might pretend at it. I, on the other hand, am, and I think it best that I look after the welfare of these two until the trial begins.*

The creature growled at that, taking a threatening step toward the Gray Man. It clearly meant to take another, was in the process of doing exactly that, when something happened.

Cutter couldn't have said exactly what that something *was.* All he knew for sure was that, one moment, the Feyling was moving toward the Gray Man, and the next, he was lying on the ground, crushed as if some giant, invisible foot had flattened him.

Green ichor leaked from the creature's mouth, and one if its arms—the arm which it had been pointing at the Gray man as it came on—was clearly broken, bent at an impossible angle. The creature mewled and cried out in terror—as did its companion. It struggled, but it was clear by its inability to move more than a few inches that it was no match for whatever magic held it.

You forget your place, the Gray Man said, and though his voice was not raised in anger, there was a coldness to it that, to Cutter at least, was far more unnerving. He had met many killers and warriors over the years, and he'd found that it was never the hot, flaming anger that worried him the most. Such anger burned itself out quickly and, quite often, was as much a danger to itself as anyone else. Instead, he had come to be wary of cold anger, the anger that a person tended over time, held onto. It was an anger that was calculated, and it was that anger he heard in the Gray Man's voice as he spoke.

You, as so many, have come to believe that because a creature does not act in violence, it is incapable of it. And you, like so many before you, will learn your mistake the hard way. I am Elder here, not Shadelaresh, and you are as nothing to one such as I. Such knowledge will not aid you here, at least, but perhaps it will be of some use in the Glade Beyond.

There was a sudden pressure, one Cutter felt all around him, as if the air had suddenly gone impossibly thick, and the next thing he knew the creature wasn't being crushed by whatever invisible force had sent it to the ground—it was crushed in truth. Green ichor sprayed out in all directions, spattering Cutter, the Gray Man, and the remaining Feyling as well as the unconscious Feledias.

Cutter stared at the creature, barely recognizable now, looking like nothing so much as a bug crushed underneath someone's boot, and could not help but marvel at the power of the Feyling, the Gray Man. He had seen some of the strange powers of the Fey before, of course, such as when one had invaded his dreams, or the creatures in Two Rivers which had taken over the town and had begun to sow discord against the kingdom. During the war he had seen others, those like the doppel which had tried to kill Matt when they'd first fled Brighton. Yet for all that he'd seen of the Fey's magic, he'd never seen anything so direct, so...forceful.

He thought, staring at that crushed body, that it was lucky for the people of the Known Lands that the Gray Man had opposed the war, for had he fought against them there was no telling what might have happened.

Now then, the Gray Man said, his voice sounding sad as he looked at the remaining Feyling, *will you, too, question me?*

The creature responded quickly, using the same language as the first had, but with a very different tone, and it bowed low to the Gray Man before scurrying away.

They meant to kill you in the night, the Gray Man said, looking at Cutter.

"Thank you," he said, pointedly avoiding staring at the crushed creature. "But...won't Shadelaresh be angry?"

Yes, the Gray Man confirmed. *Now come. I have a place where you will be safe enough until tomorrow.*

Cutter did not bother asking what would happen come the morning. He might have, but the truth was it was all he could do to keep holding Feledias, to keep his feet beneath him, and he simply did not have the energy to care.

After all, knowing would make little difference. Tomorrow would come whether he wished it or not, and only a fool thought he knew what the future held. Priest had told him, once, that the future was a shifting storm, and any man who thought he could see it caught only a glimpse of a silhouette, a flash of a shadow that might change at any moment. No, tomorrow would take care of itself. One way or the other.

For now, at that moment, he needed only to walk.

And so he did.

He followed the Gray Man through the Black Wood until, no more than ten minutes later, they reached a giant tree. Many of the Black Wood's trees were massive, ancient sentinels that seemed to have stood where they were since the dawn of time, yet the tree to which the Gray Man escorted Cutter dwarfed even these.

He would have guessed it at a hundred feet in circumference at least, but even its great size was not the strangest thing about the tree. What was, instead, was that it appeared to have grown in such a way that an opening in the vague shape of a door had grown within it and from the moonlight shining through that opening Cutter saw that much of the inside of the tree appeared to be hollow.

Come, Destroyer, the Gray Man said, starting forward. Perhaps Cutter should have been unnerved—likely he should have been—but he was far too relieved at the thought of being able to put Feledias down and rest his shoulders and back, if even for a moment. He did not hesitate, following in the Gray Man's wake.

There was a small table at one side of the inside of the tree, low enough that it was clear that anyone using it would sit on the ground. On the other side was a thick mattress of dark green moss. Cutter would have never thought, before that moment, that moss would have looked inviting to lie down on, but he couldn't remember any actual bed ever being half as appealing.

The time for your rest comes, Destroyer, the Gray Man said, *but it is not yet here. Lay your kinmate down, and I will see what can be done for him.*

Cutter didn't need to hear that twice. He moved toward the thick cover of moss and laid Feledias down as gently as he could, the muscles of his arms and shoulders screaming in protest as he did. He stared at his brother, his face pale and sickly, and now that he didn't have to focus on carrying him any longer or on just taking one step after another the worry set in.

Feledias did not look well. His face was gaunt, hollowed out...almost skeletal. There were deep, purple circles under his eyes, and he was shivering in his sleep.

Now that he was no longer focused on walking, Cutter realized that it was cold. He hadn't noticed before, had been too busy simply trying to put one foot in front of the other, but he noticed it now. He was sweating from his brief but intense battle with the Feylings as well as from carrying Feledias, and now that sweat felt like ice water running over him.

Still, it was not himself that he was worried about but his brother, and so he stood, unmoving, while the Gray Man knelt over Feledias. The Feyling reached out, placing his hand on Feledias's chest, over his heart, and closed his eyes.

It is bad with him, the Gray Man said, his voice sounding like the whisper of wind through treetops. *If left on his own, he will not last the week—likely not through the night.*

The words were like a dagger sliding into Cutter's ribs, and he felt his breath catch in his throat. Another, in Cutter's stead, might have doubted the creature—it was a Feyling, after all—but the thought never even occurred to him. After all, without the Gray Man, he and Feledias would have been killed in the Glade. In truth, he doubted they would have even reached the Glade had the creature not helped them before.

"Can you help him?" he asked, aware of the desperate, rasping quality of his voice.

The Gray Man turned to him, his expression still unreadable. *I wonder, Destroyer, should I say yes, what would you offer in return?*

"Anything," Cutter said instantly. "If it is within my power."

The Gray Man stared at him for several seconds before he spoke. *I would be very careful, Destroyer, when making such pacts. My kind do not take such words lightly.*

"Neither do I," Cutter said, his gaze traveling to his brother. "He is here because of me. Because of my doing. If there is a price to be paid, I will pay it gladly."

I believe that you would, the Gray Man said. *Though you are wrong about one thing, Destroyer—you are not the reason your kinmate is here. He is. We all make our choices. Perhaps your choices narrowed his, but that makes no difference. In the end, a living being never has less than two choices. To go or to stay. To stand or to flee. To live. Or to die.*

"Can you help him?" Cutter said again.

The creature took a slow breath, then finally nodded. *Perhaps,* the Gray Man said. *But as I told you and your kinmate before—such things come at a price. Are you sure?*

"I'm sure."

The creature nodded again then turned back to Feledias. The Gray Man closed his eyes, and Cutter felt a gathering of pressure similar, in some ways, to the way he'd felt back in the Glade when the Gray Man had grown angry with Shadelaresh and when he'd crushed the Feyling who'd attacked him. But while this feeling shared some similarities, there were differences, too. It felt subtler than the others, no less powerful but power of a different kind. He found that the hairs on the back of his neck and his arms were raising and goosebumps broke out on his flesh.

A feeling of anticipation seemed to rise within him and not *just* within him. It was as if the world itself held its breath, waiting to see what would come. Then, finally, in an invisible, silent explosion, that power, that force vanished.

The Gray Man sat back, his breath rasping as if he was in pain, but Cutter barely noticed. Instead, he was staring at Feledias. His brother lay as he had, unmoving save for the tremors that shook him from time to time.

Cutter was just opening his mouth to ask what had happened when suddenly Feledias gasped, shooting up into a sitting position. Cutter rushed forward. His brother had time to let out a squeak of surprise but no more than that before Cutter had wrapped him into a tight hug. "Fel," he said. "You were...I thought..."

"Bernard," Feledias said. "What happened? I...I had the strangest dream."

"It doesn't matter," Cutter said, glancing at the Gray Man who he saw was staring at him with an undeniably sad expression on his face. "It doesn't matter," Cutter said again, meeting the Feyling's eyes for a moment before turning back to his brother. "All that matters is you're okay."

"Are we okay, though?" Feledias asked.

Cutter sat back, starting to speak, but by sitting back he'd made the Gray Man, who had been hidden behind him up to that moment, visible and Feledias let out a hiss as he took in the Feyling. "Bernard, behind you!" he snapped, then went for the knife at his belt.

Cutter reacted instantly, catching his brother's hand before he could draw the blade. The absolute last thing they needed, he thought, was to offend the creature who had not only just undeniably saved his brother's life but also the only creature within miles that didn't seem to want them dead. "Wait, Fel," Cutter said. "It's the Gray Man."

Feledias frowned, glancing back at the Feyling. "This isn't the Gray Man. The Gray Man was bigger, made of trees, not twigs."

It is not what composes us that makes us who we are, Feledias Stormborn.

"I don't mean to quibble," Feledias said, "but it seems to me that that's *exactly* what makes us who we are. You know, the stuff we're *made* out of."

Do you truly think as much? the creature asked, sounding genuinely surprised. *Interesting.*

"What is?" Feledias asked.

My people have heard tale of you, of both princes, of course. They know your brother as the Destroyer, a great, merciless warrior responsible for the death of our king, but you, too, are known to us, Stormborn. You who are said to be one of the cleverest specimens your people have to offer with a tactical genius beyond compare. You might imagine my surprise, then, to find you so wrong.

"Wrong?" Feledias asked.

Yes. For your assertion is that we are what we are made of, and that of course cannot be true. After all, if it were, you would not call your hand your hand. You would just call it you.

Feledias's frown deepened. "What are you talking about? We just use names so that we can categorize, that's all."

Yes, your people do love to categorize, to label, don't they? For in that way they seek to understand the world around them or, at least, to fool themselves into thinking they do. Tell me this then, Feledias Stormborn: if you should lose your hand, would you be any less?

"Any less what?"

Any less you?

"Of course not," Feledias said, "what does that have to do with..." He hesitated then, frowning. "Ah."

The creature inclined its head.

Feledias sighed, glancing at Cutter. "Maybe you'd better tell me what's going on here, brother."

And Cutter did, recounting, as best he could, the events since they'd arrived in the Glade and what he knew—little enough—of what they faced tomorrow. The only part he left out was just how bad of shape Feledias had been in when they arrived at the hollowed-out tree, and even as he omitted that piece he could feel the Gray Man's eyes on him.

Feledias frowned at him as if he, too, had picked up on the fact that Cutter was hiding something. In the end, though, if he had any suspicions, he chose to let them lie. "So this ritual or whatever that's waiting on us tomorrow, they said it's because we're warriors?"

"Yes."

Feledias winced. "Did you mention that we're trying to quit?"

Cutter found himself smiling. Someone who didn't know Feledias might have taken such a comment to mean that he wasn't taking things seriously, that he was being dismissive, but Cutter knew that was far from the truth. His brother often made such jests, but beneath that he knew that that great mind of his was working, viewing the problem from more angles at once than Cutter could have done if he'd had weeks to dedicate to the task.

"I'm afraid not," Cutter said, still smiling. "It was a bit hard to do, what with fighting to keep your skinny ass alive and all."

"My ass appreciates it," Feledias commented, but in a distracted way, for Cutter could see that he was considering what they faced. "And this Path of War," his brother said, "what is it, exactly?"

Cutter shook his head to show that he had no idea either and then the two of them turned to regard the Gray Man.

The Path of War is a ritual that can be traced back to the beginnings of my people, the Gray Man said. *One which is reserved for warriors and those who have shed blood and taken lives when they wish to make an appeal to the Elders or our king.*

Feledias snorted. "That second would be pretty difficult right now, considering that Yeladrian's head is—"

"*Quiet, Fel,*" Cutter hissed.

His brother frowned, glancing at Cutter. "What, Bernard? Oh, come on, the bastard was crazy as—"

"That *bastard,*" Cutter growled through gritted teeth, "was *his* son."

Feledias's face paled at that, and they both turned to regard the Gray Man, Cutter remembering all too well how easily he had used his power to crush the Feyling less than half an hour ago. "He doesn't mean anything by it," Cutter said. "He's just…"

"What my brother is trying to say," Feledias chipped in, "is that I've always talked too much. It's a condition, I'm afraid, and the problem with talking as much as I do is that, often, I run out of intelligent things to say and am forced to say stupid ones instead." He shrugged, obviously trying to make the gesture appear casual. "It helps when speaking with Bernard, here, but it has proven otherwise inconvenient on more than one occasion."

The Gray Man nodded. *You need not hide your feelings, not from me. I know well what your people think of my son. But know this—Yeladrian was not always as you saw him. There are always more sides to a creature than even those closest to them know. He was kind, caring, considerate of all living things, including the grass that grows and the birds that fill the sky. As clever as he was compassionate, as loyal as he was loving. He...* the Gray Man trailed off then, going quiet.

Cutter glanced at Feledias but his brother gave him a shrug as if he had no idea what to do or say, and so it was left to Cutter. He reminded himself to give Feledias grief, later. After all, his brother never seemed to have difficulty in talking when it wasn't needed, and so it was convenient to find that, when something finally needed to be said, he was conspicuously silent.

"He...he sounds...exceptional."

The Gray Man turned to him then, and Cutter did not think it was only his imagination that made the Fey creature's eyes seem even more somber, what had been a storm when angered by Shadelaresh now reminding Cutter of a gray, overcast sky on one of those days when the sun never touches the surface of the world.

Yes, he was, the Gray Man said. He took a slow, deep breath, then let it out, and when he spoke again he no longer sounded quite so sad. *The Path of War is a bloody path, as it should be. Any warrior seeking audience with the Elders must prove his worth in the only way a warrior can—battle.*

"Battle with who?" Cutter asked.

The Gray Man shook his head. *In normal times, it is left to the discretion of the Fey King, but in such times as there is no Fey King, the Eldest among those who can be gathered in a reasonable amount of time will choose.*

"And who is the Eldest?" Feledias asked.

The Gray Man turned his gaze on him. *Me.*

Feledias grinned. "Well, then that's great," he said, then his smile slowly faded as the Gray Man only watched him. "Isn't it? I mean, because you want peace just like us...don't you?"

I do, but I'm afraid that will not help us, the Gray Man said.

"What are you talking about? Of course it'll help us," Feledias said. "Shit, just pick a squirrel for us to fight or something." He nodded, licking his dry, cracked lips. "Damn but some squirrel sounds pretty great right now. Never much cared for the bastards—too damned gamey for my tastes, but I suppose I'd eat one raw just now if you put it in my hands."

I'm afraid that won't be possible, the Gray Man said.

"Fine, whatever. A rabbit. A pig, if you have to, just not anything—"

I mean it will not be possible for me to intentionally choose an opponent that you might easily defeat. To do so would be to invite Shadelaresh and those who follow him to challenge my authority.

"So who gives a shit?" Feledias said. "Let them challenge it. If they get out of line, you can just squash them like you did that other poor bastard, right?"

I cannot, the Gray Man repeated. *Even if I would be victorious—and against so many as follow Shadelaresh, that cannot be certain—it would make no difference. I will not betray my people. The Law is the Law and I am honor-bound to follow it. Besides, even if it were only Shadelaresh himself who might challenge me, still the victor would be in doubt. He has grown strong in his hatred for your people, has walked the dark paths of the Wood, has given himself in the pursuit of power and like so many creatures that do so, he has found it. Such power comes at a price, but that matters little for us at the moment.*

Feledias hissed. "I thought you were on our side, damnit. So what you expect us to die for your damned honor?"

There is no greater reason for a living creature to die than for its honor, for in the end we have little else. As for the rest, if you believe me to be on your side then you are wrong. I am now, as I always have been, and as I always will be, on the side of my people.

"You say that," Feledias said, "but it seems to me that, not so long ago, you asked us to kill this Shadelaresh bastard."

It is for my people that I ask it, the Gray Man said. *Shadelaresh has walked into the shadow, has allowed it to enter into him. He has set his eyes to his path, and there is no turning back, not now. It is finished. And his hate draws my people to him as hate always does. Hate which feeds upon itself and grows stronger, larger. More and more go to him by the day. Should things remain as they are, it is not a question of if my people will war with yours once more—only when. I would save my people that suffering, if I could. Both of our people. Wouldn't you?*

"Yes," Cutter said quietly.

"Damn right we would," Feledias said. "But I wouldn't mind saving myself and Bernard here a bit of suffering too, while we're at it. Is there nothing you can do to help us?"

I have already done it, the Gray Man said, meeting Cutter's eyes.

"Damnit, you can't be—"

"Enough, Fel," Cutter said, his gaze still on the Gray Man. "Let him go—he has done what he could for us, and a damn sight more than he had to."

"So you mean to go ahead with this then?" Feledias asked. "To fight some damned champion he picks out?"

"What choice do we have?"

"Well, shit, how about we escape?"

"Escape?" Cutter asked.

"Sure," Feledias said, glancing at the Gray Man. "You said that you can't pick an easy champion, okay, fine. Why don't you just let us go?"

I cannot, the Gray Man said. *I told you, before, when we spoke in the Wood, that your quest was in vain. I warned you of what would come, but you would not listen. I have done all that I can for you—I can do no more. The rest is up to you.*

He started toward the opening in the tree then and paused at the entrance, glancing back. *They will come for you in the morning. But not before. You will be safe here, for the night.*

Feledias let out a frustrated snort, but Cutter rose, moving toward the creature, offering him his hand. "Thank you," he said, glancing back at his brother before turning back to the Gray Man. "For what you did."

The Gray Man stared at the hand as if he'd never seen anything quite like it then, after several seconds, he reached out and took it.

Cutter felt a mild shock as he did, and a tingle passed through his hand. Only for a second, then it was gone. The Gray Man gave him a firm shake before removing his hand. *What is broken might yet be mended,* the Gray Man said softly. *But it must be mended soon. You must see to it, else there is no hope for what is to come.*

Cutter nodded, frowning and glancing back at Feledias. "I'll take care of him as best I can."

I did not mean him.

Cutter glanced back at the Fey creature, confused.

Your spirit is troubled, Destroyer. You go against your own nature, work against yourself, and in so doing you rob yourself of your strength. If you are to have any chance of victory against what comes, you must embrace who you are. You must remember that man, the Destroyer, the man who you tried to shed the way a snake sheds its skin. You must find him again.

"The man you're talking about," Cutter said, his mouth suddenly, unaccountably dry, "he was a killer. A cruel murderer with no mercy or compassion in him."

Mercy and compassion will not serve you in what comes. You do not need the sheath, Destroyer—you need the blade. You must become the Destroyer once more, must find your edge again.

Cutter listened to those words, feeling more afraid in that moment of what the Feyling was saying than he'd felt even when faced with thousands of the creatures, with all of them charging toward him and Feledias, intent on their deaths. "And if I can't?" he asked.

Then both of you will die, the Gray Man said, and though there was sadness in his voice, there was also certainty. *And your deaths will only be the beginning. They will serve as no more than a prelude for the grief and despair and bloodshed that will come after. Sleep well, Destroyer,* the Feyling said. *You will need it. There is food for you and your kinmate there,* he finished, motioning with his head.

Cutter turned, following the gesture to see two squirrels, freshly killed, lying near the edge of the trunk's inner wall. At the sight of them his mouth began to water. He could not remember the last time he'd eaten and thought that was probably for the best.

"Listen," he said, turning back to the Gray Man, "I appreciate all you've done, but—" He cut off as he saw that the Gray Man was already standing outside the natural doorway formed in the tree's trunk. The Feyling met his gaze, his gray eyes shifting like dark clouds in a storm, then the trunk began to shift and move, the wood stretching out toward the opening. Cutter grunted, taking a step back. In another moment the opening where the "door" had been was gone.

"Huh," Feledias said. "Well, you don't see that every day."

"Just as well," Cutter said, clearing his throat, then he turned and moved back to his brother. "How do you feel?"

"Well, shit would be an improvement, I can tell you that much," Feledias said, then shrugged. "Still, I suppose I ought to be grateful for being alive. Thanks."

"Don't mention it," Cutter said. "Besides," he went on, grunting as he sat down, "if I let you die, who would do all the complaining?"

"It's good for a man to know his purpose," Feledias said, giving him a smile.

A silence descended, then, as Cutter started a small fire, preparing the squirrels the Gray Man had left. A silence in which each of them just enjoyed the warmth of the flames on their skin and when it was finished cooking, the taste of the hot meat.

In time they were done, and it wasn't until then that Feledias spoke.

"Well," he said, sighing. "I guess I'll get some rest. I'm damned tired, and if I'm going to die tomorrow I'd just as soon make sure I got my beauty sleep—I'd hate to leave these bastards with an ugly corpse."

"Some things can't be helped," Cutter said.

"Bastard," Feledias said, but he smiled as he lay down on the blanket of moss. "Ah, moss. Just like home. Goodnight, Bernard."

"Goodnight, Fel."

His brother gave him a nod, then turned and put his back to the flames, to Cutter.

Cutter was exhausted, but he did not immediately go to sleep. He sat there, basking in the feel of the fire's warmth on his skin, of the full belly the squirrel had left him with. He couldn't remember the last time he'd been warm, the last time he'd been full.

He stared at Feledias's back and suddenly felt a stab of panic. He'd thought he lost him. And when he'd thought it, he'd thought of all the things he hadn't said that he'd wished he had. And he thought, also, that there might not be another chance to do it. "Fel?" he asked.

But his brother was already asleep, and he did not answer.

So Cutter only sat, huddled near the warmth of the dancing flames as night stretched across the world.

CHAPTER SEVEN

There was a hand on his shoulder, shaking him.

Chall groaned. "Whatsit?" he croaked, rubbing at his aching head.

"We're here, sir," a man's voice said, managing to sound at once servile and impatient.

Chall opened his eyes, wincing at the sun light filtering into them. On more than a few occasions, during his younger—and not so much younger—days, he'd drank more than his share and woken in an unfamiliar place with no idea how he'd gotten there or why the person waking him was, almost without fail, pissed off about something.

Yet he'd discovered that, unfortunately, it wasn't the sort of thing a man got better at with practice, so he stared around in complete, baffled confusion for several seconds until he realized that he was in a carriage, and the sunlight in his eyes was coming through the open carriage door. A door at which, currently, stood a man who was staring at him with thinly-veiled annoyance.

"It's a gift," Chall muttered, wiping an arm across his mouth.

"What's a gift, sir?"

"Annoying people. Anyway, where's 'here'?"

"The castle, sir. The woman who hired me, she said to bring you to the castle as quickly as possible, that you had business here."

"The woman," Chall muttered, his brain still struggling to catch up. And why not? After all, there'd been plenty of women over the years. Too many. But then a memory came drifting back to him, one of Maeve standing over him, an apology writ clear on her face, his head aching like the left side had gotten in an argument with the right and the two had decided to go their separate ways.

Not a woman then, he realized. *The* woman. "Damnit, Maeve, what are you up to?" he asked.

"Bill."

"What?" Chall said, turning back to the man standing in the carriage door.

"My name," the man said. "It's Bill—not Maeve. And we're here, as I said. So if you are done resting..."

Chall knew when he wasn't wanted somewhere—a thing he'd also had a lot of practice at—so he stumbled out of the carriage, still dizzy from the blow Maeve had given him. He nearly fell as his feet hit the cobbles and was forced to catch himself on the carriage. "Sorry," he told Bill who was still staring at him, his disapproval considerably easier to see now. "I just got these feet yesterday."

Not his best joke, maybe, but then he *had* just woken up from being knocked unconscious by his lover while a ruthless assassin took her away so he thought that maybe under the circumstances it was pretty damned fine.

An opinion that, judging by Bill's straight face, the carriage driver did not share. "I didn't know the taverns had ale so early, sir," the carriage driver said.

"Then you've been going to the wrong taverns, Bill." The man still didn't crack a smile, and Chall sighed as he continued to stand there, staring at him. "There something else? Or do you just enjoy my company?"

"There is the small matter of payment, sir."

Chall winced. "Right, of course." He reached into his coin purse and retrieved several coins. As he did, his fingers caught on something, and he pulled it out, along with the coins, to see that it was a small piece of paper.

He ignored it for the moment, instead handing the carriage driver his payment.

Bill stared at it in obvious annoyance, clearly not satisfied with the tip. He waited for a moment, as if Chall would add more. He didn't. After all, if there was anything in the world he was used to it was disappointing people. The carriage driver gave a sniff and walked around, climbing into the carriage. He clucked at the horses and in another moment he and the carriage were heading down the road, leaving Chall standing there.

"You want a tip, Bill?" Chall said to the departing carriage. "Be less of a dick."

He realized he was still holding the scrap of paper that had been in his coin purse, and he opened it, unsurprised to see Maeve's writing.

Chall,

I'm sorry. I will be okay—you have to trust me. Find Priest, tell him about Ned. Don't come looking for me, please. Matt needs you more than me.

I love you,

Mae.

Chall read the note a dozen times as he stood there, feeling a mixture of emotions. Frustration, certainly. Frustration that she had gone off on her own again, not allowing him to protect her. Foolishness at the thought that *she* would need *him* to protect her in the first place. Annoyance and panic and fear. But mostly, he felt lucky. Lucky that such a woman would somehow choose to spend her time with him. He would have said she was perfect had it not been for her obviously terrible choice in men, but there it was.

He frowned, considering his options. He could go chasing her through the city, but he would squander precious time—time that, if he was right about Ned, they simply didn't have—and likely he wouldn't find her anyway. After all, it wasn't as if a man could just walk into the Assassins' Guild and sign up. Maeve had told him where the place was, that the Guild was disguised as a school of healers, but that didn't mean he had any chance of getting inside. After all, it was a school of *assassins,* and he thought that he had a pretty good idea of how they'd tend to handle trespassers.

Besides, the way the man, Balderath, had reached his hands into the illusions of flame Chall had created was still fresh in his mind, as was the nickname Maeve said the man had—Balderath the Brutal. In a guild that took out contracts to kill people apparently the man stood out as particularly cruel. Which, as far as Chall was concerned, was like saying he was the murderingest murderer of all the murderers. Not exactly a fellow he'd care to meet again, if given a choice.

In the end, though, it was neither his fear of assassins nor of the man, Balderath, that decided him. It was one simple fact—he *did* trust Maeve. Certainly he trusted her far more than he trusted himself, and if she thought it more important that he speak to Priest than go looking for her then likely she was right. After all, she wasn't just deadlier than him—she was also cleverer. Not that he'd ever say as much to her, of course.

Sighing and saying a quick prayer that Maeve stayed safe, Chall hurried toward the castle.

He stumbled toward the guards at the gate, wondering if Maeve had really needed to hit him so hard or if she'd maybe taken a bit of enjoyment out of the opportunity to pay him back for slights.

"Sir Challadius," one of the guards called, "is everything quite alright?"

"Is it ever, Edward?" Chall asked. "I don't mean to be rude, but I'm in a bit of a hurry."

"Of course, sir," the guard said, nodding at one of his companions.

A moment later the gates were swinging open. Chall hurried through. He didn't bother checking Priest's rooms, for if he was awake he knew that he would find the man at Matt's side. Since Prince Bernard and his brother had been sent to the Black Wood Priest was rarely anywhere else, often even foregoing sleep to watch over the king's quarters.

It had become almost an obsession of the man since Bernard left, and although he couldn't imagine how, it seemed to Chall that Priest somehow blamed himself or held himself responsible for the prince's absence. Ridiculous, of course, but then people often were—it was the one thing they could be counted on to be.

Instead, he walked down the hallways in search of a servant. Some might have asked the guards, but he knew that the guards, unless the king was in their vicinity, might well not know where he was. The servants, on the other hand, were the nearly invisible eyes and ears and heart of the castle. In order to anticipate the king's needs they always remained apprised of his whereabouts, just as they were always aware of any visitors to the castle—not that there'd been many of late. As it turned out, murders in the castle and assassinations in the city had a way of making people rethink visiting New Daltenia or taking advantage of the dubious hospitality its castle offered.

He caught sight of a servant in a minute of walking and moved toward her. "Excuse me, ma'am?"

The serving woman looked up from where she was scrubbing at what was, to Chall at least, an invisible speck of dirt on a sculpture. "Sir Challadius," she said, giving a curtsey, "how may I help you?"

"The king, do you know where he is?"

"Of course, sir," she said. "He's with Healer Malden again."

"Again?" Chall asked, confused.

Immediately the serving woman winced, a look of mild panic coming over her face as if she was afraid she'd overstepped. "That is, I think that his Majesty is in a meeting with Healer Malden."

"Has he seen the healer a lot?"

"Forgive me, sir," the woman said, "but I really must be going—the mistress will be wondering where I am."

Before Chall could say anything the woman turned and fled down the hallway, not quite running but then not all that far from it either.

Chall hesitated, staring after her in confusion but not for long. After all, he needed to speak to Priest as quickly as possible. If he was right about Ned and he tarried, there was no telling what damage the man might do. In truth, there was no telling what damage he'd done already. He could figure out whatever was going on with Matt and Healer Malden later—for now, there were more pressing matters than the king having a potential tummy ache.

He made his way through the castle hallways and up the stairs toward the healer's quarters. He was relieved to see, as he approached the stairs, that there were several guards stationed at the base of them, meaning that the serving woman was right. Or at least, if she wasn't, then the two guardsmen had decided to guard a random staircase for no apparent reason.

"Sir Challadius," the older of the two called.

Challadius recognized the guard and grinned as he approached. "Vorrun—it's good to see you. I was wondering where you've been lately—finding a likely closet to sleep in while no one's looking, I expect."

The guardsman grinned. "It has been some time since we used to go to taverns together, Sir Challadius, but as I recall it was you who ended up sleeping in closets that didn't belong to you—or beds. On that point you never seemed all that particular."

Chall winced. "No one can wound us as well as those who know us."

"Sure," the guardsman said, grinning. "Easier to stab a man in the back when he's asked you to watch it."

That hit just a touch too close to home, considering the errand that had brought Chall to the castle in such haste, and he felt the smile that seeing his old friend had brought wither on his face.

"Everything okay, sir?" Vorrun asked, picking up on his change in mood.

"Fine," Chall lied, then gave the man the most convincing smile he was capable of—that too, he'd had plenty of practice at, usually when trying to convince an angry husband he hadn't been bedding his wife or, alternatively, trying to convince the wife to let him bed her in the first place. "And you can stow that 'sir' shit, you bastard," Chall said. "I figure once you've saved me from getting my ass kicked in a dozen drunken scuffles—most of which were probably my fault—then you've earned the right to use my name. You know, almost like I'm a person."

"Seventeen, actually," the guardsman said, grinning. "But who's counting? And as for 'probably'...forgive me, but they were unquestionably your fault." He grinned wider. "*Sir.*"

Chall sighed. "Those were the good old days."

"The old days anyway," the guardsman said. "As for good, well, I'm not so sure. I remember being hungover a lot...not much else."

"Don't you see, Vorrun?" Chall said. "That's what makes them good."

"All that good damn near killed me," the older guardsman said. "I haven't had a drink in ten years and more."

"Yeah?" Chall said. "And how's life been since?"

The guardsman shrugged. "You know how it is. Some good. Some bad. At least now I remember it."

Chall nodded. "Listen, Vorrun, I'd love to catch up more later, but right now I need to speak with His Majesty. Is he upstairs?"

"Yes, sir," the guardsman said, his tone changing immediately, growing official once more. "Would you like for me to escort you?" His eyes flashed with mirth, but his expression remained serious. "The stairs can be a bit tricky."

Chall frowned. "I think I can manage, you bastard." Grinning, Vorrun stepped aside, as did the other guard, and Chall started toward the stairs, pausing to glance back at the guardsman. "Tell me, Vorrun, has Matt—that is, has His Majesty—been coming to visit the healer a lot?"

"Oh, sure," Vorrun said, nodding.

"What about?"

The guardsman blinked, looking surprised. "You don't know? I figured you knew just about everything about the king."

"So did I," Chall said.

"His Majesty's been havin' trouble sleepin'. Bad dreams and all."

"Bad dreams?" Chall asked. "Like what?"

The guardsman shrugged. "Can't say as I know, but whatever they are they've been some doozies. His Majesty woke up just yesterday mornin' screamin'. Percy and I knocked the door in, thinkin' an assassin or somethin' had broke in, only there wasn't anyone there, just His Majesty, lookin' like he'd seen a ghost."

"Really?" Chall said. "Well, if His Majesty has had trouble sleeping, why wouldn't he tell me?"

"That'd be a question you'd have to ask His Majesty, I'm afraid," Vorrun said.

Chall nodded, thinking. "Can you do me a favor, Vorrun? If anything else like this happens, can you let me know?"

"Yes, sir."

"Thanks," Chall said, then he turned and walked up the stairs.

He was sweating by the time he reached the top, and he told himself that if Vorrun made the mistake of offering his help the next time he might just take the smug bastard up on it. He walked down the hall toward the healer's door. Two more guards were stationed outside.

"Sir Challadius," one said, inclining his head in a bow.

"Hello," Chall said. "Is His Majesty speaking with the healer?"

"Yes, sir."

"And Priest, is he with him?"

The two guards shared a look, smiling slightly. "The shadow? Of course, sir."

"Shadow?"

"Yes, sir," the speaker said, grinning. "We call him that on account of—"

"He follows the king everywhere he goes," Chall said. "I get it. May I go in?"

The guard nodded. "Let me just ask, sir."

The guard vanished through the door and returned a few seconds later. "Go on in, sir," he said, holding the door open.

"Thanks."

Chall stepped inside to see Matt sitting at a single chair in the center of the room while the old healer, Malden, leaned over him, his ear pressed to Matt's chest, the back of his hand against his forehead. Priest, meanwhile, stood in the corner and gave Chall a nod as he walked in.

"Chall," Matt said, "it's good to see you." Yet despite the young man's words there was something in his tone, a sort of strain or reluctance that made Chall think maybe he wasn't as glad to see him as he might pretend. "How did you find me?"

"A serving girl told me you were here, Majesty," Chall said. "I hope everything is alright?"

"Oh, everything's fine, of course," Matt said, giving him a smile that seemed a bit strained to Chall. "Just a routine checkup, that's all."

"Routine checkup, Majesty?" Chall asked, surprised. "Forgive me, but I was led to understand that you've been coming to see Healer Malden quite often of late."

Matt cleared his throat. "I suppose I've been by a few times. I've just had a little bit of trouble sleeping, that's all. I thought perhaps Malden might have some idea how to help. He's set me up with a tea that's been working wonders."

"Trouble sleeping?" Chall asked.

"Yeah, but nothing serious," Matt said, waving a hand away dismissively. "Just worry, that's all."

"Well," Chall said slowly, "Malden is the best healer in New Daltenia, I'm sure he'll sort you out." He glanced at Priest's face, and thought he could see something in the other man's eyes— doubt. No surprise, really, for he'd been seeing that in Priest's eyes a lot lately. But now that doubt wasn't about his beliefs but instead about the king's words. And as he saw it, Chall realized something.

Matt was lying to him.

He couldn't imagine why he might do so, but he was certain that he was. After all, Chall had told enough lies in his time to know one when he heard it. "Well, that's good, Majesty," he said, because that's what was expected of him.

Matt nodded. "Anyway, how can I help you, Chall?"

"Forgive me, Majesty," Chall said, "but it's actually Priest I came here to speak to, if that's alright."

"Of...of course," Matt said. "By all means."

Chall nodded, moving to where Priest stood.

"Everything alright, Chall?" Priest asked.

Chall glanced back at Matt to see that he was currently involved in a conversation with the healer, though they were talking too low to hear. "I don't think so," he said quietly, and then proceeded to explain to Priest what he and Maeve had learned from Petran regarding the Crimson Wolves, as well as everything he'd come to believe about Ned and, finally, about their encounter with the assassin, Balderath.

"Maeve will be fine, Chall," Priest said.

"Sure she will," he said, "but if you could say a quick prayer to that goddess of yours, I've a feelin' she'd listen to you quicker than me."

The man gave him a pained smile and, instead of answering directly, changed the subject. "This third person, Lady Valencia, are you sure Petran was serious about her?"

"You ever known that bastard to make a joke?" Chall countered.

Priest frowned, nodding. "But—and I don't mean to point fingers—wasn't it you who told me to trust the carriage driver?"

"You lookin' to say 'I told you so,' that it?" Chall asked. "Look, I was wrong, alright? Shit, it isn't like it hasn't happened before. If you ask me, it's your fault for listening to me in the first place. Anyway, maybe it's not too late for us to figure out whatever the bastard's up to."

"Assuming he's up to anything," Priest said slowly. "We don't know that he is. After all, you were just reminding me how often you can be wrong."

"And we don't *know* that stickin' our head in a lion's mouth is going to end with it getting chewed on, but I'd rather not bet my life on it," Chall said, meeting the man's eyes. "We don't *know* that Ned is guilty, but it damned sure looks like it to me—after all, we've practically given him his own damned room in the castle, and all of a sudden folks start ending up dead. Seems like too much of a coincidence, if you ask me. Still..." he shrugged. "I could be wrong. We need to figure it out, one way or the other."

"And have you thought of some way that we might do that?" Priest asked.

"Don't I always have a plan?" Chall countered.

"Not that I can recall, no."

"Oh yeah?" Chall asked. "How's this? We go and see this Lady Valencia. After all, what better way to figure out if Ned's been feeding us a line of bullshit than to speak to the third founder of the Crimson Wolves?"

"Alleged third founder," Priest said.

"Oh come on," Chall said. "If it walks like a duck and talks like a duck it's probably the third founding member of a criminal organization known for brutality and murder."

"I'm not entirely sure that's how the saying goes," Priest said slowly.

"Are you in or not?" Chall said. "I'd just as soon get this done quickly, so that I can go find Maeve."

"Maeve will be fine, Chall," Priest said. "She can take care of herself."

"I know that, damnit, don't you think I know that?" Chall said. "Only...stones and starlight, Priest, they're *assassins.*"

"So is she," Priest reminded him. "And not just any assassin but the very best, the most famous and deadly to ever come out of the Guild. It is not Maeve who you should fear for but anyone who dares stand against her."

That made Chall feel better, at least a little. Not completely, though. Priest was right—Maeve *was* the most famous assassin in the world, known for being the most talented, the most skilled. But then, she was also just a woman, the woman he loved. And however talented, however skilled she was, she couldn't hope to stand against an entire guild full of people who spent their time learning how to kill things better. No one could do such a thing. Except, perhaps, for Prince Bernard, and he was far, far away.

He gave his head a shake, ridding himself of his thoughts and his worries—they would not serve him now. "Anyway," he said, "are you going or not?"

"*Of course we're going!*" Matt called.

Chall started and he and Priest turned to see Matt looking at them from across the room where he still sat beside the healer who was staring at the king with a confused expression on his face.

"Majesty?" Chall called back, glancing at Priest to see that he was as surprised as he was.

"To Lady Valencia's," Matt said, looking at them as if they were crazy. "What else do you imagine I meant?"

"But...how did you hear that, Majesty?" Priest asked, taking the question out of Chall's mouth. After all, he'd been speaking in little more than a whisper for the express reason that he hadn't wanted to trouble the king with anymore bad news.

"The same way most people hear things, I imagine," Matt said, glancing between the two of them. "Fire and salt, the two of you look like you've seen a ghost," he went on, giving a laugh. "Anyway, I don't believe that Ned would ever betray us, but we'd best make sure, just in case. And I think you're right, Chall—Lady Valencia seems to me to be the best way of doing that."

Chall was barely listening. He was too busy staring at Matt in confusion. It was impossible for the man to have heard their conversation. And yet, clearly, he had. He glanced at the healer, hoping for some sort of explanation, but the old man only gave a shake of his head. He told himself it was nothing—it had to be some funny sort of acoustics in the room or something like that. After all, Matt sat at its center, and he'd heard something before about some rooms and theaters being designed in such a way that the sound carried like that. Only, Malden was sitting at the center of the room as well and he didn't seem to have heard a thing.

Of course he didn't, you fool, Chall chided himself. *The bastard's probably damned near a hundred years old. It's a wonder he can hear anything at all.*

In the end, Chall decided to leave it. Funny acoustics—that had to be it. After all, what was the other option? Besides, it wasn't as if they didn't have enough to worry about already without looking for more. "Perhaps it would be best, Majesty, if the two of us went alone," Chall said. "No doubt you're needed here."

"For what?" Matt said. "I don't have any more audiences until tomorrow, and I'm sure we'll be back by then. Anyway, if my throne starts to float away, I'm sure that someone else's backside will hold it down as well as mine."

Chall opened his mouth, meaning to object, but the problem was he could think of no objection to voice save for the real one—he didn't want Matt to come simply because he didn't want to risk the young man, Cutter's son. Cutter was in the Black Wood now and, for anyone else, that would have been a death sentence, but if anyone could make it back from such a place it was the prince, and Chall would be damned if he was going to be the one who had to explain to him that something had happened to his son on his watch.

He turned desperately to look at Priest.

"But, the investigation, Majesty," Priest said. "Into the man, Rolph's, death. Without you here—"

"It will continue on exactly as it has," Matt said. "Commander Malex has the investigation well in hand. The only thing I can do is get in the way."

"But...well, it's late already, Highness," Priest said, glancing at a window where the afternoon sun shined into the healer's quarters. "As you said, you've had trouble sleeping. Perhaps it would be better if you lay down—you look tired and—"

"And I'll be more tired if I spend several hours tossing and turning in bed," Matt said. "Anyway, night is hours away yet. Unless you're planning to spend the night at Lady Valencia's I imagine we'll be back long before His Royal Highness needs to go down for his nappy. Unless there's some other reason the two of you are trying to keep me from going?" he finished, eyeing them both.

"Another reason, Majesty?" Chall asked.

"That's right," Matt said. "Something like...you're treating me as if I'm a child? But then that *can't* be it, can it? After all, you think I'm old enough to run a *kingdom* so surely you wouldn't worry about me going to a noblewoman's house, one that lies within the city. I mean, that would be ridiculous." He raised an eyebrow. "Wouldn't it?"

Chall had been called far worse things than ridiculous and most of those had been well deserved, so the idea of being thought poorly of wasn't really all that foreign to him. In fact, most of the time he was far more surprised by the idea that there were some people walking the face of the world who didn't want to stab him the moment they met him. But then, the prince would do far worse than stab him if he returned to discover that Chall had endangered his son.

He was just preparing to make another objection—which likely was going to amount to him grabbing Priest and running for the door—when Matt spoke again.

"Please," he said, giving him a fragile smile that seemed to Chall to be inches away from tears. "I...I feel like I've been cooped up in this castle forever. And...with not sleeping well...I could use the distraction."

He tried for a light, casual sound, but Chall could hear an unmistakable desperation in his words, could see it in the young man's eyes as he waited for what they would say. Chall glanced at Priest, but the man said nothing, leaving it to him. The bastard.

"Of course if you'd like to accompany us, Majesty, we would be pleased to have you with us."

Matt heaved a heavy sigh, as if he'd been drowning and Chall had just pulled him to shore. "Good," he said, nodding shakily. "That's good. When...when do we leave?"

Chall realized, as he stared at Matt, that the king was even worse off than he'd thought. Whatever it was that was going on with him, it was no small thing. He glanced at Priest and the man met his eyes. Although he was expressionless, Chall thought he could see a worry of his own in his friend's gaze. "Well, Majesty," Chall said, glancing back at Matt, "if it's all the same to you, now would work."

Matt nodded, smiling. "Then now it is."

CHAPTER EIGHT

"And here I was thinking your employer would want to meet for an afternoon lunch, maybe at a nice tavern." But the truth was, Maeve thought as she stared at the giant building across the street, at the sign hanging from its front, *Sir Chavoy's Academy of the Healing Arts* engraved on its face, that she would have been happier with some dark alley as their meeting place instead of where the man had taken her.

Not that she was surprised, of course, for she had assumed he'd meant to take her to the Assassin's Guild—or kill her outright. The second option hadn't been off the table by any means, for she could only think of one reason why the Guild would want to speak with her, and it wasn't a comforting one.

After all, it had only been days ago that she'd helped stage the murder of the Guild's leader, Agnes. It was likely, then, that her "invitation" had something to do with the Guildmaster. Either they *had* believed the assassination and had somehow linked her with Agnes's death, or they had not been fooled at all and had somehow become aware of Maeve's role in orchestrating the charade that allowed the prior Guildmaster an opportunity to escape.

Either way, she doubted they'd invited her for tea and cookies—not that she could have kept anything down just then anyway. Despite her assurances to Chall that everything would be alright, Maeve was worried. Terrified, in truth, but she did her best not to show it—assassins, like most people, tended to see another's weakness as opportunity.

Balderath gave a soft, polite laugh. The man had not spoken so much as a word since Maeve had agreed to accompany him, meeting her questions with polite but unbroken silence. A silence that he did not break then, only giving her a look as if to say she had come this far and might as well go the rest of the way, before turning and starting across the street toward the "healing academy."

Maeve hesitated—as anyone who knew the truth of the building's nature would—but in the end she followed. After all, what choice did she have? Another, who had less experience dealing with assassins, might have thought to run, for the man Balderath didn't look back as he moved across the street toward the Guildhouse. But then Maeve had been trained by the guild, knew well how they did things, and so she knew that they were not alone, that there would be others following them, just out of sight.

Maeve had caught a glimpse of at least two of them as she'd followed Balderath through the city. And those were just the ones she had seen. She didn't doubt that there were others trailing along around them, an invisible net that would only close it if *needed* to close, if she did something foolish like, for example, turn and flee down the street.

Inside *Sir Chavoy's Academy of the Healing Arts* dozens of young men and women—students judging by the books they carried and their simple dress—walked purposefully, moving out of or into the hallways that extended out of the entry way like spokes from the center of a wheel. Among them, Maeve noted older men and women—teachers, she suspected by the deference the students seemed to pay them as they passed.

In short, the inside of the building looked exactly like what anyone might assume an academy for healers might look like. But then, just because a mask was well-made, that didn't make it real. She wondered if any of the students that gave her and her escort a wide berth had any idea about the primary function of the academy they attended.

She didn't have long to wonder, though, for Balderath didn't hesitate, making his way through the entryway into the massive inner room of the academy, specifically to the room's center and the desk at which sat the exact same woman Maeve had met the last time she and Emille had come.

"Professor Balderath," the woman said, "I hope the afternoon finds you well."

Balderath didn't even bother glancing in the woman's direction as he continued past. Maeve expected the woman to call him down, but she said nothing, only swallowing hard and turning away as Maeve followed the man.

According to Emille, the secretary—whose name Maeve had never gotten—had no idea about the academy's dual purpose, yet she was also clearly anxious around Balderath, likely having picked up on something about the man's character that made her afraid of him. And that was good, for she was right to be afraid.

It might have been difficult to reconcile the small-framed, almost boring looking man with the terrible stories she'd heard of the infamous Balderath the Brutal, but Maeve had lived long enough to know that things were rarely what they seemed.

On the surface, Balderath might have acted and behaved like a normal man, might have appeared like nothing more dangerous than an unassuming tutor, but while his mask was good, it was not perfect, and clearly it had slipped in front of the woman at least once, enough for her to see that there was something not quite right about the man. But then Maeve doubted very seriously if the woman had any idea of just *how* wrong he was—otherwise, she suspected that she would have fled screaming for the nearest exit, something Maeve was tempted to do herself.

But things that fled were chased, and a creature who willfully chose to be prey could not act surprised when the predators came, so Maeve followed the assassin down the hall with a casual confidence, as if she were the one escorting him.

It was all an act, of course, one that became considerably harder to maintain when Balderath led her down a set of stairs, leaving the building's facade behind and taking her into the true Guild. He continued down a hallway and past a second secretary. This one, unless Maeve completely missed her guess, held the handle of a concealed crossbow behind her desk.

They walked past several doors until, finally, Balderath stopped, turning to Maeve. He bowed, opening the door at which he'd stopped, gesturing like a servant opening the door for his master.

Maeve wasn't fooled by the act, for she knew well enough that, should it be asked of him, the man wouldn't hesitate to kill her, and then she would become just another story of Balderath the Brutal's...well. Brutality.

She peered through the door into a shadowed, unlit hallway that ended in another door. "Doesn't look like much of a party," she observed.

The assassin said nothing.

"Don't guess there's someone hiding behind that door with a dagger they're looking for some place to put?" she asked, at once joking and not really joking at all.

Again, Balderath did not speak, his only answer a small smile.

Maeve didn't hesitate anymore than that. After all she could be stabbed standing where she was as well as stepping through the door. Instead, she started into the hallway, promising herself that if some bastard *did* mean to kill her and had forced her to walk all this way for it then she was going to haunt his ass for as long as he lived.

She made it to the door and then—because, as a general rule, it wasn't good to take assassins by surprise—Maeve knocked.

Her fist had barely touched the wooden surface of the door before it swung open with a swiftness that made her tense, one of her hands going for a knife hidden at her waist.

She didn't know exactly what she'd expected might wait for her on the other side of the door—the dagger she'd joked about with Balderath wasn't all that far from it—but she didn't expect what she found. The person standing on the other side of the door was not some nameless assassin ready to attack, and she did not wield a weapon, at least not openly, though the frown on her face was sharp enough to draw blood.

"It's about damned time," Tribune Silrika growled. "We've been waiting for over an hour." She glanced at Maeve's hand, frozen at her waist from where she'd started to reach for a blade.

The Tribune sneered. "You would not have been fast enough."

"Oh, do stop your carrying on, Silrika," another, older voice said, one Maeve recognized as Tribune Bethesa, the one that Agnes had referred to as "the old crone" or "ancient hag" by turns and the one that Maeve had quickly decided was by far the most dangerous of the three. "We've much to get to and little time to waste. Besides, as I recall we have already witnessed just such a demonstration once, and the results of that bout were quite...definitive."

The younger Tribune's face turned a deep, ugly shade of red, and she ran a hand through a ponytail so tight it looked as if it must have been a special kind of torture all its own. "Anyone can get lucky once," she said.

"When dealing with sharp blades, Silrika," the older woman said, "I find that once is all it takes."

The woman colored deeper at that—something Maeve wouldn't have thought was possible until she saw it. She bared her teeth at Maeve. "Well?" she demanded. "Come in—it isn't as if you haven't wasted enough of our time."

Maeve reluctantly let her hand fall away from her waist, but remained prepared to bring it back again should the woman attack—an eventuality she would not have put past her, for the last time they'd met she and Silrika had not exactly made fast friends. In truth, she wasn't sure the woman *had* friends. Any except for the assassin Felara, but Maeve had killed her when she'd tried to assassinate Matt, a fact that hadn't helped her rapport with the tribune.

Maeve tracked the woman out of the corner of her eye as she stepped past her into the room. The Tribune made a point of not moving, so Maeve was forced to squeeze between her and the doorway, thinking to herself that a woman of Silrika's age—forty-five, at least—was far too old to still be playing such childish games. Not that she planned on saying so—she wasn't exactly in the mood for a fight to the death just now.

Past the small entry hallway, the room opened into a small sitting area. A large, circular table sat at the room's center and, seated at it, were two familiar figures. The first belonged to the gray-haired, wrinkled Tribune Bethesa, whose eyes shone with a mixture of intelligence, mirth and—what appeared to Maeve, at least—anticipation.

Also seated at the table was the silver-haired Tribune Piralta or, as Agnes had so unaffectionately labeled him, "the weasel." Looking at him, at the way he studied her, his eyes slightly narrowed, his nose scrunched, Maeve thought that there was indeed something rodent-like about the man's appearance not to mention his manner.

"Ah, Lady Maeve," the man said, his voice somehow sounding servile and off-putting at once, oily, like the way a snake—or, indeed, a weasel—might sound, if it could talk. "It is a pleasure to see you."

"Speak for yourself, Piralta," Silrika growled as she moved past Maeve—intentionally shouldering into her as she did—to have a seat at the table.

"Ignore Silrika, Lady Maeve," Tribune Bethesa said. "Her bark is worse than her bite."

Considering that it hadn't been the old Tribune who Silrika had tried to "bite" quite a few times with the knives currently sheathed at her waist, Maeve wasn't so sure, but she didn't see any reason to say as much. After all, it was enough that one of the Tribunes wanted her dead openly—in secret, they likely all did— she didn't see any need to go pissing off another just to keep life interesting.

A pregnant silence descended on the room as the three studied Maeve—Silrika with a frown that made it clear she'd just as soon stick a knife in her as look at her. Piralta looked to be trying to size her up, likely trying to decide what sort of value she could offer him, how he might use her. The oldest of the three, Bethesa, studied her with a small smile on her face, the most innocuous expression of the three, yet Maeve felt quite sure it was also the deadliest. It was the smile one might expect to see on a grandmother as she watched her grandchildren at play, but she thought that the Tribune might just as easily flash that smile as she watched her victim bleed out on the ground.

An old snake, true, but Maeve had spoken to a snake tamer, once, and he had told her that while the old snakes might not have fangs as sharp as the younger, their venom was even more potent. Maeve thought that the woman, Bethesa, was like that old snake. Maybe not as agile as it once had been, but anyone who stumbled into reach of its fangs would live to regret it. Though, she suspected, not for long.

"Forgive us, Lady Maeve," the old Tribune said, "where are our manners? Please, do have a seat." She gestured to the only empty chair at the table and, Maeve couldn't help but notice that the chairs of each of the Tribunes sat on one side of the table so that anyone seated in the remaining chair would be facing all three of them at once.

"Thank you," she said, "but I really don't have much time—I was in a bit of a hurry when your man found me. There are things I need to be about." *Namely, not dying, if it's all the same to you,* she thought.

"Busy?" Silrika demanded. "You must be out of your damned mi—"

"Yes, Lady Maeve," Bethesa interrupted, "I am quite sure a woman of your status stays busy, and so I would like to thank you, truly, for accepting our invitation."

"I got the idea it wasn't the sort of invitation I would enjoy declining."

The woman smiled at that, but she didn't deny it. There was the muffled sound of something falling or being knocked over in a room beyond the one they were currently in. Maeve glanced at the door that stood half-ajar but couldn't make anything out.

"These are Guildmaster Agnes's quarters," Bethesa said in a conversational tone , drawing Maeve's gaze back to her. "But then, I guess you know that, don't you?"

Maeve felt her heart begin to race at that. She and Agnes had spent some time together as they'd planned how they would make the illusion of her assassination work, but they had never spent them in the Guildmaster's private quarters. Agnes had not trusted her quarters not to be watched—almost certainly rightly so. Still, why would the woman think that Maeve had spent any time here? Or was she just fishing?

"Lady Maeve? Are you quite alright?"

Maeve cleared her throat, smiling the best smile she was capable of back at the old woman. "I'm sorry, Tribune, but I did not know these were the Guildmaster's quarters."

She felt her heart speed up in her chest in anticipation, and she forced herself to breathe as the old woman studied her. "Oh?" Bethesa asked. "Is that right?"

"Forgive me, Tribune, but why would I?" Maeve asked. "After all, I only just rejoined the guild, and while Guildmaster Agnes and I knew each other long ago, I'm afraid there was no love lost between us." That much, at least, was true, for the two of them had been bitter rivals as anyone from their time, such as Bethesa, would well know.

"Yes," the old woman said, nodding slowly. "I am old, but I do seem to recall that the two of you didn't exactly get on famously. Still, I think you might be underestimating the respect Guildmaster Agnes had for you, Lady Maeve. After all, it was the Guildmaster herself who campaigned to have you re-inducted to the Guild, was it not? Why would she do that, do you think?"

"I'm afraid I can't pretend to know the Guildmaster's mind, Tribune," Maeve said. "I am only glad that she chose to have mercy on me."

"Mercy?" Silrika demanded, then snorted. "That old bitch wasn't known for mercy anymore than I'm known for spreading wings and—"

"That is enough, Silrika," Bethesa said, sighing as she looked back at Maeve. "Still, I must say that Tribune Silrika is not wrong. Our Guildmaster was clever and deadly, as sharp as a blade unsheathed, of that there is no doubt. But among the many qualities she possessed, I do not believe one might have counted mercy. It is surprising then that she might choose to invite someone who was, by your own admission, her long-time enemy, to rejoin the Guild. In fact, it seems more likely that Guildmaster Agnes would have used her position to make your life considerably more miserable. Or perhaps shorter."

Maeve knew what the woman was getting at, but she had no intention of doing her work for her. "Is there a question there, Tribune?"

Bethesa gave her a humoring smile. "My question, Lady Maeve, is why the Guildmaster would act against her nature in such a way?"

Maeve decided to take a calculated risk then. "I'm afraid you'd have to ask the Guildmaster, if you wanted to know her mind," she said.

"You know damned well we can't do that!" Silrika shouted. "She's dead, damn you, and—"

"*That is enough, Tribune Silrika,*" Bethesa hissed, and although her voice was not raised much above a whisper and although they technically shared the same position, Maeve could not help but notice that Silrika seemed to shrink back against her chair, her face not going crimson as it had earlier but instead pale, almost sickly.

"F-forgive me," Maeve said, putting on her best shocked expression, and she was glad, in that moment as in so many others, that she and Chall spent so much time together. After all, if there was a better actor and dissembler in all the world, she had never met him. "But...did you say that the Guildmaster is...dead?" It was a risky question but a calculated one. After all, she was well aware that the guild had yet to officially announce Agnes's death. She knew because she'd spent the last several days since their charade wondering why that might be.

"Surely you must have heard the rumors," Tribune Piralta said.

"Forgive me, Tribune," Maeve said, "but I've lived long enough to know that rumors are as useless as a man's word when he's looking for company for the night."

The Tribune colored at that, and Bethesa gave a sad smile. "Yes, well, I am sad to say that while you would usually be correct, Lady Maeve, Guildmaster Agnes was indeed killed—less than a week ago, in fact."

"Killed?" Maeve asked. "Surely you can't be serious."

"Oh, but I am," Bethesa said. "Or, at least, that is what someone would like for us to think."

Maeve felt as if someone had just poured ice water into her veins at that, but she did her best to keep her fear from her expression. "I...don't understand, Tribune."

"Yes, of course not, and how could you?" Bethesa asked, and Maeve couldn't decide if the woman was taunting her or not, thought it even odds that the woman would order her men to attack her at any moment. "You see, Lady Maeve, Guildmaster Agnes was attacked while in a tavern. Witnesses saw her stabbed multiple times before the tavern, which had caught flame somehow during the struggle between the Guildmaster's assailants and her bodyguards, went up in smoke."

"That sounds...terrible," Maeve said and here, at least, she didn't have to pretend. After all, she had been there, and it *had* been terrible. Dealing with Agnes's bodyguards had been bad enough, not to mention that the tavern actually *had* been on fire.

After all, Chall's illusion wouldn't have done much good, if the illusory smoke would have eventually cleared only to reveal a building that was completely unburned. The fire had been very, *very* real, and it had been all Maeve and the others could do to make it out of the tavern alive.

"Oh, from all accounts it was indeed," Bethesa agreed. "And from those same accounts, it was undoubtedly our Guildmaster who was killed."

"But...you don't believe that?" Maeve said.

The woman frowned consideringly. "I am...skeptical."

"Why?" Maeve croaked, then cleared her throat. "Forgive me, why is that?"

"A few reasons, actually," Bethesa said. "For one, it was an out of the way tavern in the poor quarter—not the sort of place one would expect to find Agnes who, it has to be said, enjoyed the finer things in life." She waved a hand at the ostentatious furnishings of the sitting room by way of explanation. "Secondly, it seems far too convenient for me that the killer happened to kill Agnes in the doorway of the tavern, in full view of the street, when he might have done the deed anywhere else. Why mark himself in such a way?"

"Perhaps...with the flames and everything going on, maybe he didn't think of it?"

"Maybe," the Tribune said reluctantly. "But that isn't all—you see, they never found her body." Maeve frowned at that, for she knew that she and Chall had put in a great deal of effort so that there *would* be a body there to be found. "No body?" she asked. "But I thought, according to the rumors, I mean, that they had."

"Certainly they found *a* body," the Tribune agreed, "but there is nothing to indicate that the body which was pulled from the wreckage belonged to our Guildmaster. For example, she had several rings she wore—as I said, she liked the finer things—and none of those have been found in the rubble."

Tribune Piralta sighed. "Forgive me, Bethesa, but we have been over this. Likely the rings burned up in the fire and, if not, well as you said it happened in the poor part of the city. The people who live there would risk a lot more than being singed to get their hands on the small fortune the Guildmaster used to wear on her fingers."

"As you can see," Bethesa said to Maeve, "my fellow Tribunes and I are in a bit of a disagreement. They are confident that the Guildmaster died in the fire. For my part...I am not so sure."

"But...I mean no disrespect, Tribune, but what would be anyone's reason for pretending at such a thing?"

Bethesa nodded. "I know, I know, Lady Maeve. Probably I'm just an addled old lady. Only...something about the whole business feels...off to me. As for what such a person might want, perhaps they have kidnapped our Guildmaster and are even now torturing her for information regarding the Guild. After all, who would be in a position to know more than the Guildmaster herself about the inner workings of our little club?"

Maeve thought it likely that Bethesa herself might know as much, but she didn't say so, and the woman went on. "Or, perhaps, they have taken her to weaken the Guild, to leave us without a leader in a time when we will need to be unified. It would not be the first time a rival group has tried to take over the Guild by force."

"And such groups have been put down each and every time," Silrika sneered. "Most...*forcefully.*"

"Indeed they have," Bethesa agreed, "but that has yet to stop others from trying where they have failed." She shrugged. "Or perhaps I am wrong and the Guildmaster is as dead as she appears to be. What do you think, Lady Maeve?" she asked. The question was asked casually, but there was something in the woman's eyes that made Maeve believe it was anything but.

"I'm sorry, Tribune?" Maeve asked, fighting the urge to squirm underneath that intelligent, penetrating stare.

"I only ask what you think might be a reason that someone would fake the Guildmaster's death? Or, if she was indeed murdered, who do you think might be responsible for such an atrocity?"

"I'm...sure that I'm probably the least qualified person to say, Tribune," Maeve said. "As you are well aware, I only arrived back in the city weeks ago. I have no idea about the political climate in New Daltenia, have not for a very long time."

"But that isn't *exactly* true, is it?" Bethesa asked. "After all, you were always close to Prince Bernard and now, as I understand it, you are close to his son, King Matthias. You *are* staying in the castle, aren't you? Or perhaps my information was wrong, and you are not as close to the king as I thought?"

It was a trap, that much was clear, and Maeve shook her head. "No, it's true. I have been staying at the castle. But that still doesn't mean I could guess at someone's reason to want to see Agnes dead."

"That's *Guildmaster* Agnes," Silrika snarled.

"Of course," Maeve said, "Guildmaster Agnes."

"And if she isn't dead?" Bethesa pressed. "If someone did kidnap her? If someone staged the whole charade to make it *appear* as if she died?"

Maeve's heart was hammering a staccato beat in her chest, but she shrugged, imbuing the gesture with as much nonchalance as she could. "Why would anyone do such a thing, Tribune?"

"I was hoping you might tell me, Lady Maeve," the old woman asked, watching her carefully, the way a cat might watch a mouse before it pounced. Did she know something, Maeve wondered? Or was she simply fishing, seeing what she could find out, seeing how Maeve would react? She leaned toward the latter. After all, if the three seated before her had any real inkling of Maeve's role in Agnes's disappearance she did not doubt that she'd be dead already.

"I'm sorry, Tribune," she said, "but I cannot. And, to be honest, I mean no offense, but I don't know what any of this has to do with me. As I've said, Agnes and I—*Guildmaster* Agnes and I," she corrected when Silrika opened her mouth, "were not close. We were rivals for a very long time, and even though I like to think that we made some sort of peace I was certainly not part of her inner circle, if indeed there *was* an inner circle."

"Yes, I suppose it is time you were told why you were brought here, why we interrupted your evening," Bethesa said. "As for the last, I think you might rest easy that, indeed, the Guildmaster's estimation of you grew in her last days."

"I...don't understand, Tribune."

"No, not yet perhaps," Bethesa said, "but you will soon enough." She sat back, sighing. "As I believe I mentioned, Lady

Maeve, the Guild is currently leaderless. That is, as you well know, a dangerous position for us. It leaves us weak, ununified. Should someone try to move on us now, we would have a far poorer response than normal. Do you understand what I'm saying?"

"That...the Guild needs a new leader?" Maeve asked.

"Indeed," the old woman said, nodding. "Indeed we do. And that, Lady Maeve, is why we have brought you here."

Maeve felt her breath catch in her throat. "I'm sorry...I don't understand," she said, but the truth was she was afraid, terrified, that she did.

"No?" Bethesa asked, smiling as if she understood Maeve's fear and discomfort clearly and was enjoying it. "Well, you see, Lady Maeve, we have sea—"

"Mistress?" a voice came, and Bethesa cut off, turning to regard three men who had stepped out of what had likely been Agnes's bedroom.

"What is it, Orden?" the old woman asked.

"We're finished in the bedroom," he said. "Would you like for us to check in here?"

"Later," she said, "when we're finished." She waved a hand, and the man and the other two nodded, bowing low before walking out.

Maeve stared after them, frowning.

"Ah yes, Orden is my man. The other two work for Silrika and Piralta," Bethesa explained. "We had them checking the Guildmaster's room, you see, in case they could find anything that might help us to understand what happened to her. A threatening note, perhaps, or maybe a journal that she might have kept, one that might explain to us why she went to that tavern in the first place."

Maeve's mouth went suddenly, terribly dry. "And...have they found anything?" she asked. She didn't think Agnes would have kept such a journal, of course, for when you were trying to fake your own death the last thing you wanted was for there to be a record of the plan, but then it wasn't as if she and Agnes had been close, or that she had known her well. In truth, she had no idea what the woman might or might not do.

"Nothing of consequence as of yet," Bethesa said. "Save one thing—not found at all, but brought to me and the other two

Tribunes upon the Guildmaster's death by her assistant. It is the Guildmaster's will."

"Her...will, Tribune?" Maeve asked. She felt unbalanced, wobbly, and she couldn't seem to get caught up.

"That's right," the old woman said. "Her last testament, I suppose you would say. In the documents she referenced some things she'd been working on, sharing some secrets with me and the other Tribunes for the good of the guild. Mostly mundane things of no great import. Except...for one. You see, it was in that letter, in that last testament, that Guildmaster Agnes named her replacement."

"Her replacement," Maeve repeated, feeling as if she were in one of those dreams where a person could see herself, was floating in the air somewhere above her but had no control over her body or her voice.

"That's right," Bethesa said. "She named you, Lady Maeve. So as I said, she liked you more than you think."

"That—" *bitch* she thought, just managing to keep the word from coming out of her mouth. "That...are you quite sure?" Maeve asked,   swallowing   hard.
"Oh yes, Lady Maeve," the Tribune said, "we are all quite sure. We have each of us read it over multiple times, for I must admit that it surprised us likely as much as it has surprised you. But there can be no denying it—Guildmaster Agnes put your name forward to replace her should anything untoward happen."

Maeve thought about the last time she'd seen Agnes, about the way the woman had smiled, giving her a nod and wishing her luck before she'd left. She'd thought, at the time, that the woman had just been glad that the plan had gone off without a hitch—or at least if not without a hitch then at least without any of them burning alive. Now, though, she wasn't so sure.

After all, why would the woman put her name forward? That was obvious enough, for Agnes had told her, when Maeve had first come to her, how dangerous it was to be the Guildmaster, how terrible it was. And so she had gotten her ultimate revenge by naming Maeve as her replacement.

Maeve remembered being surprised that the woman had set aside her hatred—that *they* had set aside their *mutual* hatred, so quickly. At the time she'd told herself that it was simply a matter of expedience. After all, it had been in both their best interests to let the past stay in the past. But the problem with the past was that it never stayed there. It came back to a person. Always, it came back. Sometimes in the daylight but most often in the darkness, appearing out of the shadows, a phantom from which you could not run or flee. For how could one run from herself? How could she flee from her own life? It was hers after all—bought and paid for.

Still, she had told herself, when Agnes had first put forward the plan to her that, at least for the moment, that past might be set aside, that both of them might be *willing* to set it aside. She, so that she might get the contract on her and Chall removed, Agnes so that she could escape her position as the Guild's leader. Which, thinking of it, sounded particularly stupid, and *she* particularly stupid for believing it. After all, why would the woman want to give up a position as the Guild's leader? She said that it was dangerous, that there were those—such as the three Tribunes sitting in front of Maeve—that plotted her death. Maeve didn't doubt that—she'd done her fair share of plotting Agnes's death herself, was doing some just then, in fact.

But as she sat there, the three Tribunes watching her, Bethesa with a small smile on her face, another thought struck Maeve. An unwelcome, terrifying thought. Agnes had claimed that she'd known nothing about the contract on Maeve and Chall. At the time, Maeve had accepted that—mostly because she had to—and after Agnes had proposed her deal, Maeve had largely let herself be pulled along by events. She had reacted instead of acted, had allowed fate to take the reins. Foolish, that, for fate, she'd known for years, was a cruel bitch.

Though perhaps not quite as cruel, it seemed, as Agnes herself.

"Lady Maeve? Are you still with us?"

"Yes," she said, her voice little more than a whisper. *But for how long?* After all, it wasn't a guild of bunny rabbits and grandmothers. It was a guild of assassins—of men and women who, out of all the many occupations they might have pursued, had chosen to become killers.

A guild that was so dangerous that its leader had chosen self-imposed exile, had chosen to work with her life-long enemy in order to abdicate her position.

"So?" Silrika asked, sounding as impatient as always, no doubt eager to have Maeve accept the position so that she could begin plotting her downfall. Or, alternatively, eager to have Maeve decline so that she could begin plotting her downfall. Maeve doubted she was all that particular either way.

"I...while I appreciate the Guildmaster's confidence in me, the truth is that I...wouldn't even know the first thing about being the leader of the Guild. I have been gone for a very long time, after all, and...besides, I have a lot going on just now. The war with the Fey—"

"Will be fought by warriors," Bethesa said, "or by the Fey. You are neither. You are an assassin, Lady Maeve. That first and foremost. True, you have spent an inordinate amount of time away, working with the Crimson Prince and those who accompany him. The Guild has allowed it—mostly because of the prince himself. After all, to one such as that subtlety and circumspection mean nothing and even if we have not always agreed with his methods or his choices he is our prince, and so we would not dare to set ourselves against him."

In point of fact, there had been several attempts on the prince's life over the years that Maeve at the time—and still—thought the Guild responsible for, but as was often the case when it came to the Crimson Prince, those seeking his death found their own instead and, more often than not, in a particularly brutal—and abrupt—fashion.

Still, she thought that now, with the three Tribunes facing her, several of their men within earshot, might not be the best time to bring up those failed attempts.

"Yes, and I appreciate that," Maeve said instead. "It has been my honor that the prince sees fit to make use of my talents, such as they are."

"*Saw* fit, I think you mean, don't you?"

This was from Tribune Piralta, and the man smiled as Maeve turned a questioning look his way. And although the smile looked gentle enough on the surface, Maeve thought, staring at him, at the cleverness in his eyes, that Agnes had been wrong to dismiss him as she had, seeing him a "weasel" who sought favor, a cowardly flatterer. No, there was more to the man than that—she could see it in his gaze. Besides, she thought that a person did not rise to a position on the ruling council of a guild of assassins by accident.

"I'm...not sure I understand," Maeve said in an effort to buy herself time, for the truth was, there was a growing knot of anxiety in her stomach because she thought she understood the man's point all too well.

"No?" the Tribune asked, raising his eyebrows as if in mock surprise. "Then perhaps my information is wrong, for as I understood it the prince, along with his brother, Prince Feledias, was exiled to the Black Wood by His Majesty the King."

Maeve frowned. "You make it sound as if they were sent to their deaths, but King Matthias sent them to try to bring about peace with the Fey."

"And where were they sent again?" Bethesa prompted.

"The Black Wood," Maeve said, wincing, "but that's only because—"

Silrika snorted. "Being sent to the Black Wood is a death sentence as much as if the young king had wielded the executioner's axe himself."

The woman's words were far too close to Maeve's own fears for her liking, and she shook her head. "It isn't like that. Matt...that is, His Majesty, he just wants peace for our people and—"

"If that were true, Lady Maeve," Bethesa said, "then why would he send his father? After all, if there is any man walking the face of the land who knows less of peace than the Crimson Prince, I have never heard of him. No," she went on, shaking her head, "you do not send a butcher, Lady Maeve, to comfort the pigs."

"It...it wasn't like that," Maeve said, well aware of how weak, how unsure her voice sounded.

"Wasn't it?" Tribune Piralta asked. "From what I heard, Lady Maeve, it was *exactly* like that. From what *I* heard, your prince and his brother, Feledias, were sent to the Black Wood not as emissaries seeking peace but as a punishment for your friend, Prince Bernard's crime of starting the war in the first place."

Maeve cleared her throat, lost for words, at least for the moment because that was pretty much exactly what had happened. Of course, Matt had been possessed by a Feyling named Emma at the time, one that had taken over his body and had been doing her best to destroy the kingdom of the Known Lands from the inside. The problem, though, was that if she said as much now the Tribunes wouldn't believe her, would just think she was casting about for some excuse. Stones and starlight she had been there, and she barely believed it.

Maeve was disappointed that they knew so much—disappointed but not surprised. After all, any assassin who didn't want to have an impromptu meeting with the executioner's axe understood that the greatest weapon in their arsenal was not knives or poisoned-tip arrows—it was information.

"The thing is—" she began.

"The *thing*, Lady Maeve," Bethesa interrupted, her voice sterner than it had been moments ago, "is that the Guild looked the other way years ago when you abandoned your responsibilities to follow the prince to war. But the prince is gone now, and you are here, as is the Guild. The Guild which trained you—the Guild which now needs you."

Maeve decided to try a different tactic. "Surely there has to be someone better—*anyone* better. As you've said I've been away from the Guild for years. I don't know anything of what's happened here in the intervening time."

"I'd guess that you could imagine easily enough," Bethesa said with a small smile. "After all, the Guild has done, in those years, what it has always done. Besides, Lady Maeve," she said with a laugh, "you are acting as if we are punishing you when that could not be further from the truth. To be the leader of the Guild…it is a great honor. One only bestowed upon the very best of us."

A great honor that Agnes had been desperate to give up. "What of one of you?" Maeve asked, and she was aware of the way Tribune Piralta shifted nervously in his seat. "After all," she went on, "who better to lead the Guild than one of you who worked so closely with the Guildmaster? I'm sure that the Guild would be in great hands with one of you, far better than mine."

"You're damn right it would," Silrika growled, and the old woman Bethesa turned a scowl on her with a speed Maeve wouldn't have credited her.

Instead of responding to the challenge, Silrika avoided the older woman's gaze, staring at her feet. Bethesa sighed and turned back to Maeve. "Forgive Tribune Silrika, I beg you. She has had some ambitions for the position of leader, but she understands that what we do, we do for the good of the Guild."

Maeve frowned. "I don't see how putting me—a washed up old assassin—as leader would possibly be for the Guild's good."

"Don't you?" the woman asked, sounding genuinely surprised. "I think you are selling yourself short, Lady Maeve. You are no nameless, washed-up old assassin. You are *Maeve the Marvelous,* a woman with a face as comely, it is said, as her hands are deadly. Why, during the war I could not have even counted the number of students who wanted to be just like you. You were their hero, their idol, the lofty goal to which they all aspired. Even now, years after the war, those young men and women who come to us, though they were not yet born during the height of your fame, come to us with stories told them by others, stories overheard in back alleys and in shadowed alcoves. Stories of Maeve the Marvelous, the deadliest woman in the world, desired and feared by every man walking the face of the land. You are an inspiration, Maeve, and in very large part the Guild owes its increasing numbers to you, for your legend has drawn untold souls to our ranks."

That hit Maeve like a hammer blow. As she'd gotten older, Maeve had begun to think on things she'd never paid any mind when she was young. Things like legacy, what a person left behind when they were gone. Mostly she thought what she'd leave behind was corpses. Widows and widowers, children without mothers and fathers. But then she had met the prince, and she had done some good, or at least thought she had.

Now she wasn't so sure. After all, if what the woman was saying was true—and there was no reason for her to lie—then Maeve's legacy wasn't just the corpses she'd put in the ground. It was those that would be put there by those others who'd joined the Guild because of her. Those young men and women who had no idea what they were getting themselves into. For even if they didn't die on a mission or turn up dead or missing—a common enough occurrence in a place where killers were trained and rivalries encouraged—still they would pay a heavy price. The person who they were, whatever innocence they had, would be carved away bit by bit. The instructors would begin that carving, it was true, teaching them to be hard, to be cold, teaching them to eschew such emotions as compassion and mercy and pity. But in the end, the final cuts would be made by the men and women themselves. With each contract they accepted, with each success, they would carve a little bit more of themselves away until they were not themselves at all but something else, until they were what the Guild had made them.

"Another thing to consider," Tribune Piralta said, "is that while you view your...extended absence as a weakness, I think that, in many ways, it is a strength. After all, an organization such as ours is, sadly, rife with animosities and hatreds, with rivalries and contention, and your having been gone for so long means that no one bears you any ill will."

Maeve wasn't at all sure that was true—after all, in her experience a person didn't have to know anything about another to hate them. It was one of the things they were best at. "And the reason why none of you are interested in the position?" she asked.

"As I said," Bethesa said, giving Maeve a knowing smile, "being the leader of the Guild is a great honor and one, I fear, which none of us are worthy of receiving."

"And there is the other matter to consider, too," Tribune Piralta said. "The Guildmaster herself recommended you. That is no small thing, for Guildmaster Agnes was respected and loved by the entire Guild, and the fact that she put your name forward as her replacement will go a long way toward quelling any possible objections or animosities that might arise."

Most, if not all of the man's words were bullshit—after all, it was an Assassins' Guild, full of people that weren't known for loving or respecting anyone, let alone a person who occupied a position most of them would have loved nothing more than to take from her, at the end of a knife if necessary. No, it was not love or respect that held such an organization together—it was fear.

"Well, Lady Maeve?" Tribune Bethesa asked. "What say you?"

Maeve wanted to say no. It was the only reasonable thing to say. After all, she was an old woman, and it seemed beyond foolish to accept a position she'd only recently helped someone else escape. Foolish and suicidal to boot. Another might look at it as an opportunity, for whatever else it was, the Guild was a powerful tool, a weapon that might be used against the kingdom's enemies. The problem, of course, was that if the Guild was a weapon, a dagger, say, then it was a double-edged dagger, one just as likely to cut the person attempting to wield it as anyone they sought to wield it against.

In the end, though, what made her decision was not the thought of using the Guild to her own ends. Nor was it the thought of what the three seated before her might do should she seek to refuse their offer which was no less than a thinly-veiled command.

What decided her was legacy.

What decided her were those men and women who Bethesa said joined the Guild because of Maeve, because of the stories they'd heard of her. Men and women who joined thinking to be respected, to be strong, maybe thinking that they would not have to be afraid anymore, that they could learn how to take care of themselves. People who came seeking redemption, seeking to be saved from the troubles of their lives and who had no idea that the trouble they ran to was far worse than that they left behind.

"I'll do it," she said.

And it was as simple as that. But then Maeve had always found that a person's doom, when it came upon them, never needed to be complicated. A knife in the shadows, a drop of poison in a goblet of wine.

Or three words spoken with no true idea of the consequences.

Bethesa smiled, and Maeve did not think she imagined something predatory in that expression as the old Tribune stared at her. "Very well," she said. "Then welcome back...Guildmaster."

CHAPTER NINE

The Fey were everywhere.

They were gathered in their thousands, in their tens of thousands. Creatures that were wonderful and terrible, beautiful and monstrous. Some few he had heard of before, in stories told to him when he was a boy. Others—most—he had never imagined might exist.

And among their number, in the center of that great glade, stood a green demon, one Matt had met before. A demon with a face as black as the night with eyes that blazed like emerald fire.

He spoke in a tongue Matt did not know, a sibilant, strange sound, and yet...it was familiar to him, somehow. He almost felt that he had heard it before, in a dream within a dream. And while he could not understand the individual words, he thought that he *almost* could.

And while he might not understand the individual words, he understood their meaning clearly enough. Anger. Hate. Rage. A rage that might see millennia come and go, might see oceans rise and fall, mountains torn down by time and the elements, and yet never wane, never falter. And he knew, without knowing how he knew it, at what that rage was directed.

At whom.

His father. He was out there, somewhere. Out there in the dark. And the Green Man was calling for his blood.

Even as he listened, floating above that maniacal horde, that madman's menagerie, Matt began to feel as if he could almost understand what the green demon spoke. And then not almost—he simply could.

...not allow them to do here what they did to our king, Yeladrian, will we?

Roars and shouts, hoots and hollers, growls and hisses, from the gathered throng.

We will destroy the Destroyer, will break he who wields the Breaker of Pacts, and so reclaim our honor.

The night was filled with the expectant roars of those creatures gathered, and Matt added his own to the throng.

"*Nooo!*" he shouted, and then, suddenly, that storm of sound stopped, and the demon, with his green eyes, turned and looked up at where Matt floated in the dark, seething sky of the Black Wood.

And on that creature's face Matt did not see fury or rage, not then. What he saw, instead, was surprised recognition.

The creature's green, pupiless eyes seemed to flare like the embers of a fire blown to life, and suddenly something was clutching at Matt's shoulder, pulling at him, trying to bring him down to the waiting horde.

Matt cried out, swinging his fist in a desperate effort to break his way free. He struck something, but it was not a creature or the air as he might have thought. Instead, it was something solid, something wooden, and he looked over, shocked to see that it was a wooden wall that he'd hit, was even more shocked to see that his fist had gone through it.

And this wasn't just any wooden wall. It was the wall of a carriage, the same carriage that he'd climbed into with Chall, Priest, and the two guards—Vorrun and one whose name Matt didn't know—that Commander Malex had insisted accompany him.

Not that they looked much like guarding him just then as they—along with Priest and Chall—were all leaned back in their chairs, staring wide-eyed at Matt. Or, more specifically, at his fist which was still sticking through the side of the carriage.

For a moment they all remained frozen there, as if they weren't people at all but sculptures. All staring at him, Chall's arm still outstretched in his direction from where he'd shaken him awake. Then, suddenly, everyone seemed to move and talk at once.

"Damn, what in the—" Chall began.

"Matt is everythin—"

"Majesty, are you alright?"

"I'm...I'm fine," Matt said.

"Your hand," Priest said, leaning forward and grabbing his wrist, examining his hand. "How bad is the dama..." Priest trailed off, a perplexed look coming onto his face, and Matt felt a knot of worry form in his stomach.

"What, what is it?" he said, pulling his hand back. As he did, he saw what had given the other man pause. "Not a scratch," he said, then gave a nervous laugh, glancing up at Priest. "Isn't that lucky?"

"Lucky?" Chall said, leaning forward and staring at Matt's hand as if he'd just performed some sort of miracle. "Fire and salt, you're lucky you didn't break your hand or cut it to bloody ribbons. What in the world were you thinking, Matt?" He winced, cringing. "That is...Majesty?"

Matt shook his head. "Sorry it...I had a bad dream. Someone touched me and I thought..." He trailed off, shaking his head again. "I don't know what I thought."

"Whatever it was," Chall said, glancing at the ragged hole Matt's fist had torn into the side of the carriage, "here's to hoping you don't think it again. Damn, Majesty, if you'd have told us you had something against this carriage we'd have gotten a different one—no reason to go beating the shit out of it."

Matt winced. "Again, I'm sorry," he said. He glanced over at the carriage's door where a man he took to be the driver stood. "I'll...I'll pay for all the damage, of course, I'm very sorry."

"Of course, Majesty," the man said in a concerned mumble before deciding to close the door back and move away.

Great, Matt thought. He knew that, already, the situation in the city was far from ideal. People were worried about the Fey—with good reason. Worried about their leaders, too. Much of the audiences Matt had given over the last days and weeks since becoming the king of the Known Lands were, more than anything, simply to reassure the citizens of New Daltenia that he had their best interests at heart.

Which, of course, he did. His father and uncle had entrusted him with the Known Lands, and if he failed it would not be because he did not try. Yet the hole he punched in the carriage would not help—the carriage driver would talk, and Matt couldn't blame him. After all, if *he* was a carriage driver and his latest passenger was none other than the king himself who proceeded to punch a hole in the wall then he would certainly tell anyone who would listen.

The story would circulate, growing with each telling, changing until he'd attacked the man with a knife, or perhaps rode with his face hanging out of the carriage, his tongue lolling as he panted like a dog in the wind. Either way, it would set back his and the others' efforts to gain the people's trust, and the brutal truth was that there wasn't much progress to set back.

"Are you sure your hand's okay, Majesty?" Vorrun asked.

"I'm sure," Matt said, flexing the fingers. Then, feeling everyone's eyes on him and desperate to change the subject, he glanced at Chall who was watching him with a curious expression. "So...why...why did you wake me?"

Chall blinked as if woken from some sort of trance. "Ah, right, that," he said. "Well, before you challenged our carriage to a life-or-death battle I was going to tell you that we're here."

"Here?" Matt said, his thoughts jumbled and confused.

"We've arrived at Lady Valencia's, Majesty," Priest offered.

"Oh. Great," he said, glancing at Chall to see that the magician was looking at him again, his eyes slightly narrowed as if Matt were a difficult puzzle he was trying to figure out. He was tempted to tell him that, if he did, he'd appreciate him letting him know, for he didn't understand himself either, didn't understand why he'd been plagued by dreams of nightmare creatures, of his father suffering. Dreams that felt so real that he was convinced on waking—and a little convinced even now—that they *were.*

Impossible, of course, for he was no magician or wizard like Chall to somehow cast a spell and be able to see his father and uncle miles and miles away. "So...are we going?" he asked.

Chall blinked. "Right, right, of course."

The two guards began to climb out of the carriage, along with his companions. While Matt waited his turn, he thought of the dream.

It was stress, that was all, just as Healer Malden had said. After all, it wasn't as though he didn't have plenty to stress about. Only, it hadn't been stress that had made him be able to punch a hole through the solid wood wall of the carriage and not suffer so much as a splinter.

And that was before he considered the way the Green Man had seemed to look right at him, to hear him. He would not soon forget that pitch black face, those eyes of green fire.

"Majesty?"

Matt turned to see that everyone had climbed out of the carriage and Guardsman Vorrun was staring at him with an expression that tried for casual but couldn't completely hide the man's concern.

Matt nodded, not trusting himself to answer. He climbed out of the carriage feeling shaky, unsteady. He looked around the street, taking in the palatial homes on either side, all of them with well-maintained gardens at their front and all with their own gates and fences of various make and design. Each noble family or wealthy merchant who lived on the city's richest street had their own tastes and had designed their houses accordingly so that while each individual home was beautiful in its own way, the combined effect was off-putting. So many various styles and types put so closely together, like dozens of kingdoms side by side.

And that was an analogy that held true when considering the house livery the servants wore as well as the sheer *number* of servants, many of whom he could see tending the various gardens of their masters.

Matt had been here before, on a tour of the city shortly after becoming king, and he remembered thinking that the houses along the aptly named House of Lords were beautiful, a sight to behold.

He did not find them so now.

The sun had begun to set while they rode in the carriage and shadows hung from the eves of the houses, clung to their corners and walls, settled in inky black puddles in their doorways and windows. Perhaps it was because he'd gotten very little sleep of late, or perhaps he was still troubled by the recent dream of the green demon but to Matt those windows, those doors, seemed somehow ominous, somehow scary. As if they were not doors and windows that opened up into noble's homes but instead portals to other worlds.

Worlds of darkness and shadow with green eyes that burned like fire.

They started forward and Matt stumbled, nearly falling. He managed to catch himself but not before Vorrun saw. The guardsman turned, offering his hand. "Majesty?" he asked. "Is everythi—"

"I'm fine," Matt snapped, more aggressively than he'd intended. He winced. "Sorry, Vorrun," he said to the guard. "It's been a bit of a trying day, that's all." *A trying few weeks, come to that.*

"Of course, Majesty," the guard said, giving him a mostly convincing smile, "think nothing of it."

Matt nodded, wanting to say sorry again, for he could still see a bit of hurt in the man's eyes, but he knew that it would do no good. Instead, he glanced at Chall and Priest. "Ready?" he asked.

"When you are, Majesty," the mage said.

Matt nodded and started forward, the others following suit with Vorrun at the front, the second guardsman bringing up the rear. They made their way to the gate to find that it was open about halfway. Matt thought that was odd. Why have a gate at all if you just intended to leave it open with no one, so far as he could see, to guard it?

A quick glance showed him that, indeed, all the other gates he could make out along the street were closed, and at most of them he could pick out the shadowed silhouettes of guardsmen manning their posts. Lady Valencia's gate was the only one with no one watching it. Perhaps they might have caught the guards during a shift change but, if that were the case, why was the gate left halfway open?

Judging by the wary looks he saw the others giving, he didn't think he was the only one who found it odd. With a glance at the rest of them, Chall frowned, stepping forward. "Hello the gate!" he called.

They waited for several seconds but no answer came. Chall and Priest shared a look. "Forgot to pay the guardsmen?" the magician asked.

"Perhaps," Priest said, but the tone of his voice made it clear that he doubted it.

"Don't suppose you want to call the whole thing off," Chall said conversationally, clearly speaking to Priest. "Go and get a drink, maybe?"

"There's a new tavern near here," Priest said back. "I've heard they've some fine ale."

"You must be joking," Matt said, surprised.

"Of course, Majesty," Priest said.

"Right..." Chall said, far less convincingly, then he gave a heavy sigh. "Well. Guess we ought to go and check it out."

Priest nodded at that, drawing his sword. "I'll take the lead."

"You won't hear any argument out of me," Chall said.

"What do I do?"

They both turned to regard Matt, and he couldn't help but notice a slight look of surprise on their faces, as if they'd forgotten about him altogether. "Majesty," Priest said slowly, "it would be best if you got out of here. We don't know what this is and until we do—"

"No."

"Majesty?" Chall asked.

"I'm not going back to the castle like some child being sent to bed without dinner," Matt said. "If something is happening, I want to help."

"Highness, the best help you can be is to leave so that we know you're safe and—"

"Am I king or not?"

Priest winced. "Of course, it's just—"

"If I'm king," Matt said, "then why won't you listen to me?" He knew there was a note of pleading in his voice, but he couldn't help it. Night had come on in full now, and if he went back to the castle he knew that he would try to sleep. Would try and likely fail. Or, worse, he would succeed and find himself falling into another of the dreams that did not feel like dreams at all but nightmares. "I am no child to be coddled," he said. "I am king."

Priest and Chall shared a look, and there was something in it that annoyed him, that reminded him of parents sharing a moment of mutual, long-suffering patience. "As you say, Majesty," Priest said. He shot a meaningful look at the guardsmen then turned and eased the gate open, starting through it.

Inside the gate, Lady Valencia's gardens spread out on either side of a cobbled lane. Matt didn't doubt that, in the day time, with the sun shining down from the heavens, the various shrubs and flowers that rose in ordered profusion on either side of the path were beautiful to behold, a masterpiece of colors and hues, of shapes and types that no doubt complemented each other so perfectly that many would have paid good coin to stand and admire.

But as with so many things, the shadows turned those shrubs and bushes and flowers into something else, infusing them with menace. For among those bushes, among those reaching branches and hanging vines, anything—or anyone—might be hiding among them, watching them and waiting for them to step blindly into an ambush.

That was silly, of course—a child's fear, nothing more. After all, how could anyone set a trap for them when even they hadn't known until an hour ago that they were coming here in the first place? It was ridiculous, yet knowing that did nothing to dispel the fear he felt.

They made their way down the cobbled walk to the shadowed doorway. Priest raised his fist to knock then paused, frowning.

"What is it?" Chall said in a quiet, tense voice, little louder than a whisper.

Priest glanced over at the mage before turning back and slowly, easing the door—which had been left ajar—open.

"Someone had a bit too much to drink and forgot to close it?" Chall offered, a sort of desperate hopefulness in his voice.

"Maybe," Priest said, but it was clear by the way he said it, just as it was clear by Chall's tone that neither of the men believed it.

Chall reached out, running his fingers along the door frame then nodded grimly. "Broken in," he said quietly, then frowned. "And wet."

"Wet?" Matt asked, confused, for it hadn't rained for days—he knew as it had been the topic of choice for more than a few of the farmers who'd come to have audience with him, as if they thought being king meant that he was responsible for the weather.

"Rain runoff?" Priest asked.

Chall held his fingers up, and even in the poor light Matt could see that they were dotted with crimson. "Not unless the gods decided to try a different recipe," the mage said grimly. He met Priest's gaze. "Seems we're not the only people who've taken it in mind to visit Lady Valencia tonight."

Priest nodded, turning to the guardsmen. "Stay with His Majesty," he said. "If anything happens, get him out of here, understood?"

"Of course, sir," Vorrun said.

Priest gave another nod then swung the door wide. As he did, Matt gasped for beyond the door, just inside the entry way of the home, lay an old man wearing servant's garb, a pool of blood beneath him. It was obvious what had happened—the man had been alerted by the sound of the door latch being broken and had come to investigate, only to discover his death.

Matt felt his gorge rise, and he swallowed down sharp, acrid bile, barely managing to keep from vomiting. He had seen dead bodies before, of course. Since leaving Brighton it sometimes seemed he'd seen little else. This, though, was different. Those other times, he had been in a fight himself, had been too focused on trying not to be killed to think much on the dead. But now, staring at the servant lying on his back, his lifeless eyes studying the ceiling as if contemplating a stain there, he could think of little else.

"Poor bastard," Chall said.

"Come," Priest said, his voice angry, then he disappeared through the doorway, stepping over the dead body. Chall gave a sigh and, with obvious reluctance, followed after, leaving Matt alone with the guardsmen and the dead man.

As for Vorrun and the other guard, they reacted immediately, drawing their swords and situating themselves on either side of Matt, clearly prepared to face whatever threat might present itself in order to protect him. Matt thought that odd, as he always did. After all, what strange arithmetic meant that his life added up to more value than anyone else's?

He did not know much of the other guardsman, but he did know that Vorrun, at least, had a family—a wife and two sons, both of whom were around Matt's own age. How then could the man be willing to sacrifice himself in order to protect Matt? But then when it came to death, Matt supposed very little made sense. The old man lying dead for the simple crime of doing nothing but checking on a sound he heard spoke to that truth.

And as bad as the servant's death was, as *shocking* as it was, there was another grim truth. If Chall and Priest were right in their suspicions, then it was likelier than not that Ned had been the one to take the man's life. Ned or perhaps others who were part of the shadowy organization known as the Crimson Wolves, and considering Ned had once been—and likely still was—a leader of it, Matt thought that the distinction was largely irrelevant.

He had a hard time imagining the carriage driver, a man who he'd met on multiple occasions and always found to be kind, earnest, compassionate and self-deprecating committing such an atrocity, but it seemed that he would have to. After all, it was hard to imagine that it was a coincidence that someone would choose to attack the house of the very woman who they'd come to speak with, the woman most likely to give them some answers about everything that was going on. And, from what Chall and Priest had said, that attack had been recent, perhaps as recent as only an hour or two ago.

The man or men responsible might have just left. Or they might not have left at all, might still be inside. The thought of that, of Priest and Chall walking into a house that might be filled with the gods only knew how many murderers, sent a shiver running down his spine. "We can't let them go in alone," he said. "We need to go with them."

"Forgive me, Majesty," Vorrun said, "but we cannot. We dare not risk your safety."

"*Damn my safety!*" Matt snapped. "Those are my friends, and they need our help. We can't just leave them alone!" He was thinking of the dream again, of his father, the way he had stood surrounded by that uncountable horde of creatures, all of them wanting him dead. He started for the door but came up short as Vorrun stepped in front of him.

"Majesty, please," the guardsman said. "We cannot let you go in there."

"And if I, as king, were to command you to?"

"Vorrun—" the younger guardsman began, but Vorrun held up his hand to the man, silencing him.

"Then I would still refuse, Majesty. You may not value your life, but there are those of us—many of us—who do. The people of the Known Lands have had some tough years, what with the war and...and everything else."

That everything else, it was clear to Matt, referred to his uncle and his father.

"Your becoming king," Vorrun went on, "it's the best thing that's happened for the kingdom in a long time, and, begging your pardon, Majesty, but I'll be damned if I'm going to be the guardsman responsible for lettin' you get yourself killed."

"And if I were to tell you that, should you continue to refuse me, I would have you thrown in the dungeon?"

The younger guardsman was looking sickly now, his face pale and nervous, but Vorrun only shrugged. "Then I'd only ask that you let me tell my wife first. She worries."

Matt sighed. "I'm sorry, Vorrun," he said. "I'm just..." He trailed off, shaking his head.

"You're just afraid for your friends, Majesty," Vorrun said. "I understand that. No apology necessary, of course."

"No, it is," Matt said. "You're just trying to protect me and I thank you with threats. You deserve better than that." He glanced at the other guardsman. "You both do." He sighed, heavily. "You deserve a king who listens to you, who puts you before himself."

"The whole kingdom deserves that, Majesty," Vorrun said softly, giving him a smile. "It's a good thing we got it, then."

Matt was just opening his mouth to answer that, to try to explain to the man that while he did not deserve his trust, did not deserve the faith he put in him, he was nevertheless thankful for it and would do his best to become worthy of it. But before he got a chance to say anything there was a scream from somewhere inside the noble's manse. And not just any scream but one he recognized as belonging to Chall.

Matt felt a shiver of terror run through him, and he looked at Vorrun. The guardsman hissed. "Marcus, go and see what that shouting is about. Majesty, best you come with me."

Matt wanted to argue, wanted to go and see for himself what the problem was, to see if he could help Chall in some way, but he realized he could not. They all had their roles to play, after all, and while he didn't know how much help he was to the people of the

Known Lands, he knew that he *wanted* to be a help. And to do that he needed to be alive.

So he said nothing as the pale-faced guardsman, Marcus, drew his sword and started into the manse, nor did he object when Vorrun grabbed hold of his arm with one hand, drawing his own sword and holding it in the other as he started back down the path.

Matt allowed himself to be pulled along. They were about halfway down the path when Matt heard a rustling from off to their left and a shadowy figure burst out of the bushes less than half a dozen feet in front of them.

"*Halt!*" Vorrun shouted.

The figure, who'd apparently had no idea that they were there at all, froze where it had been moving toward the half-open gate, spinning to look at them.

Matt's breath caught in his throat, for the figure, dressed all in black, was one he recognized as Ned the carriage driver. And worse than that, he recognized what was on the man's hands and shirt too, so much of it he might have taken a bath in the stuff. Blood. Blood that was almost black in the moonlight.

The carriage driver held his hands up as if to say he meant no harm, but it was clear by the amount of blood coating him that he'd caused plenty of harm already.

"Ned?" Matt asked, incredulous, his voice little more than a croaking whisper. "What have you done?"

"Isn't what it looks like, Majesty," the carriage driver said, wincing. He glanced, almost involuntarily at his waist, and Matt saw a rolled parchment sticking out of his trousers.

"Ned the blood—"

"It isn't mine," the man said, wincing again. "Listen, Majesty, I'm sorry, but I've really got to be going."

"You're not going anywhere," Vorrun growled.

Ned glanced at the guardsman then back at Matt. "I need to go," he said, desperation in his voice. "There isn't any time—that bastard is cautious, sure, but he's smart, too. Too damned smart."

"*Stand right there and do not move,*" Vorrun growled.

Ned sighed, glancing at the guard. "It's Vorrun, isn't it?"

"My name makes no difference," the guardsman said, starting forward.

Ned held up a hand.

It was a simple gesture but suddenly Matt felt as if something was gathering, as if some pressure was growing in the air.

"*Stop,*" Ned commanded, and to Matt's surprise—to Vorrun's too, based on the confused expression on the man's face—the guardsman did exactly that.

Ned shook his head, frustrated. "I'm sorry, fella. I really am. Don't like to do that, but I'm afraid I don't have a choice."

"Ned," Matt said, starting forward, "I don't know what you've done, but don't make it worse. Come back to the castle with us—"

"Sorry, Majesty," the man said, a look on his face that at least appeared to be genuine regret. "I'm afraid I can't do that. Nor can I let you arrest me just now."

"And I'm sorry, Ned," Matt said. "Because you don't have a choice. Vorrun. Arrest this man."

Vorrun trembled, yet his feet did not move. His mouth opened and closed, but neither did he speak. "Fine," Matt said, "if he can't stop you then I'll do it myself."

He started forward, and again Ned held up his hand. "I'm sorry, Majesty, to do this to you. But I ask you—I *command* you, to stop."

Again Matt felt that building pressure in the air, as if the area around the carriage driver was charged with some sort of power or force. He felt that force rise, felt it move toward him. Something seemed to flare up inside of him in response, and that power, whatever it had been, was diverted around him the way a curtain might spread around a person should he walk through it.

"Impossible," Ned said, his breath a low whisper. Then, he gave his head a shake and turned, sprinting toward the half-open gate. Matt glanced at Vorrun. The guardsman stood, still trembling, his teeth bared. He had begun to ease the smallest bit forward, as if he were moving in slow motion. It reminded Matt of the way a man might move more slowly in water but magnified a hundred times.

Matt didn't know what was going on, but he didn't have time to figure it out. Ned was getting away. He ran after the carriage driver who was surprisingly fast. But Matt was young, just barely past an age where he'd spent much of the day running and considering it a joy instead of a chore, and he caught up to the man just as he reached the gate, grabbing him by the shoulder.

"*Ned, stop!*" Matt shouted. Ned tried to jerk himself free, but Matt had a good hold on his shoulder. "Damn if you don't have your dad's strength," Ned growled as he struggled against Matt's grip. "Listen, Majesty, this really is—"

"*Hey!*"

Matt spun at the sound of a shout to see Priest and Chall emerge from the doorway to the house. They were looking in his and Ned's direction, running toward them.

"*Matt, watch out!*" Chall shouted, pointing his finger.

"Sorry about this, Majesty." He heard the words, knew them for what they were, and so he began to turn, which just meant that whatever had been aimed at the back of his head instead struck him in the temple.

There was an explosion of light in Matt's mind. He stumbled, letting out a groan. The strength went out of his legs and he fell onto his side. He landed facing the street and so was able to witness as the blurred figure that was Ned reached the gate, disappearing through it.

"*Majesty!*"

There was the sound of footsteps on cobbles and in another moment Chall and Priest were kneeling before him. "Matt, are you okay?" the magician asked.

"I'm…I'm fine," Matt said, and even as he said it the worst of the dizziness the blow to his head had caused was fading. "I…I think."

"Stones and starlight, who was that?" Chall demanded.

A stab of panic struck Matt then as his senses began to return. "It was Ned. Chall, Priest, you have to get him before he makes it away."

"Majesty, are you su—"

"Hurry!" Matt said, his voice a croaking whisper.

The two men nodded, looking at someone Matt couldn't see. "Keep an eye on him!" Then they were running and a moment later the young guardsman who'd gone into the manse to investigate the shouting appeared in front of Matt. "Majesty," he said, "are you alright?"

"I'm…I'm okay," Matt said. "Please, help me up."

The man took him by the arms, pulling him to his feet. Matt held onto the man's shoulder until the worst of the dizziness passed. When he was confident he wouldn't fall, Matt let his hand drop. No sooner had he done so than Chall and Priest returned, the former breathing heavily, an ugly red flush to his cheeks.

"Ned?" Matt asked, rubbing at his temple in a vain effort to alleviate some of the ache from where the man had struck him.

"Bastard got away," Chall panted, bending over with his hands on his knees as he gasped for breath. "Must be part gazelle."

"How about you, Majesty?" Priest said, moving forward. "How is your head?"

"Hurts," Matt said, wincing as a fresh throb of pain pulsed through his temple.

"If there's anything to be said about getting punched it's that," Chall wheezed. "And I'd know better than most."

"Which way did he go?" Matt asked. "Ned, I mean. Maybe we can follow or track him or..." But he trailed off as he noted Chall and Priest sharing a look. "What? What is it?"

"We don't know which way he went, Majesty," Priest said. "He was...he was gone when we came out of the gate."

"Gone?" Matt asked, surprised. "That quick?"

"Like I said, gazelle blood."

"What...what happened?"

They all turned at the sound of the voice, and Matt realized with a stab of shame that with everything that had happened he'd forgotten about Vorrun. The guardsman was blinking like a man who had just woken from a deep sleep.

"Vorrun!" Matt said, moving forward. "Are you alright?"

"I'm...I'm fine, Majesty," the guardsman said, looking around, "but...the criminal—where did he go?"

"He's gone, Vorrun," Matt said, surprised that the man would ask the question. After all, he had been staring right at him as Ned had turned and fled.

"Gone?" Vorrun asked.

Matt frowned. "Yes. He escaped."

"I...I don't understand."

And that sentiment Matt agreed with, for he didn't understand either. "Vorrun, are you feeling alright?"

"Fine, Majesty," the guardsman said. "Only...a bit sleepy, I suppose."

"Sleepy," Matt repeated, for that was a sentiment he most definitely did *not* share. The run in with Ned had got his heart thumping like a drum in his chest.

"Matt—Majesty," Chall said, "why don't you tell us exactly what happened?"

Matt did, speaking as quickly as he could, thinking that, perhaps, they might pick up on something he missed, something that might help them figure out where Ned had gone or what he planned to do.

He was explaining what Ned had said to him when Priest let out a hiss. "Forgive me, Majesty, what was that part? Why did Ned say he couldn't be arrested now? What were his *exact* words?"

Matt frowned, thinking back—a task made more difficult by the dull throb in his temple. "He said 'that bastard is cautious, but he's smart, too. Too damned smart.'"

Chall glanced at Priest. "You think he's talking about—"

"Catham the Cautious," Priest said, nodding. "It would seem that whatever Ned is up to, it involves Catham somehow. But please, Majesty—continue. Perhaps the man said something else that might shed some light on his motives."

Matt didn't think so, but then he didn't think Ned would have punched him in the face, either, so he proceeded as asked, describing, as accurately as he could remember it, everything Ned said, describing, also, the blood that had coated his hands and shirt.

When he was finished, Vorrun spoke. Matt had known the guardsman since coming to the castle and had always enjoyed talking with him—he was jovial and kind, confident and humble at the same time. At least, usually. Now, he sounded like none of those things except, perhaps, humble though in truth that word didn't come close to describing the shame with which he spoke or stood, his head hung low. "Majesty," he said, "I will, of course, resign my post. I...I am sorry that I failed you."

"Vorrun," Matt said softly, "you didn't fail. It just...well, Ned surprised us all, being there the way he was. It is completely understandable to freeze when a man covered in blood appears out of nowhere."

"Perhaps for some, Majesty," Vorrun said, "but not for me, not for a guardsman. We are trained specifically *not* to freeze, to be prepared for situations when others are not. And yet...I wasn't. I failed you and in doing so risked your life."

"But I'm fine, Vorrun," Matt said. "Truly. Just a bruise, that's all—nothing serious. Ned didn't kill me."

"No, Majesty," Vorrun agreed, "but he could have. And I, your guardsman, did nothing to stop it. I will speak with Commander Malex about receiving lashes for my failure before I leave the castle."

"Vorrun..." Matt began again, but he could think of nothing to say to change the man's mind, nothing to make the hurt any less.

"Before we all go falling on our swords let's just hold on a minute, alright?" Chall said. "You said you froze, Vorrun?"

The guardsman winced. "Listen, Chall—Sir Challadius—I appreciate you trying but—"

"Just swallow your damned honor and self-reproach for a minute, you bastard, and listen to me. When *exactly* did you 'freeze'?"

"I don't know what difference that makes," Vorrun said. "I froze—that's what matters."

"It was...Ned held up his hand," Matt said. "He said 'stop.' He...actually he apologized before he did it, as if he were doing something cruel."

"Taking over a man's mind," Chall said softly. "I can't think of anything crueler. It's why so many people distrust empaths and why most people—even some tutors I had at the academy—refused to believe they existed at all. You didn't freeze, Vorrun, you silly bastard," he went on, glancing at the guardsman. "You were frozen."

"I...don't understand," Vorrun said, and that, at least, made two of them, for Matt was confused as well. "What's an empath?"

"Just what it sounds like," Chall said grimly. "A man who can make people feel what he wants them to feel, and what are people if not their feelings?"

"You mean—"

"That the bastard used the Art on you," Chall confirmed. "It's got nothing to do with your courage or anything else. Anyone would have frozen in the same situation—anyone, at least, save for someone trained in the Art, for there are said to be ways a man might shield his heart and his mind against such uses, but it is something that takes a lot of training."

"I'm...not sure what you're saying," Vorrun said.

"I'm saying it wasn't your fault, damn you," Chall said. "I'm saying that there was nothing you could have done. I'm saying that anyone, *anyone* in your situation would have done the exact same thing."

"I see..." Vorrun said slowly, then his eyes got wider, and he turned to Matt. "But...Majesty, you were with me. Did...did you freeze as well?"

Matt remembered the way the carriage driver had held his hand up to him, remembered the way he'd felt some power gather then move around him like a river around a boulder. But he was aware of the others watching him and thought that if he started saying crazy things like that they'd likely never allow him to accompany them again. "Perhaps he didn't find it necessary to use the power on me," he lied. "After all, I'm not a trained guardsman—you see how easily he beat me." And the heat that suffused his face at that, at least, was no fabrication.

"Perhaps..." Vorrun said. "Only...I thought he did...didn't he? I seem to recall him reaching his hand out to you much the way he did me."

Matt was aware of Chall watching him carefully, his eyes narrowed. He might have told the man the truth then, might have told him specifics about the dreams he'd been having, about how his trouble sleeping was far worse than he'd made out and, yes, about Ned. After all, the man *had* tried to use the Art on him, or at least he thought he had. Certainly, he had felt some kind of pressure, had been aware of that pressure being swept aside from him as it came on. But he felt ashamed for some reason he didn't understand and, more than that, he was afraid. Afraid that Chall would be prompted, by his admissions, to examine him and, doing so, he would find something was terribly wrong.

So he shook his head, a confused expression on his face and that, at least, he didn't have to fake. "Maybe...maybe he was tired from using his power on Vorrun or...or maybe it...missed?"

"Missed?" Chall repeated.

Matt shrugged. "I don't know—you're the expert, not me. But it seems to me that it was either that or, as I said, he didn't see a point in wasting his power on me. After all, I've seen you use your power before, Chall. It takes a lot of energy from you, doesn't it?"

"It does," Chall said slowly.

"Well, then there it is," Matt said. "He didn't want to use his power on me because it would have taken energy to do so— energy he likely thought he would need."

"That's what you think?" Chall asked.

"What else could it be?" Matt asked, meeting the man's eyes, resisting the urge to stare at his feet.

"Right..." Chall said slowly, watching him. He felt, in that moment, as if the mage could see through him, could see into his thoughts, and so he decided it was time to change the subject.

"But what of Lady Valencia's manor?" he asked. "What was the scream we heard?"

Chall's suspicious glance vanished in an instant, replaced with an embarrassed wince. "Damned broom," he grumbled.

"I'm...sorry?"

The mage shook his head. "Who puts a damned broom in a closet, anyway? Where it'll just fall on a person who is doing nothing but minding his own business and scare the shit out of him?"

"I wonder if that's why they call them broom closets," Priest observed, and although the man kept a straight expression Matt could see the smile in his eyes.

Chall didn't answer, at least not with words, though the scowl he shot the man was answer enough.

Priest did grin then. "Well, if it's any consolation, it was a very frightening broom—as far as brooms go."

Matt smiled at Chall's obvious discomfort, but a fresh wave of pain through his temple made the smile fade quickly enough. "So...what do we do now? Go find this Catham person?"

Everyone looked at Priest, and he paused to consider. He looked at the sky, growing darker as night settled fully on the world, then finally shook his head. "No," he said. "Not tonight. It is late. Catham and whatever part he has in all of this will keep until morning. As for Lady Valencia's manse, I'll speak to Commander Malex, have him send some men to investigate." He glanced back at the manse, a grim expression on his face. "We will also need some men to take care of the bodies."

Matt swallowed. "Bodies?"

Chall nodded. "Half a dozen at least, likely more that we didn't see. Servants and two guardsmen—that bastard Ned has a lot to answer for."

"Then let's make him answer for it," Matt said, rubbing at his temple. "If he really is behind all of this, we can't wait until morning. We should go and find him or this Catham right now."

"That...would not be wise, Majesty," Priest said.

"Oh?"

"If he means to battle shadows, a wise man battles them in the day, when the sun shines and they are at their weakest."

Matt thought about arguing that. Not because Priest's words didn't make sense—after all, he thought that only a fool wouldn't listen to the man, particularly when he used to be a part of the criminal world and so was in a position to know its dangers better than anyone else.

He wanted to argue because as scary as Ned and these Crimson Wolves were, the thought of sleeping, of seeing the demon with the green eyes again, was scarier still. Better to face muggers and thieves, he thought, than to wake up in the dark, cringing against his sweat-soaked sheets, the only sound that of his own panicked whimpers and shallow, ragged breaths. Not being able to go back to sleep and growing surer and surer with each time that there was something wrong with him, something broken.

But there was no way to argue it without arousing more suspicion from Chall and the others, and so, as they all looked at him, Matt nodded. "I trust your judgement, Priest. If you think it best to wait until the morning that is what we will do."

The man bowed his head as if in gratitude. "Then, should we make our way back to the castle?"

"Very well," Matt said. They started away and, as they did, he looked up at the dark night's sky, thinking that morning had never seemed so far away.

CHAPTER TEN

Morning came slowly.

Cutter sat within the cavernous tree into which the Gray Man had led them, watching his brother toss and turn in troubled sleep, each minute stretching on into an eternity.

So it always was before a battle and so it was now.

The morning came quickly.

It felt as if Cutter had only just sat, propping his back against the inside of the tree, laying his axe down beside him, when their remaining time vanished, as if the gods had smashed the hour glass of his life and tossed the sand out onto the ground.

So it always was before a battle and so it was now.

The trunk of the tree began to reshape itself, and Cutter rose, lifting his axe from where it had sat propped beside him.

He had no sooner done so than the trunk fully pulled away, revealing an opening in which the Gray Man stood. The Feyling said nothing, but then there was nothing that needed to be said.

The time for talk was over.

Now, it was time for war.

Cutter moved to where his brother lay, kneeling and grasping him gently by one shoulder. "Fel," he said.

His brother turned and blinked deep-circled eyes at him. "It's time then?" he said.

"It's time."

"I had the most wonderful dream," Feledias said.

"Really?"

"No of course not," his brother snapped, rising to his feet. He seemed a bit unsteady, but he was standing under his own power. That was proof enough of the Gray Man's healing, for before he had seen to him Feledias hadn't even been able to so much as crawl, let alone stand.

"Are you ready?" Cutter asked.

Feledias snorted. "No. Of course not," he repeated. He glanced at the Gray Man standing in the opening of the tree then back at Cutter. "But then, Bernard, I don't think that they much care whether we're ready or not. Do you?"

"No, I don't."

Feledias sighed. He pulled on his boots, then moved to where he'd laid his sheathed swords and began strapping them onto his waist. When he was finished he walked up to Cutter. "Well then, best we get this done." He glanced at the Gray Man. "Unless, of course, we're to be given some breakfast before we fight for our lives?"

"I'm afraid not," the Gray Man said.

Feledias grunted. "Probably just as well—doubt I could keep anything down."

Cutter turned to the Gray Man, giving him a nod. "We're ready."

***

The Feyling led them away from the giant tree in which they had taken shelter and back toward the Glade. Despite the fact that it was early morning, the sun shining high in the sky, the Black Wood was full of shadows, the canopy of the giant trees blocking out all but the most stubborn of the sun's rays so that the forest existed in perpetual twilight.

And so they followed the Feyling through the shadows. Cutter was not discomfited by this, for he had spent his life in the shadow, knew of the light only from hearing of it from other, better men. What did give him pause, though, was the sheer amount of Fey gathered in the Wood, so many that they were forced to walk a gauntlet between thousands upon thousands of creatures who hissed and snarled in excited expectation.

"Almost seems like they're waiting on something," Feledias quipped, but his usual sarcastic tone was replaced by one of awe and fear. Not that Cutter was surprised. After all, it wasn't every day that thousands of creatures out of nightmare gathered to watch you die.

"Almost," Cutter agreed.

There is no need to fear, the Gray Man said as they walked, *they will not harm you, for any who undertake the Path of War may not be harmed out of turn.*

"With all due respect," Feledias murmured as they made their way through the avenue surrounded by the Fey, "I'd say there's plenty of damned reason to fear. In fact, I am quite confident in saying that I have never had more reason than now."

"Careful, Fel," Cutter said, "keep on, people are liable to think you're not enjoying yourself."

"Not that there are any *people* around," Fel muttered. "Just monsters."

The Gray Man paused at that, turning on Cutter's brother, his eyes shifting like some tumultuous thundercloud sky. *It is not our appearance, Feledias Stormborn, however strange, however alien, which makes us monsters. I would think that you should know that.*

The Gray Man did not speak with anger or threat, yet his words seemed to stab into Cutter's brother like a dagger, visibly rocking him. Feledias paled and nodded. "Right," he said, swallowing hard. "I...I'm sorry."

Feledias was clearly troubled as they continued, his grim, ashamed expression and haunted eyes reflecting his thoughts well enough. He thought of Brighton, Cutter knew, of Brighton and the other villages, other people who had suffered. Who had been *made* to suffer and with no one to blame but the two of them.

In short, he thought of monsters.

They arrived at the Glade a short while later, though one might have been forgiven for thinking it a different place altogether. It was true that the green field spread out in all directions as it had the day before, but unlike the day before the flat expanse was empty.

Or, at least, nearly so.

Shadelaresh stood in the distance, watching them. The Gray Man stepped to the edge of the Glade where the last of the line of Feylings that had surrounded them on either side stood and stopped.

Cutter stopped too, looking to the Feyling.

The Gray Man turned to him, regarding him with his bleak gray eyes. *It is your journey, Destroyer. Stormborn. I may go no farther, for now you embark on the Path of War.*

"How about the path of bunny rabbits and sweet cakes?" Feledias said, but without much feeling. "Is that an option?"

Cutter and the Gray man turned to look at Feledias, and Cutter's brother sighed. "I suppose not."

"What might we expect?" Cutter asked, turning back to the Feyling.

What one must always expect when he sets out on the Path of War, Destroyer, the Gray Man said, his voice full of regret. *Death. For when words fail, death is the only answer. That is a truth I think you, at least, have learned.*

Cutter nodded. "Thank you," he said. "For all your help."

The Gray Man bowed his head as if in acknowledgment. *You have come seeking peace, Destroyer. I, at least, believe that. But there has been much blood spilled, and to reach that goal for which you aspire there must be more yet. There is a division within you, the man you are battling the man you believe you should be, and you, as a warrior, must know that you cannot fight two battles at once. You cannot wage war within yourself and war without and hope to be victorious in both. You will forego one or the other, whether you wish it or not.*

"You're telling me to be a killer...a monster."

Yes, the Gray Man said, his voice full of sadness. *Your brother is afraid, Destroyer, and he is right to fear, for what you face is not just your own destruction but the destruction of everything you love, everything you hold dear. And you are not ready. You seek to become a good man, but a good man will not conquer the Path of the Warrior—I know this, for it has been tried before.*

"Tried before?" Cutter asked. "By whom?"

It does not matter, not now, at least. What does is that a good man cannot stand against what is in your path. For what comes, you do not need the man you would be, but the monster you are.

"I cannot do that," Cutter said quietly, his voice a harsh whisper. "I cannot become that...that person again."

You must, Destroyer, the Gray Man said. *Else you will lose not only yourself and your brother but also your kingdom...your son.*

Cutter tensed at that, a shock of fear going through him. And, as always—with him, at least—with the fear came anger. He found his muscles tensing, his fingers working, aching to go for his axe. Foolish, of course—the Gray Man was the only living creature within miles that didn't want to see him and his brother dead, not to mention the fact that he'd seen the Feyling destroy another creature with little more than a thought. But then, as always when it came to his anger, to his rage, considerations like logic and foolishness never factored into it.

It was not a question of thought, of foolish or not foolish, not a question even of morality. Or, if it was, then it was a question that could only be answered with blood. With teeth. The lion had his claws, and Cutter had his axe, the axe which his fingers ached to reach for.

You are angry, the Gray Man observed, *and that is good. There is a beast inside of you, Destroyer. A beast that you have squandered years trying to lull to sleep. But if it sleeps, then it is a troubled repose, one from which it might easily awaken. And you can do no more than that, cannot put it to sleep fully, not while you still draw breath. The beast will not sleep—it cannot.*

"Why?" Cutter grated, the words coming out in a harsh whisper, for he thought that he knew the truth. He thought that he had always known.

The Gray Man met his eyes, two pools of murky cloud shifting in an endless sky. *Because, Destroyer. The beast is you. It always has been. And such a beast never sleeps fully so long as it still draws breath.*

Cutter wanted to argue with that, wanted to claim that he could change, that he could be better. He wanted to claim it because he wanted, he *needed* to believe it. It was a fight he had fought for years, but he knew in that moment that the Gray Man was right. He had to let it go, to concede, for there was another fight looming before him, a battle that might be the most difficult battle in a life full of little else.

And so in his mind, his soul, he lay down before that beast within him, the one with which he had warred for years, and he bared his neck to it. And then the beast did what beasts always do in such situations—it moved to take him.

And with the death of everything he held dear looming before him, Cutter did something he had not done in a very long time.

He let it.

"They wait for us?" he said, his voice harsh and raw and unrecognizable. The voice of a stranger. The voice of the beast.

Yes, the Gray Man said.

"Bernard," Feledias said, the worry clear in his tone, "is everything—"

"Show me," Cutter said, ignoring his brother, for he was not important, not now. All that was important was the axe at his back, the keenness of its blade, and the flesh that it would be used against.

The Gray Man studied him for a moment then nodded. *You begin to remember yourself,* he said. *Let us hope that it is enough.*

And with that, he gestured to the Glade. Cutter, his lip pulled back from his teeth in a silent snarl, stepped into the clearing. And as he did, some part of him, some small part, cried out in terror and despair. But its cries were faint, largely drowned out by the sound of the beast's anticipatory growling, and easily ignored.

Shadelaresh tracked his approach, his anticipation obvious even on his alien features.

He was there. The enemy. The one who would, if given his way, destroy everything that mattered. The one who would destroy Feledias, the Known Lands.

Matt.

It was all Cutter could do, in that moment, to keep from launching himself at the creature as they drew nearer, but he *did* keep himself from it. The beast was slipping loose of its chains, it was true—he felt that slipping, felt it the way a man felt himself slowly sliding into a chasm of rage—but it had not fully slipped, not yet, and so his hand did not reach for the axe strapped to his back but remained at his side.

If only barely.

Ah, Bernard Paterna and Feledias Paterna. You have come, the Green Man said.

"Wouldn't miss it," Cutter growled.

Something flashed in the Green Man's eyes, then, what might have been uncertainty, but it was Feledias who spoke. "Speak for yourself," he said, glancing at Cutter with an uneasy expression, as if he were checking on a wild animal to see if it meant to attack. "As for me," he went on, turning to the Green Man, "I would have loved to have missed it."

Shadelaresh's mouth twisted into a small smile as he regarded Feledias. *You are clever, Feledias Stormborn. That is known. And, it seems, you are no stranger to sarcasm. Yet, I wonder, will you still be so clever when you are screaming in agony, when your death is upon you? I, for one, suspect not. And I suspect that, your clever brain, when dashed upon the ground, will look much like any other.*

Feledias paled at that and, for once, Cutter's brother seemed to have nothing to say.

"Enough talk," Cutter growled impatiently, for now that the thing was certain, now that there was no avoiding it, he'd just as soon get started. As always, it was, for him, the waiting that chafed the most.

Shadelaresh's smile widened. *Ah, you are eager to get started then, and that is good for so, too, am I. Tell me, Destroyer, Stormborn, you have come to the Black Wood, to the home and heart of the Fey, carrying a message from your king. Do you still wish to deliver it?*

Cutter glanced sidelong at his brother, expecting some sort of clever quip or sarcastic remark, but judging by his tight expression, Feledias had no cleverness in him just then.

"Yes," Cutter said.

Very well, the Green Man said. *Now then,* he continued, his gaze traveling back to Cutter, *you have come bearing message, Destroyer, Betrayer. You have come as an emissary, and to deliver that message you must first walk the Path of War, the path you chose long ago. To be deemed worthy of such a path one must demonstrate many qualities, many attributes. And the first of these is strength, for a creature whose strength fails him cannot make the journey required. I have heard much of your strength, as all my people have. But I wonder, Destroyer, will even your strength be enough?*

"Let's find out," Cutter said.

The Green Man's emerald eyes seemed to shimmer. *Very well—we shall.* He stepped to the side and motioned. *Go then, Destroyer and kin. Your test awaits you.*

Cutter followed the creature's gaze to the empty field behind. "I don't mean to be rude," Feledias said, "but it seems to me that this 'test' of yours is running late."

Oh, but your test is not here, Stormborn, the Green Man said. *The Glade will not be defiled with your blood. No, you journey on the Path of War, and so your path lies before you. Go then, both of you, and show us your strength.*

Cutter frowned, glancing to the side to see that the Gray Man had walked up.

It is right, the Gray Man said. He spoke further, but the next words did not seem to be spoken aloud but seemed to be spoken directly into Cutter's mind. *Be wary of what lies before you, Destroyer, for in what is to come your strength will indeed be tested. Strength of form, yes, but also strength of character.*

Cutter gave the Feyling a nod then turned to Feledias, a question in his gaze. His brother sighed.

"More walking?" Feledias asked.

"Looks like."

His brother gave a slow nod, motioning beyond the Green Man toward the tree line. "Well. After you then."

Cutter paused to glance at the Green Man, promising himself that should they fail here and should it be within his power, he would do everything he could to see the Feyling die before he fell. Knowing, even as he thought it, that it was almost certainly a vain thought.

He started forward.

As they walked, Cutter's eyes scanned the glade around them. There was nothing save what felt like an endless sea of grass and no matter how much they walked it felt to him as if they were no closer to the distant tree line than they had been.

At first, Feledias let out a steady rambling diatribe of sarcastic quips but soon even his seemingly endless well of cynicism dried up and the two of them walked on in silence.

It felt as if they walked for hours, for days, and Cutter found himself thinking they must be in the grips of some spell. Finally, he paused, glancing back, expecting to see the Green Man smiling that knowing smile, the smile that said he knew something that Cutter didn't, that he was aware of a hidden pit lying ahead of him and was eager to watch him fall in.

He was surprised, then, to find that no one was there. Not Shadelaresh or the Gray Man, not even the line of Feylings that had surrounded them as they made their way into the Glade. There was no one, nothing. Nothing, at least, save an endless field of green, an expanse of grass that seemed to reach on and on forever as far as Cutter could see.

"Don't tell me you're tired already, brother," Feledias said. Then he turned, following Cutter's gaze and hissing in a sharp breath. "What...that doesn't...it isn't possible."

Cutter stared at that empty field and thought that he had been right after all. They were, it seemed, under the grips of a spell—only it was not of the sort he'd thought. Another man might have been made afraid by that. Chall would have likely been intrigued by the power on display.

Cutter was neither.

He was only impatient. "Come on," he said, then he turned and started forward again.

He'd only taken a step, though, when his eyes alighted on a figure standing about a hundred feet ahead of them in what, moments ago, had been an empty plain.

Feledias hissed. "Fire and salt where did that bastard come from?"

"I don't know," Cutter said.

"Crawled out of my nightmares, maybe," Feledias said, his voice low and afraid. "Is...is that what I think it is?" Feledias asked, his breath little more than a whisper.

"It would seem so."

"But...I mean, that is...they're supposed to be no more than a myth."

Cutter thought of that, of how so many of his greatest fears, his greatest nightmares had come to life over the years, starting with the Skaalden's invasion. But no, that wasn't true. They had started before that, in a dark alley in Daltenia when a dueling champion had faced, for the first time in his coddled life, real danger, a real test. One that he had failed.

He thought of dreams and nightmares filled with blood and death, reflected on a life that had been filled with much the same, and turned to his brother. "Sometimes the nightmares are real," he said.

And while his brother might not have suffered all the things that Cutter had, he had suffered more than enough to know the truth of it, so he nodded. "But...but still though...an ogre?"

"Or something very much like it," Cutter agreed.

"I suppose...well, the stories have to come from somewhere, don't they?" Feledias asked.

Cutter wondered at that, for he had heard stories—as all children had—of ogres. Of trolls and bogeymen and all other manner of nighttime monsters since he was a child. But he and his people had not known of the Fey until after the Skaalden invasion and so, if ogres were real and were creatures of the Fey—which seemed a safe assumption given that one was standing in front of him—then how would his people have known of them long before they ever fled to the Known Lands and encountered the Fey in the first place?

It was an interesting question, but one he thought might better be pondered at another time and certainly by another person. After all there was a reason he was called Cutter, not Thinker.

"Suppose he's waiting for someone else?" Feledias asked.

"I don't think so."

"Maybe he just wants to have a nice chat?" his brother said hopefully.

Cutter looked over the beast. Ten feet tall if it was an inch. Ten feet of thick slabs of muscle coupled with a protruding gut and nothing but a loin cloth to cover it. The ogre's features resembled a man's but its ears and nose and brow were disproportionately large in relation to the rest of it, its yellow eyes far too small, like beady little pinpricks in its doughy face.

In its hand the creature held a club that was more tree trunk than weapon, though despite its crudeness Cutter didn't doubt its efficacy, was confident that one strike from it, powered by the creature's massive frame would be more than enough to bring a quick—and definitive—end to their journey.

"Think he's planning on planting that tree of his?" Feledias asked.

"Why don't we go ask him?" Cutter said, glancing at his brother.

"I can think of a few alternatives," Feledias said. "In case you've a mind to hear them."

"I don't think it's me you have to worry about," Cutter said.

Feledias sighed. "Right."

They started forward.

The creature stood unmoving as they drew closer, its massive features split into a buck-toothed grin, a vacant sort of look in its eyes that made Cutter think that the stories had likely gotten the idiocy of the ogres true as well as their massive frames. Though, to be fair, he supposed when you could lift tree trunks with seeming ease there wasn't much need for complicated thought.

"So what's the plan?" Feledias asked as they continued forward.

"Try not to die," Cutter said.

"Right," Feledias said slowly. "Any thoughts on how we might accomplish that?"

"Give me a minute."

They stopped about twenty-five feet from the creature. "Are you our first test, then?" Cutter asked the creature.

"I Urk," the creature said in a voice that was undeniably ogreish.

"Urk," Feledias repeated. "Like the sound someone makes when they throw up."

"Of the Vomit Urks no doubt," Cutter agreed.

The creature's thick brows drew down in an angry scowl. "You bad. Urk squash."

"Kind of straight to the point, isn't he?" Feledias asked. He raised his voice, "Violence isn't the answer, Urk. You should really learn to talk out your problems."

The ogre puffed out its naked, hairy chest, slapping its massive gut with its free hand and raising its club with the other before tilting its head back and letting out a guttural roar.

"I think that's his kind of talk," Cutter observed.

"Sure is a big son of a bitch," Feledias said, licking his lips nervously.

"So are trees," Cutter said, "but I've cut down a few in my time. I seem to remember us doing it together, back in Daltenia, before Dad...well. Before. I even seem to recall you enjoying it."

"Sure, why not?" Feledias said. "It was fun, watching those big things fall, crash to the earth the way they did. The difference, though, is that those trees weren't holding *other* trees, ones that they meant to smash us to paste with."

"Well," Cutter said, "I suppose if you're going to quibble over details. Now, if you're all done, I guess we ought to go say hello."

He hefted his axe and started forward. Feledias was right about this much, at least—the creature had little interest in talking. Or, for that matter, waiting. Cutter had barely taken a step before it let out another bellow, louder even than the first, and started forward at a run.

A run which, given the creature's enormous size, made the very ground beneath Cutter's feet tremble like the deck of a ship pitching in a storm.

As he ran to meet it, Cutter found the beast within him, that beast which he had spent so many years trying to lull to sleep, bare its fangs in anticipation just as he bared his own in a feral smile, hefting his axe.

The ogre roared as it came on, and Cutter roared back. As he rushed headlong at the ten-foot-tall monstrosity, Cutter did not feel fear, as most men might have. He did not feel worry or anxiety. Some small part of him *did* feel shame, shame at the acknowledgment of what he had become once more, shame and disgust at the realization that he had always been that person, that monster.

But more than anything, far more even than the same, Cutter felt alive. Alive in a way he had not in a very long time. Alive in a way he had only ever felt on the field of battle when testing his strength against another, his *will* against another, when the boundary between life and death could be measured on a razor's edge and oblivion, victory or defeat, were no more than a split-second away.

When they were within ten feet of each other the world seemed to slow to Cutter. As so often was the case when in battle, everything drew to a near standstill, and it felt to Cutter as if they were moving through water. But it wasn't just that. He felt completely absorbed, completely engaged. He felt the way he imagined a master artist might feel when in the grips of his talent, carried along by something bigger than himself.

It wasn't just that time seemed to slow—it was that he felt as if he knew what the ogre meant to do before it did, as if it were all just some choreographed, intricate dance, one that he had orchestrated.

He'd had the feeling before in battle. And now, like those other times, he felt taken over by it. He thought that, had he cared to, he could have traced the arc of the monster's club through the air, could have described its path as if it had been pre-destined.

But he did not, did not concern himself all that much with the club's path at all save to make sure, with a quick duck, that he was not in it. The massive tree whistled over his head, inches away, no more than that, but then in war the distance between life and death could often be measured in inches.

Inches like those separating the head of his obsidian axe from the creature's protruding stomach. Inches that vanished in another moment as Cutter finished his pivot, driving his axe into the ogre's midsection. The beast bellowed in pain as the black axe head buried itself deep in its flesh.

It stumbled backward, and Cutter followed, ripping his axe free and swinging it again, then again, the creature bellowing in pain and fear with each vicious arc of the axe. But despite the obvious pain the creature was in, it did not fall. In fact, Cutter noticed, even through the red haze that often overcame him in battle, that no sooner had the razor-sharp blade left the creature's flesh than the wounds the axe inflicted began to slowly mend and heal.

So that despite the viciousness of Cutter's unrelenting assault, the creature even went so far as to manage a counter stroke with the giant tree it wielded, one that forced Cutter to abandon his attack, at least for the moment, or else receive a blow that likely would have broken every bone in his body. He growled, frustrated at his will being balked, at being forced to retreat, as he rolled backward, underneath the ogre's strike.

He stood there, panting, regarding his foe, a slow, cruel smile coming to his face. The creature did not look so eager for the fight now. It, like so many others before it, had imagined things differently, had found that when it finally came upon the violence it had so desired, it had no taste for it.

Cutter, though, did. He knew this about himself, for he had tasted it often and each time had thought—as he now did—that there was nothing sweeter. Nothing more sustaining in all the world than to watch one's foes fall before him, to meet them in battle and best them.

Yet the beast that had awakened within Cutter, while it was creature of violence, was also a creature of cunning. Cunning as the shark swimming silently upon its prey, catching it unawares. Cunning as the lion who knows that should he offer chase too soon the gazelle might escape his jaws, and so waits until it comes close. Too close.

The ogre had half a dozen bloody rents upon its flesh, proof of the axe's attentions, but it was clear from its stance that it was not finished yet. And so, as he slowly circled it, Cutter considered what he might do.

Movement from behind him caught his eye and he shot a quick glance back to see his brother starting forward. "*Stay back,*" he said, harsher than he'd intended, his words little more than a rasping roar, and his brother froze.

In the absence of the beast's grip, Cutter might have issued the command to keep his brother safe, but the truth was that, in that moment, he did not consider his brother's safety at all. Instead, he thought of how he did not want the man getting in his way, coming between him and his prey. And, even more than that, he did not want to share the glory of victory, did not want to have any credit for his kill stolen from him.

So he forgot about his brother, for the moment. There was no Feledias, just as there was no Chall or Maeve or Priest, was no Known Lands, no kingdom to protect.

In truth, there was no *him.*

There was only the ogre, a creature who had dared to stand in his way and so must be punished for it. It would die. That death was destined, had been guaranteed since the moment it had raised its weapon against him.

The only thing left to determine was the method of that death, the means of that punishment. He stared at the creature before him, blood weeping from the touch of his axe. Bleeding but not dead, looking like it could take quite a bit more, and that was good, for he had quite a bit more to give.

More than ten feet tall, his foe, a beast bred for battle and war. But then, so too was Cutter.

When they'd first spotted the creature Feledias had likened it to a tree.

Cutter had chopped down trees before, many times, while living in his self-imposed exile in Brighton, and he decided he would cut this creature down the same way. For when a man meant to see a tree fall, its height and size did not matter, in the end.

Just so long as he was patient and started at the bottom.

The grin widened on his face, wider and wider still until it was not a grin at all but a baring of the beast's fangs.

Then he charged.

The ogre bellowed in answer to his own shout, swinging its giant weapon in a two-handed, overhead blow that would have crushed Cutter into bloody paste had he remained in its path.

He leapt to the side, barely slowing as he narrowly avoided the blow. The ground shook as the creature's massive weapon struck, but he kept his feet, rushing forward. In another moment, he was within the beast's guard, and he roared as he buried the obsidian head of his axe in the creature's thigh. Blood fountained from the wound, but he was not finished.

Once more, as he had so many years ago in Brighton, Cutter earned his name.

He spun, bringing his axe around in a deadly arc and striking the creature in the other leg, this time behind its knee. It stumbled, its leg buckling, but it did not fall, and that was alright with him. Cutter had cut down many trees for firewood in the cold wilderness of Brighton and few fell within the first two swings.

He swung again, this time striking the creature in the back of a calf that was larger than a man's waist. The ogre screamed, stumbling back.

Cutter roared, following.

And he struck again.

And again.

He was covered in his enemy's blood by the time the creature's legs finally gave way. It collapsed, striking the ground like the fist of some angry god, and the ground trembled at its fall.

The creature bellowed and shouted, but it was not fury or thirst for battle that was in its tone now. Instead it was pain. Fear.

The beast within Cutter breathed in those screams the way a man might inhale the air into his lungs, and he stepped forward, looming over the beast's form as it writhed on the ground in pain.

"This was always how it was going to end," Cutter told the creature. He did not know if it understood his words, particularly as it seemed lost to a world of pain, and he did not care. The truth did not need to be heard, to be *understood* to exist. It was there always, as keen, as powerful as a stroke of his great axe.

He raised the Breaker of Pacts above his head, glorying in that instant, that moment within moments. He roared his pleasure at the sky, preparing to bring his axe down and finish it.

"*Father, please...*"

The beast inside Cutter shirked away at that voice, the voice he knew so well, and he looked down at the figure before him, freezing. "It...it can't..." he said, his words a desperate, horrified whisper.

For what lay before him was not the ogre, not the ten-foot-tall monstrosity with which he had done battle. It was no Fey creature of death and destruction.

It was Matt.

His son.

Matt had dozens of wounds along his body, his arms and legs and chest. Wounds that Cutter recognized and how not, for like the master sculptor, he knew well his own work. Blood was spattered on Matt's face, his eyes desperate in pain.

He was looking to Cutter for help but there was no help.

He was dying.

The beast within Cutter, that rage which had spurred him on, vanished at the sight of that as if it had never been.

And then he was alone. Alone with the truth of what he was, *who* he was. Alone with the truth of what he had done.

"Matt..." he said, his voice hoarse and raw from shouting. "But...how...how can you be here?"

He was barely aware that his arms had come back down to his side, that the Breaker of Pacts dangled loosely from his hand, just as he barely noticed when he fell to his knees beside the bloody form. There was only his son lying before him.

"Matt, please, I don't...I didn't..." he said. He reached out, trying to staunch the flow of blood and knowing even as he did that there was no saving him. He had been around enough death to know when it came. And death *was* coming for his son, and he was the one who had called it.

As he struggled to staunch the wounds, some odd confusion made its way past his terrible grief and confusion. At first, he couldn't tell what was bothering him but as he continued to press at his son's wounds, he realized what it was. What his eyes saw and what his hands felt did not match.

He knew Matt's size, his height and weight, knew it better than he knew his own. After all, he had watched him all his life, had witnessed as he put on each inch, each pound. He knew him because for a long time—and in many ways, still—he was the only thing that had mattered. The only thing that had kept the knife he sometimes held to his own throat at bay.

And while the figure beneath him looked like Matt, even down to the grayness of his eyes, eyes that matched Cutter's own, what lay beneath Cutter's fingers was not Matt. He knew that as much as he knew anything, and that knowledge pierced the cloud of confusion and shock and terror that had descended upon him when he'd seen Matt lying broken and bloody on the ground.

The creature beneath him could not be Matt—Matt was miles and miles away. Matt was not in the Black Wood. He was safe back in New Daltenia, safe in the castle.

"Kill it, damnit!"

As the fog of confusion continued to lift, Cutter turned to look behind him where Feledias stood fifty feet away or so, charging toward him, his blade out.

No sooner had Cutter took note of his brother than there was a deep grunt from the figure lying at Cutter's side, one that could not have come from any human throat but one that might easily enough have come from an ogre.

He turned back.

179

Or, at least, began to. He'd only made it about halfway around, so that he was staring out at the green field somewhere between his brother and the creature lying at his feet, when he caught sight of a shape in the grass.

It was low to the ground, that shape, the tall grass covering most of it. Most but not all. Cutter noted green-gray, desiccated looking flesh, and eyes as black as pitch that almost took up the entirety of the creature's slender, emaciated face.

"What the fu—" Cutter began, but he did not get to finish.

There was another grunt from beside him, and the next thing he knew something struck him in the side with the force of a runaway carriage.

Pain exploded in his arm and side, and Cutter was flung through the air. He struck the ground hard and began to tumble end over end. He managed to take control of his careening roll, coming to his feet with one fist on the ground in front of him to keep his balance.

"*Bernard!*"

He glanced over to see Feledias running up to him, his brother pulling him to his feet. "Fire and salt why didn't you just kill the big bastard?" Feledias asked.

"It wasn't the big bastard," Cutter said, as he turned back to see the massive creature finishing climbing its way to its feet. He realized then that what had struck him had been one of its flailing arms—just as well as if it had struck him full force he'd likely have an ogre-sized hole in him.

"What do you mean it wasn't him?" Feledias said. "It wasn't me that slapped the shit out of you just now, I can tell you that. Speakin' of, how's your arm?"

"I'll let you know when I can feel it," Cutter said, wincing and shifting his shoulder. "And what I mean is, it was Matt."

Feledias frowned. "Matt? Damn, that thing must have hit you harder than I thought. Listen, brother, Matt's back in New Daltenia, him and that club of misfits of yours."

"We prefer gang of misfits," Cutter said, as the ogre continued to rise. "Anyway, I *know* Matt is in New Daltenia. What I'm telling you is that the creature, it looked like him."

Feledias frowned deeper, glancing back at the ogre which was currently bending down to retrieve its tree-club. "I don't see the resemblance."

"Damnit, Fel, now's not the time for your jokes," Cutter said.

"Well, I've got to be honest with you, brother mine, I'm not all that certain there's going to be another."

"An illusion," Cutter said. "That's what it was."

"An illusion."

"Yes."

"I don't know much about magic, but I haven't heard of a lot of magic-wielding ogres. You?"

"I don't think it was him," Cutter said.

"Well if anyone else is here, he's invisible."

"Not quite," Cutter said, keeping his voice low so they wouldn't be overheard. "Crouched in the grass about fifty feet out, that way," he said, giving the slightest nod of his head.

Feledias frowned, glancing in that direction. "I don't see anything."

"I think that's the point," Cutter said, "but he's there."

"But...I thought this was supposed to be a test of strength, us against the ogre. Isn't that what that green bastard said?"

Cutter gave a small shrug. "Seems Shadelaresh has taken it in mind to cheat."

"Damn but I hate cheaters," Feledias said quietly. "Especially when they're not me. What do you want to do?"

"Solve it the way I solve a lot of my problems."

"Talk it out, then."

"Exactly."

Feledias grunted. "Fine, but you get the ogre—I get the bastard hiding in the grass."

"Lucky me," Cutter said quietly. "And Fel? Make it fast, will you. I don't know what other tricks that damned thing has in store, but I'd just as soon not find out."

"Suppose I can put off tea until after," his brother said. Then, in a more serious tone, "Good luck, Bernard."

"Good luck, Fel."

Then he was moving, stalking through the grass. The ogre had gotten its feet now, had retrieved the giant tree and was slowly lumbering toward him. Cutter saw, as he drew closer, that the wounds he'd inflicted on the creature were completely healed. It looked as fresh and ready to fight as it had when they had first come upon it. Meanwhile, Cutter's left arm throbbed painfully.

Worse yet, he was unarmed, his axe lying at the giant creature's feet where he'd dropped it when he'd been struck. He'd fought without the axe before, of course, for years under the tutelage of his father and his father's master-at-arms, he had trained with all manner of weapons. Back in Daltenia, before the Skaalden, giant creatures of frost and death, had come to their lands, he had been a celebrated duelist, considered an expert with a sword. Worse, he had considered *himself* an expert, a notion of which he'd been disabused one fateful day in an alley when he'd been stabbed and left to die.

He had not acquired the axe until Yeladrian had gifted it to him what felt like a lifetime ago but since receiving it, it had almost become a part of him. A part of which he was often ashamed but one that he felt was no less necessary for all that. He had considered ridding himself of the weapon many times, that hateful thing which had come, to him, to represent all the worst, most violent parts of his nature. Yet he had not. He had kept it. And despite his reservations, he'd had cause to be glad of that. For without the obsidian axe he and Matt would not have escaped Brighton, would have died somewhere along the trail that had eventually led them to New Daltenia to confront Feledias.

The axe, hated or not, had saved him and those he cared for countless times, its blade, always sharp, interceding between him and death times uncountable. But it would not save him this time. This time, it would not keep the monsters at bay. He would have to do that himself.

But who will keep you at bay? He was not sure where the thought came from, if it was his own or some other force, but no sooner had he had it then he remembered the way Matt had looked lying on the ground, bleeding. Dying.

Matt who had suffered so much for many reasons, none of which were his fault. Matt who had sent them here to find peace, a peace in which the kingdom, in which *Matt,* would be safe. A peace that Cutter would never attain if he were to die here.

The thought of that, of this creature daring to stand in the way of his son's safety, made Cutter angry. And, as always, that anger, that rage, made him forget his own aches and pains, forget the numbness still not fully gone from his left arm. He forgot, too, about Feledias and the creature crouching in the grass. He would deal with them later, if there was a later.

For now, there was only the ten-foot-tall monstrosity stalking toward him, the creature which stood between him and his mission. The creature which *dared* to stand between him and his son.

A growl issued from Cutter's throat. The beast was awake once more, had returned from wherever it had slinked to when witnessing Matt lying bloody before him. It was back.

And he was running.

His feet tore at the ground in his eagerness to get to the creature, his hands clasping and unclasping in his excitement. He did not know what the ogre had expected him to do, but it was clear from the look of dumb, stricken surprise on its face that it had not thought that its unarmed opponent would choose to charge. Which just meant that it did not know of him at all. And that was alright.

It would learn.

He was on the creature in moments. It swung its great club at him in a blow that might have toppled a house but now, like before, it was too slow, for even its prodigious strength was not enough to swing the tree it held at speed. Had the creature picked a tree half as big it would have almost certainly hit him, and he would have been just as dead, but like so many men, it had not learned a very valuable lesson, one his father's master-at-arms had taught him long ago.

Just because a man could do a thing didn't mean he should and a dagger's blade was just as sharp as a sword's. Or, in ogre terms, why use a giant tree when a very large one would do?

The tree hurled toward him in a side blow, and Cutter rolled underneath it, barely slowing down before he came to his feet and continued to charge at the creature. He had no weapon, and so he knew that he had to get in close, knew that he had to take the creature's advantage away. He came in low, his arms spread wide, turning his head at the last second before he tackled the creature, hitting it in the thighs.

The creature was large, it was true. It was strong. But then so, too, was Cutter. He hit the creature low and hard, and it did the only thing it could do—it fell.

The creature fumbled its makeshift club and, in another moment, it was lying on its back, Cutter atop it. It reached for him with fingers as thick as a young boy's wrists. Cutter didn't doubt that, if given the opportunity, the creature would be capable of breaking a man's neck as easily as a man might snap a twig in his grip. So he didn't give the creature the chance.

He balled his right hand into a fist and with a roar brought it down into the creature's bulbous features. Cutter might not have been the size of the ogre, but he had plenty of practice punching people—it was largely what he was best at, as anyone who knew him or of him might have said.

He struck the creature a solid blow, and Fey strength or not, its nose *cracked* beneath his knuckles. The ogre bellowed in pain as blood spurted, and its head bounced off the ground. Even as it came back up, he struck it again, then again, each punch a hammer blow of rage as the image of Matt lying bloody, dying, flashed in Cutter's mind.

His hands ached, his knuckles were bloody and scraped raw, but he did not slow. He continued to pound his fists into the creature until its face was an unrecognizable mess of flesh and blood and bone. Finally, he sat back, heaving in deep, rasping breaths, the air like fire in his lungs.

He thought that the creature would be finished, that it *should* have been finished. Indeed, it lay still, unmoving, its hands flopped uselessly at its sides. At least for a brief time.

In a few seconds, its fingers began to twitch, and driven by whatever fel magic imbued it, the broken, battered features of the creature's face began to shift and reform, like putty being shaped by invisible hands.

"*Uhh*—" the creature began, but it never got to finish the nonword, for Cutter reached down and grabbed hold of its massive head—at least twice as large as his own—one of his hands in its hair, one underneath its chin, then with a growl he gave a savage jerk. There was a *crack* as the creature's neck broke, but Cutter had seen it heal from a dozen axe wounds, any one of which would have been enough to kill a man, just as the pummeling he'd only recently given it should have. So, with those things in mind, he decided not to leave anything to chance.

He gave the creature's neck another savage twist, then another. On the third, its flesh tore, and on the fourth its head came free from its body in a bloody fountain. "Heal that, you bastard," he told the dead, yellow eyes, then he tossed the creature's head away.

Now that the battle was done, all the aches and pains came back, and Cutter grunted as he climbed off the creature, feeling as tired, as exhausted as he could ever remember feeling. He heaved a sigh and turned to where Feledias had gone after the creature in the grass to see his brother moving toward him, sheathing his sword.

"You found it—the creature?"

"Sure, I found it," Feledias said, frowning as he rubbed his hands along his forearms where Cutter could see several thin scratches. "Nasty little bastard, though I'll admit, a touch smaller than this one here which...is he missing his head?"

"Wouldn't say he's missing it. On account of—"

"Yeah, he's dead, I get it," Feledias said, shaking his head. "You have some dark jokes, brother, and all of them with the same punchline."

"And the creature—"

"Well, he won't be performing anymore illusions anytime soon, I can tell you that much."

"Oh?"

"That's right. I asked him to stop. He was reticent at first but...well. I was convincing."

Cutter nodded. "Good," he said with feeling. After all, the image of Matt lying before him dying was not one that would be easily dismissed. It would haunt him for some time, he knew. It was not real but then that made no difference—most of the fears and concerns that haunted men during the night were not real. That gave them no less power. In fact, in some ways, it gave them more. For were they real, a man might put his hands to them, might in that way learn the shape of them and, in doing so, conquer them.

But the shadows of a man's fear had no shape, no substance upon which he might grab hold, and it was that shapelessness which was their greatest danger.

"So..." Feledias said, glancing around the field of grass that seemed to stretch on in every direction, empty save for the two of them. And the bodies, of course. There were always the bodies. "What now?"

Cutter did not know where they were going or how long it would be before something changed, yet he knew the answer to the question just the same.

What now? his brother had asked. And the answer was simple, the same answer it had always been for Cutter's entire life.

Blood.

Blood and more of it.

CHAPTER ELEVEN

Maeve sat in what had, only days before, been Agnes's quarters as several men finished packing up boxes full of the ex-Guildmaster's belongings, items ranging from a portrait Agnes had had commissioned to ledgers and reports. Ledgers and reports that one might have been forgiven for thinking were now Maeve's, considering that she had been so recently inducted—if not formally but in reality—into the position.

Maeve glanced at Tribune Bethesa where the woman sat across from her on the room's other couch, sipping at a steaming cup of tea the Guildmaster's personal servant had brought her moments ago.

Your personal servant, Maeve thought. Some might have been excited by that thought, but Maeve didn't feel excited. She felt sick. The serving woman, Amber, who appeared to be at least as old as Bethesa, had asked Maeve if she wanted anything. Maeve had declined, confident that anything even as substantial as tea that she managed to get down would, just then, have come back up with undue haste. When she'd declined, the old serving woman had smiled pleasantly and openly, ensuring Maeve that she was on hand should she need anything.

Maeve, though, was dating an illusionist—and wasn't that a thing?—and so was not so easily fooled. After all, she knew well enough that a smile and a knife cut just as deep as a scowl and a knife and a woman didn't find herself the servant at an assassin's guild by accident. Currently the woman in question was going behind the men packing up Agnes's belongings with a duster, sweeping away the dirt their work revealed. Watching her, Maeve could see the tell-tale bulge of at least one blade beneath her dress.

"And you're quite sure that none of the papers they're taking would be of any interest to me?" Maeve asked the Tribune.

The other two Tribunes had left half an hour ago, but Bethesa had remained, sitting on the edge of the divan opposite Maeve and somehow reminding her of a vulture perched on a limb, waiting for its meal to stop wriggling. It didn't take all that much wondering to figure who the meal was.

Bethesa smiled, giving a casual wave of one age-gnarled hand. "They are of no importance. Records and ledgers, that sort of thing. Quite boring and not worth your consideration."

"As Guildmaster," Maeve said slowly, "shouldn't I be the one to decide that?"

The woman lips widened again. Not a smile, not exactly, only a baring of teeth. "Of course. I apologize for the presumption, Guildmaster," she said, and it was all Maeve could do to keep from squirming at the use of the title. *Her* title. "I only sought to ensure that your induction was as pleasant as possible. It is a difficult job being Guildmaster, and I thought to take at least this small burden off your shoulders. I will, of course, have all of the papers and records brought back here tomorrow."

After you and your people have had a chance to pick through them to see if there is anything that you can use against me or use for your own gain, no doubt, Maeve thought but didn't say. As she watched the old Tribune take a relaxed sip of tea Maeve wondered what the woman would say if she demanded the records be returned this moment. Vultures were scavengers, it was true, as were jackals, but both could be dangerous if cornered, so Maeve decided not to press the point.

Instead, she sat in uncomfortable silence for another ten minutes until, finally, the three men, carrying more boxes, stepped forward, bowing. "Guildmaster," one said, then turned to Bethesa. "We're finished, Tribune."

"And the book?"

The man winced, and Maeve wasn't sure it was her imagination or not that made the man appear nervous. "It...we could not find it, Tribune."

"I see," the woman said, and although her inflection barely changed, Maeve was suddenly possessed of the certainty that Bethesa was angry. Perhaps even furious. "You are quite sure?"

"Yes, Tribune," the man said. "If it were here, we would have found it."

The woman frowned, nodding slowly.

"Is there a problem?" Maeve asked.

The woman turned to her, trying on a smile that didn't quite fit. "It is nothing to concern yourself with, Guildmaster. Only, there is a small matter of a book, a diary that Guildmaster Agnes kept. It is of no consequence to you or your duties, of course, but I had hoped it might shed some light on the dark fate that befell our Guildmaster. Amber here assures me that Agnes kept a rigorous diary."

"A diary," Maeve said.

"Just so." Bethesa sighed, working her way to her feet. "Well, Guildmaster, we have disturbed you long enough. We will now leave you to get acquainted with your quarters and get some much-deserved rest." She nodded to the three men who bowed before moving toward the door, encumbered by the stacked boxes they each carried.

Maeve watched them go, wondering how many secrets, how many bits of information that could have proven vital to her performing her role well and, more importantly, staying alive, had just been carried away right underneath her nose.

Bethesa followed the men, pausing at the door and glancing back. "Oh, Guildmaster, one last thing. If you happen upon a diary—it is a small, brown leather book, I'm told—I would be grateful should you make me aware of it."

The woman tried for casual, attempting to say it in an easily dismissed tone, but Maeve had spoken with plenty of dissemblers in her life—she was dating what was perhaps the world's biggest—and so she heard the concern, the frustration the woman tried to hide.

"This diary, it's important?" Maeve asked, making her tone sound innocent, unassuming. If the woman thought she was a fool she had no intention of disabusing her of that notion. After all, a bumbling buffoon might be controlled, might be tricked, and did not need to be stabbed in the night while she slept.

Or so she hoped.

"I am quite sure it is not," Bethesa said. *Or you at least are quite sure you want me to believe it's not,* Maeve thought.

"I only thought," the Tribune went on, "to give it to those tasked with investigating the Guildmaster's...untimely demise. In the hopes of finding who was responsible." She shrugged. "A long shot, of course, but if you find the diary it would be wise for you to tell me. After all," she said, "we are all very eager to catch whoever is out there killing Guildmasters. None more so, I imagine, than you yourself."

She smiled at that, saying the last as if she was joking, but Maeve did not think the woman meant to make her laugh. Instead, she meant to make her scared. Scared people, after all, made bad decisions, decisions like giving up a diary that held untold numbers of secrets without even looking it over. "I will, of course, let you know should I find anything," Maeve said. "After all, considering that I'm the new Guildmaster, I think it'd be in my own best interests."

"Exactly so," the Tribune said, flashing that vulpine smile again. "Good night, Guildmaster. I hope you sleep well."

I doubt if I'll sleep at all, Maeve thought, but the woman was gone in another moment, closing the door behind her.

Maeve stared at the door for a moment, frowning, then turned to regard the serving woman's back as she continued to clean. Maeve watched her, wondering who she worked for. One of the Tribunes, that much was sure. But then, for all she knew the woman worked for all three.

As if feeling Maeve's regard, the woman—Amber, yes, that was her name—turned and gave her another open, honest smile. Maeve returned the smile—because it was what you did—and a moment later the woman returned to her work.

Maeve continued to watch her. The woman's back was stooped with age, her gray, lusterless hair tied into a bun. She looked like just about the last person anyone would ever be afraid of but then that might well the point. After all, young or old, a person's fingers held a knife much the same. Suddenly, it was all too much, and the anxiety, the panic she'd been pushing down since Balderath had first confronted her and Chall in the street began to overtake her.

"I'd like to be alone, please."

The woman turned to regard her, flashing that guileless smile. "Of course, Guildmaster. I am nearly finished and—"

"*Now,*" Maeve said, shouted really, though she hadn't meant to. It was only that, suddenly, she didn't want to be alone—she *needed* to be.

The old woman recoiled as if Maeve had slapped her. "Forgive me, mistress. If I did something to offend you, that was not my intention." Her voice sounded nervous, her expression looked scared and hurt all at once, and if she was an actor then Maeve thought she was a damned fine one, one with a talent to rival even Chall himself.

"You...you have caused no offense," Maeve assured her, feeling like an ass. Perhaps the woman really was just what she appeared to be—perhaps not. There was no way to know for sure, but Maeve did know that there was also no reason to be rude. If the woman truly was only a servant, then it was bad manners, and if she was an assassin then it was unwise to give her anymore reasons to stab her than necessary. "It...it has only been a trying day, that is all," Maeve said.

"Of course, Guildmaster," the woman said, still sounding hurt as she inclined her head. "I will go, but may I send some food for you? You must be hungry. I could speak to the kitchen and get you something."

"The kitchen staff are still there this late?"

"You are the Guildmaster," the woman said simply, as if that was enough.

"Perhaps...something small," Maeve said.

"Very well, ma'am," the woman said, inclining her head, clearly pleased as Maeve had suspected she would be. "What would you like?"

In truth it made no difference, for as earlier when the Tribune was with her, Maeve didn't trust her stomach to keep anything more than air down just then. Besides which, if there was a more foolish idea than eating food prepared by the cook of a guild of assassins, many of which would have been more than happy to kill—and do quite a bit more than that—to get in her position, then Maeve didn't know it. "Why don't you choose for me," she said.

"Me, Guildmaster?" the woman said, her eyes wide as if Maeve had just asked her to turn into a bird and do a quick fly around the room.

"I trust you," Maeve said. *Just about as far as I could throw you.*

The woman, Amber, beamed at that. "Very well, Guildmaster," she said. "Thank you." And, with that, she was gone, disappearing through the door and closing it behind her.

As she did, Maeve caught sight of two figures standing in the hallway, flanking the door. Two men. She did not know them and yet she recognized them well enough. Body guards. Or, at least, that was what they would claim to be. The thing about watching someone's back, though, was that there was no one better situated to stick a knife in it.

No doubt Tribune Bethesa had seen to sending them, ostensibly to protect her, but Maeve was confident that should the old Tribune order it, those "protectors" would be all too happy to kill their charge themselves.

Maeve sighed, glancing around the Guildmaster's quarters. *Her* quarters. They were nice—far nicer than her rooms at the castle, in fact. Large and ostentatious with seemingly anything a person might want or need. Of course, none of it was real. Not any more real, at least, than the lock on her door. Not safety, not really, only the illusion of it. After all, she suspected that those men outside would be able to force their way in easily enough if they wanted to. In point of fact, it was far more likely that they had the key.

She moved to the door leading to the study where she and Agnes had first spoken what felt like a lifetime ago. Before the woman had asked for her help and, by way of thanks, had given Maeve the parting gift of recommending her for the position she herself had deemed precarious enough to prompt her to fake her own death.

Maeve pushed the door open then stood with her hands on her hips, frowning around the room, promising herself that should she see Agnes again, she would make sure to let the woman know—in no uncertain terms—how she felt about being duped in such a way. Not that such a thing was likely. After all, only a fool would fake their own death only to stick around in the same city waiting to be spotted. And whatever else she was, Agnes was no fool.

Besides, the truth was that Maeve didn't *feel* vengeful. Instead, she felt scared. And despite the fact that she was in a guild that housed hundreds—and hundreds more on top of that in the healer's academy above her head—Maeve felt very, very alone.

She found herself thinking of Chall, then. Wondering what he was doing, where he was. She missed him—she would never have thought she could miss someone as much, would never have thought she could *love* someone so much, at least not since she'd lost her family when the Skaalden had invaded Daltenia. But she'd been wrong.

She missed him, but she knew that she had to be so very careful now. They would be watching her, marking her every step, her every word, looking for the chink in her armor. And they would mark, also, every person she spent time with, and so Maeve resisted the almost unbearable urge to go running out of the Guild and to Chall, for they would see it, would find in her love for him a weakness, a flaw that might be exploited.

Instead, she sighed, walking around the desk and sitting where Agnes had sat when first asking for her help. She sat and worried and wondered how often Agnes had done the same.

"Oh, Chall," she said, "how I miss you."

Her only consolation was that however much danger she was in—and she figured that if there was a contest she was pretty much guaranteed first prize—at least the others were safe.

Not Bernard, perhaps, but then the man knew how to take care of himself and then some.

But Priest and Matt were safe in the castle.

Chall was safe.

CHAPTER TWELVE

Chall had been scared before.

In fact, sometimes, it seemed that he could not remember a time in his life when he hadn't been.

Traveling with the Crimson Prince as he led their kingdom in a war against the Fey—creatures out of nightmare, monsters that belonged in storybooks but were living for all that—pretty much guaranteed it.

But the fear he felt now was greater than all of those.

He was not anxious or worried. He was not concerned.

He was bat-shit terrified.

He would have thought, had someone asked him a week prior, that he had pretty well plumbed the depths of terror, that he had reached heights of fear and shit-yourself-horror as great as any man ever had or ever could.

He would have been surprised, then, to find that he was wrong. Would have been even *more* surprised to find that the fear he now felt, greater than all the others by such an order of magnitude as to make them of no consequence, was not fear for himself. A shock, that, considering that he had largely made a life of being just about as selfish as anybody could be.

But he was not afraid for himself, not this time.

This time, he was afraid for another. And not just *any* other.

Maeve.

Maeve who was better than he deserved. Maeve who, so far as he could see, was perfect, excepting the fact that, for reasons unbeknownst to him and, likely, unbeknownst to her as well, had chosen to spend her time with him. Once he would have suspected it was due to his charm or looks, but what looks he'd once had were long gone, and experience had taught him that he was a damned sight more charming a hundred pounds ago.

Not that any of that really mattered.

He loved her, that was it. And despite every single motivation to the contrary, she loved him as well. It had taken them a lifetime to find each other and never mind that they'd spent much of it side by side. They'd been forced to walk across fields of the dead, to wade through rivers of blood to make it here, but that love made all of it worth it.

She made it worth it. For he had finally found her, found her the way a drunk, stumbling into his house, might eventually find a candle and a flint to light it—not because he deserved to find it but because sometimes people were simply lucky.

Finally, he'd found her. And now, he'd lost her again.

She was gone.

It was a fact he'd kept coming back to since returning from Lady Valencia's with Priest and Matt. The two were sleeping now, or at least he hoped they were, for he knew Matt had been struggling in that regard. He hoped that they did not lie awake as he did, haunted by what-ifs and might-have-beens. He'd had her. Finally, he'd had her.

And now she was gone.

He and the others had returned hours ago, each of them retiring to their rooms, Matt just about as reluctant as anyone could be, and Chall all but running, sure and surer by the moment that Maeve would be there, waiting on him. That she would ask him what had taken him so long, where he'd been.

She hadn't been waiting on him though. All that had been there had been the bed, full of shadows in the dark and as cold as a coffin sat long in the grave. He'd been tempted to go out in the city and look for her then—and dozens of times in the hours since. Never mind that she'd told him not to. Let her be mad, he'd thought, just so long as she was alive to do it.

In the end, though, he had continued to lie on the bed, waiting. Not because he wanted to but because she'd told him to trust her, and he did. Fire and salt he did. *Please come back to me, Maeve,* he thought as he lay in the dark room, watching the shadows shift and sway along the wall as the moon made its slow journey across the sky toward morning.

Time dragged on, dripping by like rain drops falling from a dew-laden limb. He lay there not sleeping and not trying to, for he had given up on that some hours ago, had given up on it the moment he had opened the door and stared out into an empty room.

He was awake. Painfully, terribly awake, and so, when that same door at which he'd stood slowly began to ease open with a slight creak that would have been too low to wake a man, he heard it. Then he heard a step, and in that single step he knew it was not Maeve.

About a million things went through Chall's mind in a moment, flashing by so fast that he wasn't able to grab most of them, wasn't able even really to see them. He saw a few though. Caught a few.

He caught terror—that was repeated enough that he didn't need to try very hard. But there were others too. Most rambling, babbling, incoherent nonsense, but some not. Some thoughts, some emotions, as clear, as impossible to mistake as a mace to the head. Thoughts like—*I'm screwed. I'm dead. I'd rather be screwed than dead, haha.*

Emotions like terror and a child's desire to throw the blankets over his head, the blankets that all children knew were a barrier even the vilest of monsters could not cross. Emotions like confusion at why the monsters would come at all. Emotions like a far greater terror when he realized that they would come because they were finished with Maeve and now it was his turn.

And that brought a different feeling, one he had not expected.

Anger.

Anger that was greater even than his fear for himself. They had done whatever they had done to her, to Maeve, and now they had come for him.

He let out a roar, leaping out of the bed and charging toward the interloper. "*Where is she, you son of a bitch? What have you done with her?*" he shouted.

Or, at least, he meant to. While he *was* angry—angrier than he could ever remember feeling, in fact—he was also still an over-aged, overweight mage with far more practice crawling into bed than leaping out of it. His foot caught on the coverlet, turning his furious, charging leap into a furious, tumbling fall.

A tumbling fall that took him on a cursing, hissing, path toward the shadowed figure just inside the door and deposited him, quite unceremoniously, in a moaning, groaning heap at the figure's feet.

"*I'll...kill you,*" he told the figure looming over him, a shadow among shadows.

Chall wasn't sure what he expected—a knife to the throat was pretty close—but out of all the frightening scenarios that had rushed headlong through his panicked thoughts, what came was not what he had expected.

"Want me to help you up first, maybe you get a stretch in?" the figure asked, and as strange as the question was, stranger still was that it asked it in a voice Chall recognized.

Chall thought that he must be mistaken, that his fear had confused him or, perhaps, that maybe he had fallen asleep after all without realizing it and was now dreaming. For as the figure knelt close enough that he could make out his features, Chall saw that, indeed, his ears had not fooled him. Unless, that was, they'd gotten with his eyes and had a meeting, all decided to get together and play a trick, for the person knelt before him, a small grin on his face like was trying to hold in laughter and doing a piss-poor job of it, was none other than Ned, the carriage driver.

"*You,*" he hissed.

"Me," Ned agreed.

"Bastard."

"Sure," the carriage driver agreed. "Now—"

"You came here to kill me," Chall said.

It wasn't a question, not really, but Ned answered anyway, his eyes going wide. "Kill you?" he said as if Chall had just suggested that he grow wings and fly away. "Of course not. I came here to ask for your help. That'd be a whole lot harder if you were dead, don't you think?"

"After what you did to Matt, what you did at Lady Valencia's, I should kill you."

"Be a lot easier if you were standing," Ned said, offering his hand.

Chall stared at that offered hand like it was a serpent. And indeed he thought it probably was. The serpent's fangs weren't bared, not yet, but they might be brought out easily enough. Of that much, at least, he was certain, for he had seen those fangs at Lady Valencia's, when Ned had struck Matt, and the blood that Matt said had covered the carriage driver's shirt had been more.

But, on the other hand, he'd seen the man fight, had seen him keep up with Priest, at least briefly, a feat that was far beyond anything Chall could manage. Add in the fact that he was currently lying flat on his back, his legs tangled up in a blanket that suddenly seemed about half a dozen times bigger than any blanket should be, and Chall figured he didn't have bad odds of taking Ned in a fight. Mostly because he didn't have any odds at all.

He took the hand.

The moment he had his feet underneath him, Chall jerked his hand away. "Maybe I wouldn't be much help dead," he snapped, "but just so long as I'm alive, I can give a shout and there are several guards within earshot that'd come running." He did his best to sound confident, for while his words were true ones, what he didn't say was that the guards were at the entrance to the hall and the room in which they currently stood was at the far end. That had been Chall's idea as he'd thought to get some privacy for Maeve and himself—which just went to prove that he wasn't just fat but a fool as well.

Ned gave him a small smile, one that made it obvious to Chall that he knew as well as him that, should the carriage driver decide to attack, Chall would be long dead before the guards arrived. "So," Chall said, doing his best to sound confident, "you tell me, Ned, what's to keep me from giving those guards a shout, eh? Seems to me they wouldn't much care for the idea of you skulking around the castle uninvited."

"Never considered myself much of a skulker," the man said, giving a smile to show that he was joking.

Chall, though, was in no mood for jokes. He only stared at the man and, after a moment, the carriage driver sighed.

"You're upset," Ned said.

"Picked up on that did you?" Chall snapped.

"Okay, look maybe I should have knocked, I'll grant you that," the carriage driver said, "but, I thought, you know, given our last encounter, that it might be better—"

"To sneak in like an assassin?" Chall said. "Anyway, I don't give two shits about that. It isn't you sneaking in that's the problem and you know it." Not *quite* true as Chall's heart was hammering in his chest like a drum, and he was covered in the cold sweat of fear, but then he didn't think the carriage driver needed to know that.

Ned winced. "Guess you mean back at Lady Valencia's."

"I guess maybe I do," Chall said, frowning.

Ned nodded, sighing again. "Look, I'm sorry about…you know, about that. I ain't proud of it."

"You're not proud of it," Chall repeated.

"Well, I mean, no," Ned said. "It's just, you know, these things happen."

"These things happen," Chall repeated, shocked that the man could be so callous.

"Look, if it helps I did it for a good cause. It ain't an exaggeration to say that it's a matter of life and death. "

"I'll say," Chall growled, getting angry now as he watched the man almost seem to make a joke of his crimes.

"Okay, easy fella," Ned said, holding up his hands. "It seems to me you're makin' a bit of a bigger deal of things than you ought to."

"A bigger deal of it?" Chall demanded. "Fire and salt you can't be serious. Ned you *killed* those people!"

"I mean it isn't as if—" Ned paused, his eyes going wide. "Wait, what? What people?"

"Oh, don't play the fool," Chall said. "You know damned well who I mean—the doorman back at Lady Valencia's to start, not to mention several other servants and guards. Tell me, Ned, did the poor bastards even see it coming?"

"Look, Chall, you got it all wrong," the carriage driver said. "This whole time, I thought you meant hitting the king and usin' the Art the way I done."

"Wait…are you trying to say you didn't kill them?"

"Of course I didn't kill them," Ned said. "Stones and starlight, Chall, what do you think I am, a monster?"

The man seemed not just shocked but offended. He sounded, in short, innocent. But then Chall had met plenty of accomplished liars in his time and none more so than himself, so he knew that just because a thing *sounded* true didn't mean that it was.

"We *saw* you, Ned," he said. "Or, at least, Matt and Vorrun did."

"Vorrun the guardsman, is he?" Ned asked, nodding slowly and now, at least, he did look ashamed. "Is he...well? How's he doing?"

"Vorrun's fine," Chall said. "It's Matt who's sporting the black eye, but even he's far better off than Lady Valencia's servant and those others."

"I didn't do that, Chall," Ned said again. "As for the guardsman, I only ask as...well. Sometimes, when I use the Art on people it can...cause some issues."

"Issues?" Chall asked, frowning.

"Nothing permanent," Ned said, waving a hand. "Anyway, there's no time for that. I need you to understand, Chall, that the servant was already dead when I got there. So were the others. I won't say I haven't hurt people, haven't killed 'em when I thought it was necessary—we both know that'd be a lie—but I only done it when I thought it needed doin'. No different than the way a fella'll put down a dog that's learned to bite, one that's beyond savin'. He don't take no pleasure in it, but that don't make it any less necessary."

"And you think you're the best person to determine if the dog is beyond saving?"

"I did once. I don't anymore. All I'm tryin' to do is fix my own mistakes, to figure out who's tryin' to use the Wolves for their own purposes and make 'em stop."

"And you think you can do that all on your own?"

"No, I don't," Ned said. "That's why I'm here."

Chall frowned, considering that. "And Lady Valencia? You're saying that you didn't lie about her being part of creating the Wolves?"

Ned winced. "Right...about that, well, the thing is—"

"You lied."

Ned cleared his throat. "Yeah. I lied. I lied because I didn't think it mattered and because, years ago, I promised a friend that I would protect her identity. What about you, Chall? Would you lie to protect a friend?"

Chall found himself thinking of Maeve, of the fact that she was still missing. He thought he'd do more than lie to see her safe again. A damned lot more. He frowned. "That doesn't make it right," he said.

"No," Ned agreed. "No, it don't. Now, will you help me or not?"

Chall considered that, watching the man. He seemed innocent, but Chall couldn't tell. He wished Maeve were here. Chall might have been one of the Known Land's most accomplished liars, but if there was someone better able to see through bullshit than Maeve he'd never met them. After all, she saw through his easily enough.

But Maeve wasn't there. It was only him. Him and the man standing before him, not looking like a criminal at all but looking worried. Looking desperate. Looking, also, like a man who hadn't bathed in days, covered in dirt and blood and who knew what else. Smelling like it too, come to that.

Chall watched him, thinking. He'd always been the cynic of their group. Priest had had his faith, Maeve her cleverness, even the prince had had his axe, a way of dealing with any issues that arose that trumped any other coping mechanism Chall had ever seen. He, meanwhile, had always had his sarcasm. Sarcasm that had served him both as a shield to protect him against the worst life had to offer and as a sword to wield against it.

But the prince was gone, Maeve too. And Priest had little faith to spare. It was up to him, then. He studied the carriage driver standing before him, looking about as innocent as a big ball of innocent rolled in innocent and served on an innocent dish.

"I know that I'm askin' you to trust me, and I know that ain't easy," Ned said. "But all I can tell you is that I don't mean you and yours harm. Far from it. In fact, I mean to help in any way I can. You think I want to be out gallivantin' around the city like a man twenty years younger when Emmy's at home waiting on me? That what you think? What about you, Chall? You and the Lady Maeve, seems like you two have a bit of somethin' going on. Would you leave her waitin' on you to go off and risk your life dealin' with the worst of the worst of the city? Folks so filthy they can make dirt dirtier like that Catham bastard?"

"No, no I wouldn't," he said. "But...what's this about Catham?" he went on, angry now, remembering well the way the man had ordered a whole tavern room of people to kill him. "I wouldn't spend any time at all with that bastard—or at least no more than the time it would take to stick a knife in him." Not that he carried a knife, but then he knew a woman who had plenty to spare.

"Might be you'll get your chance," the carriage driver said grimly.

Chall raised an eyebrow at that. "What are you talking about?"

"I told you," Ned said, "I need your help. Yours and Priest's."

Chall snorted. "Look, it's one thing to expect to convince me to come with you—it's another to try to convince Priest. There was a time when it wasn't like that, a time when he believed in the goodness of people, trusted in it. But whatever trust he had, it's long gone now. Now, if he trusts in anything then he hides it well."

"And what about you?" the man asked, watching him. "What do you trust in?"

Chall considered the question carefully. There had been a time, not so very long ago, in truth, when he hadn't trusted anyone or anything, or at least had pretended not to, an illusion he'd cast even over himself. And he had thought that it was a strength. He knew, now, that that was foolish. It took courage to trust. And he *did* trust. He trusted Prince Bernard and Maeve. He trusted Matt and Priest. And, despite all the reasons he had not to, despite everything, he found that there was one simple fact looming before him, one he could not deny.

He trusted Ned.

He sighed heavily. "You better not be screwing me, Ned."

The carriage driver gave him a small smile. "Not without dinner first, anyway."

Chall snorted. A hard bastard not to like but then he'd been told much the same about himself years ago and he had been more than a bit of a bastard, that was certain. "What do you need me to do?"

"Not just you," Ned said. "We need Priest, too."

"I told you, I don't think that's going to happen. Maybe you didn't pick up on it the last time he attacked you, but Priest isn't exactly a fan of yours."

Ned considered that then shook his head. "We need him," he said simply. "Unless, that is, you have another ex-criminal stashed somewhere, one that knows that bastard, Catham, and all the other criminals running around the city."

I know more than I'd like already, Chall thought. He sighed. "Suppose not," he said.

"Alright then, let's go and fetch your buddy."

Chall winced. "I think...probably it would be wise if I did the fetching myself."

"Listen," Ned said, his usual amiable demeanor gone, "I've got a wife at home who I haven't seen in three days now. A wife who, I suspect based on our last conversation, has begun to think that I'm stepping on out her which would be the stupidest thing I've ever done and that with no small competition. A wife I'd get back to just as soon as I'm able and never mind that I'm confident I'm in for a good tongue lashin' when I do. So if you think I give a damn about pissin' off your friend, let me be clear—I don't."

"Maybe not," Chall said, "but getting in a fight with Priest isn't going to speed you along to your wife any faster. I just need an hour, no more than that. I'll convince him to help."

"And if you can't?"

"I'll convince him," Chall repeated, trying for more certainty than he felt.

Based on the dubious expression on the carriage driver's face, though, the man was far from fooled. "An hour," he said. "No more. I got a problem at home, one that's just gonna get bigger the longer I wait before I tend to it, and I don't mean to waste anymore time than necessary. I'd like to go forward with you and Priest, but I'll do it alone if I have to."

"Just tell me where to meet you," Chall said. "I'll get him there."

"Sure," the man said, clearly doubtful. "And when you do—*if* you do—do I need to be ready to defend myself?"

"The way the world is, I'd say a man ought to always be ready to defend himself."

Ned watched him for several seconds then gave a single nod. "There's a dead-end alley off Crafter's Row on the south side of the city. Meet me there." With that he turned and started back toward the door, pausing when Chall spoke.

"Ned?"

"Yeah?"

"I believe you. And I think Priest will too."

"Right."

"But...well. Probably you ought to stretch—just in case."

The man gave him a small smile. "Right. See you in an hour."

"In an hour."

With that, Ned turned and vanished through the doorway as silently as a ghost, so quickly, so quietly that Chall could have almost believed he'd imagined him. And, in truth, he almost wished he had, for while he had pretended confidence to the carriage driver, the truth was that he wasn't looking forward to his conversation with Priest.

Not even a little bit.

But he'd heard someone say, once, that if a man had a tough job ahead of him the only thing to be done was to get started as quickly as he could and get it over with. Bullshit, of course. After all there were plenty of other things to do. Things like avoidance and procrastination, things like a complete abdication of responsibility. Chall ought to know—they were strategies he'd been employing his entire life. But he didn't think those tricks would work, not this time, so he sighed and started to put on his clothes. If he was going to get murdered by a pissed-off priest he'd just as soon be dressed.

***

Chall wasn't much of a hurrier by nature—much more of a sit-around-and-do-nothinger—but he was well aware of the deadline Ned had given him and so, in less than five minutes, he was out of his room and hurrying through the castle hallways.

He rushed to Priest's quarters, where he'd left the man hours ago, but found them empty. He stopped and asked a servant in the hall about the king's whereabouts—as always, the easiest way to determine *Priest's* whereabouts—and in moments was hurrying toward Matt's quarters.

He reached the hall leading toward the king's rooms in a few minutes.

"Challadius?" one of the guards, who Chall was surprised to see was Vorrun, asked. "Is everything alright?"

"Ask me tomorrow." *Assuming I'm still alive, of course,* he thought. After all, it wasn't like he was about to go jogging through a meadow and rolling around in a bed of daisies with a puppy. He was, instead, going to meet a man who he was still not completely convinced wasn't a traitor and, best case, work with him to try to uncover the members of a conspiracy who had already proven themselves more than willing to kill to achieve their goals.

"Anything I should know about?" Vorrun asked.

Instead of answering directly, Chall chose a different tack. "I'm surprised you're not in bed—been a long night all around, hasn't it?"

The guardsman gave him a small smile, as if he knew well enough what Chall was doing. "I'm trying this new thing—going without sleep."

"Yeah? How's that working out?"

The guardsman raised an eyebrow. "Ask me tomorrow."

"Ah. Hoisted by my own petard."

"And what a petard it is."

Chall sighed. For once, he'd like to have a conversation with someone and feel like he came off the winner. "Is the king asleep?"

"In his rooms, anyway."

Chall frowned, nodding. "And Priest?"

Vorrun inclined his head down the hall, and Chall followed his gaze to the king's door at the end of it where two more guards were positioned on either side. Priest stood beside them. The man stood still, but while Chall couldn't have pointed to anything specific, he got the feeling that the man was worried.

His frown deepening, Chall glanced back at the guardsman. "See you around, Vorrun."

"Not if I see you first."

He was moving then, and the closer he got to Priest the more he became convinced that there was something bothering him. Priest must have heard his approach, for the man turned to regard him. "Chall," he said.

Chall took in the man's haggard-looking face, with sunken, purple circles under his eyes and a gaunt, hollow look to his cheeks. "Priest," he said. "You look like shit."

The man gave him a tired smile. "There's that famous charm."

"I mean it, Priest," Chall said. "Didn't you get any sleep at all?"

"A bit," the man said evasively.

"And why are you up then? Just looking to be miserable, that it?"

Priest opened his mouth to speak but, just then, there was a soft, scared cry from the other side of the door, one that reminded Chall of the way a child might sound when woken from a dream. He glanced at the door then back at Priest who frowned.

"His Majesty has not been sleeping well," the man said.

Chall thought that if the man was in a contest for biggest understatement of the year then he had a good shot at the title, for now that he was listening closely he could hear disturbed moaning coming from Matt's rooms.

"I told the guards to wake me if he had anymore trouble sleeping," Priest explained softly.

Chall winced as he listened to those tortured, scared moans. "What's going on with the lad?"

"I don't know," Priest said. "Matt fights a battle, though who or what he fights against, I cannot say."

"Will he win?"

"Does anybody really win?"

Chall ran a hand through his hair. "Damn but you're a chipper bastard. And...I'm sorry to say I've got some news, news that I don't expect is going to make you any happier."

"What's that?" Priest asked.

Chall glanced at the guards a short distance away then took Priest by the arm. "Why don't we go for a walk?"

The man frowned, glancing back at the door leading to Matt's rooms, beyond which they could even now hear more troubled moaning as the youth continued his restless sleep.

"I'm pretty sure that whatever battle Matt's fighting, it's one we can't help him with. At least, not directly, but there's another way we might help him, might take a bit of his worry away."

"Oh? And how is that?"

"I'd rather not talk about it here," Chall said. "Will you come?"

Priest watched him for a moment and Chall thought he was going to say no, was trying to decide what he would do if he did when Priest finally nodded. Chall didn't bother hiding his sigh of relief before turning and leading them down the hall.

He waited until they were away from the two guards outside Matt's door, until they were well beyond earshot of Vorrun and his second. Then, finally, he paused in the hallway, glancing around to make sure no servant might be nearby to overhear.

"What's going on, Chall?" Priest asked. "What do you want to tell me and why all the secrecy?"

"Thing is, what I'm going to tell you," Chall said, "it might lead some folks to act impulsively, might make them feel the need to wake Matt from whatever little sleep the poor lad's managing, might tempt Commander Malex to rouse a troop of guardsmen and send them on a wild chase through the city, looking to have an execution."

Priest frowned. "Surely you're being a bit dramatic. Why, Commander Malex wouldn't orchestrate such a search except for a traitor to the crown or...why are you looking like that?"

Chall winced. "What would you say if I told you I knew where Ned was?"

"I'd say that we should tell Malex," Priest said, frowning. "That we ought to get him to rouse a troop of guardsmen and start a wild chase through the city, look to have an execution."

Chall gave a nervous laugh. "Never knew you to be such a joker."

"I'm not joking."

"Right," Chall said, clearing his throat. "Look, here's the thing, Priest. Ned—"

"Ned," Priest interrupted. "The same Ned who you told me, only a day ago, was likely a traitor, one who had posed as our friend only to ingratiate himself with us so that he might do more damage. Ned who we know lied about the founding members of the Crimson Wolves, who Matt himself saw fleeing the scene of multiple murders with blood covering his tunic, who physically assaulted Matt before running away. Is that the Ned you mean?"

"That's the one," Chall said, scratching at his chin.

"Good," Priest said. "Just so long as we're clear."

"Right...well...I think maybe I changed my mind."

"You changed your mind."

"Sure, people do, don't they?"

"Changed it about which part?" Priest asked.

"Nothing major," Chall said. "Just, you know, the bit about him being a traitor and being responsible for the dead serving girl."

"I see," Priest said. "Nothing major. And you're sure about this?"

"Well...I wouldn't say *sure,* but I'm pretty confident."

"Why?" Priest asked. "The last time we spoke, you were certain he was a traitor. If now you're thinking he's innocent, what's changed?"

Chall shifted uncomfortably. "He told me he was."

"He told you."

"That's right," he said, feeling suddenly very defensive.

"Ned who also, as it happens, is an empath, a person who—according to you—is able to make a man or woman feel whatever he wants them to feel."

"Look, Priest," Chall said, "I know how it sounds—don't you think I know that? All I can tell you is that I believe him. If that makes me a fool then I'm a fool. But I trust him."

"I don't," Priest said simply.

"I'm not asking you to trust him," Chall said. "I'm asking you to trust me. To have faith."

"Faith." Priest said the word slowly, as if it was poison.

"That's right."

"I seem to recall someone telling me, once, that the only person a man could trust was himself, that faith was a shield that seemed sturdy enough right up until someone, or the world, took a swing at it."

"Sounds like a pretentious asshole," Chall said.

"It was you."

"Well, there you go," Chall said, trying a smile, one the other man did not return. He heaved a sigh. "Look, Priest, I know sometimes I've been a bit of a cynic..." He paused as the man raised an eyebrow at him. "Fine, a huge cynic. The type of fella that, when he felt rain on his head, thought it just as likely it was piss. The type of guy that figures as soon as he sticks his head out of the hole he's crawled in—usually a hole made of ale and desperation—there'll be someone or something to give it a good kick."

"And now you've changed your mind about that?"

Chall considered that for a few moments then shrugged. "Not really. But what I will tell you is this, Priest—some days it rains and some days it shines, a man won't never know until he sticks his head out. Maybe, if he stays in that hole, nothing bad will happen to him. But then nothing good will happen either. Life will just go on being a whole lot of nothing, and that *is* bad."

"And if he sticks his head out, this man, and gets stomped on?"

"Well, shit, then I guess he, like so many of us, will end up with a black eye. At least he won't be a coward."

Priest watched him for several seconds, and it was all Chall could do to keep from squirming beneath the man's gaze. "Anyway, how do you know where he is?"

"Because he told me."

"You said he told you he was innocent, too. Did he send a letter?"

"Not...exactly. He was here. In my rooms."

"In your rooms?" Priest demanded. "And you're just now saying so? Damnit, Chall, we need to—"

"To what, Priest?" Chall asked. "Send the guards, execute him? Look, if the man wanted me dead, I'd be dead. It's as simple as that. Ned says he has a lead on the Crimson Wolves, a plan, and if you ask me we should listen to him. Or is it that you've got so many ideas about how to get to the bottom of all this shit that you don't need help? That it?"

Priest frowned. "You know I don't."

"Good, because he said he needs our help and I, at least, mean to give it to him. Now, will you go? Or do you want to stick your head back in that hole of yours?"

Priest considered that for several seconds. "Okay, Chall, I will go with you, will meet him. But if it turns out that he *is* a traitor—"

"If it turns out he is a traitor, I'll deal with him myself," Chall said. But then he thought that was a lie. After all, if the man *was* a traitor then it was far more likely that, when this seemingly eternal night finally ended and morning came, he—and Priest along with him—would be dead.

CHAPTER THIRTEEN

The sun was just beginning to creep over the horizon, casting pale, cold light onto the world when Chall and Priest reached the street that Ned had told him about. The alley was deserted, likely the reason why the carriage driver had chosen it in the first place. It wasn't just that no one was around—though that was true. It was more, to Chall, that the alley seemed like the sort of place where no one had *been* around, not for a long time.

He frowned, looking around him at the empty alleyway, at the dark, wooden facades of the buildings flanking it on either side, thinking that, if there was a place in all the world built for a man to be assassinated then surely this had to be it. The cold, gray morning light did not banish the shadows—instead it gave them shape.

He frowned over at Priest who stood beside him. The man returned his stare, saying nothing. And that was good, at least. But then he didn't need to tell Chall what he thought of the situation he'd gotten them in, for Chall thought he could see the man's opinion clearly enough in his gaze.

"Well," he told the man, "the good news is it can't get much worse."

Priest raised an eyebrow at that, still not speaking and still not needing to. After all, Chall figured a knife in the back—or a whole lot of knives in the front, as the case may be—might well be worse.

He sighed. "Come on—according to Ned it's just down here."

As they continued down the shadowed alleyway, Chall found his gaze traveling over the rooftops of the buildings surrounding them, rooftops where he half-expected to see a crossbowman crouched, his weapon trained on them.

Not that he would have been likely to see such a man, anyway. The shadows, as always, seemed reluctant to give way to morning, reluctant to release the world from their grip. Some lay draped across the rooftops, others clung to the eaves. One of those shadows might, for all Chall knew, be an assassin eager for their blood. For all he knew, they all were.

It was a long walk, one of the longest of his life, but finally they reached the end of the alleyway. They stood regarding the dilapidated structure in front of them. Chall found it difficult to think of it as a *home* because for it to be considered that he thought that someone would have been willing to live in it, and to Chall anyone daring to step foot in the building didn't care all that much about living. In fact, he was certain even the homeless of Daltenia would prefer sleeping on the street than in the half-fallen in building. After all, half-collapsed building could become all-collapsed far too quickly.

"You're sure this is the place?" Priest asked.

"I'm not sure it qualifies as a 'place' at all so much as a bad day waiting to happen," Chall said. "Still, this is where Ned said to meet him."

They continued to stand there, studying the crooked home, the walls angled as if they might collapse at any moment. It was another several seconds until either of them spoke. Priest scratched his chin. "It's dark," he said.

"Darkest thing I ever saw," Chall said, staring at the unlit building.

"And you're sure that Ned doesn't, you know, want to kill us?"

"Less and less by the second."

Priest grunted. "I see. Well..." He paused, turning to regard Chall, a grin on his face. "After you?"

Chall sighed. "Just know if I get killed, I'm haunting your ass—that's a fact."

"I'll be glad of the company."

The man tried for a casual tone but he didn't quite make it. Chall stared at him, thinking that while those words seemed innocuous enough, he thought there was something buried in them. A plea for help, maybe. But whatever was going on with Priest would have to keep—the dangers of the day were more than enough to see them dead.

He gave another sigh then turned and started across the street toward the small house. He didn't turn to see if Priest was following, and it was all he could do to keep from celebrating when he finally heard the man's footsteps behind him.

He reached the door and Priest came up to stand at his side a moment later. Chall glanced at the man, raising his eyebrow, and Priest gave a small shrug as if to say he had nothing better going on.

"Reckon we should knock?" Chall asked, his gaze traveling up the crooked doorframe, along the door that hung askew, looking like a harsh word would break it off.

"If you're going to knock, I'd do it softly."

Chall nodded again, then he raised his fist and gave the door a soft knock.

"*Chall?*" a voice said from beyond the door, and despite the fact that it was little more than a rasping whisper Chall recognized it as belonging to the carriage driver. "*That you?*"

"Unfortunately," Chall answered.

The door didn't open so much as its pronounced lean became slightly more pronounced, its top half pulling away from the frame, while the bottom half remained stubbornly where it was. A shadowed face appeared in the opening and, as its owner leaned out a bit farther, Chall saw that it was indeed the carriage driver.

"You came," Ned said, sounding more than a little surprised, as if he'd thought that Chall would betray him and send the guard instead of coming. Which Chall supposed was fair considering that he had given that exact solution more than a bit of thought.

"Well," Chall said at the carriage driver, "are you going to invite us in or what?" He craned his neck, peering past Ned and into the dark room beyond. "Assuming it's big enough to fit more than just you."

"Oh, I'm pretty sure it's good for more than just me," the carriage driver said. "Come on in."

212

The man stepped to the side of the door, gesturing inside. Chall glanced at Priest who raised an eyebrow at him, making it his decision. Which meant that, should they end up impaled on a sword or with their throats cut in the next five minutes there would be no one to blame but Chall himself.

"Not planning on killing us, are you?" Chall asked.

The carriage driver gave a small smile. "Not today anyway. What about you?" he asked, his gaze traveling to Priest.

Chall followed it, regarding the man, probably just as unclear on that point as Ned himself, and he waited for what Priest would do, thinking it even odds he'd attack the man outright.

Indeed, the expression on the man's face was not the sort a man gave to his favorite niece or friend or anyone else he might not be planning on imminently sticking a blade in. Chall tensed, preparing to throw himself in between the men—as good a method of suicide as any—but to his relief Priest did not attack.

"Not yet," Priest said, watching Ned, "but I like to keep my options open."

"Sounds like words my wife might speak—though given what I've been up to lately I figure the first thing she's likely to do when she sees me isn't going to require a whole lot of talk at all. You decide to kill me," he went on, regarding Priest, "then you'll likely have to fight her for the pleasure."

"Why don't you tell us why you asked for us?" Priest asked.

It wasn't exactly a letter of safe conduct, but Chall figured it was probably about as close as they were going to get. And based on the nod the carriage driver gave Priest he thought the man knew it. "Come on in, then," he said. "Let's see if we can all go on unstabbed a bit longer, eh?"

Priest gave Chall another look, leaving it to him. The bastard. Chall heaved yet another sigh then stepped through the shadow-darkened doorway.

The inside of the home was just about what Chall had imagined it would be. A small table sat in the corner, two chairs beside it, though judging by the sorry state of them Chall thought someone would have to be awfully brave or hate their life an awful lot to risk sitting in one.

The room was not large—big enough to accommodate them, sure, but Chall didn't think there was any chance they'd be doing stretches anytime soon. A closed door that he figured must have led to the home's single bedroom stood at the back, and Chall frowned at it. The door was fine just so long as it remained closed, just so long as it didn't open and out came rushing a bunch of men and women looking for their blood.

"Looking for the assassins lying in wait, that it?" Ned asked.

Chall blinked, turning to frown at the man. "Of course not," he said, though the truth was he'd been doing pretty much exactly that. "Look, Ned," he went on, letting his gaze travel over the room—it didn't take long. "Your new home, it's uh...well. It's still standing. Mostly."

"Hold on," Ned said, "you're thinkin' I live here, that it?"

"I wouldn't say 'live' exactly," Chall countered.

The carriage driver snorted. "I don't stay here. I still live in the same house you know, along with Em. At least, I think I do..." He frowned. "Suppose I wouldn't be all that surprised if my wife had decided different and thrown all my stuff out." He got a hopeful expression then, raising his head to regard them. "Hey, has either of you talked to Emille?"

"I haven't," Chall said.

"No," Priest said. "Now, will you stop wasting time and tell us why we're here?"

Ned grunted, glancing at Chall. "Your friend ain't much for the pleasantries, is he?"

Chall frowned, for there had been a time, not so very long ago, when he'd thought Priest full of little else. "Not particularly."

Ned nodded. "Right," he said. "Well, to answer your first question," he went on, looking at Priest, "I asked you to come here because I need your help. There's a lot that need's doin', more than I can handle by myself."

"More servants to murder?" Priest asked, his voice like the metallic *snick* of a blade being loosed in its scabbard.

Ned sighed, clearly frustrated, and gave a shake of his head. "I didn't do that. I ain't gonna stand here and pretend that these hands are clean, but I promise you that whatever blood they got on 'em, it ain't from innocent servants just trying to make a bit of coin."

"And the king?" Priest said. "Was it someone else that attacked him?"

"Don't know that I'd go so far as to say I attacked him," Ned said.

"What would you call it?" Chall said. "A friendly pat on the eye?"

The carriage driver winced. "I'm sorry about that, I am. Just as I'm sorry for that guardsman, the one I had to use the Art on. But you gotta understand, I was only lookin' out for the lad."

"Sure," Priest said. "I always hit people I'm trying to look after."

"Wasn't about hurting him—it was about stopping him."

"From catching you," Priest said.

"From trying to," the carriage driver countered. "Look, since we last spoke I've been a bit busy and—"

"I'll say," Chall said.

The man frowned. "As I was saying, I've been busy. Haven't slept in...well, truth is I don't remember. Too long. Sleep...it helps. The longer a man stays awake, the bigger the shadows seem to get."

"Shadows like Lady Valencia?" Chall said. "The noblewoman who, along with you and this Robert Palden, formed the Crimson Wolves? The noblewoman who you were trying to kill?"

"I wasn't trying to kill her, damn you," Ned said. "Did you see a body?"

"Saw several, in fact," Priest said.

"I mean did you see *her* body?"

"Fine, you kidnapped her then."

"To what purpose?" Ned demanded. "If what you're saying is true, if I am behind all this and I went after Val to, what? Shut her up? Then why would I kidnap her? Why not just kill her outright? I'm telling you, I wasn't there to hurt Val."

"And we're just supposed to believe you?" Priest asked.

"Sure would speed things along if you did."

Priest frowned. "This isn't the time to be flippant."

"That so?" Ned said. "Seems to me that if a man can't be flippant when he's getting ready to be executed when can he be? That is what you're thinking about doing, right?" he went on, eyeing Priest.

Chall grunted. "You don't know Priest at all, Ned. He isn't the type of person that attacks folks out of hand."

"Maybe he wasn't," Ned said, his eyes never leaving Priest's. "But then that's the thing about bein' an empath. Folks think it's just about me bein' able to make folks feel how I want 'em to. Truth is that ain't even the biggest part. Biggest part is knowin' how folks feel," he said. "Being able to see their emotions, their feelings writ on their face like it's in a script only you can read. And that one there, on your friend's face, is all too clear. He wants me dead—wants to do it himself, in fact."

Chall snorted. "That's ridiculous." He turned to his friend. "Tell him, Priest." The man said nothing, though, only watched Ned, and Chall frowned, realizing two things in that moment. First was that, somehow, Ned was right—now that he was looking closer at his friend, he could see that the man was shaking, his body trembling with the need or, perhaps, the *desire* to attack Ned. The second was upon seeing that, a realization of just how bad it was with his friend, far worse even than he had thought, and he had thought it pretty bad.

"Tell us, Ned," he said quickly. "If you weren't there to kidnap or harm Lady Valencia, why did you go to her manse at all?"

Ned winced. "I...I can't tell you that."

Chall blinked. "You can't tell us?" he asked.

The carriage driver scratched his head, looking frustrated. "It isn't...the reason, it ain't mine to tell, that's all."

"You're going to have to do better than that," Priest said, and Chall could see in the man's eyes, could hear in his voice that he was close. Close to doing something from which he could not come back. Something from which he could not be redeemed.

"Priest, don't—" Chall began.

"Answer and answer quickly," Priest said, reminding Chall of a lion kneeling and digging its feet into the earth as it prepared to pounce. "Why did you go to Lady Valencia's manor, why did you break in?"

"I can't tell you that," Ned said, his voice full of regret and sadness but, underneath both, Chall heard determination, too. "I can only tell you that I'm not against you, any of you. That all I'm trying to do is figure out what's going on in the city, to help."

"I don't believe you," Priest said, and Chall jumped at the metallic *snick* as the man drew a knife from where it had been hidden underneath his tunic. "And you don't seem all that interested in trying to make me."

"I *am* trying to make you, damnit," Ned said.

"Try harder," Priest said, moving the hand holding the knife so that it hung at his side. "Tell me. Why did you go to Lady Valencia's if not to kill her or kidnap her? If not to keep her silent?"

There was the sound of a door creaking open. "He went because I asked him to."

Chall and the others turned to the door at the back of the room but despite Chall's earlier fears about hidden assassins, the person who stood in the open doorway brandished no weapon and, unless the Assassin's Guild's recruiters had gotten desperate indeed, was no trained killer. The woman was in her sixties, if Chall had to guess.

Perhaps it was something about her bearing, but Chall thought he knew at once who this was, who this *must* be. It was something, he thought, in the way she managed to loom and never mind that she stood a good foot shorter than him.

Priest, though, apparently didn't catch on. "Who are you?" he said, sounding confused and suspicious all at once.

"Well you ought to know, shouldn't you?" the woman countered, arching a gray eyebrow. "After all, it was my house you went traipsing through—uninvited, I might add."

Priest frowned. "I don't...that is..."

"Lady Valencia," Chall interrupted, bowing low. "It is a pleasure to meet you."

The old woman's gaze slowly traveled from Priest to Chall and whatever physical weakness she had, the woman's eyes and, he thought, the mind behind those eyes, seemed sharp enough to cut. "Is that what this is?" she asked. "A pleasure? I suppose it's getting harder to recognize in my old age. Anyway," she went on, "is someone going to offer to escort an old lady to her chair or not?"

Chall glanced at Ned, saw that the man had a frown on his face, then he turned to regard Priest who looked just at least as stunned as he felt. The woman arched an eyebrow at him in a way that somehow reminded Chall of every tutor he'd ever displeased. He found himself moving forward almost as if dragged by some unseen force, offering his arm. The woman gave a small smile, as if she knew well the impact her words had had on him, then she allowed him to lead her to the table and two chairs he'd marked earlier.

"Forgive me, lady," Chall said, "but these chairs...they seem very old...I do not know if they will hold your weight."

"Just because something is very old, young man, does not mean that is without use. Besides," she said, pausing as she sat down on the chair with a relieved sigh, "at my age, such things are worth the risk."

Chall didn't know what to do, so he gave a confused smile, turning to Ned. "But...if Lady Valencia was here, why didn't you just say so? Fire and salt, man, would you rather have fought Priest?"

"It's got nothing to do with what I would have rather done," Ned said.

"Then why?"

"Because I asked him not to," Lady Valencia said as if it were the most obvious thing in the world. "And because he loves me."

Chall blinked, feeling like someone had taken hold of his head and given him a good spin the way a child might a wooden top.

Some of his thoughts must have been clear on his expression, for the woman let out a soft laugh. "Oh my, but I think I've nearly given this one a heart attack. I would not have expected Challadius the Charmer, of all people, to be so easily scandalized."

"I don't...that is, I'm not..." Chall cleared his throat. "But...Ned, Emille—"

"Can rest assured that her husband's virtue, such as it is, remains unspoiled," the woman said. "You misunderstand, though I suppose you understand as much as such a famous cad can. You see, the love that Ned holds for me—and I for him—is not romantic in any way. Is, in fact, far closer to the love a son might hold for his mother, a mother her son."

Chall blinked, turning to regard Ned who shrugged. "I told you," the carriage driver said. "We need to talk. If, that is, your friend here can resist the urge to stab me for a few more minutes."

Chall glanced over at Priest, then at the knife the man still held at his side, the one he made no move to slide back into its sheath. "Damnit, put the blade up, Priest. If Ned tried to kill Lady Valencia then I'd say it's pretty clear it didn't take."

"And the servant?" Priest pressed.

"He was alive when we left the first time," Ned said.

"The first time?"

"Yeah, you know, when he came to save me," the old woman said. "Don't you fools get it? Ned didn't try to kill me—why, he's the only reason I'm still alive. If it weren't for him, I'd have still been in my house—sleeping or at least trying to—when Robert's men came."

"Wait...do you mean Robert Palden sent men to kill you?"

"Well, Alder didn't kill himself did he?" she snapped as if Chall was a fool when, just then, was pretty much how he felt, so difficult was he finding it to keep up with the stream of revelations.

"Alder?" he asked, confused, though he thought he might have been forgiven for it—after all, people had been dying at such a rapid pace lately it was proving difficult to keep up.

"Alder was my chamberlain," the noblewoman said, her eyes narrowed. "But more than that, he was a friend."

Chall nodded, swallowing hard at the anger in the woman's voice before he turned to Ned. "But...you said that Robert Palden wasn't back. You said he couldn't be."

"I was wrong," Ned said simply. "He's back—I don't know why, and I don't know how, but there's no denying that."

"How can you be so sure?" Chall asked.

Ned winced, glancing at Lady Valencia who sighed. "The fact that Robert is alive is the reason why I very nearly wasn't."

"I...I'm not sure I understand."

"No, I don't suppose you would," she said. "But you see, there was no one in the city who knew that I was a part of the Wolves at all. We decided that was best given my...position, in New Daltenia's nobility. Nobody, at least, save for Ned and one other person."

"Robert," Chall said.

She inclined her head like a fencer acknowledging a point. "That's right."

"But then...I mean..." Chall paused, frowning as he remembered his and Maeve's discussion with Petran Quinn. "That isn't *exactly* true, is it? I mean, there was a book that spoke of it—one from a scholar—who said—"

"I am quite familiar with Falidar," she said, her voice tight, "just as I am aware that I asked him—quite profusely and quite...*generously*—not to write of the rumors, rumors that, given an opportunity, would have, I am confident, played themselves out. But he did write about it despite my urgings—some tripe, as I recall, about artistic integrity, though no one knows better than I how completely he lacked integrity of any kind. Still, at the time I trusted that he would keep it quiet, that any suspicion of me being a member of the Crimson Wolves would fade with time."

"This Falidar must have been pretty damned convincing for you to leave so much of your future in his hands."

"Yes, well, he was not the only one that made me such a promise," she said, "not the only one who assured me that my past and my aiding in the creation and funding of the Wolves would not come back to bite me."

Ned winced, and it was clear enough from his expression who she was talking about. "I was wrong."

"You seem to be making a habit of it lately," the old noblewoman observed. "Curious that, for there was a time, not so very long ago, that it seemed to me that you were never wrong. You were, after all, the one who came up with all the plans."

"The planner, huh?" Chall asked.

"Oh yes," the noblewoman said, flashing a smile. "Ned here wasn't just a pretty face, nor was he, as he would no doubt love for you to believe, the hired help. It was him that we relied on, him whose plans we followed."

"Until it wasn't," Ned said.

"Indeed," she said, her smile vanishing as if it had never been. "Until it wasn't."

"Still, I...I don't mean any offense," Chall said, "but, surely there might be someone else that...I mean, someone who would..."

"Want to kill me?" the woman asked. "Do you fancy, Sir Challadius, that I, in my time of life, live an existence full of intrigue and high drama? The biggest danger I court is my daily rush to the privy, a rush that, it must be said, is sometimes more successful than others." She smiled at his discomfort. "Oh yes, I am afraid that I must disabuse you of any false notions—women, even rich old women, must still endure the ravages of age like everyone else. Anyway, to answer your *real* question, I do suppose it might be possible that, given my station, someone or a group of someones might have decided to find my existence offensive. After all, if there is anything the long years have taught me it's that when it comes to hurting each other, we mortals never need much of a reason."

"I won't disagree with you on that bit. But don't you see? That means that it doesn't have to be Robert Palden that showed up at all. You could all just be jumping at shadows."

"Like children cowering under the coverlet, is that how you imagine us?" the woman asked.

Chall winced. "That isn't...I mean, that wasn't—"

"Oh, relax. I would not have thought, given your reputation, that you were so easily discomfited. Still, rest assured that I have been treated far worse than like a naïve child. And you might even be right—for if there is anyone walking the face of the world who is deserving of a child's fear, then I believe it to be Robert Palden. And it *is* Robert Palden, as much as you seem to want to think otherwise. As much as *I* would love to think otherwise."

"You know this," Priest said.

"I do."

"How?"

"Because swans sow seeds of silk and shadow."

"Well...sure they do," Chall said. "On account of their thumbs."

"Thumbs," she repeated, raising an eyebrow.

"You'll have to forgive my friend," Priest said. "He tends toward flippancy when he's confused."

"Which is the same as saying he's flippant, given the amount of confusion I've seen mar his features in the five minutes since I've met him."

"The swans?" Priest prompted.

She glanced at Ned who gave her a nod. "You can trust them," he said.

"Yes, but to do what?" she asked. "Anyway, I seem to recall you telling me, once upon a time, of another man I could trust."

Ned winced. "Val, you know I'm sorry about that. I didn't—"

She waved her hand dismissively. "Yes, yes, you are sorry, and I am joking. You are quite too easy to nettle, Ned. The reason for your nickname."

"Nettled Ned?" Chall asked.

"Easily-annoyed Neddard," she countered, her face expressionless so that Chall could not tell if he was being teased or not.

"Ah. Sure, has a certain ring to it," he said slowly, feeling as if he stood, mentally speaking, on the deck of a ship listing here and there in the throes of some terrible storm, threatening to capsize at any moment.

The noblewoman gave him a small smile. "The swans, it is a passphrase. One that was recently used to access my personal records."

"I see..." Chall said.

"Not yet, but do try to keep up," she said. "The woman who accessed my records was a professional—those who I employ know Guild training when they see it. A woman with red hair. Young, pretty even. Said her name was—"

"Margaret," Chall said.

"Wait, how did you know that?"

"Because we've met," he said, frowning. "It was she that came to the castle, the one we discovered in the king's chambers, the one that killed the serving girl."

"I see," the noblewoman said, her eyes wide.

Chall glanced at Priest, and the man met his gaze, his frown making it clear that he'd had the same thought as Chall. Maybe there were two red-headed assassins running around in the city, that was possible. But to think that both of them were young, pretty women, and both were involved in the Crimson Wolves...well, that was just a bit more of a coincidence then he was prepared to believe. "So this woman, she accessed your personal records. How does that mean that this Robert Palden is back? After all, all it really means is that she somehow got your passphrase."

"Sure," she agreed. "A passphrase that was only ever known by three people."

"Well, you know what they say," Chall said. "Three people can keep a secret just so long as two of them are dead."

"Yes, but you are looking at two of those people now. I can personally assure you that I would never break into my own personal records. Nor, I suspect, would Ned. It wouldn't make much sense for him to look up a blueprint of my house, as well as the names of the guards and other information one might find pertinent to breaking into someone's home with the intention of kidnapping or killing them, only to come and save me from that same kidnapping. Not me, then, and not Ned. That only leaves one person who could have been behind it."

"Robert Palden."

"That's right. A ghost from the past come back to haunt me once more."

"But...why would this Robert Palden want you dead?" Chall asked. "I mean, the three of you, you worked together, didn't you?"

The old woman and Ned shared a look at that. "You do not *work with* someone like Robert. He was a slight man, but his emotions—his hate in particular—were some of the largest I've ever seen."

"He was passionate, then."

"To say that Robert was passionate is to say that the Crimson Prince has some violent tendencies. Yes, he was passionate—and he was far more. He was obsessed. The rest of us, Ned, myself, most of the Wolves minus a few who followed Robert the closest, still tried to have our own lives." She paused, glancing at Ned, a small smile on her face. "And, in time, our own loves. Robert, though...there was nothing for him. Nothing except the Wolves. Nothing except the killing."

Mention of Bernard made Chall think of him, and he felt a fresh stab of worry for his friend, for his prince. But he pushed it aside. There was nothing he could do for Bernard, not now. "But...I still feel like it doesn't make any sense. I mean, why would he want to kill you?"

"Assume that the ruler of a kingdom dies," she said, "and in the king's death there is no clear line of succession. There are, let us say, three different people who might take up the mantle. One of those three, wanting the crown more than anything, might well campaign for it, might try to prove his worth. But then, there is another way, one that has the potential to be far more...expedient."

"Kill the other two," Chall said grimly.

She inclined her head. "Just so. Robert is back—there is no doubt of that. He seeks to get me and, I do not doubt, Ned, out of the way. That can only mean that he intends to reorganize the Wolves in force."

"To kill criminals again," Chall said, considering that. He thought of Maeve, taken from him only recently by the same sort of people the Wolves used to hunt, and he shrugged. "I can think of worse things."

"Can you?" the woman challenged, arching an eyebrow. "And are you comfortable with a man with nothing but hate and revenge in his heart deciding who is criminal and who is not? And, if not criminal, who must die for the cause? Those like your innocent serving woman, dead only because she happened to be cleaning His Majesty's quarters."

She smiled at Chall's obvious discomfort. "Oh yes, I know all about it. Ned has told me all that there is to know. We are together in this, after all, his head just as likely to be separated from his shoulders as mine."

Likely more, Chall thought. After all, it wasn't just a psychotic, rage-filled ex-murderer turned murderer again the carriage driver had to worry about. He also had to worry about a wife who, if everything he'd heard was true, was particularly pissed off at the man just now. An *assassin* wife. Not that Ned knew that, the poor bastard.

"And the paper?"

They all turned to regard Priest. "What's that?" Ned asked.

"The paper. The one Matt saw tucked into your trousers when you fled from Lady Valencia's manse. What was it?"

Ned frowned, glancing at Lady Valencia. "Oh come on, Neddy," she said, waving a hand. "It doesn't make much sense to go to them for help if we decide to keep secrets now."

Ned nodded. "The paper...it was...a record. One from the time of the Crimson Wolves."

The old woman sighed. "What our dear Ned is finding so difficult to say is that what I sent him after—the reason he was there when you all came—was to retrieve a list."

"A list," Priest repeated.

"Just so," she said, inclining her head. "But not a supply list, this, nor even a debt ledger, though I suppose there are those that might view it as such. No, this list contains names. Names of every Wolf or, as it happens, *once* Wolf. It has the information of all our contacts, all our suppliers, those who believed in our mission years ago but who chose to limit their involvement to the indirect avenues of coin and support."

"I see," Chall said slowly, still not understanding why the man would risk his life for such a document.

"I really don't think you do," Lady Valencia said. "You see, I was the Keeper of the Records—a job they always made sound very official but one which, I believe, was little more than Ned and Robert's strategy to keep me out of the way. After all, it's not so hard to find a use for an old woman's money. It is significantly more difficult to find a use for the old woman herself."

"Val, it isn't—"

The noblewoman held up a hand, silencing Ned. "Ned would never say as much, but I am largely useless. That is another hard truth that age teaches one, whether she wants to learn it or not. Not that our friend the carriage driver would say it. He is ever polite, our Ned."

Chall thought there was a certain guardsman, Vorrun, who would disagree, not to mention Matt. After all, the king of the Known Lands was still sporting a black eye—Chall was no expert, at least not on punching people, but he thought he was as close as anyone could get as far as being punched went, and he'd never been punched politely.

"The point I'm getting at," she went on, "is that by and large, my job was no more than an opportunity for me to feel involved, to feel like a part of the solution for once instead of the problem. And keeping records is a job that it is very, very difficult to screw up. Not an important one. At least...most of the time. Now, though, I find that those records, those meticulous, specific, factual records of which I was so proud, once upon a time, are now as deadly as an unsheathed blade. More so, in fact, for the blade generally only can hurt one person at a time. This paper—these records, could hurt dozens. More."

"So...what are you saying?" Chall asked. "That someone would want to use this information to what, hurt people? To kill people who used to be Wolves?"

"Not *someone*," Ned said. "Rob. That is, Robert. Palden." He cleared his throat, scratching at the back of his head.

"You all were close," Chall said. It wasn't a question but Ned answered it anyway.

"Yes. We were. Wasn't just a job. We believed in it."

"All fanatics do," Priest said quietly. There was no note of recrimination in his voice, only sadness, regret.

"That is true enough," Ned said. "Truer than I'd like, in fact."

"But why would Robert Palden come back after all this time only to set about mass murder?"

Ned shared a troubled look with the noblewoman. "I don't think it's murder he's after," the carriage driver said, turning back to regard Chall. "It's recruitment."

"Recruitment," Chall repeated.

"That's right. He wants to start the Wolves up again. Only, this time, without me and Val here getting in the way of how he wants things done. As for what his exact plans are, I can't imagine. I am only confident that, whatever they are, they aren't good."

"So you're saying he's going around asking people if they want to get back up to the same sort of shenanigans they were doing years ago, and that he needs that list of yours to do it."

"A point for the mage," Lady Valencia said dryly.

"But it's been years, right? A lot of those folks—shit I'd think probably all of them—are going to have moved on. What interest would they have in getting wrapped up in all that shit again?"

"I don't know," Ned said. "But we're confident that Rob is going to ask."

"And if they say no?" Priest asked quietly, and by the tone of his voice Chall thought the man knew the answer to that one already.

"Three have already," Ned said. "At least, that we're aware of."

"And how did Robby take their refusal?" Chall asked.

"Not well," Ned said grimly. "Two dead, one missing. Dead too, I imagine, only the body hasn't been found yet."

"I see," Chall said. "And why didn't you just tell us all this when we saw you at Lady Valencia's? I don't know a lot, but I know this—guilty people run."

"Would you have listened?" Ned countered. "Corpses in the manse and me covered in blood? Besides, it wasn't just me I was worried about. Robert has always had a bit of a...well. Call it a temper. And from what I've seen so far, the years have only made it worse. I thought I could handle things on my own, figured that the less you all knew about it the better. Curiosity killed the cat, after all."

"And now?" Priest asked.

Ned sighed. "Now I realize I can't do it on my own. I was a fool to think I could. If it were just Robert, maybe that'd be one thing, but it ain't. He's got folks of like mind working with him, just how many I can't say. But that woman, the one that done for the serving girl, she's one. And that bastard Catham's another."

"Catham," Chall said. "Matt said you said something about him, back at Lady Valencia's. How's he wrapped up in all this? Aside from trying to see a few extra holes poked into me and Priest that is."

"I can't say, not exactly," Ned said. "But the bastard's involved, of that I'm sure."

"And about what you told Matt? About him being clever as well as cautious? What did that mean?"

Ned shook his head, frustrated. "I set a trap for the bastard, that's all, but he didn't oblige me by falling into it."

"Catham has always had an almost supernatural talent for sensing danger," Priest said. "He is no mean hand with a weapon, but it is that seeming prescience that has kept him alive for so many years, not his skills with a blade."

"Well, considering that the bastard saw my trap comin'—I was lyin' in wait for him—and damn near made me step into it myself by sending a decoy, along with half a dozen fellas with swords that looked just about ready to cut into anyone or anything that popped out, I won't disagree. That's one of the reasons I went in search of you, after all. I figure if anybody knows how to get ahead of that bastard it'd be you."

"If you tried to go against Catham in subtlety, I'm surprised you're still around to ask for help," Priest said.

"Oh?" Ned said. "And why is that?"

Priest shrugged. "Others have tried over the years. More than a few."

"And how'd they fare?"

"Well," Priest said. "They're not around to ask for help."

Ned grunted. "Right."

"What's the other reason?" Chall asked.

"What's that?" Ned said, turning to him.

"You said that Catham was one of the reasons you needed our help—well, Priest's help. I don't know Catham from anybody, and I'd just as soon keep it that way. So, what's the other reason? Why am I here?"

"Would you believe I just like your company?"

"Screw off," Chall said. "*I* don't like my company. Why am I here?"

Ned sighed, and in that moment Chall suddenly saw just how exhausted the man looked. He wondered when the last time he'd slept had been. And he was quite confident that, whenever it was, it had not been a good rest.

"I can't do this alone." He paused, wincing, before glancing at Lady Valencia. "I...that is, *we* can't do this alone."

The noblewoman rolled her eyes. "I am not so fragile as Neddy thinks," she said. "The truth is, I was very little help in the more...*martial* aspects of the Wolves ten years ago, and I am even less help now. I am not much of a threat to anyone—except my own knees, perhaps. I can barely cut my own bread, let alone imagine trying to cut a person with anything sharper than a harsh word. Assassins and blades in the night, all of that isn't really my thing."

Not my thing either, Chall thought. But then he thought of the last weeks, of how many interactions he'd recently had with assassins, including but not limited to time spent with his assassin girlfriend. Maybe it was his thing and never mind what he wanted.

"Uh-huh," Chall said slowly. "So, what, you figure I'm fat enough, I could probably catch several assassin's blades before they made it to you, that it?"

"You're sellin' yourself short, fella," Ned said. "You got a lot more goin' for you besides makin' for a good knife sheath."

"Well that's comforting," Chall said. "So what's the plan?"

"I was hoping you two could tell me," the carriage driver said. "I need to find that bastard Catham, but I need to get Val to safety."

The noblewoman rolled her eyes. "Neddy, I told you, it really isn't necessary. I'm not some maiden in need of rescue, and I'm afraid my blushing days are long over. I can stay here and—"

"Not a chance," Ned interrupted. "That's non-negotiable. We're getting you to safety and that's it. I don't know what Robert's up to, but I've lost enough friends over the years. I don't mean to lose another, not if I can help it."

The woman gave him a warm smile. "The gods save us from knights in shining armor," she said, glancing at Chall and Priest, but he could hear the pleasure in her voice.

"He's right, ma'am," Priest said. "We need to get you to safety."

"It seems I'm to be faced with a regular epidemic of chivalry," the noblewoman said, sighing.

"Forgive me, ma'am, but chivalry has nothing to do with it," Priest said. "Catham or this Robert, whoever was behind the attempt on your life, they went through a lot of trouble to see you dead, breaking into your personal records as they did. That means they had a reason—people don't risk so much for nothing."

"A reason to want to kill a dried-up old woman whose best years happened so long ago she's all but forgotten them? What reason would that be?"

"I don't know," Priest said, "but I mean to find out. I cannot speak for this Robert, though all that you have told us seems to indicate that he is very intentional in his choices. But Catham I know, and I can assure you that if he went through all of that trouble to see you dead, it is because he has decided you're a threat for one reason or another."

"Me?" the woman asked. "A threat?"

"Why else go through all the trouble?" Priest countered.

"Fine, fine," the woman said. "I see that you are all going to insist on saving me, even if it kills me. What should we do?"

"Probably best if you let us worry about that, Val," Ned said. "The less you know the better, I think. Better if you're not involved anymore than you absolutely have to be. We'll get you to somewhere safe and—"

"No."

The carriage driver paused, blinking. "No?"

"No," the woman repeated. "I was content, years ago, to sit back and let others risk their lives while I hid away, thinking that I was safe. But I'm not safe, now—he came to my *home*, Neddy. And even if I *could* remain safe, even if I could believe that Robert *would* leave me alone, still I would not stay out of it, not now. Alder was a good man. He served me for more than thirty years. The others I did not know so long, but they were good people, one and all. And for them, if for no other reason, Robert must be made to pay for his crimes."

Ned winced. "Val, I really think—"

"I know what you think," she said. "And I appreciate it, Neddy, I really do. But I'm not sitting this one out. Robert has to pay for what he's done, and I mean to make sure he does."

"And what if he finds out you're working against him and comes for you again?" Ned said. "We'll do our best to hide you, but you know Robert as well as I do—he doesn't give up easy."

"That makes three of us, then," she said, giving him a tight smile. "If Robert finds me, probably I'll die, but then I'm old, Ned. I don't have long to live anyway, and I'm okay with that. Better to die now than to live out my last few years knowing I could have helped to stop Robert and chose cowardice instead."

Ned sighed. "There won't be any stopping you, will there?"

Another tight, fragile smile. "You'd have to kill me."

"Fine," Ned said, "but will you at least let us take you somewhere safe? You can help from there," he went on quickly, "but you won't be of help to anyone if you go back to your manse and Robert comes back for you."

"Alright, Neddy," she said. "You win. But the moment I think you're keeping things from me in some misguided attempt to protect me, that changes. I want to be a part of all of it this time. Deal?"

"Deal," he said.

"So now that I've agreed to be put," she said, frowning, "where, exactly, do you plan on putting me?"

Ned frowned, clearly thinking it over.

"The castle?" Chall asked.

"The castle," Ned repeated, staring at him as if he was daft. "Do you mean the same castle where it seems like assassins come as go as they please? The castle that we know for a fact the woman working for Robert or Catham—this Margaret—has already infiltrated at least once? The castle where, unless I'm misremembering, there was an attempt on your and Lady Maeve's lives what, a week ago?"

Maybe I am daft after all, Chall thought.

"Oh come now," Lady Valencia said. "I'm sure you're exaggerating, Ned."

"He really isn't," Chall said.

"Ah, right. Well," she said, "nowhere is completely safe and nobody can be *made* completely safe. Unless, that is, you've intentions of locking me in a padded room, filing my fingernails and pulling my teeth in case I take it in mind to hurt myself."

"I do not think it would be wise," Priest said. "The castle is...troubled, right now. There must be somewhere else in the city, somewhere better that you might take shelter."

"Must there?" the noblewoman asked. "What about you, then?" she asked, glancing at Chall. "Have any spare safe houses lying around?"

Chall winced. "Fresh out, I'm afraid."

"Well then," she said, "seems like the castle it is," and if Chall hadn't known better he would have thought the noblewoman was excited about the prospect of staying in the castle and never mind the fact that Ned had essentially just told her it was full to the rafters with assassins. Which was nowhere near as much of an exaggeration as Chall would have liked.

"Maybe not," the carriage driver said.

The woman turned to him, a flash of what might have been annoyance on her face, caused apparently by the thought of missing her opportunity to stay in a king's castle. Having stayed there—and nearly been killed there multiple times—himself, Chall might have assured her that castle living wasn't all it was cracked up to be.

He didn't get a chance, though, for in another moment Ned spoke. "You can stay at my home."

"Your home," the woman said. "You wish for me to leave my well-guarded, gated manse to go and stay in your...no offense, Neddy, but significantly less well-guarded, and though I'll admit I've never been invited for supper, I would guess ungated, home?"

"Your gate and guards didn't help when Robert's men came," Ned reminded her. "Anyway, everyone knows where the great Lady Valencia, one of New Daltenia's most admired noblewomen lives."

"Richest, you mean," she said, rolling her eyes.

"Either way, pretty much no one knows where my home is," he said.

She frowned, clearly not liking it but also clearly struggling for a reason to dismiss the idea. "And your wife," she said slowly. "She will be there too, yes?"

"I hope so," he said, and in those three simple words Chall could hear the level of the man's concern.

"And you think that she will be okay with all of this, is that it?"

"I don't know," Ned said, wincing. "Emille and I...we haven't been as...close, lately, as I would like. But what I do know is this—if you go home, you'll die. Robert is many things but one thing he certainly is not is the type of man who leaves things to chance. You have to go somewhere, somewhere safe, somewhere nobody from the old days will think to look."

"And you do not believe that Robert will think to check at your house? Or do you believe that he will *think* to do it, but would refuse to attack me—or *you,* for that matter—at your home out of some sense of...sentimentality? Because, as you said, Robert is many things, but neither is sentimental one of them. At least not anymore. If he came for me, he will come for you."

"He would," Ned agreed, "if he knew it was my home. He doesn't."

"And you are sure of that?" she countered.

"Positive," the carriage driver said instantly. "I'm not the cleverest man, I'll admit, but I'm not a complete fool. When we disbanded the Wolves I set out to leave that life behind me, and I did."

"Sometimes, a man has to turn around and look behind him to see his past and, sometimes, he finds it standing before him, refusing to be ignored."

They all turned to regard Chall, as surprised as he was to hear the words come out of his mouth. "What was that then?" Ned asked. "From a book?"

"Stones and starlight no," Chall said. "There was a friend of mine, a long time ago. The bastard liked to talk just about as much as he liked to drink, and he really, really liked to drink."

"A drunken philosopher," Lady Valencia said, raising an eyebrow.

Chall shrugged. "A drunk, anyway. Point is," he pressed on, not caring, at the moment, to revisit his own past, a past full of things he wasn't proud of, "sometimes a man tries to leave his past behind him but sometimes—maybe *all* times—his past has other plans." He turned to regard Ned.

The carriage driver seemed to consider it then, finally, shook his head. "No. No, maybe your drunk friend was usually right, but not this time. I left that past behind me. Left it just about as sure as any man can leave anything. Haven't revisited it once, avoided anywhere my business took me, back then."

"*Any*where?" Chall pressed.

"It's a big city," Ned said, nodding. "Broke contact with all the old folks, too. Lost some friends in the process, some that, time was, I thought of as more family than friends. Didn't want to do it at first—fact was, there was a time or two, or a hundred, where I thought about reachin' out. Only...I met Emille, and I didn't want her to be a part of that. I signed up for that danger, that risk. She didn't. She's innocent."

Chall, who was aware that the man's wife was an assassin, an active member of the Guild and, according to Maeve, damn good at her job, found himself clearing his throat.

"An innocent," Lady Valencia said, "who will be put into danger, should we do what you suggest. You did not risk your wife before, Neddy. Why risk her now?"

"Because I don't have a choice," he said simply but with feeling. "Whatever's happening, whatever Robert's up to, it's big— he wasn't ever one for half-measures. Until we find him, until we *stop* him, nobody in the city is safe. Not Emille, not anyone."

"I see," Lady Valencia said slowly. "And how will you explain my presence to your wife, I wonder? What will you tell her?"

"The truth," Ned said instantly. "It's been a long time comin', after all."

"The truth," Priest said in a solemn voice, "is man's greatest weapon and his greatest fear—rightly so. For the truth cuts. It separates. A man from his illusions, a woman from her hopes and, sometimes, a family from their loved ones."

"I don't doubt you're right," Ned said. "But Emmy deserves the truth. She needs to hear it, and I need to tell it. After all, a fish might lie to a bird and tell her he has wings, but when it finally comes time to fly he's the one who's the fool, not her. I've got a dark past, it's true, but I don't want to have a dark future. Not if I can help it, and the only way I see to do that is to tell Emmy the truth."

"And if she decides that it's too much? If she decides to leave you?" the noblewoman asked.

A look of pure terror at the thought crossed the man's face then and in that expression Chall saw clearly just how much the carriage driver loved his wife, just how much the loss of her would kill him. "Then she leaves," Ned said, his voice dry and hoarse with emotion. "Emmy deserves the truth and finally I'm going to give it to her. After all, she's never been nothing but open and honest with me."

Chall winced, glancing at Priest. The man returned his troubled expression. Priest also knew the truth of Emille's identity, knew that she was far from innocent. He wondered, for a brief moment how, in a city full of tens of thousands, such a man and such a woman might find each other. After all, there had to be some clerks that *were* just clerks, some house wives that didn't have to think on keeping their cooking knives and murdering knives separate. But then he didn't wonder for long. Like attracted like, that was all. A man can't go traipsing around in the mud and expect anyone he finds there to be without blemish or stain. But then it wasn't Chall's place to go pointing such a thing out—in fact, he couldn't think of anyone worse suited. No, in the normal course of events he would have much preferred to leave it alone, to stay out of it and let things sort themselves out however they would. And from the look on Priest's face, the other man would have liked to have done the same thing.

The problem was...they couldn't.

"Listen, Ned..." Chall began slowly, turning to the man. "It...that is..." He hesitated, unclear of how to begin. After all, if there was a gentle way to break the news to a man that his innocent, loving house wife was an assassin and a member of the most dangerous guild in the Known Lands then he didn't know it.

The carriage driver gave a confused grin at his obvious discomfort. "You alright, Chall? You look like you got somethin' on your mind. Either that or you're havin' a stroke, and it'd be a damn terrible time for it."

"No," Chall said, giving a smile that vanished instantly. "No stroke." Though he thought maybe that'd be less painful than what he had in front of him. He glanced at Priest, seeing if the man had any intention of jumping in, but it was clear by the way he watched Chall that he did not. Bastard.

"The thing is, Ned, I mean...all I was going to say. You know, no one is *completely* innocent. Completely...*good.*"

"Maybe you're right," the carriage driver said, "but I don't think so. I think maybe it's just that when a man spends too much time in the dark, when the light finally comes, it's hard not to look away. I know Emille ain't perfect—anyone who's had her roasted chicken knows that. But I reckons my Em's just about as close as anyone walkin' the face of this world comes."

Getting worse by the minute, Chall said. It was as if he stood at the face of a mountain, one that looked damn near impossible to climb and even as he was contemplating the immense—likely impossible—task before him, that mountain was growing, getting taller, its trails steeper, its rocks...rockier.

"All I mean," Ned said, "is that if she ain't perfect, she's perfect for me. Shit, you ought to know as good as anyone what I mean, Chall. After all, you and Maeve—I've seen the way the two of you are."

Gods help me. "She's an assassin, Ned!" he blurted, the words exploding out of him in desperation.

He wasn't sure what he expected—disbelief, maybe. Anger. Confusion. He got none of those things, though. Instead, the carriage driver only stared at him as if he were daft—and if he was looking for an argument on that score, he was going to be disappointed. "Sure, sure—the finest one I've ever heard of it's true. But then folks are complicated, Chall. It ain't nothin' to be held against her."

Chall blinked, at once shocked and relieved by how well the man was taking it. And here he'd thought this was going to be difficult. He grinned. "Wait, you knew?"

Ned snorted. "Of course I know. How not? I'm not blind or deaf, am I? And a man'd have to be both not to know about Maeve the Marvelous. "

Chall laughed. "I can't tell you how—" He cut off, frowning. "Wait, what did you say?"

"I said that everyone knows who Maeve the Marvelous is, Chall. Shit, there's damn near as many stories about her and the rest of you as there is about the Crimson Prince himself."

Oh Chall, you fool, he thought. *You damned fool.* "Not Maeve, Ned. Emille."

The man frowned, and now he did look confused. "What?" he asked. "What about Emille?"

"Maeve's not the assassin," Chall said, then paused, frowning. "No, wait, well, she *is* an assassin or...or was? It's complicated. But the point is, *Emille* is an assassin."

Ned gave him an awkward smile. "That uh...that's an odd joke, Chall. Can't say as it's your finest."

"It would be odd," Chall agreed, meeting the man's eyes. "If it was a joke."

Ned stared at him, paling. "I don't...I can't...that's ridiculous."

"Is it?" Chall asked, watching the man who was frowning, thinking. Some part of him had recognized the truth, some part that was even now putting the pieces of that truth together and, as was often the case with the truth, not much caring for the shape it took. "Think, Ned. There must have been signs."

"Signs," the carriage driver repeated. "Like me comin' home early and findin' her stabbin' some poor bastard, that what you're thinking?" The words might have been a joke, but then the man looked just about as far from laughing as any man could get.

"She's an assassin, Ned," Chall repeated. Not because he wanted to say it but because he thought the man needed to hear it.

"I like you, Chall. But you watch your mouth. That's my wife you're talking about. The sweetest, cleverest, kindest person I know. A person who, unless I very much misremember, saved your life when you came to her wounded after getting yourself kebabbed on the end of a *real* assassin's blade. Or have you forgotten that?"

"I haven't forgotten, Ned," Chall said. "I know what Emille did for me, what the two of you have done for all of us. And I'm telling you, whatever else she is—and, for what it's worth, I believe almost all of it good—Emille *is* an assassin."

"You won't be offended if I just don't take your word for it, just swallow the idea that you know my wife better than I do."

236

"But I think you do know, Ned," Chall said sadly, hating that he had to press the man but knowing that he had to just the same. "I think that some part of you is realizing that this makes sense. And you don't have to take my word for it—take Emille's herself."

"What do you mean by that?" the carriage driver said. He tried for challenging, but he just sounded scared, tired.

Chall began to recount all that he knew of Emille since first discovering from Maeve that she was an assassin. He continued by telling the man about what they'd done to help the old Guild leader so that they could get the hit on their heads removed. It took about fifteen minutes, and Ned stood, silent, for the entirety of the telling, his expression growing grimmer and grimmer by the moment.

Even once Chall had finished, the man did not speak, only stared at him. Stared at him the way, Chall imagined, a child might stare at his parent when his parent told him that faeries were real after all—and that they all hated him.

"If all this is true—"

"It i—"

The carriage driver held up a hand, silencing him. "If all this is true," he repeated, "then why are you telling me now?"

Chall cleared his throat. "Look, Ned, I wanted to tell you, I did. But...I mean, it just didn't seem like my place. After all—"

"You misunderstand me, Chall," the man said quietly. "I'm not asking you why you didn't tell me before. I understand—shit, I wouldn't have told me either. After all, who wants to be the bearer of *that* news? I'm not curious about why you didn't tell me—I'm curious about why you did."

Chall winced. "Well, isn't it obvious? You were talking about taking Lady Valencia to your home, sheltering her there, and I thought...well. Maybe that isn't such a good idea. You know, since Emille..."

"Since Emille what?" Ned asked, frowning.

Chall fidgeted and glanced at Priest. "You going to talk or what, damnit?"

"He means since she is an assassin," Priest said.

"Even if she is—and I'm not completely sold on that—what does that have to do with anything?"

"She works for the Guild," Priest said. "The same Guild which, according to all that I've heard, the Crimson Wolves set themselves against so many years ago. Along, of course, with all the other criminal enterprises. I cannot help but think that the Guild would be thrilled at the idea of having one of the founding members of the organization which caused them so many difficulties in the past right under their noses."

Ned frowned, a dangerous expression coming to his face. "You're saying you think Emille would, what? Want to kill Val?"

"I'm saying that if the Guild finds out that you're harboring a founding member of the Crimson Wolves in your house, if they find out that *you* yourself are a member, what Emille wants might not matter."

"You think they'd ask her to kill us, that she'd do that. That she'd kill me."

"Nobody's saying that," Chall said. "Look, Ned, Emille loves you—a blind man could see that. Just as anybody can see that you love her."

"I hear a but comin'."

"*But,*" Chall said, "I don't know if she's going to have the same affection for a strange woman out of your past."

They turned to regard Lady Valencia. "No," Ned said after a moment, shaking his head. "No, Emmy wouldn't do that, wouldn't murder someone in cold blood."

Chall thought that was pretty much *exactly* what assassins did but now wasn't the time to say it, so he shook his head. "No one's saying that, Ned."

"No?" the carriage driver asked, rounding on him. "Because it sounds to me like that's *exactly* what you're saying."

Chad opened his mouth to speak, to utter some defense, but he found that, in that moment, he could think of nothing to say, for the fact was that he *was* concerned that Emille might kill Lady Valencia. She was a secret *assassin* after all, not a secret nun or closet cat lover.

But he could find nothing to say that he thought would let him go on the next few minutes without the shit beaten out of him, so he was glad when Priest came to his rescue.

"Emille isn't the only assassin in the Guild's employ, Ned," the man said. "And while no one is claiming that your wife would hurt you or even Lady Valencia, she might very well feel obligated to share these revelations of, if not your identity, then at least Lady Valencia's with them."

Ned watched him for several seconds, his expression grim. Then, finally, he shook his head. "No. No, Emille wouldn't do that. Not my Emmy. I have faith in her. I trust her."

"Faith, like hope, is a flimsy shield against reality's truths," Priest said, and in the man's voice, in his face, Chall could hear, could see the pain of whatever was troubling him.

"I think you're wrong," Ned said, "but setting that side for a moment, what would you suggest? Do you know of another place that we can take Val? Besides my house, I mean? A place where she would be safe?"

"The castle?" Val suggested, once more showing a surprising eagerness at the thought.

"No," Priest said immediately. "Ned is right—the castle is not safe. Perhaps, in time, it might be made so, but...not now. No, I think you are right," he went on, turning to the carriage driver. "Your home is the safest place. At least, that is, given one, small adjustment to our strategy."

Chall was just about to ask what the man meant by that but, before he could, Ned spoke. "You don't want me to tell Emille the truth," the carriage driver said. "About who Val is—about who *I* am. Or, at least, who I was."

It wasn't really a question but Priest answered it anyway. "Yes," he said.

"You want me to lie," Ned said. "To my wife."

"Oh, Neddy," Lady Valencia said, "it isn't as if you haven't been doing that already."

The carriage driver frowned. "I don't want to do it anymore."

It was Priest's turn to hesitate, his turn to look at Chall for help. And why not? After all, if there was any person walking around breathing air that had a larger reputation for dissembling and lying than Chall he'd never heard of them. "We're not asking you to lie to Emille, Ned," Chall said.

"No?"

"No," Chall said, glancing at Priest then back at the carriage driver. "We're only asking that you...delay telling her the truth. For a little while. Until we get all this sorted out."

"Delay telling her the truth," the carriage driver repeated.

"That's right."

"You know, Chall," he said, "I try not to speak for my wife, but I'm pretty damned sure she'd consider that lying."

"Probably she would," Chall agreed.

The carriage driver watched him for several seconds, turned to regard Priest, then Lady Valencia, waiting for any of them to object, to put forth another idea. When no one did, he sighed heavily. "I love my wife," he told Chall.

"I know you do."

The carriage driver nodded. "Well, let's get on with it. Val will stay with me."

"And how will you explain it?"

Ned shrugged. "For anyone who asks, I'll say she's an aunt of mine, come to visit."

Chall glanced at Lady Valencia who nodded. "Better aunt than grandmother, I suppose," the noblewoman said.

Chall looked to Priest, and the man nodded. "It sounds good to me."

"What about Catham, then?" Ned asked. "How are we going to get that bastard?"

"You're not," Priest said.

The carriage driver frowned. "Now, look here. It was me that come to you with this, not the other way around."

"I know that," Priest said. "And there was a reason you came to us. I know Catham—I know the people he knows, the places he knows. I will find him."

"And once you do?" Ned asked.

"They didn't call me Valden the Kind," Priest said grimly.

The carriage driver scratched his chin. "Maybe not, but that bastard's slippery. You could use some help."

"And I'll have it," Priest said, glancing at Chall with a small smile, one that Chall didn't return for hunting down a murderer known for his cleverness wasn't exactly on his bucket list. "You, on the other hand, have your own task before you," the man went on, turning back to Ned.

"Oh?"

"Well, sure," Chall said. "It ain't as if we can take Lady Valencia to your home, say she's one of our aunts, can we?"

Ned frowned. "I see. And what of you two?"

Priest glanced at Chall. "We'll go find Catham, ask him what he knows about the Crimson Wolves, about Robert."

"I'd prefer a nap, maybe going for a drink," Chall said, "but I suppose everyone has their own idea of a good time."

Ned grunted, turning back to Priest. "And if he doesn't want to answer?"

Priest flashed a humorless smile that sent a shiver down Chall's spine. "We'll convince him."

Ned nodded slowly. "Bastard'll likely say anything you want to hear, if he thinks it'll protect him. Don't make it true."

"I'm fairly good at telling when someone's lying to me," Priest said.

"Holdover from life as a priest?"

"From life as a criminal."

Ned sighed. "Okay, but I don't like it."

"What's to like?" Chall said.

"And when are you thinking to get started?"

Priest glanced at Chall who grunted. "Might as well. I won't be getting anymore sleep this morning," he said. "Maybe ever."

Priest nodded, turning back to Ned. "Now's as good a time as any."

"Not that we don't appreciate your hospitality," Chall said, glancing around at the ruined house surrounding them. "But I'm afraid if we hang out in here much longer I'll end up catching something." *A disease, maybe, or, perhaps, a punch in the face from a pissed-off husband who I've just told I've been keeping important information about his wife and who I have just convinced to lie to her.*

"Alright," Ned said. "We've got a plan—or at least enough of one that they can inscribe it on our tombstones when it all goes tits up. Suppose the only thing left to do is do it."

Or die, Chall thought, *as the case may be.* "Right," he said, trying to keep the fear from his voice and pretty damned certain he failed.

"How will we get in contact with you?" Chall asked. "I don't think it'd be wise for us to be seen going to your house."

"Not sure it's going to be wise for me to be there either, once Emille finds out the truth," Ned said, then held up a hand, glancing at Priest. "I know, I know, don't lie just...don't tell the truth."

"At least not yet," Priest said.

"Anyway," Ned said, "I'll come here for half an hour every day at noon. You got somethin' to tell me, you can meet me here."

"And if you need to get in contact with us?"

"No offense, Chall, but you ain't all that hard to find," Ned said.

Chall winced, remembering the assassin that had climbed up to his and Maeve's window or the *other* assassin—the fact that there was more than one was proof, so far as he was concerned, that he'd made some poor life decisions—who'd accosted them in the street. "Right," he said. "Ned...listen, about Emille—I'm sorry."

"Me too," the carriage driver said. "Now, why don't you two go on ahead? I'll lock up."

"Why bother?" Chall asked, glancing around the tiny room, dirty and looking in danger of falling down at any moment. "If anyone stole something they'd be doing you a favor. Not much but dirt and rotten wood anyway."

Ned gave him a humorless smile. "Dirt, sure. But my dirt. Good luck to both of you."

"Good luck to you as well, Ned," Chall said.

The words felt weak. After all, the man was going to be forced to try to trick his wife—an almost impossible job—and this man's wife just happened to be an assassin. Not to mention the fact that Robert Palden, Catham, and whoever else worked for them would be looking to make him dead, though if he knew anything about women—in truth, very little—Chall thought they'd have to get in line behind Emille.

But weak or not, they were the best words he had, so Chall gave the man a nod then shared a look with Priest, starting toward the door.

Priest followed him then stopped, turning back. "For what it's worth, Ned, I am sorry. For not trusting you."

"Don't be sorry yet," the carriage driver said. "There's still plenty of time for you to regret it. Anyway...thanks. It's worth plenty."

Priest nodded at that, turned back to Chall, and they left, stepping out of the shadowed confines of the dilapidated house and into early morning sunlight.

CHAPTER FOURTEEN

He stood in a field of the dead.

There were hundreds, thousands of them. More dead than he could have ever imagined seeing all at once. More *people* than he could have ever imagined seeing all at once.

They lay sprawled like so many broken dolls, dolls spattered in crimson, great gashes cleaved through their flesh. Many were missing limbs, some their heads, and others still appeared to have been split in half by a blow of incredible force.

There were no scavengers to pick at the corpses, no crows cawing or coyotes howling at the feast. There was only the silence of the dead, a silence greater than any the living could ever hope to match.

He stood atop a small rise staring about him. Corpses as far as he could see. Sightless eyes staring, limp limbs unmoving in death. A field of the dead, stretching out in every direction to the edges of his sight and beyond.

Wake up, he told himself.

But he did not wake.

He could not. He could not force himself to awaken anymore than a man could force himself to go to sleep. As always, sleeping and waking came upon a man like a thief—or, he thought, like an assassin, his midnight blade gleaming.

He remained as he was, staring at that devastation, wondering where he was, who the dead men were. But as he looked closer, he saw that the corpses littering the ground were not just those of men. There were others too. Others that he recognized as Feylings, creatures that were often as different from each other as they were from the mortals they lay beside.

Dead of all kinds, that and nothing else.

Until there was.

He caught sight of something in the distance. A hill, one that he was sure had not been there before. Or, at least, he was as sure as any man might be when traversing the land of dreams.

And he *was* dreaming, of that he was sure. Yet that knowledge did nothing to quell the terror that gripped him, offered no comfort for the grief he felt at the sight of so many dead. Perhaps some had been good men, perhaps some had been bad. But seeing them there, it did not matter. They were the dead, and the dead were all dead alike.

He stared at the distant hill then, in a decision that was not really a decision at all, the way it often was in dreams, he began to walk toward it.

The dead stretched on for miles. It should have taken hours to navigate through them, and yet, he found that the journey was one of mere moments. He had barely started out, had just stepped past the corpse of a dead man with a jagged line cleaved through his chest, when he was standing at the base of the hill.

He blinked, staring up the hill in shock.

"*So many dead,*" a voice said from beside him.

Matt screamed, spinning, and reaching for the sword at his side only to realize that it wasn't there. Which was likely just as well, for the man who stood beside him did not seem intent on attacking him. In truth, he barely seemed like a man at all, more like a youth of no more than eighteen or nineteen years, only a couple of years older than Matt.

In fact, the stranger wasn't even looking in Matt's direction. He stared out at the field of corpses, a grim expression on his face. His jaw was hard set, his eyes as the cold gray blue of a misty morning sky, and he had shoulders wider than nearly everyone Matt had ever met save his father. He was young, but there was a hardness to his gaze, to his expression that seemed to say that despite his age he had seen, had experienced much more tragedy than most. "Who are you?" Matt demanded.

The figure still did not turn to look at him. "So many dead," he repeated, his voice a growl, and there was something familiar about that voice, something Matt couldn't put his finger on. "He killed them."

"Who killed them?" Matt asked, confused and scared all at once.

"The dead speak, sometimes," the youth told him. "Most people don't think they can, but the dead have a voice. They speak." The young man's words came out hoarse, a tortured quality to them.

"What...what do they say?" Matt asked. It wasn't the question he meant to ask, yet in the way of dreams it came out of him of its own accord.

The man did turn then, fully facing him. "They all say the same thing," the stranger told him.

"What do they say?" Matt asked again.

The man opened his mouth as if he meant to answer but before he could there was a loud, deep sound from somewhere farther up the hill. So loud that it seemed to come from *inside* Matt's head, so deep that it shook the ribs in his chest. It sounded similar to a powerful rushing wind or the cacophony of some terrible storm. But more than either, it sounded like something else...like the growl of some great beast. Matt stared up the hill, licking his lips nervously, then looked back at the stranger.

"It is nearly time," the stranger said, his voice sounding sad and full of regret.

"Time for what?" Matt asked, but there was something about the young man's demeanor that made him unsure of whether or not he wanted to know the answer.

The man turned to him, studying him with eyes so pale blue as to be almost white. Come," he told Matt. "Come and see, if you will."

He started up the hill.

Matt hesitated.

He did not want to follow the stranger. The thought of seeing whatever had made that sound, of whatever lay beyond his sight at the top of the hill filled him with icy dread. He could not climb that hill, could not see it.

And yet, he found his feet moving forward against his will. His heart began to thump a rapid beat in his chest as he fell into step beside the stranger. "What...what is it?" he asked.

The other man did not answer, though, only walked on and Matt noticed a slump to his wide shoulders. Saw, in that slump, in the stranger's trudging walk, the countenance of a man who knows he has a dark path ahead of him and no choice but to walk it.

It should have been the work of moments to reach the top of the hill, five minutes, no more. But instead it seemed to Matt to take an eternity, opposite to the shortened amount of time it had taken him to cross the field of the dead.

In time, they arrived at the top. Or, more precisely, one step away from the top. The young man paused, grabbing Matt's arm to keep him from moving forward then turning his pale gaze on him. "Do not show fear. It responds to fear."

Matt didn't like the sound of that, but before he could manage to get any objections past the sudden lump in his throat, they were moving again, the young man walking, Matt pulled along by whatever invisible force had taken hold of him.

They reached the top then and despite the young man's warning, Matt could not avoid the sharp *hiss* he let out as he sucked in his breath in terror at what waited for them there.

A giant beast. A creature of claw and teeth, its muzzle stained with blood, its razor-sharp claws gleaming crimson. It shifted, and Matt started to scream, sure that it was turning to come barreling at him, this beast the size of half a dozen carriages, with a mouth that could swallow a small cottage whole.

But before he could utter a sound, the young man clamped his hand around Matt's mouth, and he turned his gaze on him to see the stranger give a grim shake of his head. There was something incredibly familiar in that simple expression, but before Matt could pin down what that might be, the young man spoke.

"Do not scream," he said. "The screams...they nourish him. They are part of what he lives for. Most, maybe."

"What...what is it?" Matt asked, turning to stare at the creature, seeing that its eyes were closed and what he'd taken for it charging toward them was, instead, just its restless turnings as it shifted in what was a clearly troubled sleep.

The young man, though, did not answer him. At least not directly, and when he spoke Matt could not tell whether he spoke to him or to himself. "It sleeps," the young man said. "It has slept for a long time now, but it will not sleep much longer. It awakens. Do you see?"

Matt watched the creature move and shift. "I see," he said, terrified at the thought of being here when the creature opened its eyes.

"It is hungry," the stranger said, turning back to regard the field of corpses spread out all around them. "It is always hungry."

"Are...are you saying it did this? That it...that it killed them?"

"The beast awakens," the young man said, then he turned to Matt, his expression tense, hard, but Matt could see the worry, the fear, in his cold blue-gray gaze. "And I cannot stop it. Not anymore."

"What...what will it do? When it wakes?" Matt asked, staring at the giant creature as it shifted in its sleep.

"What it always does," the young man told him. "I have put it to sleep once before...I do not think I can do it again. You should go now. Get as far away as you can. Soon the beast wakes and, when it does, it will feast."

Matt turned and stared out at the river of corpses, then he turned to regard the beast. But despite his fear, despite the icy-cold dread that gripped him, he found his gaze settling on the man standing beside him. Young. Dark hair, steely eyes. There was something familiar about him, and Matt thought that he should know him, that he *would* know him, if not for the magic of dreams.

"Who are you?" he asked the young man.

The young man did not answer, though, and in another moment there was a growl, one that sent shivers down Matt's spine. "You had best go," the young man said. "Now."

Matt saw the beast shifting, looking as if it might awaken at any moment, and he nodded.

He started away. Or, at least, he tried to. For some reason his feet refused his commands. There was another growl, and he shot a look at the beast. Still asleep, but based on the way it was moving, stretching its giant paws, he did not think it would remain so for long.

He tried to move again. And, like before, his body refused to listen.

"*Go!*" the young man yelled.

"*I can't!*" Matt shouted back.

There was another noise from the beast, but this one sounded different, and they both turned, as one, to regard it as it rose to its feet, stretching its giant legs. Then it lowered its head and its eyes opened. Matt did not think he could have been anymore scared than he already was, but when the creature's eyes opened, he found that he was wrong. Pale blue eyes, the same as the stranger's only larger, stared at him.

The beast took a step toward him, and the young man suddenly lunged in front of Matt, holding up his hands. "*No,*" he roared. "*You can't have him! Not him!*"

And then, suddenly, Matt knew who the stranger was, the pieces clicking into place like a puzzle. Not that it was so difficult, for the figure standing before him, interposing himself between Matt and the beast, was not that of the young man he'd first seen standing at the base of the hill anymore. It was a much larger form with shoulders twice as wide as Matt's, a form he recognized well, and how not? After all, it belonged to his father.

"*You cannot have him,*" his father yelled again. The beast hesitated but only for a moment before starting forward again, taking its time, its teeth bared wider in anticipation.

"F-father?" Matt asked, his voice coming out in little more than a whisper. And as he stared at the man who he had not seen in days, in weeks, another emotion rose in him, one greater even than his fear. Relief. His father was here. His father was still alive.

"*You shouldn't be here,*" his father growled, grabbing him by the shoulders.

"I-I tried to leave but—"

"There is no time. Goodbye, son." His father pivoted, his inexorable strength pulling Matt along with him, and in another moment he was hurtling through the air, sailing over the fields of corpses. His father's strength was so great that it carried him through the air, beyond the hill, beyond the fields, and to the very edge of the dream, crashed him through it and into wakefulness where he jerked out of bed with a gasp, his body covered in sweat.

Early morning light streamed in through the window of his quarters, seeped underneath the crack of the newly installed door to his rooms, casting the room in a mixture of pale light and shadow.

Matt barely noticed. There could have been an army of assassins lurking creeping toward his bed, and still he would not have seen them. For all he saw, all he considered, were those last seconds before he'd exploded out of the dream.

Seconds in which he'd been flying through the air, seconds in which he had turned to look back. And as he had he had seen the fields of corpses, and his father standing among them, surrounded by death. But that was not all he had seen. He had seen the beast, too. The beast which had been lunging at his father, its great maw opened wide in anticipation. And for his part, his father had not even seemed to note the beast's approach, for his eyes had not been on it at all. Instead, his blue gray gaze had been locked on Matt, and there had been a small smile on his face.

The beast would take him in moments, Matt was sure, but his father had paid it no heed, and as he thought of that last image of him standing among the corpses, the beast coming for him, the last words of his father echoed in his mind.

Goodbye son, he'd told him.

And Matt, sitting in a puddle of his own sweat, his breath rasping from his lungs, felt tears gather in his eyes. He hoped, he prayed, that they would not be the last words he heard his father speak.

CHAPTER FIFTEEN

Cutter sat up from his bedroll, draping his arms over his knees. He'd had a lot of unpleasant dreams in his time, a lot of unpleasant visions. Products, no doubt, of a life made up of a lot of unpleasantness. But that dream, it had been a bad one. Matt standing in that field of the dead, men and creatures who Cutter himself had slain. Matt looking somehow different than the last time he'd seen him, a little older, a little harder. And staring at him without any of the hate or malice with which he'd seemed to regard Cutter when he'd sent him on his mission to the Black Wood what felt like a lifetime ago.

"So what's this beast then?"

Cutter glanced over to see Feledias sitting on his bedroll. His brother had several pieces of long thin grass and was weaving them in and out of each other the way somebody might crochet a quilt. It was something he'd done when they'd been kids, and seeing it brought Cutter back to a time long ago, back before all of the horrible things, back before his *life* had happened.

For a moment, he could almost see Feledias sitting before him. Not the Feledias of now, the Feledias whose hate had eaten away at him over the years, but the child he'd once been. The hopeful child with an intelligence that, even at a young age, had surpassed nearly everyone else, had certainly surpassed Cutter's own.

"Couldn't sleep?" Cutter asked.

"I find that being lost in hostile territory where seemingly every inhabitant save one has made it their personal mission to see me dead wreaks havoc on my body's rhythms." Feledias shrugged. "Anyway, I can always sleep when I'm dead. You know, like tomorrow."

"You don't think we'll die until tomorrow?" Cutter said. "That's unusually optimistic for you, Fel."

"It seems that imminent death brings out your humor, Bernard," his brother said, raising an eyebrow. "More's the pity. Now, what of the beast?"

"What beast?"

"The one you kept growling about in your sleep, of course." He waved a hand at the green fields all around them, an expanse that had remained unbroken by anything so much as even a single tree since they'd left the ogre and the illusionist creature's corpses behind them. "Unless there's a beast lurking in the grass somewhere, though if he's small enough to be concealed by it then I don't think he'll be too much of a worry."

That brought the dream back to him, brought Matt's frightened expression back, brought back the shameful incongruity of him standing among those fields of corpses, like a single flower remaining in a mud-churned bloody field as battle waged all around it. A flower that could only be smashed underfoot.

"Well?" his brother pressed. "Who is this beast then?"

It's me, Cutter thought. *It has always been me.* "Just a dream, nothing more."

"Sure," Feledias said. "And we're just in a field in a wood that's just a wood. But if you wish to keep your dreams to yourself, I will not stop you. Why bother trying to understand each other now, after all, with death so close?"

Cutter winced. "I dreamed about Matt."

"Ah yes, my dear nephew, the author of our current predicament."

"I think you know better than that," Cutter said. "We made our choices. Matt's not responsible for where we are, where our walking has brought us."

"Of course you're right," Feledias sighed. "Still, wouldn't it be easier if he were?"

"We've never taken the easy path," Cutter said. "Why start now?"

Feledias nodded at that as he glanced around them. Not that there was much to see. Fields unending, nothing else. "Well," he said. "It's morning." He glanced at the bleak sky where the sun seemed to cower behind the clouds, so that it did not seem to brighten the day at all so much as outline its shadows. "Or, at least, what passes for morning here. A new day. How would you like to spend it? Perhaps we might visit one of the new cafes in the city—I hear there is a fine one on Baker's Street. I always loved Baker's Street, the smell of freshly made bread, the angry shouts of the bakers. Or perhaps you'd like to go to a pub, have some ale. A trip along the tourney grounds—"

"Who's dreaming now?" Cutter asked.

Feledias sighed. "Ah, but what a dream. I'm not so picky as all of that though. I'd be more than satisfied with a new pair of trousers, perhaps a shirt to go along with them."

"What?" Cutter said, raising an eyebrow as looked at the shirt his brother wore, ripped in several places, old blood stains marring it. "Don't like what you've got on now?"

"Oh I love it—at least what's left of it. I'm only concerned that, at this point, it likely doesn't qualify as a shirt at all. Scraps, maybe."

"But scraps fit for a prince."

Feledias grunted sourly, and Cutter grinned. "As for what we're to do...I suppose we might go for a stroll."

"I was afraid you'd say that," Feledias said, sighing.

It didn't take them long to pack up their belongings, for they had very few belongings to pack. Their bedrolls, travel sacks that contained little more than a change of clothes that looked no better than what they currently had on, crumbs from bread that was nothing but a memory, and waterskins that were far more skin than water.

And his axe, of course. There was always the axe, the Breaker of Pacts. Cutter lifted it from where he'd set it on the ground and strapped it onto his back in its usual place.

And then they were walking. Not toward anything specific but he didn't think that mattered. After all, men rarely knew what they moved toward in their lives, and Cutter thought that often it wasn't what lay somewhere down the path that mattered. Instead, it was that a man walked the path before him. Not the destination then—but the moving. Just that he was going forward, just so long as he did not stop.

"You know," Feledias said after they'd been at it for a few minutes, "out of all the many ways I thought the Fey might kill us, I had not counted boredom among them."

Cutter had to admit he was surprised too. He had not been shocked when they'd been allowed a night's rest, but he had expected the challenges to resume promptly the next morning. After all, he was well aware of just how eager the Green Man and all the other Fey were to see him and his brother dead.

Yet as they continued on, the fields of green remained unbroken by form or figure. Feledias hissed a quiet curse from time to time, but Cutter did not share his brother's frustration. It was good to be moving, good to feel his muscles working, heating in the cold morning chill.

He had always lived his life guided by the belief, that a man could never lose, could never fail, until he stopped. Until then, failure was not failure, it was only a steppingstone on the pathway to success, as necessary in its way as every step that came before it and every step that might come after.

And it wasn't just the walking, wasn't just the warming of his body, though that was a part of it. It was also the quiet, the peace. After the dream he'd had, he thought he would like some quiet, and while he knew what peace he enjoyed would not last, as it never could, he refused to take the brief moment of respite for granted.

"This is bullshit," Feledias said. "It's one thing to make us fight an ogre, it's another to make us walk for no other reason than to be assholes."

"I'm terribly sorry to hear they've inconvenienced you, Fel," Cutter said, not bothering to hide his sarcasm.

"I'm just saying, if they're going to kill us, why not do it already? Why I'd almost rather face another one of those damned monstrosities than spend one more minute—"

"Wait," Cutter said, holding up a hand to silence his brother.

They stood in the quiet, listening. Cutter let his gaze travel around the field, still empty so far as he could see. He could not have said, for sure, what had alerted him. A sound, perhaps, or a smell. It might have been some flickering movement out of the corner of his eye. Or maybe it had been something he'd picked up not with any of his regular senses but with that other sense, the one that men had possessed from time immemorial. The one that had allowed them to exist, to even thrive in a world full of creatures far more deadly than them, creatures of fang and teeth, built for destruction.

A sense, an instinct that told him danger approached. That told him that he—*they*—were not alone. And so he stood the way the rabbit stood, its ear flickering as it tried to hear the great cat stalking through the high grass toward it.

"Fine, Bernard," Feledias said, "I'll stop griping, but I can't promise for how long. After all, you have to admit it isn't exactly—"

"Not that," Cutter said. "Something's here."

"Where?" Feledias asked.

"I don't know," Cutter said, his gaze traveling along the grass as he slowly turned. He saw nothing, but that did not matter. What a man saw or, in this case, did not see, did not change what he knew. And something *was* there—he knew it. Knew it as much as he had ever known anything.

"Are you sure?" Feledias asked. "Because I've got to be honest with you, Bernard, the only thing I'm seeing is nothing and more of it."

You yet live, came a rasping voice like the sound of fallen leaves rustling in the wind or the creak of branches beneath the frost.

Cutter turned to his left to regard the field that, a moment ago, had been completely empty. A familiar shape stood, twenty five feet away. "Shadelaresh," he said.

Destroyer, the Feyling responded, his pupilless emerald eyes flashing. *You have conquered your first trial, that of Strength.*

"I suppose the medals ceremony is to be later then?" Feledias asked.

The Green Man turned to regard Cutter's brother but said nothing before turning back. *But then even a brute, such as that creature you faced, has strength.*

"Well," Feledias interjected, "not anymore. Unless, that is, you plan on putting that poor bastard back together, a task I wouldn't envy you as Bernard here did a pretty thorough job of taking him apart."

The creature's emerald gaze turned on Feledias once more. *Oh, Stormborn, but you do love to hear yourself speak, don't you?*

"You can't blame a man for appreciating the sound of intelligence when he hears it."

Quite, the Green Man said, his eyes flashing. *I wonder, though, will you enjoy the sounds of your screams as much?*

That left Feledias without much to say—a rare occurrence—and the Green Man's ebony face shifted in a smile as he turned back to Cutter. *You have conquered the Trial of Strength, Destroyer, but I would not celebrate yet, were I you. For you travel the Path of the Warrior, and it takes far more than brute force to reach its end. For a warrior, a* true *warrior possesses not just strength but courage. Trust. Wisdom and Honor. Qualities which you know nothing about.*

"And patience—let's not forget patience," Feledias said.

The Green Man's face twisted in fury. The look was gone in another moment, but however brief the expression had been, however alien the Feyling's features, neither had stopped Cutter from seeing the insane hatred in his gaze.

I will enjoy watching you die, Stormborn, the Green Man hissed, the sound like dried leaves being crushed underfoot. *I will revel in it, and ere your soul departs your body I will ensure that an eternity of suffering is visited upon you. I will scour you out, tear you apart from the inside, and the shadows will feast on your fear. You cannot fathom the depths of despair which I will lead you t—*

"Enough," Cutter growled, and the Green Man cut off, rounding on him.

You dare to interrupt me?

"I would dare much more than that," Cutter said. "But then I don't think that's allowed. Or am I wrong?"

The Feyling sneered at him. *You are right in this, if nothing else. Very well, Destroyer. I will leave, as is the Law. But know this. Your time and the time for your clever brother comes.*

There was a burst of wind, a silent *pop* of force in the air, and then, in another moment, the Green Man vanished, leaving Cutter and Feledias standing alone in the endless field once more. Cutter turned to his brother, saw that Feledias's face was pale, his hands trembling with fear. Cutter understood his brother's fright, for it was not every day that one received a personal threat from one of the most powerful of the Fey, a creature who matched or even exceeded the nightmare visages attributed to demons and bogeymen.

"You should not provoke him," Cutter said.

Feledias cleared his throat. "Sorry," he said in a voice that wasn't quite steady. "It must be something about having my life threatened that makes me a bit peevish. Besides—" he paused, a smile trying to wiggle onto his face but quickly falling away—"it isn't as if he can kill me twice, is it?"

"There are worse things than dying," Cutter said quietly.

Feledias winced. "You really know how to comfort a man, Bernard."

"I'm not trying to comfort you, Fel. I'm trying to keep you alive. To keep both of us alive."

Feledias looked at him as if he were daft. "Haven't you realized it yet, Bernard? We're not walking out of here. Even if we somehow conquer all their little trials, beat all their little games, still we will not leave. We were dead the moment we set foot into the Black Wood."

"You don't know that."

"Don't I?" his brother countered. "You tell me, Bernard, does that green demon seem like the type to play fairly to you? He seem like the type to forgive and forget?"

"It isn't just up to him."

"No? Because I was back there at the Glade, just like you were, Bernard, and while I saw the Gray Man stand for us, I didn't see anyone else all too eager to do so. What about you? Did you see a lot of friendly faces?"

"Hard to tell," Cutter said. "What with the teeth and scales and all."

Feledias gave him a humorless smile. "Such a burgeoning comedic talent. It is a shame that you have discovered this particular interest so soon before we die a gruesome death."

"Maybe."

His brother raised an eyebrow. "Maybe what? Are you trying to say that you think we might survive somehow?"

Cutter shrugged. "Maybe. We should be—"

"You can't be serious," Feledias said. "Damnit, Bernard, look at what we face—we're dead. Doomed. There's no way we're making it out of the Black Wood alive. You do *know* that, don't you?"

Cutter stopped scanning the surrounding fields and turned to regard his brother. "What I know, Fel, is that a year ago I would have been sure—completely *sure*—that we would never come close to any sort of reconciliation. I would never have imagined that instead of killing each other we would be sent on a mission together—"

"A suicide mission."

"A *mission,*" Cutter repeated, "to seek peace in the Black Wood, an opportunity for me to try to seek some penance, some atonement for my sins. An opportunity for both of us."

"You really think we can atone for the things we've done? And even if we could, do you really think peace with the Fey is even possible? That's ridiculous, Bernard."

"Maybe," Cutter said. "But I have to try. The question is, will you try with me?"

"What choice do I have?" Feledias countered.

Cutter opened his mouth to answer, but before he got a chance something began to happen.

He frowned as the world began to darken around them. He turned his gaze to the sky, his frown deepening as what had, seconds ago, been a blue sky, began to grow darker and darker.

"Am I completely losing it, or is it not morning?" Feledias asked, also staring overhead.

"It was," Cutter said quietly.

"Then...what's happening?"

"Didn't you say, earlier, that you would rather something attack us than walk anymore? Well, Fel, I think you're about to get your wish."

Feledias turned, looking around the quickly darkening fields as shadows began to stretch out inky black fingers, like a great hand that meant to grab hold of the entire world. "What do we do?" he asked.

What it sometimes seems I have done my entire life, Cutter thought. "We fight."

"Fight *what?*" Feledias asked. "I can't see a damn thing. How are we meant to—"

"Quiet," Cutter hissed, for he had heard something. The whisper-swish of grass as someone—or something—moved through it.

To his credit, Feledias did as was asked, and Cutter listened. He listened not just with his ears, ears that could tell something was moving around them, brushing through the grass but which had a very difficult time telling where exactly that thing was and had no idea at all of *what* it was. He listened, also, to that part of him that he could not exactly define. Perhaps it was the beast, perhaps not. It was the part that had saved him countless times over the years, the part that knew battle and nothing else, and so knew it well.

It was the part that told him that he was *meant* to hear the creature moving in front of him and off to his left. And it did not take much consideration to wonder why anything or anyone that approached with ill intent would want to be heard.

"Bernard, are you su—"

It was a feeling more than anything else. Hot breath on the back of his neck. A chill running down his spine. A tightening in his shoulders, a rippling in the muscles of his arms, his chest, as that part of him, that primal part of him that perhaps belonged to the men of ancient times, warned him of danger. But he did not think so, did not think that it was the part of him that was a man at all.

It was the beast.

"Down!" he roared. Feledias was too slow, though, could only be too slow, and so Cutter put his hand on his brother's back, shoving him down. Fast enough to manage that much, at least, but not fast enough to raise his axe in time.

Which meant that the figure he'd sensed, the form that had leapt out of the grass toward them did not strike Feledias. It struck him.

It hit him in the chest with a blow that felt like the kick of a horse. He staggered but did not fall as claws raked at him. He didn't know what it was, not exactly. Something like a wolf, he thought, but all he could make out were its luminous amber eyes shining in the darkness, the flash of fangs closing inches in front of his face as its great maw snapped shut one time, then, growing closer still, a second time.

There was not a third.

Cutter grabbed hold of one of the creature's furred limbs then with a roar pivoted, spinning and launching the creature into the darkness.

There was a *thump* as it landed in the distance, accompanied by a yelp of pain.

Cutter glanced to his side, grabbing hold of his brother's arm and helping him to his feet.

"Fire and salt, what is it?" Feledias groaned.

"Angry," Cutter said, running his fingers along his chest and the cuts there. "And not alone." He slowly turned, listening to the sounds of the others moving through the grass around them. Half a dozen, perhaps more—it was hard to tell for sure in the darkness, but they were out there, slinking in a slow circle around him and his brother.

"You hurt?" Feledias asked.

"I've been hurt before."

"And likely will be hurt again and that sooner than either of us would like. How do you want to do this?"

"Back to back. Stay behind me."

"Happily, though I'm afraid that there's more than enough to go around, brother," Feledias said, and Cutter heard the metallic whisper of his brother's swords leaving their scabbard.

"Good luck, brother."

"And to you, Bernard. Once more into the fray."

Once more into the fray.

They were words from another lifetime, when they had both been kids. Words Feledias had said to him before a difficult test from their tutors or a lesson from their father's master-at-arms. Words he'd said when Cutter had gone courting his first girl and when he had gone courting his. They brought Cutter back to another time, back when they had not become what they were or, at least, had not *known* what they were. Feledias had said his part, and so it was left to Cutter to say his. "See you on the other side."

They waited, then, as the creatures circled around them, vague shapes in the darkness and, sometimes, not shapes at all. Only sounds.

"What are they waiting for, damnit?" Feledias asked after the creatures had still not attacked them.

"Easy, Fel," Cutter said, for he could hear his brother's fear in his voice, thought that was the point. He had fought in countless battles, and he knew that while bows and blades presented their own dangers, no sword was as sharp, no arrow nearly as deadly as a man's own fear. He had seen warriors of great skill fall to those with far less because they allowed that fear to grip them, to rob them of their strength.

Feledias didn't answer, and Cutter knew what that meant. His brother's fear had gotten hold of him. He could not blame him, for in the dark, where a man's eyes were of no use, it was easy to be afraid, easy to think, to *know* that he was alone, that there was nothing beyond those shadows but death, a death that was coming for him. And if that fear continued to pull at him, it would drag him down, and he would die, for fear robbed a man of his strength, robbed him, too, of his wits.

"What was that boy's name again? The one that used to pick on you when we were younger?"

"What?" Feledias said, sounding confused and annoyed at once.

"You know, that big kid with the gut and the red hair."

Cutter couldn't see his brother in the darkness, but he could feel him tense beside him at the memory. Thirty years and more it had been, but few memories were as powerful, he'd found, as those from a person's childhood. "Alvin Gunderson," his brother said, and though Cutter couldn't make out his brother's features, he could hear his frown in his voice.

"That's right, Alvin," Cutter said, though the truth was he'd remembered the boy's name well, enough. The same way that he remembered going to his father after the third or fourth black eye Feledias received and told him he wanted to handle it. After all, Alvin had been closer to his age than Fel's. But his father had refused, claiming that Feledias had to learn to fight his own battles, and now that he was older, Cutter realized he'd been right to do it. "He used to beat the shit out of you. Whatever happened to him anyway?" Another question he knew the answer to, but he thought that Feledias needed to hear it from himself, needed to be reminded of it.

"He beat the shit out of me," his brother said sourly.

"Until?"

"Until I beat the shit out of him...you bastard. I know what you're doing."

"No idea what you're talking about, Fel. Now, are you ready?"

"I'm ready," Feledias said, and when he spoke it was no longer fear that Cutter heard in his brother's voice but anger, anger that the memory of that long-ago bully had produced.

And with that, they waited for what would come.

They did not have to wait long.

The slow, methodical sound of the grass moving suddenly grew far louder, far faster, and Cutter tensed in anticipation as he watched yellow eyes rushing toward him out of the darkness.

As the closest set of eyes hurtled toward him, Cutter swung his axe in an upward strike, aiming at the amber glow. He missed the eyes, but that was alright, for he struck flesh. There was a terrible, wailing keening as the obsidian axe cleaved deeply into the wolf-like creature, flinging it away. Cutter paid it no more attention, however, for there were more eyes hurling toward him, and he decided that his estimation of the creatures' numbers had been woefully off.

He could only hope it had not been fatally so.

"*Bastard!*" Feledias yelled behind him, but Cutter couldn't turn to check on his brother for there were two more sets of eyes charging toward him out of the inky darkness.

He swung his axe in a wide sweep, striking flesh and moving through it, striking more, blood splattering his face and hands. And then the eyes were gone. Not that it mattered much, for there were plenty more to replace them, darting toward him.

Cutter struck again, the back swing of his axe cleaving deep into the flesh of his enemy, but before he could bring his weapon back up another of the creatures pounced on him. He would have fallen under the weight of the creature's body—a hundred pounds at least, he judged—had he not fetched up against Feledias's back where his brother stood behind him.

He couldn't bring his axe to bear, not with the creature so close, and his single free hand wasn't enough to keep the creature's attacks at bay, a fact evidenced by the claws scoring his upper arm and chest. So, reluctantly, Cutter let go of the Breaker of Pacts, letting it fall to the ground and bringing his now free hand up. His fingers quested in the darkness, moving through damp, dirty fur until he caught hold of what he was confident was the creature's neck. Then he used his other hand, wrapping it around it. The creature, apparently aware of his intentions, squirmed and kicked, not breaking loose but keeping him off balance so that he couldn't gain any leverage to twist its neck. He might have tried anyway, but he chose a different route.

He squeezed.

The creature let out a tortured croak as his grip tightened around its neck, one that cut off abruptly as he squeezed harder. Something *crunched* beneath his grip, and the creature's struggles ceased, its body hanging limp in his hands. Cutter let it drop, reaching for his axe, but before he was halfway there another creature leapt at him. He raised his left hand, more by instinct than anything else, catching the creature in the air. He slammed it down on the ground, stomping on what he hoped was one of its more important bits. The first stomp struck the creature's jaw, and it let out a yelp. The second time, though, his booted foot came down on the creature's snout which smashed beneath the blow.

Then, the creature dead—or, at least, a mewling, broken, dying mess lying at his feet—Cutter took the brief moment of respite to retrieve his axe.

He roared as more came on, seeming from every direction, dozens, hundreds of them. The beast inside roared with him.

And then the real bloodletting began.

He didn't know how long it went on.

He knew only that his arms burned like fire, and his legs felt as if they were made of stone. On and on they came, and on and on they fell before him. He slew one, then another, his axe reaping a bloody harvest, until finally one rushed toward him, and he brought his axe down in a two-handed blow, burying it in the head of a creature charging at him and driving it into the ground with bone-shattering force. Another leapt at him before he could pull his weapon free, and he roared as its teeth sank deep into the meat of his forearm. He shortened his grip on his axe and buried it deep in the creature's head, and its teeth let loose their hold. Then, Cutter ripped his axe free, letting the corpse fall to the ground. He stood straight once more, preparing to defend himself against the next opponent only to find that there was no next. No more amber eyes floated in the darkness, no more growls and hisses filled the air.

There was only the sound of his rasping breathing, and Feledias's grunt and a squelching sound as his brother ripped his own blade free of his latest kill.

"Done?" Cutter asked.

"Gods but I hope so," Feledias said, sounding exhausted. "Because if they're not then I'm getting ready to be. Anyway, what were you doing while I killed a hundred of those bastards? Taking your ease?"

"Something like that," Cutter said. He had barely finished speaking when he noticed something change. Or, rather, he *saw* it change. The unnatural darkness began to lift, like a curtain that had covered the face of the world being drawn away. It was uniform in its drawing, far different than the normal transition of night to day when the sun rises, much faster.

In moments, they were left standing in what was, if not broad daylight, as close to it as the Black Wood, the sanctuary and home of the Fey, ever got.

"You bastard."

Cutter turned to his brother to see that the man was staring at the pile of corpses lying at Cutter's feet then to the significantly smaller pile at his own. "And you let me do all that shit talking about you taking your ease?"

Cutter shrugged wearily. "You like to talk. Didn't see the harm in letting you."

"Wrong, brother. Perhaps on most days I like to talk. But just now..." He paused, glancing around once more at the beasts lying scattered around them, then at his own—and Cutter's—blood-soaked, scratched forms. "Well, just now, I don't think I like anything."

"Me neither," he said, but then he thought that wasn't exactly true. The beast wasn't completely awake yet, no, but it was restless in its slumber, and that part of it which was cognizant was pleased at the slaughter, rejoiced in it.

He blinked, giving his head a shake, shoving the thoughts away. They did not go far. But then they never did. "What are they?" he asked, thinking to get his mind off those dark, red thoughts. "Wolves?"

"Not any wolves I've ever seen," his brother said, kneeling down to examine one of the creatures. Feledias retrieved his belt knife and used it to pry open the creature's mouth, frowning. "And not unless wolves have poison in their teeth."

"Poison?" Cutter asked, blinking as a sudden bout of dizziness, no doubt caused from exhaustion and malnutrition, swept over him.

Feledias used his knife to lift away the creature's lip farther, revealing teeth that were coated in a slimy green substance. "That's my guess, anyway," he said. "Certainly not something I'd want wandering around in my body, that's for sure. It's a good thing neither one of us were bit."

"Yeah," Cutter said, blinking in an effort to banish his suddenly blurred vision. "Good thing." His legs felt weak and uncertain beneath him, and he wavered, frowning. "Bernard?" Feledias asked. "You didn't get bit, did you?"

Cutter frowned deeper, thinking. He had never been as clever as Feledias, a man who seemed to figure out in moments, what most others took hours, sometimes days of deliberating to discover, but he had never been a fool, either. Clever, in his way, or perhaps cunning would be closer to the truth, cunning like many beasts are. Only...he did not feel cunning now. He did not feel clever or smart. He felt like a fool. It was as if some fog had settled over his thoughts, and where they would have normally been easy enough to reach out and grab, now he felt like he was groping blindly in some impenetrable mist, and whatever thoughts he managed he did so not out of any skill or talent on his own part but out of pure luck.

"Bitten..." he said slowly.

Feledias gave a soft laugh, still eyeing the wolf-creature. At least, Cutter thought he was. In truth, his brother—and the entire world, come to it—had become little more than a vague blur. "That's right. If I'm any judge, a man would be better off playing free in one of New Daltenia's most...let us say *inexpensive* brothels. Though truth to tell, in my less proud moments I have found myself in one or two such places, and with some of the goods—or 'bads' as the case may be—on hire looking little better than our friends here." The blur shook its head. "No, I definitely would not want to have..." His brother turned, or at least Cutter thought he did, then paused.

"Bernard? Are you alright?"

"Sure. Why not?"

"Well, you're lying on the ground for a start."

Cutter frowned as he realized that was true. An odd thing not to notice, falling, but then he wasn't noticing a lot just then. All, that was, except for a darkness that seemed to be creeping into his vision.

"*Shit,* Bernard, your arm—one of those bastards bit you, didn't it?"

Cutter said something. Or, at least, he tried to. Was pretty sure he tried to. But whatever came out wasn't understandable to him. If it came out at all.

The truth was, he really wasn't all that sure.

The only thing he *was* sure of, just then, was that the darkness was getting closer. Not creeping into his mind now but rushing in, a great tidal wave of darkness crashing into his mind, into *him.*

And then, a moment later, there was no him at all.

Only the crashing...

Only the darkness.

CHAPTER SIXTEEN

"Tea, madam?"

Maeve glanced up from her massive desk in the Assassin's Guild, currently littered with an equally massive amount of papers and reports ranging from ledgers cataloguing every expenditure all the way from snacks down to assassination contracts, to see Amber standing in the doorway of her office. Standing there for what Maeve estimated could be no less than the tenth time in an hour. "No thank you, Amber."

The serving woman nodded, flashing her a smile before closing the door again.

Maeve stared at it, wondering how Agnes had managed to get anything done with the constant interruptions. She wondered, also, how the woman had managed to read so many reports and ledgers, logs and letters without committing outright arson—if not murder. Part of her—*all* of her—regretted making a point to Bethesa the day before about wanting to see all the papers.

Maeve's eyes were beginning to cross, and her fingers were sore from leafing through one parchment after the other. All documents, Bethesa had assured her via yet *another* cursed-letter, that were integral to her position, though how the amount of grain—an exorbitant amount—that was purchased to feed the teachers and students of the Assassins' Guild and the healers' academy above could be important she could not imagine.

Nor, in fact, did she wish to. When she'd first arrived, escorted by Balderath, she had been confident that her death was imminent. It seemed that she was right, though those plotting against her had not been so kind as to offer her a knife in the back—or chest or neck, at this point she wasn't all that particular. Instead, they had doomed her to a slow, painful death by a thousand paper cuts. She wondered how Agnes had been able to face it every day without murdering someone. Much more, and Maeve thought she would do something drastic, perhaps take her own life and save the assassins the trouble.

She wondered, also, about what Chall was doing, about Priest and Matt and, of course, Bernard, her prince.

What she did *not* wonder was why Agnes had sought to escape her role as Guildmaster for after the dozenth letter—each written in a smaller, even more cramped hand than the last, as if they'd had some sort of contest, one at which, to Maeve's mind, they were all winners—she understood the Guildmaster. After the twentieth, she hated her.

She would have given it up already and chosen something less tedious—like counting straws of hay, maybe, or walking in circles—except for one thing. She wasn't looking, despite appearances, to read every sheet of parchment with writing on it that existed in New Daltenia. Instead, she was looking to read only one—namely, the one that detailed the assassination attempt on her and Chall and, more specifically, *who* had put the contract out on them to begin with. Agnes had gotten the contract removed—her payment for them helping her—but Maeve still thought that if someone wanted her and Chall dead, it'd be nice to know who.

She hadn't found it yet, and she thought it likely that, lost in the sea of paperwork in which she'd waded—and drowned—for the last several hours since waking, she never would.

She hadn't wanted to stay at the Assassins' Guild, but she hadn't dared to go back to the castle, to Chall and the others. After all, the Tribunes could smile and nod all they wanted to, but Maeve was not a fool. Or, if she was, then at least she wasn't a *complete* fool. They might smile to her face, but behind her back they were plotting, looking for signs of weakness.

She didn't doubt that the Tribunes had begun digging into Maeve's life the moment they'd received the letter where Agnes had named her as her replacement. Looking into every friend, every acquaintance she'd ever had, searching for leverage. If she went back to the castle to see Chall she would put the man in even more danger than he already was. She knew this life, knew it for she had lived it for many years, and she knew how people like Bethesa and Piralta—even Silrika—thought. She knew because once she had been one of them. Snakes lurking in the grass, waiting for their opportunity to strike. Coyotes slinking in the darkness, their teeth bared in what might have been smiles, only they were not.

So as much as she would have liked to see Chall or Priest or any friendly face that didn't hide a blade, she didn't dare go to them. It was her mess, that was all, and she would be the one to clean it up.

She sighed, sitting back in her chair. A person might think that the one benefit of being scared for your life was that at least you wouldn't be bored. As it turned out, though, they would have been wrong. She went back to work. A short while later, the door opened once more.

"Ma'am, is there anything I can do for you?"

Has it been thirty seconds already? Maeve thought, only half-jokingly. She looked up to see Amber standing in the doorway. She considered asking her if she slept or ate, or even used the privy, and how she fit that into her constant checks. In the end, though, she decided against it. "No, thank you, Amber," she said to the stooped serving woman.

"Very well, ma'am," the old woman said, inclining her head, her constant smile plastered in place. Maeve wondered, as the woman, turned and started back through the door, if she practiced that friendly face in a looking glass, thought it likely she did.

Maeve rubbed at her eyes, trying to work up the courage to dive into the mountain of paperwork before her once more. She slumped into her chair, thinking again of Agnes. Wondering where she was, what she was doing, how she had managed all of this. Mostly, though, she wondered how difficult it would be to track the woman down and murder her.

Of course it was just a dream and one far beyond her reach. After all, even if she did somehow manage to extricate herself from the mountains of paperwork around her, even if she managed to get to feet that were numb from sitting, still she was not sure that she would even be *allowed* to leave the Guild. She had mentioned to Amber that she was considering going for a walk a couple of hours ago and had been met with a scandalized expression as if she'd just suggested parading through the streets naked. Then she'd proceeded to start away with the intention of summoning a guard contingent—her word—at which point Maeve had changed her mind.

Maeve wanted to scream. She wanted to talk to someone, anyone. Well, almost anyone. She didn't much care to have another conversation with the old serving woman who somehow managed to project an aura both of servility and disapproval at the same time. She couldn't imagine how Agnes had done it, how she'd endured the frustrations for so long without having someone to confide in.

She realized she was stalling, casting about for anything to contemplate, anything to consider save for the piles of papers on her—and, if the world was fair at all what should still be Agnes's— desk. It was for this reason that her eyes alighted on the front of the desk itself, on a particular part where the wood was the slightest bit lighter than the other, as if it had been worn away from being touched or rubbed often.

Maeve frowned at that. Nothing, probably. Nothing except some spot on the desk that Agnes had fidgeted at in order to keep herself from committing murder. Or, at least, anymore murder than she intended. Still, Maeve reached for it, running her finger along it. It was a small space, only about as wide as her hand with only the slightest discoloration, a thing she wouldn't have noticed at all if she hadn't spent the last several hours sitting here, staring at the desk and the insurmountable mounds of work it contained.

But she had noticed, just as she noticed the way it seemed to give the slightest bit beneath her fingers. Which was odd. What was odder still was that, when Maeve pushed on it, it popped open, sliding out no more than six inches, a tiny drawer apparently connected to some invisible hinge.

Her curiosity fully aroused, Maeve bent down to look at the drawer and found, sitting inside, a small, bound book. The front binding was blank, bearing neither title nor author, and Maeve frowned as she opened it. The writing inside was in a slanted scrawl, and it took only a moment of perusing to realize that she held what could only be Agnes's diary.

And based on the thickness of it—heavy enough to knock somebody out if it was swung with some feeling—Maeve adjusted her earlier opinion. Agnes *had* had someone to confide her frustrations with her role as Guildmaster in—namely, herself.

"Forgive me, Guildmaster, can I—"

Maeve looked up and was unsurprised to see the old woman, Amber, standing in the doorway. She was surprised, however, that the woman had stopped in the middle of her usual question. "Guildmaster, if you don't mind my asking, what is it that you are reading?"

Maeve shrugged. "It would appear that Tribune Bethesa was right, and Guildmaster Agnes did have a diary after all."

"I see," the woman said. "Very well, then with your permission I will go and let Tribune Bethesa and the others know. They will be most pleased to hear that you have located the diary." The woman bowed, turning to start away, but paused as Maeve spoke.

"Hold a moment, Amber."

The serving woman glanced back at her. "Guildmaster?"

Maeve looked at the small diary, thinking. She was in a precarious situation—there was no denying that. A position which, until recently, Agnes had occupied for years. Years in which she had managed to survive the machinations of the Tribunal as well as a guild full of assassins and schemers, many—perhaps all—of whom would have been more than happy to have taken her position. Which meant that, contained within her diary might well be information that could prove invaluable to Maeve, not just in staying alive—though that was certainly a concern—but also in dealing with the other members of the Guild.

"Let's...wait on telling the Tribunes for now."

"Ma'am?" the woman asked, giving her that shocked look again. "Surely you jest. That is...the Tribunes asked us to tell them if we found the diary. Tribune Bethesa said to let her know right away and—"

"And Tribune Bethesa is not Guildmaster," Maeve finished. "I am. Aren't I?"

She met the woman's eyes and, in a moment, the older woman looked away nervously. "O-of course, Guildmaster."

Maeve winced inwardly. *Nice job, bullying an old woman. Aren't you so tough?*

"I-I'll leave you alone then, Guildmaster. If...if that's alright?"

"Yes, it's fine. Thank you, Amber."

The woman gave her an anxious smile then started away, pausing once more. "Guildmaster, would you like anything? Some breakfast, perhaps?"

"No thank you," Maeve said, giving the woman the best smile she could. Amber gave her a nod, glancing at the diary once more before turning and walking out, closing the door behind her.

She started to leaf through the diary. Much of it was complaints of one thing or another—several passages were Agnes going into great detail of what she'd like to do or, in some instances, have done to the Tribunes. Others referenced the Guildmasters, certain contracts, and at least one, Maeve saw, were several pages that were dedicated, solely, it seemed, to complaining about the mounds of papers on her desk, a complaint with which Maeve personally sympathized.

She continued to thumb her way through the diary until a familiar name popped out at her. Not one of the Tribunes—though they had been mentioned plenty. Instead, it was the name Amber, the same name as that of the serving woman.

She had plenty she needed to be about—specifically looking for any information regarding the contract that had been taken out on her and Chall and who was responsible—but Maeve's curiosity got the better of her.

She'd just started to read the entry when the door opened again, and she looked up to see the old serving woman standing there. The woman held a tray upon which sat a cup of what, based on the steam rising from it, Maeve judged to be tea. "I apologize for the interruption, Guildmaster," the woman said, bowing her head as best she could while holding the silver tray with both hands, "but I have returned with your tea."

Maeve frowned, quite confident that she had declined the woman's offer of tea. She considered saying as much but, in the end, let it go. Amber was probably lonely, that was all, and based on the way she was watching her, expectant, nervous, Maeve thought she must have brought the tea as a sort of peace offering, hoping to get back into Maeve's good graces after she'd snapped at her. And should Maeve decline, it would be as if she declined the woman herself.

"Ah, thank you very much, Amber. Some tea would be nice."

The woman smiled, clearly pleased, as she brought the tray to the desk, carefully setting it down on the one empty spot—a spot that had taken several hours' worth of work to clear—on the large surface.

"Is there anything else, mistress?" the woman asked, and Maeve didn't miss the way she kept glancing at the diary in her hands.

"No, thank you, Amber, that will be all," Maeve said, giving the woman a smile.

The serving woman bowed her head, and Maeve returned to the entry she'd seen.

—I do not know which of them she works for, but I am confident she works for one of them, Agnes wrote. *The old hag, perhaps, or the mad dog but then it is possible that the weasel pulls her strings. After all, he, like so many cowards and flatterers, is clever. Any rate, I do not trust her. She makes out to be a sweet old lady, bent with age, but I do not believe it. Besides, even a dull blade can cut, if given opportunity enough.*

Maeve frowned. It did not take much thinking to figure out about whom Agnes spoke. After all, Maeve herself had heard Agnes refer to the Tribunes as the hag and the weasel multiple times. Mad dog was a new one, but then she was confident the woman referred to Silrika. She looked up and was surprised—and, given what she'd just read, more than a little unnerved—to see the serving woman, Amber, staring at her, a smile fixed on her face.

"Yes?" Maeve asked. "Is there something else, Amber?"

"It's only your tea, ma'am. I made it myself, my own recipe, and forgive me, but I must admit to a certain degree of eagerness to see what you think."

I don't doubt you do, Maeve said, giving the woman a smile as she glanced down at the cup. It looked like tea and nothing else, but then she suspected poison would be considerably less effective if it was obvious to all those who were meant to drink it. Likely she was being paranoid—probably she was. After all, what possible reason would the woman have to want her dead? None that she could think of. Or, at least, it was more accurate to say no reason other than those the Tribunes had already possessed when she'd first arrived. No, if they'd wanted her dead they'd needed only to say as much and she did not doubt Balderath the Brutal would have been happy to oblige.

Sure, she was probably being paranoid—probably *Agnes* had been paranoid as well. But the thing was, a person rarely regretted being careful—in her experience, they almost always regretted not being careful enough.

Maeve offered the woman the best smile she was capable of, taking her hand away and putting it on her lap. "Perhaps later," she said. "I will be sure to let you know how it tastes."

"Please, ma'am, but you surely would be doing your servant a kindness," the woman asked, her old, grandmotherly features stretching into an ingratiating smile. She looked one step away from offering Maeve a treat or some earthly wisdom, so perfect was the act. If, indeed, it *was* an act. After all, Maeve thought that surely *someone* walking the face of the world had to be who they appeared to be, though admittedly she wouldn't expect to find such a specimen in the Assassin's Guild of all places.

And while the woman's grandmotherly act was convincing, there was a hardness, a *sharpness* to her gaze that one didn't expect to see in a grandmother. "I said I will try it," Maeve said. "Later. Now, if there is nothing else, Amber, I have a lot to do."

"Just the one thing, Guildmaster," the woman said. Part of Maeve had expected something, yet even still she nearly died, for the woman moved with a speed Maeve wouldn't have credited her, withdrawing a wicked-looking blade from inside her simple servant's shift and lunging forward. The blade traced a line in the air, one that would end in Maeve's chest. Or, at least, would have.

She'd been ready for just such an eventuality, so while she might not have normally been able to parry such a quick attack, expecting it made all the difference, so as soon as the woman reached for the blade Maeve was already moving.

Maeve used the ridge of her hand to knock the woman's strike wide even as she rose from her seat with enough speed and force to send it hurling over its end and, in one smooth motion, buried the blade she'd drawn when bringing her hand down to her lap in the woman's chest.

The old woman staggered back, fetching up against the wall and staring at the dagger embedded in her chest with obvious surprise. She raised her face, then, and the look of pure hatred she gave Maeve eliminated any thought of her as a kind old lady. "*Bitch,*" the woman sneered, bloody spittle going down her mouth. "You're...going to die."

"You first," Maeve said softly.

The woman bared her crimson-stained teeth and took a step toward Maeve before promptly collapsing to the floor of her study. Maeve looked at the diary lying on her desk, blinking. "Alright, Agnes," she said quietly. "We're even." She turned back, staring at the body, feeling stunned. She'd seen dead bodies before, of course—the fact was that she thought there was a good chance she'd seen more of the dead than the living in her lifetime. But still she found herself staring at the woman, the woman that might have been anyone's grandmother, that should have been enjoying her twilight years in relative peace instead of colluding with assassins.

Easy there, she told herself idly. *You're not far away from those twilight years yourself, and you're not just colluding with assassins—you're their Guildmaster.*

Idle thoughts from a mind that was casting about trying to decide what to do. The woman was dead—that was the thing, and it wasn't as if Maeve could ask her to remove her dead self from her quarters. Which meant that it was up to her. But Maeve was older than she had been, and she thought it likely that her corpse-moving days were behind her, if she'd ever had them at all.

Besides, even if she could somehow move the body herself, there was no way she could make it past the two "bodyguards" stationed outside her quarters without them seeing. That would be asking for two miracles in a row, and in her experience the world was not so giving as that. And should those men who pretended to be her bodyguards but who were, she did not doubt, loyal to one of the Tribunes, be tasked with removing a dead body, they would waste no time telling their master. Which would be bad. After all, the Tribune—or Tribunes—in question would be forced to wonder how much Maeve had learned from their agent before her death.

She hadn't learned a thing, of course, but then they wouldn't know that. They would also, no doubt, wonder about the *reason* the woman had attacked Maeve in the first place, and Maeve found that she did not much care for the idea of explaining that to them. After all, Bethesa had tried to hide it, but Maeve had not missed how much she'd wanted the diary. Which meant that she believed that there was important information contained in its pages and, considering that it had just saved her life, Maeve was tempted to agree.

No, she could not risk alerting the Tribunes to the truth, it was as simple as that.

But what options did she have?

It wasn't as if she had a bunch of assassin friends that she could call on to help her.

No, she told herself, *but you do have one.*

One who had been a member of the current Guild for more than a few days, one who was familiar with all the players and one who would not arouse any suspicion should she be seen coming to Maeve's rooms. Or, at least, not *much* suspicion. Assassins, as a general rule, were not a particularly trusting bunch.

But even as talented as Emille was—having seen the woman dispatch several crossbowmen with incredible ease, Maeve could attest to that—even as *clever* as she was, she would still not be able to make a body disappear without a trace. At least, not without leaving the room and that, unfortunately, was exactly what was required.

Luckily, though, Maeve knew somebody who could do exactly that.

She didn't like the idea of involving Chall, and her reasons for not liking it were the same as they had been half an hour ago. But then she didn't have much choice. It wasn't as if she could tell the two bodyguards stationed outside her door to go have lunch and not expect them to be suspicious.

She sighed. "You know, you have just made things really inconvenient for me," Maeve told the dead woman.

The dead woman, unsurprisingly, had little to say on the subject. And, Maeve supposed, that even though her own situation was bleak and getting bleaker with each moment that the blood was left to soak deeper into the carpet, it was not quite so bleak as the dead woman's. Life was a pain in the ass. Death was worse.

Or so she'd heard.

She didn't like the idea of involving Chall, but if she wanted to go on living she thought that was exactly what she was going to have to do. She sighed, thinking it over. After a moment, she came up with an idea. A dangerous idea, one that was all too likely to end up with a knife in her back—or maybe her front—but considering that it was the only one she had, it pretty much won out by default.

She took a deep breath. "I'll be back," she told the dead woman, then she stepped out of her study. She started across the sitting room where, the night before, she had sat with the Tribunes, wondering when they would kill her and how much it would hurt.

She moved to the door, pausing in front of it to glance at her clothes and make sure she hadn't gotten any of the woman's blood on her. Satisfied, she took a slow, deep breath, putting on a blank expression as she'd been taught so long ago. An expression that didn't say much of anything, that certainly did *not* say that she'd just murdered a woman in her study.

Then, Maeve opened the door.

The two men were standing as she'd last seen them. Whatever else they were—likely assassins hidden in plain sight, prepared at a moment's notice to take her life—Maeve had to admit that the men were vigilant. "Edgar, wasn't it?" she asked the older of the two.

The man stared at her with a blank expression. "Phillip, ma'am."

"Right, just so. Listen, Phillip, I have some work I need to get done and for it I require some assistance."

"Of course, ma'am," the man said, bowing his head. "If you will inform us about what it is you require we will make sure to find someone that will best suit your needs."

"Actually, I already have a someone in mind."

"Oh?"

"Two someones, in fact," Maeve said.

"Forgive me, but are you quite sure you would not rather one of us find those you need? After all, you have been gone a long time and—"

"Guildmaster."

The man frowned. "What's that?"

"You meant 'forgive me, Guildmaster,'" Maeve said.

The man watched her for a moment, and though there was no expression on his face, Maeve knew that he was weighing her. Weighing her the same way wolves might eye an aging alpha, deciding if they thought they could take it down. Maeve tensed, preparing to go for one of the knives she'd hid on her person. She doubted she would get to it in time if the man decided to attack, but like a noblewoman rushing toward an awning in hopes of not getting wet by a sudden shower, she was ready to give it a damned good try.

In the end, though, the man did not attack. Maeve couldn't say what exactly changed. One moment she could feel the tension building in the air. The next, he only nodded, glancing at his companion before moving his gaze back to her. "Of course, Guildmaster," he said. "I beg your pardon. I did not mean any offense. If I may be so bold, ma'am, I grew up on stories about you and...and I just want to say, it's an honor to meet you. For both of us."

Maeve glanced at the other man who was nodding. They seemed genuine enough but then, so too had Amber, right up until she'd tried to murder her. "You want to pay me back, how about keeping anyone from murdering me." *Including yourselves.*

"Of course, Guildmaster."

She nodded. "Good. Now, there are two people I need brought here and I would much prefer if we kept this to ourselves."

The guard, Phillip, glanced at his companion, who gave a nod then back to Maeve. "Yes, Guildmaster. We're listening."

And that, she did not doubt, they were doing with alacrity. After all, whichever Tribune they worked for—assuming they did work for one, and when it came to assassins Maeve found it always better to assume such things—would want to know as many details as possible. Still, it wasn't exactly as if she was spoiled for choice. After all, as Chall had so recently intimated, you had to trust someone sometime.

And that was true.

The problem, of course, Maeve thought as she began to issue her instructions to the waiting men, was that while it might be true that a person had to trust someone sometime, that wasn't the only truth.

There was another. Everyone had to die sometime, too.

CHAPTER SEVENTEEN

"Em?"

He stood at the door.

It was locked, and that was no surprise. He had the key, just as his wife did. And why not? It was their house. *His* house. And yet the thought of letting himself in with his key felt far too much like trespassing. And so, he had knocked. Knocked the way a stranger might. Knocked the way someone might who was unsure of the welcome they might receive.

"Em?" he called again. "Are you there?"

Still no answer.

"Everything alright?" Lady Valencia asked from behind him, and Ned thought he could hear what might have been amusement in her voice. Which just went to show that the woman didn't have a wife—if she had, then she'd know that a pissed-off wife was no laughing matter. More of a run-and-hide matter, really.

"Fine," he said. But then he wasn't really sure about that, not at all. He'd lost count of how many days it had been since he'd spoken to Emille—if getting yelled at could be counted as speaking. Three? Two? Too many, anyway, that was for sure.

He sighed, reaching into his pocket and retrieving his key. Then, taking a slow breath, he slid it into the lock. *"Em,"* he called as he swung the door open. *"It's me. Ned. Your husband."*

He wasn't sure why he felt the need to remind her of that just then, wasn't sure, in truth, if it would make him less likely to get hit over the head with something if she was inside—or more likely. He only knew that he had never felt as distant from his wife since meeting her as he now did, and he did not like that distance, not at all.

He stepped into the home. *His* home.

He knew in a moment that she was not there, and while he was worried about what she might say when she saw him, what she might *do,* Ned found himself letting out a regretful sigh. Angry or not, she was his wife, and he missed her. He missed her terribly.

"Nobody home?"

He glanced back at Val standing in the doorway, peering inside. "Apparently not."

"Does your wife normally get such an early start?"

No, he thought, *no she doesn't.* But he didn't answer, didn't want to. He was worried. Not for himself as he had been on his way over here, but for his wife. She should have been home—he'd been confident that she would be. Even when she had not answered he had chalked that up to her anger with him, anger that he'd expected to get the full weight of when stepping inside. Either in yells or shouts or in the cold, frigid silences that, in his experience, were far worse.

He wondered, for a moment, if he'd been wrong. Had Robert and Catham and whoever else they were working with somehow tracked down his home? Had they come here to find him only to find his wife instead? The thought made Ned break out into a cold sweat, and his heart began to thunder in his chest, beating so hard he thought it a wonder it didn't rip its way out.

For a second, a very long, stretched second, he had the nearly undeniable urge to sprint out of the door, to run through the city streets shouting his wife's name or to run to the poor district and find the bastard, Catham, and demand to know where his wife was.

In the end, though, he stopped himself from acting so foolishly reckless, if only just. After all, he reasoned with himself, Chall and Priest were already hunting down Catham, and he was confident they could handle the man. Besides that, if he allowed himself to be ruled by his emotions, he would make mistakes, mistakes that would cost not just him but Lady Valencia, Chall and Priest, and the gods alone knew who else. No, he would trust Chall and Priest. He would trust them because they had not let him down yet and because, in the end, he had no choice. After all, it wasn't as if he didn't have his own problems to deal with.

On the other hand, without her, without Emille, none of the rest of it mattered. He'd been dead when he met her. Dead, and he hadn't even known it. And she, being the healer that she was, had brought him back to life again. And now that she had, now that he'd seen what it meant to live, to really *live*, he was not ready to give it up again.

Perhaps what Chall had told him was true—perhaps she really was an assassin working for the Guild, though how such a thing might have passed unnoticed between them he could not imagine. But then he was not mad at her. How could he be? After all, he had his own secrets. For now.

"It isn't much," Ned said, looking around his home, "but you'll be safe here." And that was true, only not in the way he'd meant it when he said it. It wasn't much—it was everything. It was their place, his and Emille's, their place that they had built together. The place they lived in together.

"Oh, I think I'll manage, Neddy," Val said. "But tell me, where do you keep your servants? The cupboard? Or, if they are not live-in servants, what time do they arrive? I shall be wanting breakfast soon, I expect."

Ned blinked, opening his mouth to answer—or, at least, to try to—but before he could she let out a laugh, shaking her head.

"Clever and a fool all at once," she said. "It seems that nothing's changed."

No, Ned thought, smiling as he looked around his home. *Everything's changed, and I wouldn't have it any other way.* "There is food here and clean water. A spare bed in the back room there," he went on, nodding his head. "Make yourself comfortable. You'll be safe here."

"Oh?" she asked, sounding surprised. "You're not staying?"

"I'll be back soon," he promised. "Only, I have some things to take care of first." *I'm going to find my wife.*

"I see," she said slowly, and by the look in her eyes, he thought maybe she did. "Your wife, she is a good woman?"

"Better than I deserve."

Lady Valencia nodded. "I am happy for you, Ned. Truly. I know that many believe that I married my departed husband for money and status, and while it is true that my mother and father arranged the marriage, I did come to love Edward, in my way. Yet even that love, I think, pales in comparison to that you share with your lady love. But remember what your friend the mage said—for the love you bear her, it is better that she knows nothing of what is really happening."

"More lies."

"Are lies told to protect someone really lies?" she countered. "Or are they more a shield to stand in the way of those things, those *people*, we love and those things which might do them harm?"

Ned considered that but not for long, for he knew the answer well enough. They were lies. And a man never lied for others—he only ever lied for himself. "I've got to go," he said. I'll be back to check on you before the day's out." *And, the gods willing, I'll be with my wife.*

He started toward the door.

"Neddy?"

He paused, his hand on the door, and glanced back at her. She looked...smaller than he remembered. Val had always been strong. Not physically, maybe, but with a strong personality, more of a force of nature than a woman. Imposing, with no patience for foolishness and always confident in herself. She did not seem confident now. She seemed, more than anything, scared. No surprise, really, considering that in the last couple of days she'd had what had once been a close friend try to kill her and had several of her servants and household guard killed as well. Ned cursed himself for his callousness, for in his rush to get to Emille he'd done almost nothing to comfort his old friend.

He moved toward her, taking her hands in his, aware of the way they trembled, aware of how frail they seemed. "It's going to be okay, Val."

"Oh, Neddy," she said softly, and he saw what might have been tears in her eyes. "I am old, and I know that I don't have many years left—"

"Val, you'll live a lot longer ye—"

"Nonsense. I know my time approaches just as the sun knows when the time has come for it to sink below the horizon once more. My morning, after all, was a very long time ago. Longer than I sometimes like to admit, even to myself."

He opened his mouth to speak, but she held up a hand, silencing him. "My *point*," she said, "is that some might think that a person, knowing her end approaches, might find some peace, but I have not found that to be true. When we are young, we have much time—or, at least, believe ourselves to—and so we give it little thought. But when we are old, when we can see the sands of the hourglass draining before our very eyes, then it seems to me that we grip what's left all the tighter. I'm afraid, Ned."

"I know," he said. "Me too. But it will be okay. Everything's going to work out."

"Do you really believe that?"

"I have to believe somethin'," he said. "I choose to believe that."

She nodded slowly, not saying anything for a moment, and while he was eager to set out and go about looking for his wife, he could tell that there was something else on Val's mind. He didn't rush her though and, in another moment, she spoke.

"Did you ever think...that is, have you ever considered that...maybe we were wrong, all those years ago?"

"What do you mean?"

"I think you know what I mean," she said, meeting his gaze. "Robert wanted to keep going, after...well, after what happened at Lord Banham's house—"

"You mean after he murdered an entire family. Innocents, Val."

"Yes, I know," she said. "It was atrocious, terrible, I'm not saying it wasn't. Only...we did good back then, Neddy. Didn't we?"

There'd been a time when Ned had thought they had. Now, though, in retrospect, he wasn't so sure. Now, it felt all too much like they'd tried to put out a fire by throwing more fire on it. "I don't know," he said.

"And if we did," she pressed on, "then wouldn't that good that we'd done outweigh even the death of that family, tragic though it was?"

He frowned then, but before he could say anything she spoke on. "I guess what I mean, Neddy, is if you could kill one innocent to save a thousand, would you do it?"

"Such a thing isn't within my power."

"But what if it was?"

Ned considered that. He'd heard such questions before, of course. It was the dreaded hypothetical, the way in which men and women tried to justify so many of their actions. The way in which he, some time ago, had tried to justify his own. Finally, he shook his head. "I'll tell you what I think, Val. I think that if a man wants to do good, he should do good, not do evil and hope that good comes of it. And as for your question, I think that the best that we can do is to live the life we have, not to be a good person but to be a good person in the moment. I think that some of the world's greatest evils reside in what-ifs. Why? Do you feel differently?"

"Of course not," she said. "I just...I just needed to hear you say it, I guess. After all, we are committed. *I* am committed. I set my feet on this path many years ago, and I am too far down it now to change course, even if I wanted to, and I do not."

Ned watched her for a minute, waiting to see if she would say more, and she rolled her eyes, waving a dismissive hand. "Go on with you, then. Go about your business."

"You're sure you're alright?"

She gave him a smile. "A man I once called the closest of friends wants to kill me, I've fled my home, and now, on top of it all, I don't have access to *any* of my dresses. What could possibly be wrong?"

Ned winced. "I'm sorry, Val."

"Sorry? About what?"

"About...everything, I guess. Sorry about you having to leave your home, about Robert being back. Sorry about your servant, too."

"Is that all?"

He frowned. "What?"

"I had a pretty bad fall last year. Broke my wrist. Are you sorry about that?"

"I don't—"

"Or what about my husband dying? Are you sorry for that? Are you sorry for the fact that I've put on fifteen pounds in a year and that my knees ache when it's going to rain?"

"I'm not sure what—"

"My point, Ned, is that you have nothing to be sorry for. I'm a big girl, and I made my own decisions. You didn't make them for me—you couldn't have made them for me, even if you'd wanted to. I've made my bed and now I'll lie in it. I can only hope, can only pray to whatever gods might be listening, that I don't die in it too. Now go on, take care of your business. I can look after myself."

He didn't think things were great with her. He thought she was troubled, somehow, but that concern paled in comparison for the concern he had for his wife, the impatience digging at him to go, to find her. "Very well. I will be back soon," he said. "Then we will talk." And with that, he turned and walked to the door and stepped out into the city to find his wife.

CHAPTER EIGHTEEN

Chall arrived back at the castle alone.

He'd meant to go with Priest—that had been the plan when they'd discussed it with Ned and the Lady Valencia—but no sooner had they left the small, decrepit building than Priest had told him he was going alone. Chall had challenged him on this, but Priest had told him that to find Catham he would need to meet and speak with people from his past, people who as a rule didn't care for strangers. And Chall, partly because he didn't want to end up with any fresh holes in him but mostly because he didn't really have a choice—if Priest decided he was going alone all it would take would be a slow jog and he'd leave Chall behind—he had reluctantly agreed.

His initial thought was to go to his quarters. Perhaps Maeve would be there and, failing that, she might have left a note or sent word. But he thought he needed to check on Matt first, so he moved through the castle corridors and, in a few minutes, stood at the hallway leading to the king's rooms.

He nodded to the two guards there who nodded back before he continued on. Outside the king's door, two more guards stood in position on either side, and Chall was unsurprised to find that Vorrun was one of them. As he walked up, he noted what appeared to be a troubled expression on the older guard's face, noted, also, two trays sitting near the door, both laden with food. Both, it appeared, completely untouched.

"Vorrun."

"Challadius," the man said, trying for a smile but not quite getting there. "It is good to see you. I had hoped you might come."

"I take it not because you wanted to play a game of cards?"

"I'm afraid not."

Chall sighed, glancing at the door. "How bad is it?"

"I don't mean to speak out of turn, but—"

"How bad, Vorrun?"

"Bad, I think. His Majesty did not sleep much last night, if he slept at all. And he has not eaten in at least two days, perhaps more."

Chall winced, fighting back the urge to curse. Assassins seemed to be coming and going as they pleased in the castle, a group of murdering vigilantes seeking justice had re-formed and seemed a lot more interested in murder than justice, and Maeve had been taken by a man nicknamed Balderath the Brutal. It was the worst possible time for the king to be going through...well. Whatever it was he was going through.

He hesitated, thinking it would have been better if Priest were here for this. But Priest was off hunting criminals, and so he was not here. And even if he were, with the way the man had been acting lately, Chall was not so sure that would have been a good thing. "Alright if I go see him?"

"He's asked to be left alone," Vorrun said.

"Ah, right—"

"But I've lived long enough to know that often times the things we want are rarely what we need."

"Sergea—" the other, younger guard began, but Vorrun held up his hand, and the man cut off.

"Good luck," Vorrun told Chall, then he opened the door.

Chall gave a brief thought to how a man might find himself going through so many doors he doesn't want to go through in so short a time before walking through.

Inside, the king's quarters were a mess. Clothes were tossed haphazardly around the room, hanging from the backs of chairs, lying in heaps on the table. The sheets and coverlet of the bed were in disarray, balled up and twisted.

And that was far from all.

There was another tray sitting on the table with some old meat and bread, flies buzzing around it, and one of the table's chairs—or at least what was left of it—lay in a broken heap, looking as if someone had taken it in both hands and slammed it against the floor until it had come apart. A particularly *determined* someone, for they were good chairs and well made. There was a smell, too. The smell of the ruined food, yes, but more than that, the smell of stale sweat.

If desperation had a smell, Chall thought, if it had a *look,* then this was it. His gaze traveled across the terrible state of the room to the window where Matt stood staring out at the early morning sun.

"Good morning, Chall," Matt said without turning, a low, rasping, empty quality to his voice that Chall did not like.

"Majesty, how...how did you know it was me?"

"I told Vorrun not to let anyone in," Matt said as if Chall hadn't spoken. "I suppose I'll have to punish him."

"Vorrun was only doing what he thought best, Majesty. He's trying to help you."

Matt did turn then, and as he did Chall saw the deep, purple circles under his eyes and the shrunken appearance of his cheeks. The king gave Chall an exhausted, humorless smile. "Help," he said. "No one can help me."

Chall hesitated, thinking of what he might say, doing his best to overcome his shock at the king's haggard, terrible appearance. He'd known Matt was troubled, but he'd had no idea just how bad it was. "I...I know it sometimes it seems like no one can help, Matt, but—"

"It seems like it because it's true," Matt said. Not angrily or snappish—in truth, Chall would have preferred either. Instead, the young man's voice sounded empty. Dead.

"The dreams again?" Chall asked.

Matt gave a soft, tired snort without feeling. "Again implies they stopped, and they have not. They have only grown worse."

Chall nodded. "I'll go get Healer Malden," he said. "He'll—"

"You don't think I've tried that?" Matt said, and there was an emotion in his voice now—desperation. "Malden can't help me."

"Fine," Chall said, "then we'll get someone else." Though where they would get anyone as experienced or knowledgeable as the old healer he couldn't imagine—after all, the man hadn't achieved his role as castle healer by accident. There had been a reason, and it damned sure wasn't his personality, at least as far as Chall was concerned. If they ever started having grumpy old man contests, then the healer could retire and spend his life criticizing and complaining. Chall thought he'd probably like that. "Anyway," he went on, "we'll get another healer and—"

"Come on, Chall," Matt interrupted. "We both know there's no point. Malden's the best in the kingdom—it was you that told me that."

Chall winced. First Priest used his words against him, then Matt. He really ought to start watching what he said. "Malden's good, but he doesn't know everything. We'll figure out these dreams and—"

"Damnit, Chall, it isn't just the dreams!" Matt shouted. "Don't you get that? It's...it's...you wouldn't understand."

"Pretty hard to, lad, if you don't tell me what's going on," Chall said softly, feeling his heart reach out to the boy, so pitiful, so *desperate* did he look.

Matt sighed wearily. "You wouldn't believe me if I told you."

"You're young, lad, so I'll forgive you for saying that. But the truth is, following your dad as I did so many years ago, I saw things I never would have thought existed. Mostly bad, it's true, like monsters that'd eat your face off. But some good, too. The stories you and your friends used to tell each other? I was there when those stories happened, when they weren't stories at all."

"Right, I'm just some stupid kid who doesn't know anything, is that it?"

"No, lad. That's not it at all."

"Then why are you telling me this?"

"I'm telling you so that you'll realize that you might be surprised at what I'll believe. And you want to know the truth, Matt?" he went on. "The absolute truth? It's something I usually avoid, but here it is—I trust you. If you tell me something's happening, whatever that something is, I'll believe you."

"You'll believe me."

"That's what trusting a person means, doesn't it? If you only trust them when it's obvious they're telling the truth, well, that don't seem much like trust at all to me."

Matt stared at him for several seconds, a small, fragile smile coming to his face. "And if I were to tell you that I could sometimes...tell what people are thinking?"

Chall blinked. Whatever he had been expecting, it hadn't been that.

Matt nodded, his smile fading like a wilting flower. "You see? I don't have to be able to read your mind to see your thoughts. You think I'm crazy."

"No, lad," Chall said after a moment. "Not crazy. I was just...surprised, that's all. Now, to answer your question proper, if you told me you could read thoughts, then I'd definitely ask you to hang around the next time I saw Maeve. That way I'd get a good idea of what she thought of me. Though, now that I think on it, I'm not all that sure I want to know."

Another frail smile. "Funny," he said. "But I'm afraid if you're looking to make jokes, Chall, I'm a poor audience just now."

"Sorry," Chall said, wincing. "We all have our shields, lad. I'm afraid mine's always been sarcasm, jokes. Making light of heavy burdens so that I might try to carry 'em a bit better." He shrugged. "It's what some do."

"And others," Matt said, "destroy their rooms and hide away."

It was Chall's time to give a small smile. "We all have our methods, though mine at least allows eating." He glanced at the spoiled food on the table then down at his ample belly, scowling. "More's the pity. Now, will you sit, and tell me what's going on?"

Matt hesitated long enough that Chall thought the young man meant to say no or kick him out. In the end, though, he walked over to the table and sat.

"I...I'm not sure where to begin."

"Times like these, Matt, I don't think it matters all that much where you begin. Just so long as you do."

Matt nodded slowly. "It's been happening for some time now," he said slowly, "pretty much since Emma...did what she did," he finished. "First it was the dreams. Always of my father and uncle."

Chall frowned. "All of them?".

"All of them," Matt agreed.

"That's odd," Chall said.

"You don't know the half of it. They were small dreams, at first. Dreams of them walking through the woods but...they got worse."

"Worse how?"

"Worse," Matt repeated. "I started dreaming of Feylings attacking them, hundreds of them. And the Green Demon, the Feyling with a face as black as pitch and green eyes."

"Shadelaresh," Chall said, frowning. "That bastard always has been a pain in the ass. What else?"

"Else?"

"You said the dreams were the beginning of it—what else was there?"

Matt winced. "It...it's hard to explain. It's like I can see into other people's thoughts. Not always...just...sometimes."

Chall was aware of the young man watching him. He was trying for casual, but Chall could see the hurt and worry in his eyes. Worry that Chall would not believe him, likely. Worry that Chall would not be able to help. "Is that all?" he asked.

"Isn't it enough?" Matt asked ruefully. "Anyway, no, that isn't all. There was the thing with Ned, too."

"What thing with Ned?"

"Remember back at Lady Valencia's? When he used his power on Vorrun?"

"I remember," Chall said. He'd been wading through a manse of dead men and women at the time, and he didn't think he'd forget that night anytime soon, no matter how much he might wish to.

"Well, I think...that is, I think he tried to use it on me too."

Chall raised an eyebrow. "You didn't mention this before."

"No, I didn't," Matt said.

"Why not?"

"Because...because I wasn't sure I didn't imagine it. I guess...I thought that, if I told you, told anyone, it would make it real...that's stupid, maybe."

"No," Chall said. "Not stupid, lad. Just wrong. You want stupid, I'll give you a lesson but later. For now, explain to me what happened at Lady Valencia's manse."

"I'm...not sure I can."

"Try."

"It...he reached his hand out to me, like he did Vorrun, and...I felt something. Something...building. Like...well, it was like the air got thicker, like it was pressing in on me. Then I felt that pressure, whatever it was, grow and move toward me."

"Then what happened?" Chall asked, realizing idly that he was sitting forward in his chair.

"That...force, whatever it was, it...parted around me. Like...like a river around a giant stone."

"A river around a stone," Chall repeated.

"That's right."

Chall nodded slowly.

"So...what do you think?" Matt asked, giving a nervous laugh. "Am I doomed?"

"No more than the rest of us anyway," Chall said distractedly, for he was busy thinking, considering the problem before him. It certainly seemed, based on the way Matt had described it, as if he'd felt the flows of magic, of the Art, but that shouldn't have been possible. The boy didn't have any ability with the Art. Or, at least, not as far as Chall had seen.

"Chall?"

"Hmm?" he asked, glancing up to see Matt staring at him.

"Is everything okay? You're worrying me."

"Fine, of course."

"Is it? Because you don't look like everything's fine."

"I'm just thinking, lad, that's all."

"So...what are you thinking?"

Chall shook his head slowly. "The things you're describing—the way you felt, I mean, when Ned used his power—it isn't uncommon in those who find that they have a talent for the Art. Being able to detect the weaves of magic of another, that is often—not always, but often—the way a person first comes to know that they have a propensity for the Art."

"But...then, that's a good thing, isn't it?"

Chall could hear just how much of the young man's hope was in that question, could see it in his gaze, the desperate need to be assured. "Yes," he said. "It's a good thing. That said, I will look into it more. For now, I must be off, and—"

"Off to where?" Matt said. "Can I come?" He winced at his own childish, excited tone. "That is, is it something I might help you with?"

"I'm afraid not, Majesty. Just some things that I have to take care of, that's all."

"But...but I want, Chall, I think I *need* to get out of this room, if only for a little while."

"Forgive me, Majesty, but what you need is food and some sleep." He gave Matt a small smile. "Maybe a bath."

Matt laughed, clearly immensely relieved by the knowledge that he wasn't, in fact, going insane. "Fine, fine, a bath, and I will ask Mistress Ophasia after the meal she sent. But...Chall, as for sleeping...the dreams..."

"You need sleep, Majesty," Chall repeated. "There are many things a man can go without, but sleep is not one of them."

Matt sighed, nodding. "As you say, but you'll forgive me if I'm not excited about it."

"Then it seems, Majesty," Chall said, thinking of Catham, of Maeve, "that we both have tasks ahead of us that we dread."

"And will you tell me what your task is?"

"I will, Majesty, but I ask that you let me do it later. After you've had some sleep. There is no great urgency." That wasn't exactly true. In fact, it was a complete lie, but he thought that the king had more than enough on his plate now without Chall adding to it.

"Thanks, Chall," Matt said. "I...I know I can be difficult sometimes, but...I appreciate it. You...you are a true friend."

Considering that he'd just lied to the lad that hurt quite a bit, a knife jabbing into him, but Chall did his best to keep that pain from his features. "Sleep well, Your Majesty—I'll see you soon."

Matt smiled. "Sleep well, Chall."

Chall tried to return the youth's smile but in truth he wasn't sure that he'd managed it before he turned and headed for the door. After all, while their conversation might have given Matt some comfort, it had only made Chall even more worried, an occurrence he wouldn't have thought possible before he'd spoken with the king. He closed the door, nodding his head to the question on Vorrun's face. He wanted to stop and talk to the man, but he couldn't bring himself to, not just then, for his mind was on other things as he made his way to his room, hoping Maeve was there, for he needed her wisdom.

What he'd told Matt about the sensing of another's Art being one of the first signs many experienced to indicate that they, themselves, had some talent for it had been true. But what he had lied about—or, at least, hadn't been honest about and, as Maeve was so forcefully teaching him, there was really no difference between the two—was the other part, the dreams. The discovering of one's talent with the Art took many shapes but, at least so far as Chall knew, dreams was not one of them. Nor were the reading of men's thoughts. In fact, he had never heard of anyone doing such a thing. The closest user of the Art he could think of was an Empath like Ned, but Empaths could only get a vague sense of a person's emotional state—yet even with that they were feared by nearly everyone in the Known Lands.

Troubling, more questions to which Chall had no answer, and so he started walking faster, hoping against hope that Maeve would be waiting in his quarters when he arrived. He reached the rooms they shared a short while later, stepping inside. He started to close the door when his eyes caught sight of a figure standing and staring out the window, the same window through which an assassin had tried to shoot him and Maeve with a crossbow what felt like yesterday.

The room was cloaked in shadows, the figure blocking most of the meager, early morning light that would have made itself into the room from its single window, and so Chall could not make it out clearly. And yet, he could see enough to know that the person waiting staring out the window of his rooms was not Maeve.

He sighed, heavily. "Damnit, Ned, you nearly gave me a fright. I hadn't expected to see you back so soon."

"Forgive me, Sir Challadius," the figure said, "but it seems that there has been a misunderstanding."

The shadowed figure turned away from the window, and a chill shot up Chall's spine as he saw that it was not Ned the carriage driver after all but Balderath.

Balderath, an assassin who, according to Maeve, was known for his brutality—and that among men and women who killed people for a living. "Balderath," he said, his voice coming out in a mixture of a rasp and a squeak.

"Sir Challadius," the man said, bowing his head.

"What...that is, what are you doing in my rooms?"

"Why, I'm waiting for you, of course, sir."

"And...why are you waiting for me?" Chall asked, preparing to turn and run at the first sign of any assassiny shenanigans.

"The Guildmaster wishes to see you," the man said.

Chall blinked. "I don't suppose we're talking about the Guildmaster for the Healers? Or, maybe the head of the Merchants' Guild?"

The man gave him a small smile that was of just about as much comfort as an alligator flashing its teeth. "Indeed, the reputation you enjoy for your quick wit, Sir Challadius, is well earned. If you do not mind my saying so, sir, you are a clever man, indeed."

"A clever man wouldn't live the life I have," Chall said. "Anyway, can I ask why the Guildmaster wants to see me?"

"Because she wishes to speak with you."

"And what does she want to speak to me about?"

"I do not know, sir, but you will be able to ask the Guildmaster when you see her."

"And when would that be?" Chall asked. He supposed he might have carried on the fiction that he had a choice but there really didn't seem to be much point. He was an illusionist, not some battle mage. True he'd been in battle, more than a few times, but that had always been despite his best efforts to the contrary. Either way, the man before him had already showed that he held no fear for Chall or his Art. Meanwhile, Chall had plenty of fear of the man himself and whatever weapons he no doubt had secreted on his person.

"Now would suit, sir," the man said.

"Alright..."

The assassin bowed, gesturing to the door. "After you, Sir Challadius."

Chall winced but started out of his room. "Don't bother closing the door," he told the assassin, frowning. "There really doesn't seem to be much point."

***

After an hour of his heart hammering in his chest, an hour of being certain, absolutely *certain* that any second the man named Balderath was going to turn and attack him, they reached the healing academy Maeve had told him doubled as the Assasssin's Guild. "Are the others coming with us?" he asked as Balderath started forward.

"What others, sir?" the man said, speaking for the first time since they'd left his room.

"The other...you know, assassins."

"There are no others, sir," the man said, frowning. "Please, this way."

Chall frowned at that as he followed after the man. He supposed he should have been glad that the man was alone, but instead he found himself being offended. After all, when Balderath had come for Maeve there'd been at least four others, likely more.

But he had come this far, so offended or not, he followed as the man led him through the doors and then through a hallway and down some stairs. They traveled down several more twisting, turning hallways until they approached a door at which stood two men. Chall didn't know much about assassins—though far more than he'd like, truth be told—but the two men standing at the door looked dangerous indeed, like two knives standing there waiting to stab someone.

"Brother Balderath," one said, bowing.

"I have brought Sir Challadius, as asked," Balderath said.

"Well done. They await inside."

The man opened the door and nodded his head to Chall. Chall started to ask who "they" were but figured he'd discover that soon enough. He walked toward the open door, wondering, as he had since leaving his rooms, why the Guildmaster of the Assassins' Guild would want to see him at all. And not just him. Maeve, too. It seemed that whoever had replaced Agnes was particularly interested in the two of them and, when it came to assassins, Chall thought that could never be a good thing.

So, Chall reached the door, took a deep breath, then, with one more glance at the two expressionless men on either side, he stepped inside the room.

He half-expected to find a dozen assassins waiting with loaded crossbows—not that it would take so many to do the job and do it well. He was surprised, then, as the door closed behind him, that instead of assassins with gritted teeth and bared blades, he saw two women seated upon two separate divans, facing each other.

One's back was to him, but Chall grunted in surprise as he recognized the one facing his direction. "Emille?"

"Good to see you again, Challadius," she said. "How's the wound?"

"Well I'm alive, thanks to you. But considering where I am, I think it all too likely that that will soon change."

"Oh, always so dramatic," another voice said, one he recognized as well, if not better than his own. The second woman stood up from the divan, turning to face him, and Chall felt his breath catch in his throat.

"M-Maeve?" he asked.

"Hi, Chall," she said, giving him a smile.

"How...I...I don't understand."

She winced. "I'm sorry for not getting to you sooner. I wanted to but—" She cut off as Chall rushed forward, pulling her into a tight hug.

He felt her lay her head against his shoulder, the way he liked so much, and for a time they just stood there, the two of them, sharing in the moment.

They continued to stand that way until Emille—who Chall had very nearly forgotten was there—cleared her throat. He pulled back. "It's good to see you, Mae," he said.

"It's good to see you too," she said, grinning.

"But...but what are we doing here?" he asked. "Are we their prisoners or what?" A thought occurred to him, and he tensed. "Oh, stones and starlight, have they somehow figured out about Agnes and—"

"No one knows anything," Maeve said quickly.

"Then...what?" Chall asked. "I don't understand. Balderath said the Guildmaster wanted to speak with me."

"Indeed she does," Maeve agreed.

"Well?" he said. "Where is she?"

Maeve didn't answer, at least not with her words. Instead, she only stared at him and, after a second, his eyes went wide. "Wait, do you mean...you? You're the new Guildmaster?"

She frowned. "Don't seem so surprised."

"Well, Maeve, I *am* surprised. The last I saw of you, you were being led away by what you said was the most brutal assassin in the Guild. Now, I'm summoned only to find that you're the new

Guildmaster—you've got to admit, that's a damned strange turn of events."

"Not so strange," Maeve said, "when you take into account that Agnes left a document recommending me as her replacement."

"A replacement for the job she hated so much she went through all the trouble of teaming up with what was likely her greatest rival to fake her own death in order to escape it?"

"That's right."

"That bitch."

"I won't disagree with you, if that's what you're looking for," Maeve said.

"So...you're the one that sent for me?"

"Of course," Maeve said. "I needed to speak with you—and Emille."

"Right," Chall said.

"What, what's wrong?"

"Nothing, just...so it was you that sent Balderath?"

"Yes," she said slowly.

"*Just* Balderath?"

She blinked. "Wait, is it...are you upset that I didn't send more assassins to fetch you?"

He frowned. "It's just, well, they sent five for you, didn't they? I only got one. Doesn't' seem fair, you thinking that one would be enough to get me here."

"But...wasn't he?"

"That's not the point," Chall said, feeling a bit uncertain. She looked at him saying nothing, eyeing him in the way she did, the way that told him he was acting a complete fool. Which, of course, he was. He sighed. "Okay fine maybe that's *exactly* the point, but it didn't feel nice."

"Would it help you to know that there were five more stalking your and Balderath's movements through the city?"

"Five more," he said slowly. "That's six in all. That's more than came for you."

"Yes, it is."

He nodded slowly. "Is it true?" he asked then, before she could say anything, he held up his hand. "You know what, I don't want to know. I've gone this long in my life avoiding the truth, I don't see any reason to stop now. Anyway, I'm glad to see you, Maeve. I was worried about you. What with all that's going on with Matt and Ned, it's good to see that at least one person is okay."

Maeve frowned. "What's going on with Matt and Ned?"

"That's a long story," he warned.

She gave him a small smile. "What is it that Bernard used to say to us all the time, back during the war? Sooner started..."

"Sooner finished," Chall said sourly. "Very well, but can we sit down?" he went on, motioning to the divans. "I've just spent the last hour being led through the city by an assassin known for violence. My legs, I'll admit, feel just a bit unsteady."

Maeve smiled. "Of course," she said. Once they were seated, she nodded for him to go on, and Chall glanced at Emille then back to Maeve, a question in his eyes.

"You can talk freely, Chall. I trust Emille."

Chall eyed Emille consideringly. He had trusted her too, just as he had trusted her husband only to find out that she was an assassin, and her husband was...well. Not guilty, maybe, like they thought. So...maybe he trusted him again. Still, the woman looked tired, a grim expression on her face as if she'd had a rough few days. Somehow he didn't think telling her all that her husband had been up to of late would do much to better her mood. And one of the rules Chall lived by was not to piss off assassins if he could help it.

He began recounting as quickly and—to begin with, at least—as accurately as he could the events that had transpired in the half a dozen lifetimes since Maeve had been taken away by Balderath. He avoided mentioning Ned, replacing the man with, in turns, a castle servant, a castle guard, and once—as more of a flourish than anything else—an overweight baker. He was particularly proud of that last one. Soon he came to their trip to Lady Valencia's and ended his tale by stating that, without options and not daring to bring her to the castle, he and Priest had brought her to Ned and Emille's home.

When he was finished, both the women were watching him, Maeve with an expression that said she knew that if not all of what he'd said was a lie, plenty was. Emille, though, watched him with an expression that was a mixture of anger and worry. "And Ned?"

"What about Ned?" Chall asked, tensing in preparation for a scolding, wondering what lie she'd detected, inwardly cursing himself for the baker bit. He knew it had been too far, but he hadn't been able to resist.

But instead of snapping at him, she cleared her throat, looking uncertain. "I...that is, did you see my husband? At the house or, maybe, at the castle? I thought...I thought perhaps he might have come to speak with you."

Chall wasn't sure if it was a trap or not, and if it was then falling into it would make her question everything else he'd said. "Well..." he hedged, "it's a big castle and all, but...I mean..." He glanced at Maeve and thought he detected the slightest hint of her shaking her head, almost imperceptible. He couldn't be sure, but considering he didn't have much of a choice, he went on, "But...no. I'm afraid to say I haven't seen your husband."

He tensed nervously. After all, it might not have been a shake of the head at all, really, probably just Maeve taking a breath or stretching her neck.

"I see," Emille said quietly.

"Anyway," Chall said, turning to Maeve, eager to change the subject, "what am I doing here?"

"Can't a girl just want to spend time with her lover?" Maeve countered.

Chall felt his face heat at that. "O-of course she can," he said, clearing his throat. "Only...since we're sitting in an Assassins' Guild instead of a nice tavern or going for a stroll I feel like maybe you had something else on your mind."

Maeve winced. "Right...about that...I've got something to show the both of you."

Chall and Emille shared a glance at the odd tone of Maeve's voice. But before either of them could question it, Maeve rose from her seat and started away, moving toward a door at the other end of the room.

She paused at the door, glancing back at them, then opened it, stepping through. Chall shared another look with Emille before following her into what, if the bookshelves and giant desk with papers scattered across it were anything to go by, a study.

One that looked very similar to dozens of other studies he'd seen in the manses of wealthy nobles or in the castle itself. Very similar but with one significant difference.

"Huh," Emille said softly.

"Maeve," Chall said.

"Yes, Chall?"

"Are you aware that there's a dead body lying on your floor?"

"Yes."

"And…judging by the pool of blood spreading out from underneath her, am I to surmise that she did not die of natural causes?"

"Well now, that depends. When someone is stabbed in the heart with a sharp implement—say a dagger—naturally, they tend to die."

"I see," Chall said, still staring at the dead body. "And…if I were to guess who did the stabbing…"

"I did," Maeve said.

"Right, right, sure, well, that's…ordinary. Listen, are you telling me that you killed this woman?"

"Yes, but she tried to kill me first," Maeve said, sounding defensive.

"By doing what?" Chall said, staring at the woman lying there, looking like the deadest grandmother that ever grandmothered. "Bouncing you on her knee? Feeding you too many treats?"

"Poison," Maeve said. "Then a knife. That one there. She's still holding it."

"So she is," Chall said, suddenly feeling very hot, thinking it'd be nice to have a quick lie-down. He considered the fact that he was lying to Maeve about Ned, about Lady Valencia, and thought that she knew it. Thought, too, that it was the sort of thing women tended to be upset about. "Are you…that is, are you feeling stabby now?"

"Stabby?" Maeve asked, raising an eyebrow. "Not particularly. Why, should I?"

"No!" Chall blurted. "That is, no," he continued, trying for a calmer tone. "So anyway…what do you need our help with? I mean…it looks like you handled it pretty well. It isn't as if we can kill her twice."

"True," Maeve said, "but then we can't exactly wake her up and ask her to walk out of here either, can we?"

"So you called us to help you lug around a dead body?"

"Sure, why not? You didn't have anything on, did you?"

"No but I'd have found something, if I'd have known this is what you had in mind," Chall grumbled. "Anyway, why not get those two big bastards out front to do it? Shit, the way they looked, they'd probably consider disposing of dead bodies a holiday."

Maeve shared a look with Emille. "Because," Emille said, "she doesn't want them to know that the woman is dead."

Chall blinked. "You want to, somehow, walk a dead body past the two guards outside without them knowing it?" He snorted. "That'd be a nifty trick."

"Yes," Maeve said slowly, giving him a small smile. "And another word for that might be..."

Chall sighed. "An illusion. Right. I get it. You know, you don't pay me enough."

"Oh, I'll make sure to make it worth it," she said, giving him the smile he loved so well, one that managed to make him forget, at least for the moment—at least mostly—the dead body sprawled on the floor.

"Fine," he said, "but after this, a moratorium on dead bodies and visits to the Assassin's Guild. Deal?"

"I'm not sure that's up to me," Maeve said.

While Chall was thinking of a way to answer that, at least one that didn't involve some choice words, Emille knelt by the body, turning the face to look at it. *Bloody assassins,* he thought. *It isn't enough to kill them, they have to play with their bodies afterward. Like cats playing with their food.*

"Wait," Emille said, "I know her. This is Amber—she was Guildmaster Agnes's personal valet."

"Yes," Maeve said. "And then mine...briefly."

"I'm guessing you didn't care for the job she was doing," Chall said.

"Actually, it was she who decided to sever our relationship, as it were," Maeve said.

"But...why?" Emille asked. "She served Agnes for several years. Why would she attack you?"

"She attacked me as soon as I found this." Maeve said, reaching inside of her shirt and producing a small, leather-bound book.

"What is it?" Chall asked.

"A book," Maeve said, raising an eyebrow. "Don't worry, it won't hurt you."

"There are thousands who'd disagree, I think, considering that it is books—and the words they contain—that have led to countless wars."

"Countless?" Maeve said. "Is that right? I didn't know you were a historian, Chall—trying to take Petran's job, is that it?"

"Gods forbid," Chall said. "Anyway, what does it say?"

Maeve shrugged. "I didn't have much of a chance to look through it before Amber attacked me. Though, Agnes did mention in it that she didn't trust Amber."

"Well," Chall said, glancing at the corpse, "I'd say she's one for one then, isn't she?"

"I'd have to agree," Maeve said. "What I do know is that Amber was working for one of the Tribunes—"

"Which one?" Chall asked.

"I don't know," Maeve said, sighing.

"It doesn't really matter in any case, does it?" Emille asked, and they both glanced at her. The woman shrugged. "It seems to me that who she worked for is largely irrelevant—what matters is that she isn't working for them *now*. And while it would be nice to know, I think what we really should be focused on is the diary. After all, what is obvious is that she—and by extension, her employer—was willing to risk her position to retrieve it. Which tells me that whatever is contained within its pages—"

"Is worth killing for," Chall finished.

"More than that," Maeve said quietly. "It's worth giving up a huge advantage, the information that the woman could have shared with them for weeks, months, possibly even years. They traded all that for what is or, at least what they *believe* is contained within its pages."

"Information," Emille said.

"Sure, yeah information's important," Chall agreed, thinking of all the times that knowing when a woman's husband was coming home had kept him alive and all the times when he *hadn't* known that had nearly made him quite dead.

Maeve frowned as if she had some idea of what was going on in his mind—not much, he was confident, or else there would be two corpses in the room instead of one—but more than he'd like. "So what's your plan for the body, then?" he asked, eager to redirect her attention.

She gave him a small smile, as if she knew well what he was doing, but after another moment shrugged. "I was hoping the two of you might have some ideas."

Chall grunted. "You ask me, this Guildmaster job of yours isn't all it's cracked up to be. I mean, what's the point if you can't even make use of your guild's resources? I have to think a guild of assassins has people they train to get rid of bodies."

Maeve frowned, opening her mouth to speak, but before she could, Chall was thankful to hear Emille beat her to it. "Have you eaten today?" she asked.

Maeve continued to frown at Chall for another moment before turning to regard the other woman, raising an eyebrow as she did. "It seems that I've lost my appetite—someone trying to kill me tends to have that effect."

"No, no it doesn't," Emille said, "at least, not this time. This time, you have a very great appetite. So, it must be said, do I and Chall."

Chall grunted. "Speak for yourself, I—"

"A lot of food," Maeve said, giving a small smile as she regarded Emille.

"Quite a lot," Emille agreed, sharing a smile.

"Look, I enjoy eating as much as the next fat man," Chall said, "but I don't see what—"

"So much they'll have to wheel it in on a cart," Maeve said, raising an eyebrow at Chall.

"Right," he said slowly. "A cart."

"A big one," Maeve said.

"Well, it'd have to be to carry all that food," Emille agreed, her eyes flashing, and they both turned to regard Chall.

Chall had no idea what was expected of him, felt that sinking in his stomach that had always accompanied one of his tutors at the Academy asking him a question. "A...a metal cart?" he offered.

"A big cart," Maeve repeated, frowning at him and shaking her head. "One that might carry food or..." She paused, glancing at the corpse meaningfully.

Finally, realization came the way it never had with his tutors, and Chall found himself grinning. "For the dead body!" he said, only, in his excitement, he realized that he didn't say it so much as yelled it.

"Not so loud," Maeve hissed.

"What, do you want to bring the whole Guild down on us?" Emille said.

"Sorry," Chall said, his face heating. "And I suppose I'm to cast an illusion on it, one that will make it—"

Suddenly, there was a knock on the door, and Chall's words turned into a terrified squeal.

"Excuse me, Guildmaster?"

They all stared at each other, looking like nothing so much as three frightened children trying to sneak out and hearing their parents' footsteps.

"Guildmaster, is everything alright?"

"F-fine," Maeve called in a weak voice then, trying again. *"Fine, what is it?"*

"There's a man here, Guildmaster, seeking admittance.

Maeve shared a look with the two of them then walked out of the study, toward the door to her quarters. Meanwhile, Chall eased the door to the room including him and Emille—and, of course, the incredibly-incriminating corpse—shut so that only a crack remained open.

Maeve glanced back from the door, and he gave a thumbs up through the crack. She nodded then turned back, opening the door. "Tell him to go away—I am busy at the moment, and I do not have time for an audience."

"Forgive me, Guildmaster," Chall heard the man say, "but he is persistent—and he has not come to speak with you but Sister Emille."

"Wha—" Maeve began, then there was a pause. "Ned?" she said. "Is that you?"

Chall turned to regard Emille in shock, and the woman, her eyes wide, shook her head to show that she didn't know what her husband was doing here.

"You know him, Guildmaster?" the guard asked in a tone that said that, should she ask it, he would have no problem murdering Ned outright.

"Y-yes," Maeve said, clearly overcoming the worst of her shock with an effort. "I-I know of him. Through Sister Emille. He is her husband."

"Would you like us to get rid of him, Guildmaster?" the man asked, and even though the guard wasn't talking about Chall he found himself breaking out in a sweat at the man's tone.

"No, no," Maeve said quickly, "that won't be necessary. Come, sir, your wife is within, though she and I will have some difficult words later."

Maeve stepped to the side and, in another moment, the carriage driver walked into the room, eyeing the two guards.

"Will there be anything else, Guildmaster?" a voice called.

"No, that will be quite a—" Maeve began, and Chall gave a hiss, one he hoped the men outside didn't hear. "Oh, there is one thing," she said. "I would like some food delivered."

"Of course, Mistress. What would you like?"

"Surprise me—but we are famished, and there is much work to be done, so deliver a cart full."

"As you say, Guildmaster."

Maeve closed the door, and Chall opened his own. He and Emille joined the other two in the sitting room, and they, as well as Maeve, stared at the carriage driver.

"Ned," Emille said, her voice a dry, rasping croak, "what...what are you doing here?"

"What?" he said, giving her a small smile. "Can't a man visit his wife at work?"

Emille's eyes went wide at that, and it seemed to Chall that she was lost for words. He, though, had plenty. "Are you out of your damned mind?" he asked the man. "Do you have any idea what this place is? How did you even get in here?"

"The way most people do, I imagine," the carriage driver said. "I walked. And, yes," he said, turning to regard Emille. "I know," he said in a tone that made it clear he meant more than just knowing about the nature of the building in which he stood.

"You...know?" Emille said.

"I know," Ned repeated.

"But...how?"

"Chall told me."

They all turned to look at him then, Maeve and Emille with murder in their eyes, and Chall decided it was a good time to look at his boots, assess the state of them. Not great, that was sure, though he thought they still had one or two more run-for-your-life's left in them, thought it likely he was about to find out for sure.

"Why would you do that?" Emille asked.

"Don't blame him," Ned said, though it was clear by their expressions that that was *exactly* what the two women were doing. "He did what he thought was right. That's the best anyone can do."

"Ned, listen, I...I'm sorry. I don't—"

"You don't have anything to apologize for, Em," he said.

Whatever the woman had been expecting, clearly it hadn't been that. She blinked, staring at him as if he were some creature she'd never seen before. "I...I'm not sure what you mean."

"What I mean is that we all have our pasts, love," he said softly. "We both had our lives before we met each other—you did, and so...well—" he glanced at Chall who gave him what he hoped was a covert shake of his head—"well, so did I."

She frowned. "I shouldn't have kept it from you though," she said, stepping forward, holding his hands in hers. "I'm sorry."

"Well, I'll admit," he said, giving her a small smile, "if I'd have known, I probably wouldn't have made fun of your cooking so much." He winced, then, the smile fading. "Anyway, everybody has their secrets."

"What does that—"

"Later," Maeve said, and Chall did his best to hide his sigh of relief. "For now, we have too much to deal with. By coming here, Ned, you may have put yourself in danger."

"I wanted to see my wife," the man said simply, and Chall didn't miss the way Emille smiled. *Women,* he thought. *They do love their grand gestures.* He only hoped that *this* grand gesture didn't end with all of them murdered.

"Romantic," Maeve said, "but you still couldn't have picked a worse time to come, Ned. It's dangerous here."

"Didn't seem all that dangerous," Ned said. "I mean, I got in without much trouble, just asked after Emmy."

"Just asked?" Chall said.

"Well," the man said, giving him a smile. "Maybe I was a bit persistent."

"Anyway," Chall said, "bear traps and Assassin's Guilds have one thing in common, Ned. It isn't the getting in that's the hard part—it's the getting out."

"Don't worry," the carriage driver said, giving him a wink before glancing at his wife. "I've got an inside woman."

Emille gave him a half smile, half wince. "It's...a bit more complicated than that, Ned."

Chall snorted. "Complicated?" He walked to the door leading to Maeve's study, threw it open, and gestured for Ned who frowned, walking forward and peering inside.

"That," Ned said after a moment, "is a very old, very dead woman. Did she deserve it?" he asked, turning to regard them.

Chall decided that maybe the man wasn't so far removed from the person who'd first created the Crimson Wolves as he thought, but it was Maeve who spoke. "She tried to kill me."

"Well," Ned said, "looks like she failed. Maybe you'd all better tell me what's going on."

And they did, as quickly as they could. Mostly, it was Maeve who spoke, but Chall jumped in from time to time, doing what he had often found himself doing to protect lies he'd told—telling more. It wasn't his finest work—in truth, he kept getting confused and having to remind himself of who knew what—but he thought it was good enough, namely because, when they'd finished, he was still just as unstabbed as he had been.

The large pushcart of food had arrived when they talked and so, as soon as he'd finished, Chall picked up a roll and began to eat it. Not because he was hungry—his appetite had left the building sometime around the third attempt on his life this week—but to give his hands, and his mouth something to do instead of what they wanted to do. Namely, fidget and, in the case of his mouth, tell the truth. A death sentence if there ever was one.

"Well, seems like you all have had a hectic couple of days," Ned said, glancing at Chall.

"I'll say," Chall agreed.

"So...what do we do now?" Ned asked, glancing between them.

"We get the two of you out of here as quick as we can," Maeve said, looking at Chall and Ned.

"Wait a damned minute, you're the one that had me brought here, remember?" he said.

"Yes, because I needed you, but if everything you've told me is true, then you need to get back to Matt."

"But—"

"He's alone, Chall," Maeve said. "With Priest gone, he'll have no one to talk to."

Chall winced, thinking. "Fine, I'll go, but you're coming with me. All of us. It isn't as if—"

"I can't," Maeve said.

"Sure you can—it's like Ned said, you just have to walk."

"I'm not sure they would let me leave, not alive at least," Maeve said. He started to speak, but she held up a hand, silencing him. "And even if they did, it would make no difference. They were willing to kill in order to get their hands on this diary. That means it's important—there's no telling just how important."

Chall frowned. "It's a book, how important can it be?"

"Weren't you the one telling me so recently that wars had been fought over them? Anyway, I need to be here. I need to dig into the diary, yes, but not just that—I want to figure out who put the contract out on us. I think...I think if I stay, I can do some good."

"You know more about all this than I do, Maeve," Chall said, "but I don't think people come to an Assassins' Guild to do good."

"I need to do this, Chall," she said softly, meeting his gaze. "Will you trust me?"

Chall sighed. "When will I see you again?"

"As soon as I'm able," Maeve promised.

He shook his head. "Fine, but the next time you send someone for me, why not make it a pretty young girl instead of the most brutal killer in the Guild, eh?"

She frowned. "Keep it up, and I'll ask Balderath to do more than fetch you."

He swallowed at that. "I was kidding," he said.

"I wasn't."

"So what do you want us to do, exactly?" Ned asked.

"Whatever you can," Maeve said. "Help Priest, help Matt. And keep Lady Valencia safe. We're going to need to make sure she's protected—after all, there was a reason this Robert Palden wanted her dead." She glanced at Chall. "In truth, you shouldn't have left her alone."

"Right," Chall said, trying to keep from glancing at Ned. After all, it was the carriage driver, in truth, who had left the noblewoman alone, not him. "I shouldn't have done that. You're right."

Maeve blinked. "You haven't often agreed with me so quickly," she said, her eyes narrowing suspiciously.

"What can I say?" Chall asked. "Being around so many assassins makes me agreeable." He tensed, waiting for what she would say. Maeve was clever, and she did not miss much. He hated hiding the truth about all of it from her, but she was the Guildmaster and the less she knew about Ned's origins, the better. Not to protect him or even to protect Ned, but to protect her. "Anyway," he said, fighting the urge to squirm under her suspicious gaze, "I'll go check on Matt."

"Lady Valencia first," she said, still frowning at him. "Matt has a castle full of guards to protect him—she has no one."

"As you say, darling," Chall said sarcastically, but she stepped forward and pulled him into a tight embrace, giving him a kiss that was most definitely not sarcastic at all.

It ended quickly, far too quickly as far as he was concerned, but even so short a kiss as that made the last few days of harrowing almost-death worth it. Mostly.

"Be safe," Maeve told him as she pulled back.

"You too," he said. Then he turned, starting toward the door. "Not going to get murdered leaving, are we?"

"No, you'll be alright," Maeve said. "Oh, and Chall, before you go…"

"You want me to cast a spell on a corpse and make it look like food."

She gave him a timid smile. "Could you?"

He sighed. "Fine." He moved to the study, closing his eyes and beginning to weave a spell over the old woman's corpse. It was the work of a few minutes to make sure that the illusion would stay even after he left. When it was done, he stepped back into the sitting room, giving Maeve a nod before he glanced at Ned. "You coming?"

"Wait for me outside," the carriage driver said. "I'd speak with my wife for a moment."

Chall frowned, remembering all too well how much the man had wanted to tell his wife the truth. "Don't be long," he said, looking at the man meaningfully.

Ned returned the stare. "No longer than I have to," he agreed.

Chall sighed and, for the second time of the day—two too many, so far as he was concerned—he walked out of the door and into a guild of assassins.

CHAPTER NINETEEN

Matt parried his opponent's attack, focusing on his footwork as he stepped back the way he'd been taught. Another blow came, lightning fast, and he brought his weapon up just in time, narrowly deflecting it.

It felt more like magic than anything else that made his sword interpose itself between him and his opponent's third strike. But whatever magic it was, it was not good enough to protect him from the fourth blow that struck him in the arm.

He grunted, stepping back and bringing his free hand to his arm. Even though the blade was dulled, even though he wore a padded doublet, his arm felt numb from the strike.

"Majesty," his opponent said, his tone worried as he moved forward, "are you alright?"

"I'm fine, Vorrun," he said, giving the man a smile he did not feel. It wasn't the pain that made it so bad, not really. It was the losing. He'd lost—again—and that made him angry. Not at Vorrun, for the man was only doing what Matt had asked him to, sparring with him without complaint despite the early hour and the fact that the man should have been off duty over thirty minutes ago.

After Chall had left, Matt had picked at his food, but everything had made his stomach roil, and so soon he had given it up. And after an hour of tossing and turning in his bed he had given up on the idea of sleep as well. So they had come here to the sparring ground reserved for the king and his guests, one that, he was told, his uncle had made use of often, inspired to train by his hate for his brother, Matt's father.

He had come here many times since he'd been freed from the Feyling Emma's possession. He'd come here to fight, to battle not just a practice opponent but the demons that lurked inside of him, doubt and shame, regret and hatred. And anger. That most of all. It seemed to Matt lately that he was always angry. And that anger, more often than not, was at himself.

Anger like he was feeling now.

"I'm fine," he said again, shifting his arm in an effort to work the numbness out of it. "I know that you need to get home to your family, Vorrun, but might we do one more round?"

"Of course, Majesty," the guardsman said, bowing.

Matt nodded his gratitude, stepping forward and holding his sword out, trying to stay on the balls of his feet as his father had shown him. In another moment, they were at it again, their blades flashing. He was fast, was pretty confident that he was faster than the older guardsman, but try as he might, he couldn't seem to make that speed work to his advantage.

He lunged forward, lighting quick, his sword leading, but Vorrun stepped to the side, as if he'd expected the attack, and knocked the blow away. Matt pivoted into the momentum of the parry and spun, lashing out. Again the guardsman's blade seemed to appear right where it needed to be. Again and again Matt struck, and again and again his blade was knocked away, until finally his weapon was knocked wide, and he didn't recover fast enough.

Vorrun's blade whipped around, and he planted it in Matt's sternum as gently as the touch of a moth landing on his chest. Matt wanted to scream, he wanted to growl and shout in anger, but instead he only inclined his head. "Well fought, Vorrun," he said, doing his best to keep the bitterness out of his voice.

"Well fought, Majesty," the guardsman said, taking the blade away. "If you don't mind my saying so, sir, it is incredible to see how quickly you have progressed. You are a natural talent, sir."

A natural talent at losing, maybe, Matt thought. He flashed the guardsman the best smile of which he was capable, taking his practice sword. "Thank you, Vorrun. Tell your wife I said hi."

"She'll be flattered, Majesty," the guardsman said. "Is there anything else?"

"Nothing," Matt said, giving the man another smile, one that remained in place while the guardsman bowed and vanished the moment he turned away. Matt waited until the man was out of the door, leaving Matt alone in the arena then he moved to a bench and sat the practice swords down. That done, he began to remove the padded tunic. As he did, he took slow, deep breaths in an effort to curtail his anger.

It did not help.

He kept replaying the fight with Vorrun in his mind over and over again. By the time he'd stripped off the padded tunic and was left in his sweat-soaked night shirt, his anger had risen to a fever pitch, and he found himself picking up one of the practice blades. He took several swings with it, focusing on his footwork as he moved through some of the forms his father—and Vorrun—had shown him. He was still doing this when one of his feet was too slow in the movement, and he tripped, nearly falling. He let out a growl of frustration at that and then, with an angry shout, he slammed his practice sword down on the ground and was shocked as it shattered, snapping in half like a frost-weakened branch.

Matt stared at the broken sword in his hand in shock. Someone cleared their throat behind him, and he spun to see the gray-haired Commander Malex standing near the door, his hands clasped behind his back. He bowed upon catching Matt's attention. "Forgive me, sir, I did not mean to interrupt, only you asked me to come as soon as I could."

"So I did," Matt said, feeling his face heat. He glanced at the remains of the practice sword in his hands, winced, then tossed it to the ground, walking toward the commander.

"If you don't mind my saying so, Majesty," Malex said, "you possess your father's strength."

And his anger, too, Matt thought, suspected the commander was thinking much the same, though he would never say it. "Thank you," Matt said. "Though, in truth, I am more than a little frustrated. It seems that no matter how much practice I put in, I cannot best Vorrun."

"Guardsman Vorrun is an accomplished swordsman, Majesty. One of the best of all the guards. He has been practicing the blade for longer than you've been alive. If you will forgive the impertinence, you cannot expect to best him after less than six months' training."

Matt winced. "Sorry, Malex. I'm afraid I'm the one being impertinent, not you. So, about what I sent you to check on?"

The older man did a fine job of hiding his feelings—in fact, his expression didn't change in the slightest. And yet, while his features did not betray any emotion, a thought suddenly came to Matt.

Please, don't do this. It is a mistake. Malex's thoughts, coming into his mind as if spoken aloud.

Matt winced, rubbing at his head where a sharp, throbbing pain suddenly spawned in his temple.

"Majesty?" Malex asked. "What's wrong?"

"It's nothing," Matt said, waving his hand. *Nothing anyone can fix, anyway.* Except, perhaps, for Chall. He hoped the mage would find an answer to what plagued him, but the truth was he doubted it. Chall had tried to seem confident, but Matt had sensed something of the man's worry before he'd left. "Now," he said, pulling his thoughts away from Chall and his troubles, at least for the moment, "what I asked you to check on?"

Malex bowed formally. "Of course, Majesty. The army will be ready and able to march within seven days."

Matt nodded, trying to keep his frustration from his face. Seven days. Seven days before he could go to his father and uncle's aid. Not so long in the normal course of things, but when the two of them were in the Black Wood, trying to survive while surrounded by thousands of the Fey, it was a lifetime. "No sooner?" he asked.

"Even a week will be pushing it, Majesty," the older man said. "Our supply lines will not be well established, among other concerns, but I am aware of the urgency with which you would like to depart."

A mistake, the thought came again, in Malex's voice and never mind that his mouth didn't move.

Matt watched the man for several seconds. "What do you think of going to the Black Wood, Commander Malex?"

I think it's a mistake. "It is not my decision to make, Majesty. I will, of course, serve you in whatever way you see best. Though..."

"Though what?"

"Though, perhaps, you may want to speak with Priest or Sir Challadius or, better still, Lady Maeve. They would no doubt like to know and their help would be invaluable."

Would no doubt like a chance to talk me out of it, you mean. He felt his anger rise at that. "They are not king in New Daltenia, I am."

"Of course, Majesty," the man said, his eyes widening slightly.

"Forgive me, Malex, I did not mean to...I have not been sleeping well, and I am only eager to help my father and uncle. I will speak to them about it, for I value their counsel."

"No offense taken, Majesty," the man said, inclining his head. "Forgive me for asking, Majesty, but...are you alright?"

"I'm fine," Matt answered, doing his best to give the man a smile. "Just tired, that's all."

"Of course, Majesty. Is there anything else I may do for you?"

Can you block my dreams? Matt thought, rubbing at his head where the headache was growing and confident, based on recent history, that it would get worse before it got better, so bad that even the slightest bit of light would feel like a dagger slid into his temple. "No thank you, Commander," he said. " That is all—you may go."

Malex nodded, bowing, and then he turned and walked away.

He watched the commander go, regretting lying to the man, lying to him the same way that Chall had lied to Matt only a few hours ago when he'd pretended like what Matt was going through was normal.

No, Malex, he thought at the man's departing back. *I don't think I am fine. Not at all.*

316

CHAPTER TWENTY

Chall paced back and forth in the street, waiting impatiently for what could have been no more than fifteen minutes but what felt like a lifetime before he finally saw the carriage driver emerge from *Sir Chavoy's Academy of Healing—and Killing,* he thought— *Arts.*

"About damned time," he said as the carriage driver walked up. "I was beginning to think the bastards had decided to use you for practice. What did you tell her?"

"No more than I needed to," Ned said.

Chall nodded. "Good. You know it was the best way, don't you?"

"Sure, the only way. We lie because we care."

"Right," Chall said, frowning. "Now, are you ready to go?"

"When you are."

Chall glanced around at the street that was, given the earliness of the hour, nearly empty. "Your carriage?"

"I don't have it."

Chall sighed. "What's the use of a carriage driver without a carriage?"

"That a joke?"

"If it is, it isn't a funny one," he said. "Come on—the sooner we go check on Lady Valencia the sooner I can look in on Matt and

Priest. And, if I make it through all of that without getting killed, then maybe I'll even get the chance to take a nap."

"Here's hoping. About the nap, not the getting killed," Ned said, baring his teeth in a smile. "Probably."

"You're a bit of a bastard, aren't you?" Chall asked.

Ned shrugged. "We all have our gifts. Now, if you're done talking, let's get moving, eh?"

And before Chall could answer—likely with a couple of choice curse words—the man started away and, based on his whistling, he knew well enough the annoyance he'd just caused.

"Being killed isn't the only option," Chall said, frowning at the man's back. "Murder's still on the table too." And then, since he really didn't have any choice, he started walking.

***

Over an hour later they reached the front of Ned's home. As they moved toward it Chall tried to ignore the ache in his feet. "Did we really have to walk all over the city?" he asked, knuckling at his sore back.

Ned shrugged. "Wanted to make sure we weren't being followed. Anyway, I thought you'd appreciate a nice stroll."

"I could stab you."

"Have a knife, do you?"

"I could get a knife."

Ned nodded slowly. "Well, we all have to have goals. Come on—let's check on Val."

Chall followed as the man started forward, waiting as Ned unlocked the door. The inside of the house was dark, lit only by the pale morning light filtering in through the open doorway.

Chall frowned. "You sure you brought her here?"

"Of course I'm sure," Ned said. "She must be sleeping, that's all. She's had a long few days."

"I can sympathize," Chall said.

Ned grunted, stepping into the shadowed home. "Val?" he called. "You here?"

Chall followed him inside, glancing around the house as Ned started toward a door at the back of the room, the same door through which he—not too long ago—had been brought, dying, the same place where Emille had saved his life.

There was no sign of a struggle, nothing seeming out of place or amiss, and yet a clarion bell began to ring in Chall's mind. A sixth sense—developed over years of sneaking out of windows and out of beds—warned him of danger. "Ned—"

"Just a second," the carriage driver said, opening the door and looking inside the room. "Val?"

"Ned, maybe we ought to go."

"Oh, it's too late for that," a voice said from somewhere behind him. "Far too late."

Chall let out a squeak, spinning and feeling a shiver of terror as he saw the criminal, Catham, standing in the doorway. That was bad. Worse, though, were the men—at least eight, all of which held crossbows—filing in behind him.

Chall closed his eyes, preparing to cast an illusion, calling on his Art. But before he'd managed it, something *thudded* into his thigh, and he screamed, his eyes shooting open. He stared down at his agonized leg and saw a crossbow bolt sticking out of it.

"No tricks," Catham said. "I am well aware of what you—what *both* of you," he paused, glancing at Ned—"can do. And if either one of you tries, you'll regret it, though not for long."

Chall was already regretting it, in point of fact. His leg throbbed painfully, and he felt as if he was going to be sick. He shot a questioning glance at Ned, and the man gave an almost imperceptible shake of his head. Then Chall turned back to Catham, saw the man giving him a small, knowing smile, and he remembered Ned's words.

Not just cautious, he'd said, *but clever too.*

"What do you want?" Chall said, doing his best to sound threatening and, considering the pain he was in—and the fact that there were eight crossbows trained on him and Ned—he failed miserably.

"It's not about what I want," Catham said, smiling and drawing his sword from the sheath at his waist. "It's what the person I work for wants."

"I take it you don't mean the woman that took over for Belle. What was her name, Nadia?"

"Afraid not," Catham said.

"And what does this boss of yours want?" Ned asked.

Catham smiled. "Well, now, that's the thing. He wants the two of you dead."

Chall stared at those crossbows, at the sword in the man's hand, as blood ran down his leg. *I'm sorry, Maeve,* he thought. *I'm sorry that we didn't have more time.* And then, he stood and waited for his death to come.

CHAPTER TWENTY-ONE

He woke to pain.

It wasn't the first time, but then it wasn't the sort of thing a man got used to.

His stomach felt as if it were turning flips inside him, and his arm throbbed with the heat of sickness. He was hot, covered in sweat. All of these things he noticed in an instant.

In the next, he noticed something else. He was moving. Or, more accurately, he was being moved. Dragged, in fact. And he could hear panting. He craned his neck, trying not to throw up at the sickening dizziness the movement caused. Looking above him, he saw Feledias's back, his brother's hands holding onto two wooden bars attached to the travois upon which he was dragging Cutter.

He winced as the travois—which Feledias was pulling at breakneck speed—struck a rock, nearly tumbling him off. "Fel," he croaked, "what's happening?"

"Can't...talk, right now," his brother panted. *"They're...coming. Right...behind us. Fast but...not just that."*

"Who? Who's behind us?" Cutter rasped, looking down at his upper arm where the wolf-like creature had bitten him, the bandage wrapped around it stained a mix of crimson and a sickening green.

"We are in the land of monsters, brother, the land of death," Feledias panted. *"So you ask me what chases us? Monsters, brother. Death. What else?"* Feledias hissed a curse, then stumbled and fell to one knee. "That's it," he rasped. "I can't...can't go any farther." Cutter's brother let go of the travois and turned around and, in doing so, Cutter saw just how exhausted, just how haggard his brother's face was.

"Can you stand, brother?" Feledias asked, offering his hand, his eyes scanning behind them. "If it helps, I do not think you will need to for long."

Cutter took the hand, grunting as he was pulled to wobbly legs, struggling to keep back his rising gorge at the sudden movement. He turned, following his brother's gaze to look behind them. The sun had set while he was unconscious. It was dark now, the area lit with the glow of the moon. And in that glow, Cutter saw that they were still in the unending fields of the Black Wood.

"What is it, Fel?" he asked. "What's coming?"

"The only thing that ever comes in the land of the dead, brother," Feledias said, glancing at him. "Are you ready?"

For death? he thought. *I think I was born ready.* "Yes," he said. "But I thought we would not have another test until tomorrow."

"It seems that the green demon has decided to change the rules, brother."

"He can do that?"

"He's doing it," Feledias said, then turned to him, giving him a smile sharp enough to cut as he drew his swords. "Once more into the fray, then?"

Cutter nodded, hefting his axe and looking at the shadowed fields before him as they came alive with movement. "See you on the other side."

And now we have come to the end of *A Warrior's Path*. I hope you enjoyed revisiting Cutter and his companions as much as I did. The next book in the Saga of the Known Lands will be coming your way soon.

In the meantime, I've got a few other series to keep you occupied.

Want another story of an anti-hero in a grimdark setting where a jaded sellsword is forced into a fight he doesn't want between forces he doesn't understand?
Get started on the bestselling seven book series, The Seven Virtues.

Interested in a story where the gods choose their champions in a war with the darkness that will determine the fate of the world itself?
Dive into The Nightfall Wars, a complete six book, epic fantasy series.

Or how about something a little lighter? Do you like laughs with your sword slinging and magical mayhem? All the world's heroes are dead and so it is up to the antiheroes to save the day. An overweight swordsman, a mage who thinks magic is for sissies, an assassin who gets sick at the sight of the blood, and a man who can speak to animals...maybe.
The world needed heroes—it got them instead.
Start your journey with The Antiheroes!

If you enjoyed *A Warrior's Path*, I'd really appreciate it if you'd take a moment to leave an honest review. They make a tremendous difference, and I would love to hear from you.

If you want to reach out, you can email me at Jacobpeppersauthor@gmail.com or visit my website at JacobPeppersAuthor.com.
You can also give me a shout on Facebook or on Twitter. I'm looking forward to hearing from you!

Turn the page for a limited time free offer!

Sign up for my new releases mailing list and for a limited time get a free copy of *The Silent Blade*, the prequel book to the bestselling epic fantasy series *The Seven Virtues*.

Go to JacobPeppersAuthor.com to get your copy now!

NOTE FROM THE AUTHOR

And so that brings us to the end of *A Warrior's Path*. It is my sincere hope that you enjoyed the time you spent with Cutter and Maeve, with Priest and Chall and all the rest. Things are bad with the kingdom of the Known Lands, and they only seem to be getting worse. But then, Cutter and his companions have faced bad before, and they know plenty about worse.

Things are bad, it's true, but they're still breathing. And as long as there is breath in their lungs, there is hope. And whatever else might be said for Cutter, this much we know to be true—he will fight. He will stand until he is no longer able to do so.

The next journey with Cutter and the rest of his companions will be coming your way soon so stay with me, won't you? Stay with *us*. After all, in the war for the Known Lands, every person will be needed.

I'd like to take this time, as always, to thank the many people who have helped to make this book better or who have, for reasons beyond my understanding, blessed my life with their presence.

Thank you to my wife, Andrea. This life's a wild, crazy ride, but I wouldn't change it for anything, and I'm grateful that I get to go on it with you. Thank you, also, to my children, Gabriel, Norah, and Declan. You are all a blessing I don't deserve, but I promise I'll keep trying to.

Thank you also to my beta readers. It's impossible to overstate how helpful your thoughts and opinions are or how grateful I am for the time and energy you dedicate to them, so I'll simply say thank you.

And last, thank you, dear reader. Books, I've always thought, are a kind of magic. Maybe the best kind. After all, who sits around hoping someone will hand them a pigeon out of a hat or that quarters will start falling out of their ears? But if books are magic—and they are—then I am not the magician. The stagehand at best. The real magic comes from you.

So thanks for coming back, for bringing the magic with you. The next book in *Saga of the Known Lands* is coming soon so take your seats, get comfortable.

The curtains are about to be drawn.

Happy Reading and until next time,
Jacob Peppers

About the Author

Jacob Peppers lives in Georgia with his wife, and his children, Gabriel, Norah, and Declan, as well as their two dogs. He is an avid reader and writer and when he's not exploring the worlds of others, he's creating his own. His short fiction has been published in various markets, and his short story, "The Lies of Autumn," was a finalist for the 2013 Eric Hoffer Award for Short Prose. He is the author of the bestselling epic fantasy series *The Seven Virtues* and *The Nightfall Wars.*

Printed in Great Britain
by Amazon